OXFORD WORLD'S CLASSICS

THE LIBRARY OF GREEK MYTHOLOGY

APOLLODORUS is the name traditionally ascribed to the author of the *Library*. Although he was formerly identified as Apollodorus of Athens, a distinguished Alexandrian scholar of the second century BC, it is now recognized that the *Library* must have been written at a later period, probably the first or second century AD. It is not known whether Apollodorus was the author's true name; in any case we know nothing about him. Essentially an editor rather than an original writer, he compiled this brief but comprehensive guide to Greek mythology by selecting and summarizing material from the works of earlier writers. Based in the main on good early sources, it is an invaluable reference work.

ROBIN HARD studied Greek at Aberystwyth and Reading, writing a doctoral thesis on Plato's *Symposium*, and is currently combining writing and translating with the part-time teaching of ancient philosophy and Greek.

OXFORD WORLD'S CLASSICS

*For over 100 years Oxford World's Classics have brought
readers closer to the world's great literature. Now with over 700
titles—from the 4,000-year-old myths of Mesopotamia to the
twentieth century's greatest novels—the series makes available
lesser-known as well as celebrated writing.*

*The pocket-sized hardbacks of the early years contained
introductions by Virginia Woolf, T. S. Eliot, Graham Greene,
and other literary figures which enriched the experience of reading.
Today the series is recognized for its fine scholarship and
reliability in texts that span world literature, drama and poetry,
religion, philosophy and politics. Each edition includes perceptive
commentary and essential background information to meet the
changing needs of readers.*

OXFORD WORLD'S CLASSICS

APOLLODORUS

The Library of Greek Mythology

Translated with an Introduction and Notes by
ROBIN HARD

OXFORD
UNIVERSITY PRESS

OXFORD
UNIVERSITY PRESS

Great Clarendon Street, Oxford OX2 6DP

Oxford University Press is a department of the University of Oxford.
It furthers the University's objective of excellence in research, scholarship,
and education by publishing worldwide in

Oxford New York

Athens Auckland Bangkok Bogotá Buenos Aires Calcutta
Cape Town Chennai Dar es Salaam Delhi Florence Hong Kong Istanbul
Karachi Kuala Lumpur Madrid Melbourne Mexico City Mumbai
Nairobi Paris São Paulo Shanghai Singapore Taipei Tokyo Toronto Warsaw

with associated companies in Berlin Ibadan

Oxford is a registered trade mark of Oxford University Press
in the UK and in certain other countries

Published in the United States
by Oxford University Press Inc., New York

British Library Cataloguing in Publication Data

Data available

Library of Congress Cataloging in Publication Data

Apollodorus.
[Bibliotheca. English]
The library of Greek mythology / Apollodorus; translated by Robin Hard.
(Oxford world's classics)
Includes bibliographical references and indexes.
1. Mythology, Greek.   I. Hard, Robin.   II. Title.   III. Series.
PA3870.A73 1997   29.1'3—dc20   96–34135

ISBN 0–19–283924–1 (pbk.)

7 9 10 8 6

Printed in Great Britain by
Clays Ltd, St Ives plc

CONTENTS

INTRODUCTION

THE *Library* of Apollodorus is a concise but comprehensive guide to Greek mythology. It covers the full span of mythical history from the origins of the universe and the gods to the Trojan War and its aftermath, and between these limits it tells the story of each of the great families of heroic mythology, and of the various adventures associated with the main heroes and heroines.

This is the only work of its kind to survive from classical antiquity. Although the Greeks developed an extensive and varied mythographical literature in Hellenistic and Roman times, the few handbooks which have been preserved are mostly specialist anthologies, recording myths of the constellations, for instance, or tales of transformation, and many of the stories contained in them are relatively obscure and of late origin. The author of the *Library*, by contrast, wanted to provide his readers with a general handbook which would offer them an account of the most important myths as related in the earlier tradition (with only the occasional late or recondite variant). Otherwise we possess only two works which are at all comparable. There is a Latin compendium, the *Myths* (*Fabulae*) of Hyginus, probably dating to the second century AD, which was based on a Greek predecessor, but conveys its contents in a very imperfect form; it presents summaries of myths and various catalogues in many separate chapters. Although it is a valuable source for myths or versions of myths which would otherwise have been lost, it is disorganized and sadly unreliable, and has to be approached with caution. Secondly, when Diodorus of Sicily was compiling his historical compendium in the first century BC, he departed from the more austere practices of many fellow historians and included a section on the mythical history (or pre-history) of Greece. Although it contains a useful biography of Heracles and other interesting material, Diodorus' account of Greek myth is not nearly as complete as that in the *Library*, and much of it is based on inferior Hellenistic sources.

It may seem surprising that this unpretentious handbook should have survived when the most important works of the ancient mythographers have been lost. Fortune, of course, plays a large part in such matters; all surviving manuscripts of the *Library* derive from a single archetype. But if it is unpretentious to a fault, the *Library* encloses a mass of reliable information in a short space, and it is clear that the scholars of later antiquity found it exceptionally useful for that reason. It is often cited in the scholia (explanatory comments on the works of the classical authors) and similar sources, and in the twelfth century the Byzantine scholar John Tzetzes made extensive use of it. This suggests that the preservation of this particular handbook was not simply a freak of fortune, and that the writers of this later period thought that it had its virtues, at least from a purely practical point of view. As it happens, we know directly what one of the finest Byzantine scholars thought of the *Library*, for Photius, patriarch of Constantinople in the ninth century, registered his opinion in a brief review. While travelling abroad on a diplomatic mission, Photius kept a record of his reading for his brother, and in this record, after summarizing the contents of another mythical work, he noted:

In the same volume, I read a small work by the scholar Apollodorus; it is entitled the *Library*. It contained the most ancient stories of the Greeks: all that time has given them to believe about the gods and heroes, and about the rivers, and lands, and peoples, and towns, and thence everything that goes back to the earliest times. And it goes down as far as the Trojan War, and covers the battles that certain of the heroes fought with one another, and their exploits, and certain of the wanderings of the heroes returning from Troy, notably those of Odysseus, with whom this history of ancient times concludes. All in all, it is a general summary which is by no means lacking in usefulness to those who attach some value to the memory of the ancient stories.

If the *Library* had been lost, like so many of the works reviewed by Photius, we might feel some regret on reading these words; as it is, we can refer to the original and judge for ourselves whether for the modern reader too it fulfils the claims that Photius makes for it. These claims are by no means extravagant. It is indeed a useful synopsis of the mythical history of Greece; and, it may be added, it is based for the most part on good early sources, and the author was content to summarize them as he found them without imposing his own interpretations, or attempting to reconcile conflicting traditions, or making any alterations for literary effect.

In the manuscripts, this book is entitled the *Library of Apollodorus of Athens, the Grammarian*. 'Library' was a title applied to compendia; for a compendium, which draws together material from a multitude of other books, could be regarded as a library in itself. Diodorus called his much larger historical compendium the *Historical Library* for the same reason. In Photius' copy of the *Library*, a little poem was placed at the beginning in which the book itself addresses the reader and expresses this thought directly. It ran like this:

Now, due to my erudition, you can draw upon the coils of time, and know the stories of old. Look no longer in the pages of Homer, or in elegy, or the tragic Muse, or lyric verse, and seek no longer in the sonorous verses of the cyclic poets; no, look in me, and you will discover all that the world contains.

Whether this was really written by the original author is impossible to say, but none the less it seems appropriate and suggestive, even if the mixed metaphor at the beginning is not altogether fortunate. Time is pictured as a serpent, and the succession of ages as the serpent's coils which the learning embodied in the book will enable its readers to 'draw on' (as though drawing water from a well). For rather than search through a whole library of ancient poems, they have merely to look within this 'Library' to discover all that they could wish to know about the myths and legends of early Greece. And there is some truth in this, even if we would be happy to have the same opportunity as its author to consult all these early poetic sources in the original, and there is a certain philistinism in the suggestion that a work of these dimensions could enclose 'the world'.

The attribution of the work to Apollodorus of Athens, a distinguished scholar (or 'grammarian') who worked at Alexandria in the second century BC, is more problematic. Although Apollodorus had wide interests and also wrote on literary, historical, geographical, and other matters, he appears to have been most highly regarded in antiquity for a treatise on Greek religion entitled *On the Gods*, which would have contained extensive discussion of divine mythology. Thus the *Library*, which is largely devoted to heroic mythology, could be seen as a complementary work; and if the attribution were correct, we would possess a book by one of the most learned authors of the greatest age of Greek scholarship. The reference to 'the scholar (grammarian) Apollodorus' in Photius' review shows that he too considered this Apollodorus to be the author, and the attribution was accepted by modern scholars until quite recently, although it was increasingly recognized that it raises serious problems. Not until 1873, when the publication of a thesis on the *Library* by Carl Robert forced a reconsideration of the matter, were these problems fully confronted.

There is one very definite indication that the *Library* could not have been written during the lifetime of Apollodorus of Athens: it contains a reference to the *Chronicles* of Castor of Rhodes (p. 59). This was a study in comparative chronology which is said to have contained tables which extended to 61 BC; and the date of its author is confirmed by a report that he married the daughter of Deiotarus, an eastern king who was defended by Cicero in 45 BC. Unless the reference to Castor was added to the text at a later period (and there is no reason to suppose that it was) the *Library* must have been written a century or more after the death of Apollodorus of Athens.

In view of the difficulty raised by this citation, we must ask whether the *Library* is in any case a book which we could reasonably accept as the work of a scholar of Apollodorus' stature and period. In truth, it is not at all what we would expect from a learned Alexandrian scholar. Rather than an original synthesis achieved through the author's own research and reflection (as was surely the case with Apollodorus' treatise on the gods), we have an elementary handbook which the author compiled by consulting and epitomizing standard sources. And the author made no attempt to interpret the myths and explain their meaning in rationalistic terms, as was characteristic of Hellenistic mythographers. In relation to the gods, for instance, many writers of this period would explain that they represented forces of nature, or that they had originally been human beings who later had divine status attributed to them. Although it is explicitly attested that Apollodorus of Athens adopted such an approach, there is not a trace of it in the *Library*; nor was the author disconcerted by the fabulous element in many heroic myths (unlike Diodorus, who often provides rationalized versions, following Hellenistic sources). He simply accepts the myths as enjoyable stories which formed an important part of the Greek heritage, a characteristic attitude in later times. Furthermore, there are features in the author's use of language which suggest that the book was written at a later period than the second century BC. In short, there is every indication that the attribution to Apollodorus of Athens can be confidently rejected.

Apollodorus was a fairly common name, and it is conceivable that the *Library* was compiled by an author of that name who was later confused with the famous scholar of an earlier period; but it is more likely that our book is sailing under a flag of convenience. Perhaps, as Robert suggested, the author was too timid to launch the work under his own name, or perhaps later copyists found it to their advantage to pass it off as the work of a distinguished scholar. In any case, we know nothing about the author. Accordingly, the author is sometimes referred to as the pseudo-Apollodorus, particularly in the continental literature; but it is more convenient to use the traditional name, with due reservation.

Accepting that the traditional attribution reveals nothing about the author, can we infer anything about his time of birth, or his origins, or perhaps even his character from the book itself? It must be stated from the outset that a compilation of this kind is of its very nature unlikely to reveal much about its author, and in the present instance some features which might be of help in that regard are lacking. There is no dedication, and there are no incidental allusions to things that the author has seen or experienced. Nor does he make any reference to recent or contemporary events; indeed, the only historical event mentioned by him is the Phocian War (p. 163), which took place in the fourth century BC. It is possible, however, to draw some conclusions about when the *Library* may have been written, and perhaps about the origins of its author.

The reference to Castor (the latest author to be cited) shows that the *Library* could not have been written before the first half of the first century BC. To establish a later limit with equal certainty, it would be necessary to find a reference to the *Library* in another work which could be dated to a sufficiently early period. In practice, however, this approach is unproductive. Although, as was remarked above, the *Library* is cited quite frequently in the scholia and elsewhere, all the relevant sources are either hard to date or were certainly written at a much later period. We must therefore rely on internal criteria. Let us consider first the author's use of language, which might be expected to provide the most definite indications.

Although the author's Greek is generally unexceptional, there are features in his vocabulary and idiom which are more characteristic of later Greek. He occasionally uses words in senses which are not attested before the early Christian era, and sometimes the verb forms and minor points of grammar and expression are suggestive of later usage (even if they are not entirely unparalleled in the works of earlier authors). On these stylistic grounds, it is commonly agreed that the *Library* would be best dated to the first or second century AD (although some would place it somewhat earlier or later); and the author's general attitude and approach is consistent with such a dating. It has been remarked that in contrast to many Hellenistic writers, he is uncritical in his approach to myth. This is not because he accepts all the stories as being literally true, but because his approach is that of an antiquarian, so the question of truth or falsity is no longer relevant. This antiquarian approach, accompanied by a taste for the archaic and picturesque, and the desire to take stock of aspects of the Greek heritage, were characteristic of authors writing under the early empire. One has only to think of Plutarch or Pausanias. In preparing this summa of Greek myth, the present author was writing on a lesser scale in a work that belonged to an inferior genre; but the literature of epitomes and popular handbooks was itself characteristic of the age, and in its way, witnessed to the same tendencies.

To pass from the question of chronology to that of the author's origins, we must consider whether he shows any special interest in (or disregard for) particular areas of the Mediterranean world. Here a measure of caution is required; in a handbook

Introduction

devoted to the main early myths, there will inevitably be an emphasis on stories associated with the heartland of Greece and the Aegean. None the less, many readers have felt that the author is curiously neglectful of myths relating to Italy and the west; and some have detected a bias to the east. Apollodorus' account of the life history of Heracles is broadly similar to that in the historical compilation by Diodorus of Sicily. Yet his coverage of Heracles' adventures in Italy when returning with the cattle of Geryoneus (pp. 80–1) is very scanty when compared with the full account in Diodorus; and he makes no allusion to the tradition that Heracles was supposed to have visited the site of Rome. Indeed, he never mentions Rome or the Romans, and disregards the aspects of Greek mythology which were of most concern to them. Thus he tells how Aeneas escaped from the sack of Troy carrying his father on his back, but we would never gather from the *Library* that there were traditions connecting him with Latium and the origins of Rome. Although a similar attitude can be detected in other authors at that time and the matter raises questions of wider interest, with regard to the specific question of the author's origins we can surely conclude that it is most unlikely that he came from Italy or the west. Some have tried to draw more positive conclusions, but it is doubtful whether there is sufficient evidence to support them. Robert suggested that the author was an Athenian (like the Hellenistic Apollodorus); but the coverage of Athenian mythology, although quite extensive, is not disproportionate in terms of the place that Athenian myth occupied in the general tradition, and it can hardly be accepted that references to topographical features like the 'sea' of Erechtheus (p. 130) are explicable only on grounds of local knowledge. Again, it could be argued that Apollodorus shows a special interest in the east, and it is quite possible that he lived there, but we cannot say more than that.

There is no suggestion in Photius' review that he regarded the *Library* as an introductory work for schoolchildren or the uneducated, and the citations in the scholia show that in late antiquity at least it was used by scholars as a reference work. We have no corresponding evidence of how it was viewed in earlier times, or whether it was widely used. It may be suspected, however, that readers of much education would have preferred more solid fare, and scholars at that period would surely have found little use for an elementary work of this kind when they could refer to more scholarly and comprehensive handbooks by the Hellenistic mythographers.

A modern reader leafing through the *Library* is likely to gain conflicting impressions about its general level and the kind of audience that the author would have had in mind when writing it. Unlike many of the mythographical works which survive from antiquity, this is not a specialist study, and the author is happy to recount the most familiar stories; and most of them are summarized quite briefly. If the *Library* is used merely as a mythological dictionary and consulted for the stories associated with the main heroes, the reader may feel that it is very elementary, containing little that any moderately educated ancient reader would not have known already. Thus the story of Perseus is summarized in three pages, that of Oedipus in about a page, and the plot of Sophocles' *Antigone* in two sentences. Many have concluded that the *Library* was written as a primer for school-children, or perhaps for semi-Hellenized adults in the eastern reaches of the Roman empire; such a view has been held by scholars whose opinion is worthy of respect (and some have advanced specific arguments in its favour, suggesting, for instance, that certain stories have been bowdlerized for a youthful audience).

On the other hand, if the *Library* is read consecutively, the reader may feel that it is not as elementary as all that. Within its brief confines it contains a remarkable quantity of information, and much that a reader with a fairly comprehensive knowledge of Greek mythology would not expect to hold in mind. Perhaps the work was intended not as a primer, but as an epitome of mythical history for a general if unsophisticated readership. As we have already observed, there was an extensive literature of this kind in the Roman period, and the part that popular handbooks and epitomes played in transmitting many aspects of Hellenic culture to a broad public should not be underestimated. For their knowledge of philosophy, for instance, many Greeks of that period would have relied on handbooks summarizing the opinions of the different schools on each of the standard questions. Works of such a kind may have been aimed at a relatively uncultivated audience, but they were not written specifically for use in schools.

Taken as a whole, the *Library* amounts to far more than an anthology of mythical tales. For it offers a full account of each of the main cycles of myth, and thence a complete history of mythical Greece, organized on a genealogical basis, family by family; all the main stories are there, each situated in its proper place in the overall structure. From this perspective it could well be argued that the author wanted to provide the general public with a summa of Greek myth in epitome form; and that in a modest way, his aim was encyclopaedic. In a recent French edition of the *Library*, J.-C. Carrière has advanced some interesting arguments in favour of this view. Although this is ultimately a matter of judgement, and a full consideration of the question would require the examination of a number of different issues, I would like to consider a single aspect of the work which seems to favour such a view.

Even a casual reader of the *Library* will be struck by the profusion of names. The narrative may often be brief and bare, but the author was immensely thorough in recording the names of all the figures associated with the heroic families and the main episodes in heroic mythology. Most of these names appear in various catalogues, or in the genealogies which punctuate the histories of the great families of heroic mythology; let us first consider the catalogues, which serve less of a practical function than the genealogies.

In such a short work, the author devotes a surprising amount of space to these catalogues, which sometimes take up more than a page. Instead of merely reporting that the fifty daughters of Danaos married the fifty sons of Aigyptos and, with one exception, murdered them on their wedding night, Apollodorus lists all the brides and their husbands, and tells us who their mothers were (pp. 61–2). Only two of the Danaids are of any significance thereafter. Similarly, the fifty sons of Lycaon, who met a premature death, are listed by name, and all the suitors of Penelope (although there is no such list in the *Odyssey*, Apollodorus' main source at this point), and the many children of Heracles by the fifty daughters of Thespios and other women.

Introduction

In certain cases such catalogues could be of practical interest even to those first approaching the study of Greek mythology, as with the catalogue of the Argonauts (pp. 49–50), or the catalogue of ships (pp. 148–9), which gives the names of the Greek leaders at Troy, and their origins and the relative strength of their contingents. But generally this is gratuitous information. Such catalogues were nevertheless valued in the Greek tradition, as in many other mythical traditions, as a matter of record, and it is understandable that our author should have wished to include the more important catalogues when summarizing the tradition. It may be doubted, however, that any author would wish to burden a digest for schoolchildren with catalogues listing over six hundred and fifty names (excluding patronymics).

The genealogies are equally comprehensive. The histories of the heroic families are interspersed with genealogies which list the full succession in each family, even if no significant stories are associated with the figures in a particular generation, and usually catalogue all the known children of each marriage, even if most are not mentioned again (and may be otherwise unknown). In this way, complete family trees are built up for each ruling line, partly as a matter of record (and here completeness can be seen as a virtue in itself, even if many of the names which appear are no more than names), and partly because these genealogies provide the main principle of organization in mythical history. In many mythical traditions, the myths tend to tell of events that happened 'once upon a time', in an indefinite past. This is rarely the case in Greek mythology, and heroic mythology in particular was ordered into a fairly coherent pseudo-history. This history was necessarily organized on a genealogical basis, because the succession of generations in the families ruling in each centre provided the only possible chronological measure. Only when plausible family trees had been constructed was it possible to locate each figure or mythical episode at its appropriate position in time, and thus construct a history in which these could be viewed in due relation. Considering the multiplicity of the independent centres in Greece, and the mass of mutually inconsistent myths and legends which would have been transmitted in the oral tradition within these various centres, the economy of the pan-Hellenic genealogical system recorded in the *Library* is impressive. There are only six main families, and each family tree is sufficiently detailed to allow each figure or story to be assigned to its definite place. To gain a full understanding of this body of myth as a coherent history, it is necessary to master this system. The genealogies in the *Library* give its readers the resources to do so. In this respect, it cannot be said that the book merely records matter that a well-educated person would have known; for the genealogies are by no means simple, and would not easily be committed to memory.

To draw a tentative conclusion from these brief reflections, there are aspects of the work which suggest that the common (but by no means universal) view that the *Library* was written for use in schools is open to serious question. It could well have been written as a summary handbook for a more general audience (although schoolmasters may also have found it useful), and the author's concern for completeness and inclusion of full genealogies ensures that it has genuine virtues both as a summary of the tradition and a reference work. The shortcomings of the work derive from its extreme brevity rather than any essential flaw in the compiler's approach to his task.

The material in the *Library* is drawn from a wide variety of sources, whether original poetic sources, from early epic to the learned compositions of the early Hellenistic poets, or mythographical compilations which offered prose summaries of mythical tales. Since the author's main purpose was to provide an account of the most important early myths, we might expect that he would have been interested primarily in earlier sources, in particular early epic and the works of the fifth-century chroniclers, who were amongst the earliest prose writers. If we consider which sources are cited most frequently by name, we find some confirmation of this. Of poets, Hesiod is named most often (eleven times) and then Homer (five times), and of prose writers, two less familiar figures, Pherecydes (thirteen times) and Acousilaos (ten times), who wrote on mythical history in the fifth century BC. This provides only an approximate measure because Apollodorus sometimes cites authorities for specific traditions or variants, but rarely indicates the main source that he was following in each stage in the work. The emphasis on early historical and epic sources is nevertheless significant.

The question of sources concerns not only the origin of individual stories, but also the structure and organization of the various cycles of myth. The Greek mythological tradition, as summarized in a broadly representative manner in the *Library*, is in many respects a peculiar one. It is dominated to an unusual degree by heroic mythology, and the material from heroic legend is organized in such a way that it provides an unusually coherent pre-history of the regions covered. As has been remarked, stories are rarely located in an indeterminate past; each is fitted into its appropriate place, whether in relation to the history of a specific place and the successive generations of its ruling family, or to the development of a great adventure or the life history of a major hero. For the most part, this systematization was not the work of the scholarly mythographers of the Hellenistic era, but was achieved at a relatively early period by the epic poets and by prose writers who regarded themselves as historians rather than mythographers. Indeed, the beginning of the process by which the mass of often mutually inconsistent myths in the oral tradition was ordered into a coherent pseudo-historical pattern can be traced to the earliest Greek literature to be recorded in writing, the Homeric epics and Hesiod's *Theogony*, and the process was brought to fruition in the works of the fifth-century mythographer-historians—precisely the sources most frequently cited in the *Library*. First we must consider the nature of these early sources and their contribution to this process, and then how the author of the *Library* made use of them.

Until the development of prose literature in the latter part of the sixth century, Greek literature was exclusively poetic, and the richest sources for myth and legend were the works of the epic poets. The earliest epics to survive, the two Homeric epics and Hesiod's *Theogony*, were probably written about the same time towards the end of the eighth century. Although they belong to the same broad genre, the poems attributed to these authors are quite different in nature. Homer was a story-teller on a grand scale and each of the Homeric epics is constructed on the basis of an overall plot running through the whole poem.

But Hesiod organized his *Theogony* on a genealogical basis; and generally speaking, in a genealogical poem of such a kind the stories associated with the various figures are inserted successively as the figures are introduced in the genealogies, and the narratives are relatively brief and self-contained. These contrary approaches can be related to the two main ways in which the mythical material is organized in different parts of the *Library*, the narrative ordering in the histories of great adventures like the voyage of the Argonauts and the Trojan War (or in the life of Heracles), and the genealogical ordering in large stretches of the histories of the great families, where we find an alternation between genealogical sections and narratives recounting the stories associated with the heroes and heroines as they are successively introduced in the genealogies. We will examine first how the works of the epic poets who could be regarded as the successors of Homer contributed to the establishment of standard accounts of the greater mythical adventures, and then how the Hesiodic approach was extended in a later epic to cover heroic mythology, resulting in the development of an all-embracing genealogical system.

The main action of the *Iliad* covers only a few days in the tenth and final year of the Trojan War, and the *Odyssey* describes the return voyage of only one of the Greek heroes, although both poems assume a much broader background of Trojan myth and they contain many allusions to stories not directly covered in the poems themselves. The exceptional quality of the Homeric poems seems to have impressed itself on their audience from the beginning, and it is understandable that poets in the century following their composition should have wished to compose epics covering the elements in Trojan mythology not already covered by Homer, and, in effect, fill in the gaps. And so it came about that a cycle of epics was composed which, taken together, built up a sequence narrating the entire history of the Trojan War. Although only a few fragments have survived, we know their general contents from a series of summaries attributed to a certain Proclus, and can see how they were constructed around the Homeric epics. Thus the origins of the war and all events up to the angry withdrawal of Achilles which marks the beginning of the *Iliad* were covered in a single long epic, the

Cypria; and then three shorter epics (partly overlapping in content) continued where the *Iliad* left off, covering the final period of the war and the sack of Troy. Then the *Returns* told of the return voyages of the surviving Greek heroes, except for Odysseus, and last of all, the later history of Odysseus was recounted in the *Telegonia*, which formed an eccentric supplement to the *Odyssey*. Although there is reason to think that by Homeric standards the artistic quality of these poems was not high, they were of great importance from a mythographical viewpoint for the part that they played in the establishment of a canon of Trojan myth. By selecting and ordering material from the oral tradition and earlier lays, and 'fixing' it in long poems which were transmitted to future generations, the authors of such epics made a major contribution to the formation of standard histories of adventures like the Trojan War. The account of the war in the *Library* is ultimately dependent on these epics for its general structure and much of its contents. Other epics composed in the seventh century or somewhat later fulfilled a similar service with regard to other mythical episodes, such as the Theban Wars, or the voyage of the Argonauts (although, as we shall see, Apollodorus followed a Hellenistic epic for that adventure).

In his *Theogony*, Hesiod sought to organize the traditions concerning the gods into a coherent pattern by developing the comprehensive genealogical system which forms the basis of his poem. Beginning with a mythical cosmogony presented in genealogical terms, he tells of the origin and descent of the earlier gods and the establishment of Zeus as supreme ruler, and concludes with a catalogue of Zeus' marriages and his offspring by his wives and other women. A supplement was added later which includes a catalogue of the children born to goddesses by mortal men. As a story-teller, Hesiod is short-winded and often clumsy, although his material is naturally of great interest. The approach adopted by Hesiod is largely determined by the peculiar nature of his subject matter; but later, probably in the sixth century, another poet composed a continuation to his poem extending the same approach to heroic mythology. This epic, which survives in fragments only, is known, somewhat misleadingly perhaps, as the *Catalogue of Women*, because the origin of each line is traced to the offspring of a god by a mortal woman. Its importance for

Greek mythography cannot be emphasized too strongly; for it was here that the heroic genealogies were first ordered into a coherent pan-Hellenic system. The pattern of heroic genealogy which we find in the *Library* is still similar in general outline (although, of course, it often reflects later developments). And the *Catalogue* offered far more than sequences of names; for most names suggest a story, and the relevant narratives were inserted at the appropriate points in the presentation of the genealogies. This approach was subsequently adopted by prose mythographers and, as we have observed, it is in evidence in many parts of the *Library*.

Historians were prominent amongst the earliest prose writers. Some concerned themselves with purely local matters, but others (including those mentioned amongst the authors most frequently cited by Apollodorus) had broader ambitions and covered the traditions associated with many parts of the Greek world. They could not extend their researches any distance into the past without engaging with what we would regard as myth; and in the present context, it is their contribution to mythography which interests us. But they regarded themselves as historians, and while they were not always totally uncritical, they were willing to accept myth and legend as reliable sources of historical truth. In this respect, they differed from the scholarly mythographers of the Hellenistic era, who were critical in their attitude to myth and regarded mythography as a separate area of investigation. These earlier authors, whose qualities must be judged from fragments and testimonies, are sometimes referred to as logographers to distinguish them from more critical historians like Herodotus and Thucydides; but since this term (which simply meant 'prose writers' in ancient usage) can be misleading if it is thought to describe a specific school of historians, it is safer to describe them merely as historians (or mythographer-historians or chroniclers).

If these mythographer-historians were uncritical with regard to the basic nature of their material (and were rarely worried by the fabulous element in myth), they were by no means uncritical regarding the historical implausibilities which can arise from deficiencies in chronology and internal inconsistencies within the mythical narratives. With regard to chronology, they continued the enterprise begun in the Hesiodic *Catalogue* by refining and further developing the heroic genealogies, and trying to improve the synchronisms between families. In other respects, these authors could also be seen as heirs to the epic poets in the Homeric tradition. Many composed extensive narratives and most undertook to collect together the myths associated with the various cycles, and where necessary reconcile or choose between conflicting versions, and iron out contradictions to establish a convincing narrative.

The works of the two mythographer-historians explicitly cited by Apollodorus were complementary in character. Acousilaos of Argos probably wrote at the end of the sixth century, as a contemporary of Hecataios (although some would place him somewhat later). He aimed to provide a systematic account of the entire mythical tradition, rigorously organized on a genealogical basis. The material was ordered in much the same way as in the *Library*, although on a far larger scale; as in the *Library*, most of the figures in heroic mythology were assigned to one or other of a small number of important families, and the history of each of these families was narrated separately from beginning to end. In this regard, Acousilaos used the Hesiodic *Catalogue* as his model, developing or modifying the genealogies as he thought necessary. As might be expected in an author of Argive birth, Acousilaos seems to have stressed the centrality of the Argive traditions in his account of Peloponnesian mythology.

Pherecydes of Athens composed his history somewhat later, probably in the first half of the fifth century. His writings were more copious than those of Acousilaos, and it seems that his prime concern was to gather together as complete a collection as possible of the traditional myths. He was correspondingly less interested in genealogical matters, and the organization of his works would necessarily have been much looser in view of the quantity of diverse material collected within them. Indeed, the principles that he followed in this respect are not at all clear from the surviving evidence. He is the mythographer-historian most frequently quoted by the scholiasts, who (like Apollodorus) clearly valued him for his copious records of early myth, narrated in a pleasantly ingenuous style. Since the narratives preserved from the works of later mythographers are generally so lacking in charm, it is a particular shame that the works of this mythographical Herodotus should have been lost. Sometimes we detect something of their flavour in the summaries in the *Library*.

Another mythographer-historian should also be mentioned who was certainly consulted by the author of the *Library* although he is not cited by name. Hellanicos of Lesbos, who wrote in the second half of the fifth century, was closer in spirit to Acousilaos than to Pherecydes, for he was important above all for his contribution to the fine-tuning of the genealogical system. He was less interested in the narration of myth, and the passages preserved by the scholiasts suggest that his writings were marked by a certain dryness and a rationalizing tendency rarely in evidence in the works of his predecessors. He was nevertheless an important authority on certain aspects of mythical history, notably the Trojan War.

In the main, and allowing for a few important contributions from tragedy and later sources, the *Library* summarizes the canon of myth as it was defined in the works of these mythographer-historians and in early epic poetry; and for much of its organization, the *Library* relies on the genealogical system developed in the Hesiodic epics and further refined by the early prose mythographers. The author's dependence on epic (and other poetic sources) would often have been indirect. Most of the stories from early epic would have been summarized in prose in the works of the mythographer-historians, and collections of summaries of epic and tragic plots became widely available in the Hellenistic era. These would have provided our author with the models for his own summaries, and would usually have served as his immediate sources. Indeed, it can be assumed that he would rarely have worked directly from a poetic source. He seems, however, to have had a thorough knowledge of the Hesiodic *Catalogue*, and, as would be expected, of the Homeric epics. Although the theogony at the beginning of the *Library* is largely based on Hesiod's *Theogony*, the author preferred to follow other sources on some significant points (as is remarked in the Explanatory Notes).

In many parts of the *Library*, the narrative can be regarded as being, in all essentials, a brief epitome of relevant sections from the works of the mythographer-historians (and much of its interest and value could be said to have derived from that). Pherecydes seems to have served as the author's main model, although he also followed other historians when they were the main authorities on a particular area, as was Acousilaos on Argive myth, or Hellanicos on the myths connected with Troy. Not all scholars have agreed, however, that the author of the *Library* drew his material directly from these early prose sources, even where we can be certain that it was ultimately derived from them. For he had all the resources of Hellenistic mythography available to him, including handbooks which would have contained summaries of material from such writers. In his influential study, Carl Robert argued that the *Library* is little more than a précis of an earlier handbook by a Hellenistic author; and amongst German scholars at least, such a view came to be widely accepted in the early part of this century. Because we have to rely on fragments for our knowledge of most of the *Library*'s earlier sources, this is by no means an easy question. Nevertheless, the most detailed examination of the evidence hitherto (in the article by M. Van der Valk cited in the Select Bibliography) gives reason to suppose that the author referred directly to the writings of the mythographer-historians when he was following one of them as his main source in a particular part of the work.

The author of the *Library* also drew on a variety of other sources. Besides epic poetry, his earlier sources would naturally have included lyric and elegiac poetry, and the 'tragic Muse', as was stated in the little poem attributed to him. The great Attic dramatists of the fifth century generally relied on heroic mythology for their plots, in particular the stories associated with the Argive and Theban royal families and the Trojan War. But they adapted the traditional stories with considerable freedom, whether for dramatic effect or to develop a moral of their own, and were thus responsible for some striking innovations which had a marked influence on the development of the tradition. In certain cases the tragedians contributed the canonic version of a particular story, while in many others they provided appealing variants. Both aspects of this influence are evident in the *Library*. Thus the account of the life of Oedipus is in the main a summary of Sophocles' version in his Oedipus plays, for this became the canonic version, largely displacing the very different accounts in early epic; but the plot of a play by Euripides on Alcmaion (p. 114) is included merely as an interesting variant, in a supplement to the main account based on the earlier tradition.

To proceed to the Hellenistic poets, Apollodorus based his account of the voyage of the Argonauts on the *Argonautica* of Apollonius of Rhodes, a relatively late epic written in the third century BC. As was common in that age, Apollonius was a scholar as well as a poet, and he made extensive use of the early sources in composing his poem. For certain stories, however, such as the murder of Apsyrtos (p. 54), the author of the *Library* prefers to report a more primitive version than was found acceptable in this late epic. Otherwise his interests diverge from those of the Hellenistic poets, who tended to concern themselves with the more recondite aspects of the tradition, and he draws on them only for the occasional learned variant. As to the mythographical literature of this period, it was observed above that he would have made use of the resources that it provided. It is likely that some of his narratives are based on Hellenistic summaries of epic or tragic plots; and mythical variants, collections of references, and alternative genealogies may often have been drawn from Hellenistic handbooks. Apollodorus would have valued such literature as a source of instant erudition, but there is nothing to indicate that the *Library* is marked in any deeper sense by Hellenistic scholarship, and the author had no interest whatever in the rationalistic interpretations favoured by many Hellenistic scholars.

Over a millennium has passed since Photius suggested that the *Library* was not without its value to those who attach some importance to the memory of the ancient stories. Does this still apply for the modern reader? And even if the *Library* is of some practical use for its summaries of the main myths and the other information that it provides, is that the most that can be said for it?

As the only comprehensive mythical history of Greece to survive from antiquity, it is certainly the case that it has been used extensively by scholars and amateurs of myth in modern times.

It is no accident that the major mythographical work of C. G. Heyne, the founder of modern scholarly mythography (who was responsible for introducing the word 'myth' into modern usage), should have been an edition of the *Library* accompanied by an exhaustive commentary. And ever since, authors of mythological dictionaries and compendia have relied heavily on the *Library* for their accounts of the main myths. This will be readily apparent if relevant passages from Robert Graves' *Greek Myths*, for instance, or Pierre Grimal's dictionary of classical mythology are checked against the text of the *Library*. It must be said, however, that despite the undoubted usefulness of the *Library*, writers on Greek mythology tend to refer to it with condescension or even disdain, and the neglect of it in the scholarly literature confirms that it is generally regarded as a work of no great substance.

In reaching a judgement on the value of the *Library*, we must take due account of the genre that it belongs to; for a summary handbook of this kind, compiled by collecting and epitomizing material from earlier sources, belongs to a mediocre, or at least a secondary, genre. The value of such a work will not derive from any originality or serious scholarship on the author's part. He is simply an editor. Nor should we expect such a work to have any literary merit (beyond a tolerably clear presentation of the mythical narrative, which is generally the case with the *Library*). If Apollodorus' main sources had survived, the *Library* would be no more than a historical curiosity, and the work as a whole would possess no greater value than the summary of the *Iliad* on p. 153. But if his main sources are taken to be primarily the works of the early mythographer-historians, very little of them has been preserved, so we must ask: can a compilation of this kind convey anything of value from them, and in the present case, is it reasonable to assume that it does? Now this is surely an area in which a writer of very modest capabilities could perform a useful service. Mythology is not at all like philosophy, for instance, where subtleties of thought and essential points in the reasoning can easily be lost in the process of summarization. If a mythical epitomist shows reasonable discrimination in the selection of resources, he merely needs the ability to summarize the stories clearly and accurately, and to be thorough in transmitting genealogical and other information which may be of less immediate appeal but is essential if the individual stories are to be ordered into a coherent mythical history. In this respect, the author of the *Library* certainly demonstrates the necessary thoroughness, and where his narratives can be compared with surviving sources, we can see that his summaries are generally reliable.

Furthermore, a lack of originality and of scholarly and literary ambition are not necessarily defects in an epitomist; for the mediocrity of his aims prevents our author from ever standing in the way of his sources. He never tries to rationalize the myths or impose his own ideas on them, or to alter and embellish them for literary or rhetorical effect. And he willingly accepts conflicting traditions without attempting to reconcile them.

If the author had modest aims, he can be said to have fulfilled them in a satisfactory manner. Of its kind, and allowing for its brevity, the *Library* is a work of surprisingly high quality. It is founded for the most part on good authorities of early date, and reports them with a high degree of accuracy. Naturally we would prefer to have the works of Pherecydes and Acousilaos (and the early epics too), but we should be grateful to fortune that at least we have this little summary of the mythical history of Greece as it would have been depicted in the works of the earliest mythographers. If only because so much else has been lost, it is indispensable to anyone who has more than a passing interest in Greek mythology.

NOTE ON THE TEXT
AND TRANSLATION

ALL surviving manuscripts of the *Library* are descended from
a single original, a fourteenth-century manuscript in the Bibliothèque Nationale in Paris. Unfortunately this breaks off before
the end of the work, during the section on Theseus (p. 138),
which meant that, until quite recently, the valuable account of
the Trojan cycle was entirely lost. But the situation was improved
at the end of the last century by the discovery of two epitomes,
or abridgements, of the *Library*, which provide a very service-
able summary of the end of the work. They were found quite
independently, in the Vatican Library (the Vatican epitome) and
the monastery of Saint Sabbas in Jerusalem (the Sabbaitic epitome), in 1885 and 1887 respectively.

The standard modern text, that of Richard Wagner in the
Teubner series (1926 edn.), has been used for the present translation, although alternative readings have sometimes been preferred, and account has been taken of the more recent literature
mentioned in the Select Bibliography. The Greek text in
Frazer's edition in the Loeb series is largely based on that of
Wagner.

The two epitomes are not identical either in content or, where
they cover the same episodes, in expression, and Wagner prints
both texts, using parallel columns where necessary; but in a translation, Frazer's procedure of combining the two to provide a
single continuous narrative is clearly preferable. In practice this
raises few problems, except occasionally when both epitomes tell
the same story but express it in a slightly different way. Only
at a very few points have I felt it necessary to question Frazer's
judgement on the selection of material (and it was considered
desirable in any case that the translation should correspond as
far as possible to Frazer's Greek text).

This is a utilitarian work which offers no promise of literary
delight. The prose of Apollodorus is plain and colourless, and
so simple in expression that a translator has little latitude. Without misrepresenting the original, it is hard to prevent a translation

from reading like a story-book for young children; but I have
tried to bring out the possible advantages of a plain style, and
hope that the reader will find the mythical narrative brisk and
clear, and if ingenuous, at least agreeably so.

I have benefited from a long familiarity with the translation
by Sir James Frazer. Despite the archaisms and a tendency to
euphemism on sexual matters, it is a work of quality. I have also
consulted the elegant and precise French translation by Carrière
and Massonie.

According to the traditional arrangement, the work is divided into three books followed by the Epitome. Each of these
is further divided into numbered chapters (here indicated in the
margin) and subsections (indicated within the text); and correspondingly, three figures (or two for passages from the Epitome)
are cited in references in the scholarly literature (e.g. 2, 4, 6, or
Epitome 7, 18). The paragraph numbering found in some editions has been omitted to avoid confusion; I have added italicized headings to make the work easier to consult.

Greek names. These present a real problem because the
Latinized forms are not only more familiar, but in many cases
have become part of our language and culture. Nevertheless, in
a comprehensive work of this kind, containing so many genealogies, it is surely preferable that the original Greek forms should
be used. If the Greek names can look strange and unattractive
in an English text, this is largely because of the *k*s (e.g. Kanake,
Kirke, Lakonia); but there seems to be no particular disadvan-
tage in using a *c* (properly a hard *c*) for Greek kappa, and I have
followed that course in the present translation. For very familiar figures, however, like Oedipus and Achilles, the traditional
forms have been preserved (except in some cases where the Latin
form differs markedly from the original); and for place names,
modern or Latinized forms have been used much more frequently.
Some guidance on pronunciation and possible sources of confusion is offered at the beginning of the Index. The Greek forms
differ most frequently from the Latin in the use of *-os* instead
of *-us* at the end of masculine names, and of *ai* and *oi* instead
of *ae* and *oe* (thus Aigimios and Proitos rather than Aegimius
and Proetus).

Note on the Text and Translation

Square brackets are used to indicate (1) additions to the original text, and (2) passages where the surviving manuscripts may misrepresent the original text.

1. *Additions.* Short gaps in the surviving text are usually filled by the insertion of an invented phrase (if the content of the missing passage can be inferred from the context, or from another source) or of a brief passage from another source which can be reasonably assumed to be related to, or dependent on, the original text of the *Library*. For the most part, the added passages correspond to those in Wagner's and Frazer's texts. Again, significant additions are explained in the notes.

Very occasionally, I have added a phrase for the sake of clarity. For minor additions—where it has been indicated, for instance, that a particular place is a mountain, or that a child is a son or daughter, although this is not stated explicitly in the original text—square brackets have not been used.

2. *Dubious passages.* These are of two main kinds. Something in the content of a passage may give reason to suspect that the text has been corrupted in the course of transmission and no longer corresponds with the original; or occasionally, for reasons of style or content, we may suspect that a passage is a later interpolation (typically a marginal note which has found its way into the main text). Significant instances are discussed in the notes.

NB. Some interpolations which interrupt the narrative (and also a dubious passage from the Epitome) have been segregated to the Appendix. A *dagger* (†) in the text indicates where each was inserted. Each of the passages is discussed in the accompanying comments; although not part of the original text, four of them contain interesting material.

Etymologies. The ancient mythographers liked to explain the names of mythical figures, or of places involved in mythical tales, by etymologies which were sometimes valid, but often fanciful or even absurd. Because these depend on allusions or wordplay in the original Greek which cannot be reproduced in a translation, the presence of such wordplay is indicated in the text by the appropriate use of *italics* (see, for instance, p. 88) and explained afterwards in the Notes.

SELECT BIBLIOGRAPHY

Editions and Translations of the Library

There have been three English translations:

J. G. Frazer, Apollodorus, *The Library*, 2 vols., Loeb Classical Library, London, 1921. (The extensive notes give full references to the ancient sources, and contain a mass of disordered information, mythographical and ethnographical; thirteen appendices on specific themes and episodes, citing parallels from the folklore of other cultures.)

K. Aldrich, Apollodorus, *The Library of Greek Mythology*, Lawrence, Kan., 1975. (With accompanying notes; the translation is more modern in idiom than Frazer's.)

M. Simpson, *Gods and Heroes of the Greeks: The Library of Apollodorus*, Amherst, Mass., 1976. (The translation is not always reliable.)

A recent French translation should also be mentioned:

J.-C. Carrière and B. Massonie, *La Bibliothèque d'Apollodore*, Paris, 1991. (Excellent translation; the copious notes concentrate primarily on textual and linguistic matters, but many mythological points are also discussed; relevant passages from the scholia are often cited in translation.)

The best edition of the Greek text is:

R. Wagner (ed.), *Apollodori Bibliotheca* (*Mythographi Graeci*, vol. 1), Leipsig, 1926 (2nd edn. with supplementary apparatus).

On the text, two subsequent articles should also be consulted, along with Carrière's notes:

A. Diller, 'The Text History of the Bibliotheca of Pseudo-Apollodorus', *TAPA* 66 (1935), 296–313.

M. Papathomopoulos, 'Pour une nouvelle édition de la Bibliothèque d'Apollodore', *Ellenica*, 26 (1973), 18–40.

Secondary Literature

The scholarly literature on the *Library* is very scanty. The only full commentary was written in the eighteenth century:

J. G. Heyne, *Apollodori Atheniensis Bibliothecae libri tres et fragmenta*, 2 vols., Göttingen, 1803, 2nd edn. (Text, with accompanying notes in Latin; a landmark in the scholarly study of myth, and still of more than historical interest.)

Select Bibliography

As it happens, the most comprehensive modern study is in English:

M. Van der Valk, 'On Apollodori Bibliotheca', *REG* 71 (1958), 100–68. (Primarily on the sources of the *Library*, arguing in particular that the author often referred directly to his main early sources, rather than relying on a Hellenistic handbook; much of the argument is technical, and citations in Greek are not translated.)

Otherwise the following should be mentioned:

C. Jourdain-Annequin, *Héraclès aux portes du soir*, Paris, 1989. (Contains some suggestive observations on Apollodorus, and his treatment of the Heracles myths in particular.)

C. Robert, *De Apollodori Bibliotheca*, Inaugural diss., University of Berlin, 1873. (The work that first established that the *Library* was not written in the second century BC by Apollodorus of Athens. Robert argued that it should be dated to the second century AD.)

C. Ruiz Montero, 'La Morfologia de la "Biblioteca" de Apolodoro', *Faventia*, 8 (1986), 29–40. (Not seen.)

E. Schwartz, 'Apollodoros', *RE* 1, 2875–86.

Other Ancient Mythographical Works

Two have been translated into English:

Hyginus, *The Myths*, trans. and ed. M. Grant, Lawrence, Kan. 1960. (A chaotic and often unreliable Latin compendium, probably dating from the second century AD; this volume also includes a translation of the *Poetic Astronomy*, the largest surviving collection of constellation myths, which forms Book II of Hyginus' *Astronomy*.)

Antoninus Liberalis, *Metamorphoses*, trans. F. Celoria, London, 1992. (An anthology of transformation myths dating from *circa* second century AD; the stories are of Hellenistic origin for the most part.)

There are also French translations of Antoninus Liberalis and Hyginus' *Astronomy* in the Budé series.

The summaries by Proclus of the early epics in the Trojan cycle are translated in Hesiod and the Homeric Hymns in the Loeb series.

Book IV of the universal history by Diodorus of Sicily is a mythical history of Greece; for a translation, see Diodorus Siculus, vols. 2 and 3, in the Loeb series. (It is less complete than the *Library* of Apollodorus, and the stories are often rationalized; the biography of Heracles is especially interesting.)

Mythological dictionaries and compendia

The excellent dictionary by Pierre Grimal is available in two different editions, as the *Dictionary of Classical Mythology* (Oxford, 1986, complete edn., with references to ancient sources), or the *Penguin Dictionary of Classical Mythology* (Harmondsworth, 1991, a convenient abridged edn.). William Smith's *Dictionary of Greek and Roman Biography and Mythology*, 3 vols. (London, 1844) is still of value for the mythological entries by Leonhard Schmitz, which are long, generally reliable, and give full references. Robert Graves' compendium, *The Greek Myths*, 2 vols. (Harmondsworth, 1955) is comprehensive and attractively written (but the interpretative notes are of value only as a guide to the author's personal mythology); and Karl Kerényi in *The Gods of the Greeks* (London, 1951) and *The Heroes of the Greeks* (London, 1974) has also retold many of the old stories in his own way. H. J. Rose's *Handbook of Greek Mythology* (London, 1928) has not aged well, but it is useful on divine mythology in particular.

Other Books on Greek Myth

The literature is vast, and only a few suggestions can be offered here. For those first approaching the subject (and others too), Fritz Graf, *Greek Mythology: An Introduction* (Baltimore, 1993), can be recommended unreservedly, as a concise but remarkably complete survey, examining the varieties of Greek myth and also changing attitudes to the myths and their interpretation in ancient and modern times, with helpful bibliographies. To this, three other works may be added which, in their different ways, convey an idea of the distinctive nature of Greek myth: K. Dowden, *The Uses of Greek Mythology* (London, 1992), a lively introductory work; G. S. Kirk, *The Nature of Greek Myths* (Harmondsworth, 1974), and above all, R. C. A. Buxton, *Imaginary Greece: Contexts of Mythology* (Cambridge, 1994), a very rich and suggestive study.

Timothy Gantz's *Early Greek Myth* (Baltimore, 1993) is an invaluable guide to the literary and artistic evidence on the early mythological tradition. T. H. Carpenter, *Art and Myth in Ancient Greece: A Handbook* (London, 1991) offers a useful introduction to the treatment of myth in the visual arts. M. L. West, *The Hesiodic Catalogue of Women* (Oxford, 1985), explains the origins and nature of the genealogical scheme for heroic mythology which was adopted and developed by the early mythographer-historians, and thence by the author of the *Library*.

Paul Veyne, *Did the Greeks Believe in their Myths?* (Chicago, 1988), examines the complex and inconsistent attitudes of the Hellenistic and later Greeks to their traditional myths, and M. Detienne, *The Creation of Mythology* (Chicago, 1986), the development of our modern conception of mythology. On modern approaches to the interpretation of Greek myth since the eighteenth century, see Graf's discussion, and also the illuminating survey by J.-P. Vernant in *Myth and Society in*

Ancient Greece (Brighton, 1966). And finally, two volumes of essays may be mentioned which show some of the ways in which scholars of the present day approach the interpretation of myth: J. N. Bremmer (ed.), *Interpretations of Greek Mythology* (London, 1987) and L. Edmunds, *Approaches to Greek Myth* (Baltimore, 1990).

THE LIBRARY OF
GREEK MYTHOLOGY

CONTENTS

THE original text of the *Library* contains no formal subdivisions or chapter headings; at most, the author occasionally indicates that he has concluded his account of one family and is passing on to the next. This can make a modern edition difficult to use, even where it is prefaced with an analytical summary, and a reader first approaching the work is likely to feel, quite mistakenly, that it is formless or even chaotic. To overcome these problems, and to make the work's implicit structure immediately intelligible, I have divided the book into titled chapters and subsections, as summarized in the following table. In the text, these headings, which form no part of the original text, are italicized.

The basic pattern should be apparent at a glance. Greek mythical history begins with the Theogony, accounting for the origin of the world and the divine order within it, and culminates with the Trojan War and its aftermath; and everything that happens in between forms part of the history—or can be related to the history—of the great families of heroic mythology. Considering the richness of the mythological tradition and the multiplicity of independent centres within the Greek world, there are remarkably few main families, only six here (or seven, depending on whether the Pelasgids in Arcadia are considered to be independent from the Inachids). A thorough grasp of their history is evidently the key to an understanding not only of the present work, but of the whole pattern of Greek mythology. Genealogical tables have therefore been added after the Contents (together with some brief remarks on the heroic families and their geographical setting). The roman figures (IA, IB, etc.) in the Contents refer to these tables, indicating which part of the text is covered by each table.

3

Contents

Contents

Contents

Contents

GENEALOGICAL TABLES

The following tables cover the six main families, as follows:

I The Deucalionids
   A The early Deucalionids
   B The Aetolian line
   C The sons of Aiolos and their descendants
II The Inachids
   A The early Inachids in Argos and the east
   B The Belid line in Argos
   C The Agenorid line: the descendants of Europa in Crete
   D The Agenorid line: the descendants of Cadmos in Thebes
III The Atlantids
   A The Laconian royal line, and the usurpers at Thebes
   B The Trojan royal line
IV The Asopids (the family of Achilles and Aias)
V The Athenian royal line
VI The Pelopids (the family of Agamemnon and Menelaos)

Most of these tables depict the mythical royal line in one of the main centres in Greece. Only one of the six families covered by the tables, namely the Athenian, conforms to the simplest possible pattern, in which a single family provides the ruling line in a single city. Generally the genealogical system is more economical, and the ruling lines in two or more cities are traced to a common ancestor and so united within the same family. Thus separate branches of the Inachid family provide the royal families of both Argos and Thebes, the two greatest centres in mythical Greece, and also of Crete. Accordingly, the family trees of the first three families, which are the largest and are divided in this way between different centres, have been subdivided in the tables.

Although the adventures of various members of these families take them to many different parts of the Mediterranean world, it is natural that the main centres of rule associated with the great families should be located in the heartland of Greece. There

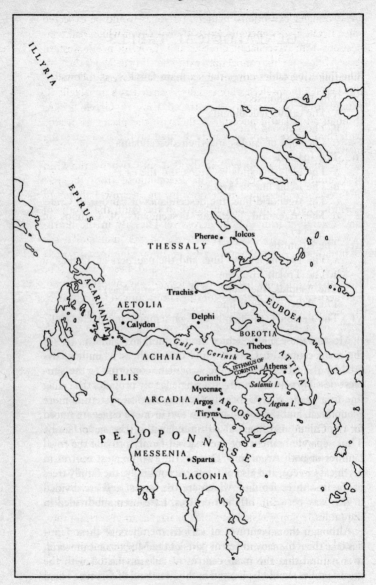

are two major exceptions, namely, Crete, as would be expected since it was a very ancient centre of civilization which had connections with Mycenaean Greece, and Troy, in north-western Asia Minor, for its connection with the Trojan War, the culminating adventure in the mythical history of Greece. Although the Trojans themselves were usually regarded as a non-Hellenic people, the ruling family was traced back to Greek origins through an Atlantid ancestor. Otherwise the places associated with these various families can be located on the accompanying map.

The mainland of Greece is divided into two by the Gulf of Corinth, which separates the Peloponnese from the rest of Greece, being joined to it only by the narrow Isthmus of Corinth. Starting immediately north of the Gulf, the swathe of land extending from Aetolia across to Thessaly in the northeast is the area primarily associated with the first family, the Deucalionids. Although this was an important area in early myth, there were many separate centres, and these tended to be associated with major heroic myths for only a generation or two. Furthermore, many members of this family moved to fresh areas at various stages and established new dynasties, whether in the north, or in the western Peloponnese and the south. As a result, the structure of this family is rather complex, and we do not find extensive lines within individual centres as in most of the following families. The Aetolian royal line covered in the second table (1B) was descended from a daughter of Aiolos; the most important town in Aetolia was Calydon, the site of the first great adventure which drew heroes from all parts of Greece, the hunt for the Calydonian Boar. The descendants of the sons of Aiolos covered in the third table (1C) were primarily associated with Thessaly (but also with the western Peloponnese and elsewhere); here Iolcos, the home of Pelias and Jason, and Pherae, the home of Admetos and Alcestis, are the most significant towns.

South of the Gulf of Corinth, in the Peloponnese, the most important region was not Laconia (Sparta) as in historical times, but Argos with its great Mycenaean cities, Mycenae, Argos, and Tiryns. Here the second family, the Inachids, provided the main ruling line. Although it was of Argive origin (the Inachos was the largest river in Argos), other branches of this family ruled

11

in Crete and in Thebes. Passing north from Argos and then across the Isthmus of Corinth, Boeotia, with Thebes as its main city, lies to the left, and Attica to the right. In mythical history Thebes ranked with Argos as the most important centre.

Of the Atlantids, two main lines are covered in the following tables, the earliest royal line in the second main centre in the Peloponnese, Laconia, and the Trojan royal line.

The Asopid family tree is exceptional, as it was developed to account for the common descent of the two greatest heroes of the Trojan War, Achilles and Aias (who came from different areas) as grandsons of Aiacos (who reigned in a different area again). This was a relatively late development; in the *Iliad* the pair are not related. Aiacos was the first king of Aegina, a small island in the Saronic Gulf, which lies between Attica and the Peloponnese. Both of his sons were exiled. Telamon, father of Aias, went to the island of Salamis, not far to the north; Peleus eventually arrived in Thessaly where he became the father of Achilles by the goddess Thetis.

This leaves the Athenian royal line and the Pelopids. The Athenian genealogies were systematized at a relatively late period, and none of the figures before Aigeus and Theseus are associated with major heroic myth. The first four kings were earthborn. The Pelopids provided the second royal line in each of the main centres of the Peloponnese, Argos and Laconia; for Agamemnon, who ruled in Mycenae at the time of the Trojan War, and Menelaos, who ruled in Sparta, did not belong to the original ruling families covered in tables IIB and IIIA, but were descended from Tantalos, who lived in Asia Minor, and his son Pelops, who became king of Pisa in the north-western Peloponnese. The Pelopids were displaced when Tisamenos, who ruled in both Argos and Laconia, was killed by the returning Heraclids (who were of Inachid descent).

In the following tables:

The parentage of children is indicated by *swung dashes* (~); where both parents are mortals, these will usually indicate a marriage also.

The names of successive kings within each centre are set in **bold type**, and the order of succession is indicated by small letters before their names (*a*, *b*, *c*, etc.). The order of succession is not indicated for the Argive line in IIB because of the complexities which arise after the kingdom is divided between Proitos and Acrisios.

In IC only the Iolcian line is indicated, and in V only the Mycenaean. For the Laconian succession after Amyclas, in IIIA, the account in 3.10.4 is followed; 3.10.3 should be consulted for alternative genealogies.

Where it has been necessary to divide family trees into two or more tables, the names of pivotal figures who appear in more than one table are enclosed in *boxes*.

NB. There was disagreement on many genealogies. These tables show the main lines as presented in the text of the *Library*, without indicating alternative traditions recorded in other sources, or variants mentioned within the *Library* itself.

The purpose of these tables is to give a clear picture of the descent and interrelationship of the more important figures, and they are by no means complete. In particular, many marriages yielded more children than are named in the tables, and the fact that names have been omitted is not always indicated; and for reasons of clarity, the names of mothers have sometimes been omitted, and children are not always presented in their order of birth. For the full picture, the text should be consulted.

The tables for the Deucalionids and Atlantids do not cover all branches of the family.

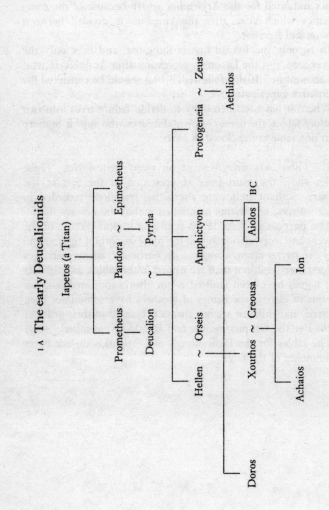

I A The early Deucalionids

Iapetos (a Titan)

Prometheus   Pandora ~ Epimetheus

Deucalion ~ Pyrrha

Hellen ~ Orseis   Amphictyon   Protogeneia ~ Zeus

Aethlios

Aiolos BC

Doros   Xouthos ~ Creousa

Achaios   Ion

14

1 B The Aetolian line

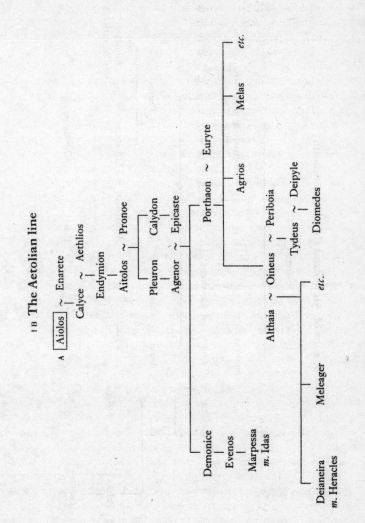

1c The sons of Aiolos and their descendants

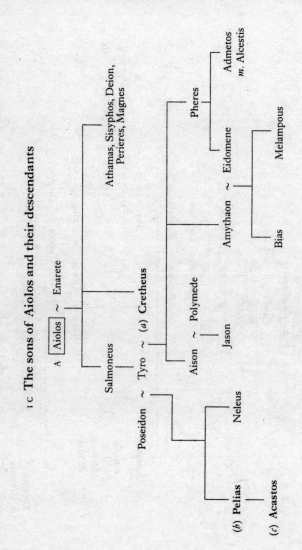

IIA The early Inachids in Argos and the east

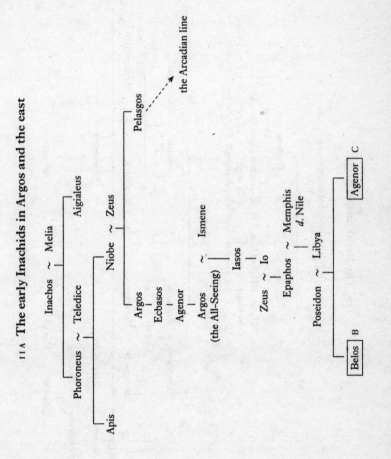

IIB The Belid line in Argos

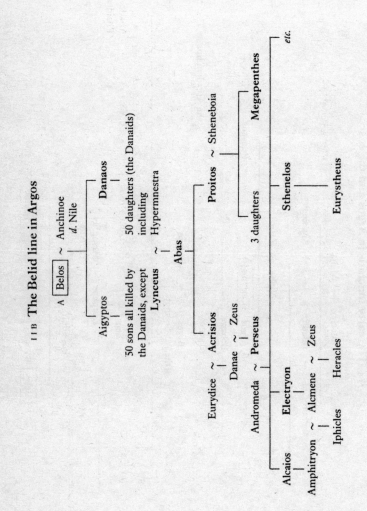

```
A  [Belos]  ~  Anchinoe
               d. Nile
   ┌──────────┴──────────┐
Aigyptos              Danaos
50 sons all killed by    50 daughters (the Danaids)
the Danaids, except           including
Lynceus      ~          Hypermnestra
               │
             Abas
   ┌──────────┴──────────┐
Eurydice ~ Acrisios    Proitos ~ Stheneboia
         │           ┌──────┴──────┐
Danae ~ Zeus    3 daughters    Megapenthes
         │                              etc.
Andromeda ~ Perseus    Sthenelos
         │                   │
Electryon          Eurystheus
         │
Amphitryon ~ Alcmene ~ Zeus
Alcaios    │           │
       Iphicles    Heracles
```

11C The Agenorid line: the descendants of Europa in Crete

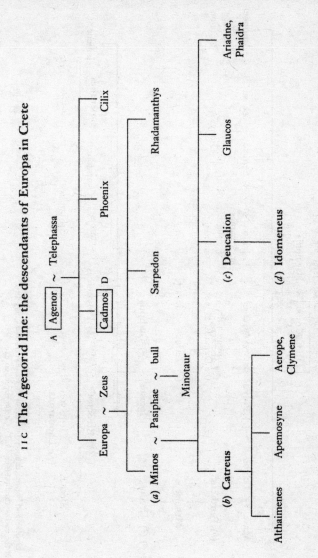

11D The Agenorid line: the descendants of Cadmos in Thebes

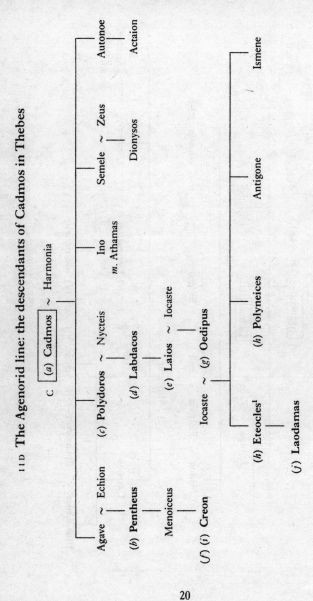

c (a) **Cadmos** ~ Harmonia

Agave ~ Echion

(b) **Pentheus**

Menoiceus

(f) (i) **Creon**

(c) **Polydoros** ~ Nycteis

(d) **Labdacos**

(e) **Laios** ~ Iocaste

Iocaste ~ (g) **Oedipus**

(h) **Eteocles**[1]

(j) **Laodamas**

(h) **Polyneices**

Antigone

Ismene

Ino
m. Athamas

Semele ~ Zeus

Dionysos

Autonoe

Actaion

[1] Eteocles and Polyneices agreed to rule in alternate years, but quarrelled at the end of the first (see 3.6.1). Creon succeded Eteocles either as king or as guardian of Laodamas.

IIIA The Laconian royal line, and the usurpers at Thebes

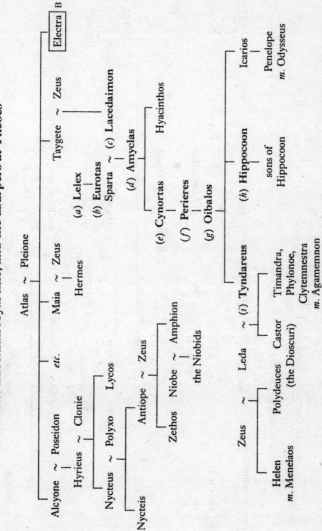

111B The Trojan royal line

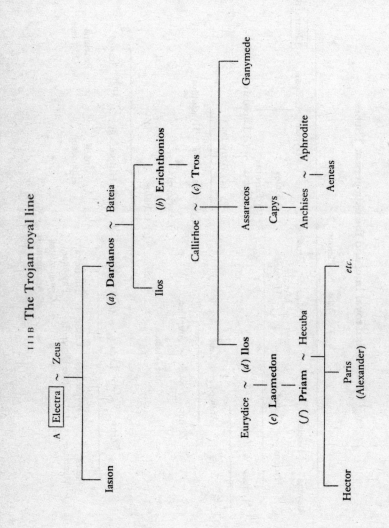

A Electra ~ Zeus

Iasion

(a) Dardanos ~ Bateia

Ilos   (b) Erichthonios

Callirhoe ~ (c) Tros

Assaracos   Ganymede

Capys

Anchises ~ Aphrodite

Aeneas

Eurydice ~ (d) Ilos

(e) Laomedon

(f) Priam ~ Hecuba

Hector   Paris
(Alexander)   etc.

IV The Asopids (the family of Achilles and Aias)

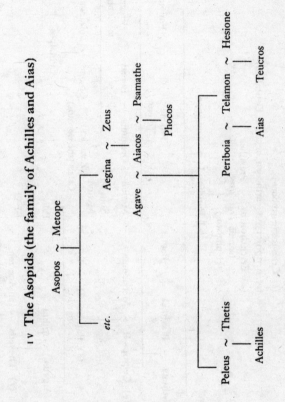

Asopos ~ Metope
     Aegina ~ Zeus
          Aiacos ~ Psamathe
     Agave ~   Phocos
  etc.

Peleus ~ Thetis   Periboia ~ Telamon ~ Hesione
  Achilles   Aias   Teucros

Genealogical Tables

v The Athenian royal line

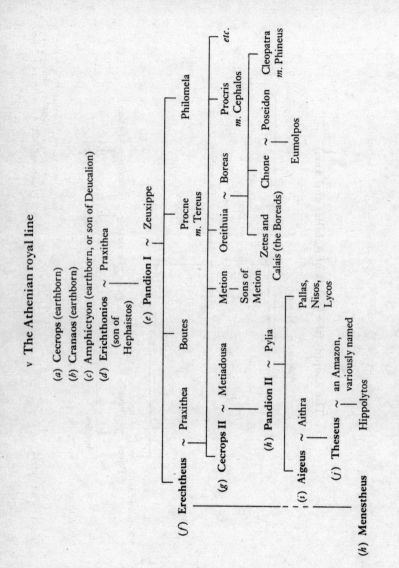

(a) Cecrops (earthborn)

(b) Cranaos (earthborn)

(c) Amphictyon (earthborn, or son of Deucalion)

(d) Erichthonios ~ Praxithea
(son of Hephaistos)

(e) Pandion I ~ Zeuxippe

Boutes · Erechtheus ~ Praxithea · Procne *m. Tereus* · Philomela

(f) Erechtheus ~ Praxithea

(g) Cecrops II ~ Metiadousa

Metion · Sons of Metion

Oreithuia ~ Boreas

Procris *m. Cephalos*

Zetes and Calais (the Boreads)

Chone ~ Poseidon

Eumolpos

Cleopatra *m. Phineus*

etc.

(h) Pandion II ~ Pylia

Pallas, Nisos, Lycos

(i) Aigeus ~ Aithra

(j) Theseus ~ an Amazon, variously named

Hippolytos

(h) Menestheus

24

vi The Pelopids (the family of Agamemnon and Menelaos)

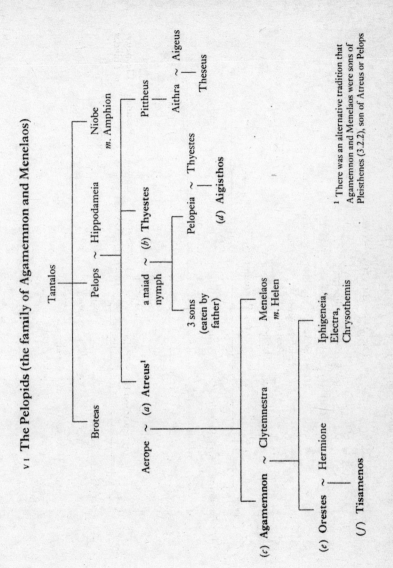

1 There was an alternative tradition that Agamemnon and Menelaos were sons of Pleisthenes (3.2.2), son of Atreus or Pelops

BOOK I

1. Theogony

Ouranos, Ge, and the birth of the Titans

1 ¹ OURANOS was the first ruler of the universe. He married Ge,* and fathered as his first children the beings known as the Hundred-Handers, Briareus, Cottos, and Gyes, who were unsurpassable in size and strength, for each had a hundred hands and fifty heads. ² After these, Ge bore him the Cyclopes,* namely, Arges, Steropes, and Brontes, each of whom had a single eye on his forehead. But Ouranos tied these children up and hurled them into Tartaros (a place of infernal darkness in Hades,* as distant from the earth as the earth from the sky); ³ and he then fathered by Ge some sons called the Titans, namely, Oceanos, Coios, Hyperion, Creios, Iapetos, and the youngest of all, Cronos, and some daughters called the Titanides, namely, Tethys, Rhea, Themis, Mnemosyne, Phoebe, Dione, and Theia.

The revolt of the Titans and rule of Cronos

⁴ But Ge, angered by the loss of her children who had been thrown into Tartaros,* persuaded the Titans to attack their father, and gave an adamantine* sickle to Cronos; and they all attacked him, apart from Oceanos, and Cronos severed his father's genitals and threw them into the sea. (From the drops of blood that flowed out* the Furies were born: Alecto, Tisiphone, and Megaira.) When they had driven their father from power, they brought back their brothers who had been thrown down to Tartaros, and entrusted the sovereignty to Cronos.

⁵ But he bound them once again and imprisoned them in Tartaros, and married his sister Rhea; and since both Ge and Ouranos had prophesied to him that he would be stripped of

his power by his own son, he swallowed his children as they were born. He swallowed his first-born, Hestia, and then Demeter and Hera, and after them, Pluto and Poseidon.

The birth of Zeus and his war against Cronos and the Titans

6 Angered by this, Rhea went to Crete while she was pregnant with Zeus, and brought him to birth in a cave on Mount Dicte.* She gave him to the Curetes* and to the nymphs Adrasteia and Ida, daughters of Melisseus, to rear. 7 So the nymphs fed the child on the milk of Amaltheia* while the Curetes, fully armed, guarded the baby in the cave, beating their spears against their shields to prevent Cronos from hearing the child's voice. And Rhea wrapped a stone in swaddling clothes and passed it to Cronos to swallow as if it were the newborn child.

2   1 When Zeus was fully grown, he enlisted the help of Metis,* the daughter of Oceanos, and she gave Cronos a drug to swallow, which forced him to disgorge first the stone and then the children whom he had swallowed; and with their aid, Zeus went to war against Cronos and the Titans. When they had been fighting for ten years, Ge prophesied that the victory would go to Zeus if he took as his allies those who had been hurled down to Tartaros. So he killed Campe, who was guarding them, and set them free. And the Cyclopes then gave Zeus thunder, lightning, and a thunderbolt, and they gave a helmet* to Pluto, and a trident to Poseidon. Armed with these weapons, they overpowered the Titans, and imprisoned them in Tartaros, appointing the Hundred-Handers as their guards; and they shared power* between themselves by casting lots. Zeus was allotted sovereignty over the heavens, Poseidon over the sea, and Pluto over the halls of Hades.*

Descendants of the Titans

2 The Titans had the following offspring: to Oceanos and Tethys were born the Oceanids,* Asia, Styx, Electra, Doris, Eurynome, [Amphitrite,] and Metis; to Coios and Phoebe were born Asteria and Leto; to Hyperion and Theia were born Dawn

and the Sun and Moon; to Creios and Eurybia, daughter of
Pontos, were born Astraios, Pallas, and Perses; 3 and to Iapetos
and Asia were born Atlas who bears the sky on his shoulders,
and Prometheus, and Epimetheus, and Menoitios, whom Zeus
struck with a thunderbolt during the battle with the Titans and
hurled down to Tartaros. 4 To Cronos and Philyra, Cheiron
was born, a Centaur of twofold form. To Dawn and Astraios
were born the winds and stars, and to Perses and Asteria, Hecate;
and to Pallas and Styx were born Nice, Cratos, Zelos, and Bia.*

5 Zeus caused oaths* to be sworn by the waters of Styx,
which flow from a rock in Hades. He bestowed this honour on
Styx in return for the help that she and her children had brought
to him in his war against the Titans.

Descendants of Pontos and Ge

6 To Pontos* and Ge were born Phorcos, Thaumas, Nereus,
Eurybia, and Ceto. To Thaumas and Electra were born Iris
and the Harpies, Aello and Ocypete; and to Phorcos and Ceto,
the Phorcides and the Gorgons, who will be considered below
when we tell the story of Perseus. 7 To Nereus and Doris were
born the Nereids,* whose names are Cymothoe, Speio, Glau-
conome, Nausithoe, Halie, Erato, Sao, Amphitrite, Eunice,
Thetis, Eulimene, Agave, Eudore, Doto, Pherousa, Galatea,
Actaie, Pontomedousa, Hippothoe, Lysianassa, Cymo, Eione,
Halimede, Plexaure, Eucrante, Proto, Calypso, Panope, Cranto,
Neomeris, Hipponoe, Ianeira, Polynome, Autonoe, Melite,
Dione, Nesaie, Dero, Evagore, Psamathe, Eumolpe, Ione,
Dynamene, Ceto, and Limnoreia.

Various children of Zeus and Hera; children of the Muses

3 1 Zeus married Hera and fathered Hebe, Eileithuia, and Ares;*
but he had intercourse with many other women, both mortal
and immortal. By Themis, daughter of Ouranos he had some
daughters, the Seasons, namely, Eirene, Eunomia, and Dice,*
and the Fates, namely, Clotho, Lachesis, and Atropos; by
Dione he had Aphrodite;* by Eurynome, daughter of Oceanos,
the Graces, namely, Aglaie, Euphrosyne, and Thaleia; by Styx,

Persephone;* and by Mnemosyne the Muses, firstly Calliope, and then Cleio, Melpomene, Euterpe, Erato, Terpsichore, Ourania, Thaleia, and Polymnia.

2 Calliope bore to Oiagros—or really, it is said, to Apollo— a son, Linos,* who was killed by Heracles, and Orpheus, who practised the art of singing to the lyre, and set rocks and trees in motion by his singing. When his wife, Eurydice, died from a snake-bite, he went down to Hades in the hope of bringing her up, and persuaded Pluto* to send her back to earth. Pluto promised to do so, provided that on the way up Orpheus never looked round until he had arrived back at his house. But Orpheus failed to obey him, and turning round, he caught sight of his wife, and she had to return below. Orpheus also invented the mysteries of Dionysos. He was torn apart by the Maenads,* and is buried in Pieria.

3 Cleio fell in love with Pieros, son of Magnes, through the anger of Aphrodite (for Cleio had reproached her for her love of Adonis*); and she had intercourse with him and bore him a son, Hyacinthos, who aroused the passion of Thamyris, son of Philammon and a nymph Argiope, the first man to love other males.* But Hyacinthos later died at the hand of Apollo, who became his lover and killed him accidentally when throwing a discus.* And Thamyris, who was exceptional for his beauty and his skill in singing to the lyre, challenged the Muses* to a contest in music, on the agreement that if he proved to be the better, he could have intercourse with them all, but if he were defeated, they could deprive him of anything they wished. The Muses proved to be superior, and deprived him both of his eyes and his skill in singing to the lyre.

4 Euterpe bore to the River Strymon a son Rhesos, who was killed by Diomedes at Troy;* but according to some accounts, his mother was Calliope. To Thaleia and Apollo were born the Corybantes;* and to Melpomene and Acheloos, the Sirens, who will be considered below in our account of Odysseus.

The births of Hephaistos and Athene

5 Hera gave birth to Hephaistos without prior intercourse (though Homer describes him as another of her children by

Zeus).* Zeus threw him down from heaven for coming to the aid of his mother when she was put in chains; for Zeus had suspended Hera from Olympos for sending a storm against Heracles when he was sailing home after capturing Troy. Hephaistos fell to earth on Lemnos and was lamed in both his legs, but Thetis came to his rescue.*

6 Zeus had intercourse with Metis, although she changed into many different forms in the hope of escaping it. While she was pregnant, Zeus forestalled future developments by swallowing her; for [Ge]* declared that after having the girl who was due to be born to her, Metis would give birth to a son who would become the ruler of heaven. It was for fear of this that he swallowed her down. When the time arrived for the child to be born, Prometheus, or according to others, Hephaistos, struck the head of Zeus with an axe and from the top of his head, near the River Triton,* leapt Athene, fully armed.

Artemis and Apollo

4 ¹ One of Coios' daughters, Asteria, took the form of a quail and threw herself into the sea to escape the embraces of Zeus; and a city was named Asteria after her, for this was the former name of what was later called Delos.* His other daughter, Leto, had intercourse with Zeus, and was chased all over the earth by Hera until she arrived at Delos, where she gave birth first to Artemis, and then, with the aid of Artemis as a midwife, to Apollo.

Artemis devoted herself to hunting and remained a virgin, while Apollo learned the art of divination from Pan, son of Zeus and Hybris, and went to Delphi where, at that time, the oracles were delivered by Themis;* and when the guardian of the oracle, the serpent Python, tried to prevent him from approaching the chasm,* he killed it and took possession of the oracle.

Not long afterwards, he killed Tityos also, who was the son of Zeus and Elare, daughter of Orchomenos; for after making love with Elare, Zeus had hidden her under the earth for fear of Hera, and had brought up to light the child that she was carrying in her womb, the enormous Tityos. Now when Leto came to Pytho,* she was seen by Tityos, who was overcome by desire and seized her in his arms; but she called her children to her aid, and they shot him down with their arrows. Tityos suffers punishment* even after his death, for vultures feed on his heart in Hades.

2 Apollo also killed Marsyas, the son of Olympos; for Marsyas had discovered the flute that Athene had thrown away because it disfigured her face,* and he challenged Apollo to a musical contest. They agreed that the victor should do what he wished with the loser, and when the test was under way, Apollo played his lyre upside down and told Marsyas to do the same;* and when he was unable to, Apollo was recognized as the victor, and killed Marsyas by suspending him from a lofty pine tree and flaying him.

3 Artemis, for her part, killed Orion on Delos. They say that he was born from the earth, with a body of gigantic proportions; but according to Pherecydes, he was a son of Poseidon and Euryale. Poseidon had granted him the power to walk across the sea. His first wife was Side, who was thrown into Hades by Hera because she had claimed to rival the goddess in beauty; and afterwards he went to Chios, and sought the hand of Merope, daughter of Oinopion. But Oinopion made him drunk, blinded him* as he slept, and threw him out by the seashore. Orion made his way to the forge [of Hephaistos],* where he snatched up a boy, and setting him on his shoulders, told him to guide him towards the sunrise. When he arrived there, his sight was rekindled by the rays of the sun, and he was able to see again. 4 He returned with all haste to attack Oinopion; but Poseidon had provided him with an underground dwelling constructed by Hephaistos. Dawn fell in love with Orion and carried him off to Delos (for Aphrodite caused her to be continually in love because she had gone to bed with Ares).* 5 According to some accounts, Orion was killed because he challenged Artemis to a contest in throwing the discus, while according to others, he was shot by Artemis* because he tried to rape Opis,* one of the virgins who had arrived from the Hyperboreans.

The children of Poseidon; Demeter and Persephone

6 Poseidon married Amphitrite, [daughter of Oceanos,] who bore Triton to him, and Rhode,* who became the wife of the Sun.

5 1 Pluto fell in love with Persephone and, with the help of Zeus, he secretly abducted her;* but Demeter, bearing torches,* wandered by night and day all over the earth in search of her. When she learned from the people of Hermion* that Pluto had carried her off, she abandoned heaven in her anger at the gods, and came to Eleusis in the likeness of a woman. First she sat down on the rock which is called the Laughterless Rock because of her, and then made her way to Celeos, who was king of the Eleusinians at the time. There were some women in the house, and when they invited her to sit down amongst them, an old woman called Iambe joked with the goddess and made her smile; and that, they say, is the reason why the women make jokes at the Thesmophoria.*

Metaneira, the wife of Celeos, had a young child, and Demeter took it over to nurse. Wanting to make it immortal, she would lay the baby in the fire at night, stripping it of its mortal flesh. But because Demophon (for that was the child's name) was growing at such an extraordinary rate each day, Praxithea* kept watch over him, and when she found him buried in the fire, she screamed aloud; as a result, the baby was consumed by the fire, and the goddess revealed her identity.*

2 For Triptolemos, the eldest of Metaneira's children, Demeter fashioned a chariot drawn by winged dragons, and she gave him wheat,* which he sowed over the whole inhabited earth as he was carried through the sky. Panyasis says that Triptolemos was a son of Eleusis, for according to him, that was whom Demeter had visited. Pherecydes, for his part, says that he was a son of Oceanos and Ge.

3 When Zeus ordered Pluto to send Kore* back to earth, Pluto, to prevent her from remaining too long with her mother, gave her a pomegranate seed to eat;* and failing to foresee what the consequence would be, she ate it. When Ascalaphos, son of Acheron and Gorgyra, bore witness against her,* Demeter placed a heavy rock over him in Hades, but Persephone

was forced to stay with Pluto for a third of every year,* and the rest she spent with the gods.

6   ¹ Such is the story of Demeter.

The revolt of the Giants

Ge, angered by the fate of the Titans, brought to birth the Giants, whom she had conceived by Ouranos.* These were unsurpassable in size, unassailable in their strength, and fearful to behold because of the thick hair hanging down from their head and cheeks; and their feet were formed from dragons' scales. According to some accounts, they were born at Phlegrai, or according to others, at Pallene. And they hurled rocks and flaming oak trees at the heavens. Mightiest of all were Porphyrion and Alcyoneus, who was even immortal as long as he fought on the land of his birth. It was he, moreover, who drove the cattle of the Sun from Erytheia. Now the gods had an oracle saying that none of the Giants could be killed by the gods [acting on their own], but if the gods had a mortal fighting as their ally, the Giants would meet their end. When Ge heard of this, she searched for a herb to prevent the Giants from being destroyed even by a mortal; but Zeus forestalled her, for he ordered Dawn, and the Moon and Sun, not to shine and plucked the herb himself. And he sent Athene to summon Heracles as an ally.

And first Heracles shot Alcyoneus with his arrows, but when he fell to the earth, he recovered some of his strength. On the advice of Athene, Heracles dragged him beyond the boundaries of Pallene, and so it came about that the Giant met his death. ² In the course of the fighting, Porphyrion launched an attack against Heracles and Hera. But Zeus inspired him with a lust for Hera, and when he tore her clothing and tried to rape her, she cried for help; and Zeus struck the Giant with his thunderbolt, and Heracles killed him with a shot from his bow. As for the others, Apollo shot Ephialtes in the left eye with one of his arrows, while Heracles shot him in the right. Eurytos was killed by Dionysos with a blow from his thyrsos,* Clytios by Hecate with her torches, and Mimas by Hephaistos with missiles of red-hot iron. Athene hurled the island of

Sicily on Encelados as he fled; and she flayed Pallas and used his skin to protect her own body during the fight. Polybotes was pursued through the sea by Poseidon and made his way to Cos, where Poseidon broke off the part of the island called Nisyron* and threw it down on him. Hermes, who was wearing the cap of Hades, killed Hippolytos in the battle, and Artemis killed Gration;* and the Fates, fighting with bronze cudgels, killed Agrios and Thoon. The others were destroyed by Zeus, who struck them with thunderbolts; and all of them, in their death throes, were shot with arrows by Heracles.

The revolt of Typhon

3 When the gods had defeated the Giants, Ge, whose anger was all the greater, had intercourse with Tartaros and gave birth to Typhon* in Cilicia. He was part man and part beast, and in both size and strength he surpassed all the other children of Ge. Down to his thighs he was human in form, but of such immense size that he rose higher than all the mountains and often even scraped the stars with his head. With arms outstretched, he could reach the west on one side and the east on the other; and from his arms there sprang a hundred dragons' heads.* Below his thighs, he had massive coils of vipers, which, when they were fully extended, reached right up to his head and emitted violent hisses. He had wings all over his body, and filthy hair springing from his head and cheeks floated around him in the wind, and fire flashed from his eyes. Such was Typhon's appearance and such his size when he launched an attack against heaven itself, hurling flaming rocks at it, hissing and screaming all at once, and gushing mighty streams of fire from his mouth. Seeing him rush against heaven, the gods took flight to Egypt,* and when they were pursued by him, transformed themselves into animals. While Typhon was still at a distance, Zeus pelted him with thunderbolts, but as the monster drew close, Zeus struck at him with an adamantine sickle, and then chased after him when he fled, until they arrived at Mount Casion, which rises over Syria. And there, seeing that Typhon was severely wounded, he engaged him in hand-to-hand combat. But Typhon enveloped him in his coils and

held him fast; and wresting the sickle from him, he cut the tendons from his hands and feet. And raising him on his shoulders, he carried him through the sea to Cilicia, and put him down again when he arrived at the Corycian cave. He placed the tendons there also, hiding them in a bear's skin and appointing as their guard the she-dragon Delphyne, who was half beast and half maiden. But Hermes and Aigipan* made away with the tendons and fitted them back into Zeus without being observed. When Zeus had recovered his strength, he made a sudden descent from heaven on a chariot drawn by winged horses, and hurling thunderbolts, he pursued Typhon to the mountain called Nysa, where the fugitive was tricked by the Fates; for persuaded that he would become stronger as a result, he tasted the ephemeral fruits.* Coming under pursuit once again, he arrived in Thrace, and joining battle near Mount Haimos, he began to hurl entire mountains. But when they were thrust back at him by the thunderbolts, a stream of *blood** gushed from him onto the mountain (which is said to be the reason why it was called *Haimos*). When he set out to flee across the Sicilian sea, Zeus hurled Mount Etna at him, which lies in Sicily. This is a mountain of enormous size, and there rise up from it, even to this day, eruptions of fire* that are said to issue from the thunderbolts hurled by Zeus. But that is quite enough on this matter.

2. The Deucalionids

Prometheus and early man

7 1 After he had fashioned men* from water and earth, Prometheus also gave them fire, which he had hidden in a fennel* stalk in secret from Zeus. But when Zeus learned of it, he ordered Hephaistos to nail his body to Mount Caucasos (a mountain that lies in Scythia). So Prometheus was nailed to it and held fast there for a good many years; and each day, an eagle swooped down to feed on the lobes of his liver, which grew again by night. Such was the punishment suffered by Prometheus for having stolen the fire, until Heracles later released him, as we will show* in our account of Heracles.

Deucalion, Pyrrha, and the great flood

2 Prometheus had a son, Deucalion, who ruled the area around Phthia, and married Pyrrha, the daughter of Epimetheus and of Pandora, whom the gods had fashioned as the first woman.* When Zeus wanted to eliminate the race of bronze,* Deucalion, on the advice of Prometheus, built a chest, and after storing it with provisions, climbed into it with Pyrrha. Zeus poured an abundance of rain from heaven to flood the greater part of Greece, causing all human beings to be destroyed, apart from those few who took refuge in the lofty mountains nearby. It was then that the mountains of Thessaly drew apart and all the lands outside the Isthmus and the Peloponnese were submerged. But Deucalion was carried across the sea in his chest for nine days and as many nights until he was washed ashore at Parnassos; and there, when the rain stopped, he disembarked, and offered a sacrifice to Zeus, God of Escape. Zeus sent Hermes to him and allowed him the choice of whatever he wished; and Deucalion chose to have people. On the orders of Zeus, he picked up stones and threw them over his head; and the stones that Deucalion threw became men, and those that Pyrrha threw became women. That was how people came to be called *laoi*, by metaphor from the word *laas*, a stone.*

The immediate descendants of Deucalion

Deucalion had two sons by Pyrrha, first Hellen (though some describe him as a son of Zeus), and secondly Amphictyon, who became king of Attica after Cranaos; he also had a daughter, Protogeneia, who later bore Aethlios to Zeus.

3 Hellen had three sons, Doros, Xouthos, and Aiolos, by a nymph, Orseis; and those who were called the Graicoi he named Hellenes* after himself. And he divided the land amongst his sons. Xouthos received the Peloponnese, and by Creousa, daughter of Erechtheus, he had two sons, Achaios and Ion, after whom the Achaeans and the Ionians were named. Doros received the country opposite the Peloponnese* and named its inhabitants the Dorians after himself. Aiolos became king of the lands around Thessaly and named their inhabitants the

Aeolians. He married Enarete, daughter of Deimachos, and became the father of seven sons, Cretheus, Sisyphos, Athamas, Salmoneus, Deion, Magnes, and Perieres, and five daughters, Canace, Alcyone, Peisidice, Calyce, and Perimede.

Ceux and Alcyone; the Aloads; Endymion

Perimede bore Hippodamas and Orestes to Acheloos; and Peisidice bore Antiphos and Actor to Myrmidon. 4 Alcyone became the wife of Ceux, son of Heosphoros. Both of them died because of their arrogance: for Ceux said that his wife was Hera, and Alcyone that her husband was Zeus, and Zeus changed them into birds, making her a *halcyon** and him a *sea-swallow*.*

Canace bore Hopleus, Nireus, Epopeus, Aloeus, and Triops to Poseidon. Aloeus married Iphimedeia, daughter of Triops, but she fell in love with Poseidon, and went down to the sea again and again, where she would scoop water from the waves with her hands and pour it into her lap. Poseidon had intercourse with her and fathered two sons, Otos and Ephialtes, who are known as the Aloads.* They grew a cubit broader every year and a fathom* higher; and when they were nine years old, and nine cubits across and nine fathoms in height, they resolved to fight against the gods. They piled Ossa on Olympos and Pelion* on Ossa, and threatened to use these mountains to climb up to heaven; and they said that by filling the sea with mountains they would turn the sea into dry land and the dry land into sea. And Ephialtes sought to win Hera, and Otos to win Artemis; they also imprisoned Ares.* But Hermes freed him surreptitiously, and the Aloads met their death on Naxos* as the result of a subterfuge by Artemis; for she changed herself into a deer and leapt between them, and in their desire to hit the beast they struck one another with their javelins.

5 Calyce and Aethlios had a son, Endymion, who led the Aeolians out of Thessaly and founded Elis. It is said by some, however, that Endymion was a son of Zeus. Because of his exceptional beauty the Moon fell in love with him; and when Zeus allowed him the choice of whatever he wished, he chose

to sleep for ever and so remain untouched by either age or death.

Early Aetolian genealogies; Evenos and Marpessa

6 By a naiad nymph, or according to some, by Iphianassa, Endymion had a son, Aitolos, who killed Apis, son of Phoroneus,* and fled to the land of the Curetes.* There he killed the sons of Phthia and Apollo who had welcomed him, namely, Doros, Laodocos, and Polypoites, and called the country Aetolia after himself.

7 By Pronoe, daughter of Phorbos, Aitolos had two sons, Pleuron and Calydon, after whom the two cities in Aetolia were named. Pleuron married Xanthippe, daughter of Doros, and had a son, Agenor, and three daughters, Sterope, Stratonice, and Laophonte. To Calydon and Aiolia, daughter of Amythaon, were born two daughters, Epicaste and Protogeneia, who bore Oxylos to Ares. Pleuron's son Agenor married Epicaste, daughter of Calydon, and fathered Porthaon and a daughter, Demonice, who bore Evenos, Molos, Pylos, and Thestios to Ares.

8 Evenos had a daughter, Marpessa, who, while she was being courted by Apollo, was carried off by Idas, son of Aphareus, in a winged chariot which he had received from Poseidon. Chasing after him* in a chariot, Evenos went as far as the River Lycormas, but finding it impossible to catch up with Idas, he slaughtered his horses and hurled himself into the river, which is now named the Evenos after him. 9 Idas went on to Messene,* where Apollo happened to meet him and tried to take the girl away from him. As they were fighting for her hand, Zeus separated them and allowed the girl herself to choose which of them she preferred to live with; and Marpessa, fearing that Apollo might leave her when she grew old, selected Idas for her husband.

10 By Eurythemis, daughter of Cleoboia, Thestios had three daughters, Althaia, Leda, and Hypermnestra, and four sons, Iphiclos, Evippos, Plexippos, and Eurypylos.

By Euryte, daughter of Hippodamas, Porthaon had five sons, Oineus, Agrios, Alcathoos, Melas, and Leucopeus, and

a daughter, Sterope, who is said to have borne the Sirens to
Acheloos.*

Oineus, Meleager, and the hunt for the Calydonian boar

8 1 Oineus, the king of Calydon, was the first to receive a vine
plant from Dionysos.* He married Althaia, daughter of Thestios,
and fathered Toxeus—who was put to death by Oineus himself for jumping over the ditch*—and two further sons, Thyreus
and Clymenos. He also had a daughter, Gorge, who became
the wife of Andraimon, and another daughter, Deianeira, who
is said to have been Althaia's child by Dionysos. Deianeira drove
a chariot and practised the arts of war; and Heracles wrestled
with Acheloos to gain her hand.

2 Althaia also bore to Oineus a son, Meleager, whose real
father is said to have been Ares. When he was seven days old,
it is said that the Fates appeared and announced that Meleager
would die when the log burning on the hearth was fully consumed. In response, Althaia snatched it from the fire and
placed it in a chest.* Meleager developed into an invulnerable
and valiant man, but met his death in the following manner.
When Oineus was offering the first-fruits from the annual harvest in the land to all the gods, he forgot Artemis alone. In
her anger, she sent a boar of exceptional size and strength,
which prevented the land from being sown, and destroyed the
cattle and the people who encountered it. To hunt this boar,*
Oineus summoned together all the bravest men in Greece,
announcing that he would give the beast's hide to the man who
killed it, as a prize for his valour.

These are the people who gathered to hunt the boar:
Meleager, son of Oineus, and Dryas, son of Ares, both from
Calydon; Idas and Lynceus, sons of Aphareus, from Messene;
Castor and Polydeuces, sons of Zeus and Leda, from Lace-
daimon; Theseus, son of Aigeus, from Athens; Admetos, son of
Pheres, from Pherae; Ancaios and Cepheus, sons of Lycourgos,
from Arcadia; Jason, son of Aison, from Iolcos; Iphicles, son
of Amphitryon, from Thebes; Peirithoos, son of Ixion, from
Larissa; Peleus, son of Aiacos, from Phthia; Telamon, son of

Aiacos, from Salamis; Eurytion, son of Actor, from Phthia; Atalante, daughter of Schoineus, from Arcadia; Amphiaraos, son of Oicles, from Argos; and with the aforementioned, also the sons of Thestios.

When they were assembled, Oineus entertained them as his guests for nine days. On the tenth, when Cepheus, Ancaios, and some others considered it beneath their dignity to take part in the hunt with a woman,* Meleager—who wanted to have a child by Atalante although he was married to Cleopatra, the daughter of Idas and Marpessa—compelled them to set out with her on the hunt. When they had surrounded the boar, Hyleus and Ancaios were killed by the beast and, by accident, Peleus struck down Eurytion with his javelin. The first to hit the boar was Atalante, who shot it in the back with an arrow, and the second, Amphiaraos, who shot it in the eye, but Meleager struck the death blow by stabbing it in the side. And when he received the skin, he gave it to Atalante. The sons of Thestios,* however, took it amiss that a woman should get the prize when men were present, saying that it belonged to them by right of birth if Meleager chose not to take it. ³ Angered by this, Meleager killed the sons of Thestios and returned the skin to Atalante. But Althaia was so distressed by the loss of her brothers that she rekindled the log, bringing Meleager's life to a sudden end.

It is said by some,* however, that Meleager met his end not in that way, but as follows. The sons of Thestios raised an argument about the hunt, saying that Iphiclos had been the first to hit the boar, and because of this a war broke out between the Curetes and the Calydonians. When Meleager marched out and killed some of the sons of Thestios, Althaia cursed him, which so enraged him that he confined himself to his house. But when the enemy forces were drawing close to the walls, and the citizens approached him as suppliants and asked him to come to their aid, he was persuaded by his wife, though with difficulty, to march out, and after he had killed the other sons of Thestios, he met his own death in the fighting. After the death of Meleager, Althaia and Cleopatra hanged themselves, and the women who wailed over his dead body were transformed into birds.*

The later history of Oineus, and the birth and exile of Tydeus

4 After Althaia's death, Oineus married Periboia, the daughter of Hipponoos. According to the author of the *Thebaid*, Oineus received her as a prize after the sack of Olenos, but according to Hesiod she had been seduced by Hippostratos, son of Amarynceus, and her father sent her away from Olenos in Achaea to Oineus,* who lived some distance from Greece, with orders that he kill her. 5 Or according to some, Hipponoos discovered that his daughter had been seduced by Oineus, and he sent her away to him when she was already pregnant. It was by her that Oineus fathered Tydeus. Peisandros says, however, that Tydeus was born to Gorge; for in accordance with the will of Zeus, Oineus conceived a passion for his own daughter.

When Tydeus grew to manhood, he was exiled for having killed, according to some accounts, Alcathoos, a brother of Oineus, or according to the author of the *Alcmaeonid*, the sons of Melas* who had plotted against Oineus, namely Pheneus, Euryalos, Hyperlaos, Antiochos, Eumedes, Sternops, Xanthippos, and Sthenelaos. According to Pherecydes, however, he killed his own brother,* Olenias. When Agrios tried to bring charges against him, he fled to Adrastos in Argos, and married Adrastos' daughter, Deipyle, who bore him a son, Diomedes.*

6 Tydeus joined Adrastos in the expdition against Thebes, where he was wounded by Melanippos and died. The sons of Agrios—Thersites,* Onchestos, Prothoos, Celeutor, Lycopeus, and Melanippos—robbed Oineus of his kingdom and gave it to their father, and furthermore they imprisoned Oineus (who was still alive) and ill-treated him. Afterwards, however, Diomedes arrived in secret from Argos with Alcmaion and killed all the sons of Agrios, apart from Onchestos and Thersites, who had fled beforehand to the Peloponnese; and since Oineus was now an old man, Diomedes gave the kingdom to Andraimon, who had married Oineus' daughter, and took Oineus back with him to the Peloponnese. But the two sons of Agrios who had managed to escape laid an ambush for the old man near the Hearth of Telephos in Arcadia, and killed

him. Diomedes took his body to Argos, and buried him at the place where a city called Oinoe, which is named after him, now lies. After his marriage to Aigialeia, the daughter of Adrastos (or according to some, of Aigialeus), Diomedes took part in the expeditions against Thebes and Troy.

Athamas, Ino, and the origin of the golden fleece

9 1 To proceed to the sons of Aiolos, Athamas ruled in Boeotia, and had a son, Phrixos, and a daughter, Helle, by Nephele. He then married Ino, and had two sons by her, Learchos and Melicertes. But Ino began to scheme against the children of Nephele and persuaded the women to parch the wheat-grain;* and they took the grain and did so, in secret from the men. When the earth was sown with this parched grain, it failed to produce its annual crop, so Athamas sent envoys to Delphi to ask how they could be delivered from this barrenness. But Ino persuaded the envoys to say that, according to the oracle, the infertility would come to an end if Phrixos were sacrificed to Zeus. When Athamas heard this, he was compelled by the inhabitants of the land to bring Phrixos to the altar; but Nephele snatched him away together with her daughter Helle,* and gave them a ram with a golden fleece which she had received from Hermes. Carried through the sky by this ram, they passed over land and sea alike; but while they were over the stretch of sea that lies between Sigeia and the Chersonese, Helle slipped into the waters, and the sea where she died was named the *Hellespont* after her. Phrixos for his part went to the land of the Colchians, which was ruled by Aietes, son of the Sun and Perseis, and brother of Circe and of Pasiphae, who became the wife of Minos. Aietes welcomed Phrixos and offered him one of his daughters, Chalciope, as a wife. Phrixos sacrificed the ram with the golden fleece to Zeus God of Escape, and gave its fleece to Aietes, who nailed it to an oak in a grove sacred to Ares. By Chalciope Phrixos had four sons, Argos, Melas, Phrontis, and Cytisoros.

2 Later, through the wrath of Hera,* Athamas was also deprived of his children by Ino; for he himself, in a fit of madness, killed Learchos with an arrow, and Ino threw herself into

the sea with Melicertes. Exiled from Boeotia, he asked the gods where he should settle, and was told by the oracle to settle at the place where he was offered hospitality by wild beasts. After he had crossed large expanses of land, he chanced upon some wolves as they were sharing out morsels of sheep; and when they caught sight of him, they fled, leaving behind the food that they were sharing. So Athamas founded a colony there, calling the land Athamantia* after himself, and married Themisto, daughter of Hypseus, who bore him four sons, Leucon, Erythrios, Schoineus, and Ptoos.

Sisyphos, Salmoneus, and other sons of Aiolos

3 Sisyphos, son of Aiolos, founded Ephyra, now known as Corinth,* and married Merope, daughter of Atlas. A son, Glaucos, was born to them, and by Eurymede, Glaucos had a son, Bellerophon, who killed the fire-breathing Chimaera.* Sisyphos undergoes the punishment in Hades* of rolling a rock with his hands and head in an attempt to roll it over the top of a hill; but however hard he pushes it, it forces its way back down again. He suffers this punishment because of Aegina, daughter of Asopos; for Zeus had carried her off in secret, and Siyphos is said to have revealed this to Asopos, who went in search of her.

4 Deion, who reigned over Phocis, married Diomede, daughter of Xouthos, who bore him a daughter, Asterodia, and four sons, Ainetos, Actor, Phylacos, and Cephalos, who married Procris, daughter of Erechtheus. But afterwards Dawn fell in love with him and carried him off.*

5 Perieres took possession of Messene, and married Gorgophone, daughter of Perseus, who bore him several sons, Aphareus, and Leucippos and Tyndareus, and also Icarios. But many say that Perieres was a son not of Aiolos, but of Cynortas,* son of Amyclas; and for that reason, we will tell the story of his descendants in our account of the family of Atlas.

6 Magnes married a naiad nymph, and had two sons, Polydectes and Dictys, who colonized Seriphos.*

7 Salmoneus lived in Thessaly at first, but later went to Elis

and founded a city* there. A man of great arrogance, he wanted to put himself on a level with Zeus and suffered punishment for his impiety. For he claimed that he himself was Zeus, and depriving the god of his sacrifices, he ordered that they should be offered to himself instead. And he dragged dried animal skins and bronze kettles behind his chariot, saying that he was making thunder; and he hurled flaming torches into the sky, saying that he was making lightning. Zeus struck him down with a thunderbolt, and destroyed the city that he had founded, with all its inhabitants.

Pelias and Neleus

8 Tyro, the daughter of Salmoneus and Alcidice, was raised by Cretheus, the brother of Salmoneus, and she fell in love with the River Enipeus. She would constantly wander down to its flowing waters and tell them of her sorrows. Taking on the appearance of Enipeus, Poseidon had intercourse with her,* and she gave birth in secret to twin sons, whom she exposed. As the babies lay abandoned on the ground, a mare belonging to some passing horse-trainers knocked one of them with its hoof, leaving a black and blue patch on its face. The horse-trainer recovered the two children and brought them up, calling the one with the *black-and-blue* patch *Pelias*,* and the other Neleus. When they were grown up, they found their mother and killed her stepmother, Sidero.* For learning that their mother had been ill-treated by Sidero, they set out against her, but she forestalled them by taking refuge at the sanctuary of Hera, only to be killed on the very altars by Pelias, who refused ever afterwards to pay due honour to Hera.

9 Later the brothers quarrelled, and Neleus was driven into exile. Arriving in Messene, he founded Pylos,* and married Chloris, daughter of Amphion, who bore him a daughter, Pero, and twelve sons, Tauros, Asterios, Pylaon, Deimachos, Eurybios, Epilaos, Phrasios, Eurymenes, Evagoras, Alastor, Nestor, and Periclymenos. Poseidon granted the last of these the power to change his form; and when Pylos was sacked by Heracles, he transformed himself as he fought, now into a lion, now into a snake, now into a bee, but he was killed by

Heracles* along with the other sons of Neleus. Nestor alone survived because he was brought up amongst the Gerenians; and he married Anaxibia, daughter of Cratieus, who bore him two daughters, Peisidice and Polycaste, and seven sons, Perseus, Stratichos, Aretos, Echephron, Peisistratos, Antilochos, and Thrasymedes.

10 Pelias settled in Thessaly and married Anaxibia, daughter of Bias (or according to some, Phylomache, daughter of Amphion), and fathered a son, Acastos, and four daughters, Peisidice, Pelopeia, Hippothoe, and Alcestis.

The earlier history of Bias and Melampous

11 Cretheus founded Iolcos and married Tyro, daughter of Salmoneus, by whom he had three sons, Aison, Amythaon, and Pheres.

Amythaon, who lived in Pylos, married Eidomene, daughter of Pheres, who bore him two sons, Bias and Melampous. Now Melampous lived in the country, and in front of his house there was an oak tree which housed a nest of snakes. After these snakes had been killed by his servants, Melampous gathered some wood and burned the reptiles, and then reared their young. When they were fully grown, they came up to him while he was asleep, and placing themselves at either shoulder, purified his ears* with their tongues. Melampous rose up in great alarm, to find that he could understand the cries of the birds* flying overhead; and making use of what he discovered from them, he began to predict the future to mankind. He also learned how the victims at sacrifices can be used for divination, and after he had met with Apollo on the banks of the Alpheios, he was the best of diviners from that day forth.

12 Bias sought to marry Pero, the daughter of Neleus; but since his daughter had many suitors, Neleus said that he would give her to the one who brought him the cattle of Phylacos.* These cattle were kept at Phylace, and were guarded by a dog which neither man nor beast could approach without being detected. Finding himself unable to steal the cattle, Bias sought his brother's help. Melampous promised his assistance,* and predicted that he would be caught in the act as he

tried to steal the cattle, but would finally acquire them after he had been imprisoned for a year. After offering this promise, he departed for Phylace and, as he had predicted, he was caught in the act when he attempted the theft, and was then put in chains and kept under guard in a cell. When the year had almost elapsed, he heard the woodworms talking in the hidden part of the roof: one of them was asking how much of the beam had already been consumed, and the other replied that hardly any of it remained. Without delay, Melampous asked to be moved to a different cell, and not long afterwards, the first cell collapsed. Phylacos was astonished, and realizing that Melampous was an excellent diviner, he released him and asked him to say how his son Iphiclos could come to have children. Melampous promised to tell him if he were given the cattle in return; and then, after sacrificing two bulls and cutting them up, he summoned the birds. When a vulture arrived, he learned from it that Phylacos, as he was gelding lambs one day, had laid down the knife, still covered with blood, next to Iphiclos; and when the child took fright* and ran away, Phylacos had stuck the knife into the sacred oak, and its bark had grown around it and covered it over. The bird went on to say that if the knife were found, and Melampous scraped off the rust and gave it to Iphiclos to take in a drink* for ten days, he would father a son. Discovering all this from the vulture, Melampous found the knife, scraped off the rust, and gave it to Iphiclos for ten days in a drink; and a son, Podarces, was duly born to him. So Melampous drove the cattle to Pylos, and when he was given the daughter of Neleus, passed her on to his brother. He remained in Messene for a time, but when Dionysos drove the women of Argos mad,* he cured them in return for a share of the kingdom and settled there with Bias.

13 Bias and Pero had a son, Talaos, who had six children by Lysimache, daughter of Abas, son of Melampous, namely Adrastos, Parthenopaios, Pronax, Mecisteus, Aristomachos, and Eriphyle, who became the wife of Amphiaraos. Parthenopaios had a son, Promachos, who joined the Epigoni in the expedition against Thebes, and Mecisteus had a son Euryalos, who went to Troy. Pronax had a son, Lycourgos; and Adrastos and Amphithea, daughter of Pronax, had three daughters,

Argeia, Deipyle, and Aigialeia, and two sons, Aigialeus and Cyanippos.

Admetos and Alcestis

14 Pheres, son of Cretheus, founded Pherae in Thessaly, and fathered Admetos and Lycourgos. Lycourgos settled near Nemea, and, marrying Eurydice (or according to some, Amphithea), he had a son, Opheltes, who was later called Archemoros. 15 Admetos for his part became king of Pherae, and at the time when Apollo was serving him* as a labourer, he wanted to win the hand of Alcestis, daughter of Pelias. Now Pelias had announced that he would give his daughter to the man who could yoke a lion and a boar to a chariot; so Apollo yoked them and gave them to Admetos, who took them to Pelias and obtained Alcestis as his wife. While offering the sacrifices at his marriage, however, he forgot to sacrifice to Artemis; and as a result, when he opened up the marriage chamber, he found it to be filled with coils of snakes.* Apollo advised him to propitiate the goddess, and demanded of the Fates that when Admetos was about to die, he should be released from death if somebody would freely choose to die in his place. When the day came for him to die, neither his father nor his mother was willing to die for him, so Alcestis died in his place. But Kore sent her back* to earth again, or, according to some accounts, Heracles fought with Hades for her* [and returned her to Admetos].

3. Jason and the Argonauts

Pelias orders Jason to fetch the golden fleece

16 To Aison, son of Cretheus, and Polymede, daughter of Autolycos, a son, Jason, was born; and Jason lived at Iolcos, which was ruled by Pelias, who had succeeded Cretheus.* When Pelias consulted the oracle about his kingdom, the god told him to beware of the man with one sandal. At first he could make no sense of the oracle, but afterwards he came to under-

stand it. For when he was about to offer a sacrifice by the sea to Poseidon, he summoned Jason, together with many others, to take part in it. Jason, who lived in the country because of his passion for farming, hurried off to the sacrifice, but as he was crossing the River Anauros, he emerged with only one sandal, after losing the other in the current. So when Pelias caught sight of him, he knew what the oracle meant; and going up to Jason, he asked him what he would do (assuming he had the power) if he had received an oracle saying that he would be murdered by one of his fellow citizens. In response—whether as chance would have it, or as a result of the wrath of Hera,* who wanted Medea to come as an affliction to Pelias (for he had failed to honour the goddess)—Jason declared, 'I would order him to fetch the golden fleece.'* As soon as Pelias heard his reply, he told Jason to set out for the fleece. It was to be found at Colchis* in a grove sacred to Ares, hanging on an oak tree and guarded by a dragon that never slept.

When he was sent for the fleece, Jason summoned the assistance of Argos, son of Phrixos; and Argos, on the advice of Athene, built a ship with fifty oars, which was named the *Argo* after its builder.* To the prow of the ship, Athene fitted a piece of wood that came from the oak at Dodona* and had the power of speech. When the ship was built, Jason consulted the oracle, and was told by the god that he could sail after he had gathered together the finest men in Greece.

Catalogue of the Argonauts

The men who assembled were the following: Tiphys, son of Hagnias, who steered the ship; Orpheus, son of Oiagros; Zetes and Calais, sons of Boreas; Castor and Polydeuces, sons of Zeus; Telamon and Peleus, sons of Aiacos; Heracles, son of Zeus; Theseus, son of Aigeus; Idas and Lynceus, sons of Aphareus; Amphiaraos, son of Oicles; Caineus, son of Coronos; Palaimon, son of Hephaistos or of Aitolos; Cepheus, son of Aleos; Laertes, son of Arceisios; Autolycos, son of Hermes; Atalante, daughter of Schoineus; Menoitios, son of Actor; Actor, son of Hippasos; Admetos, son of Pheres; Acastos, son of Pelias; Eurytos, son of Hermes; Meleager, son of Oineus; Ancaios,

son of Lycourgos; Euphemos, son of Poseidon; Poias, son of
Thaumacos; Boutes, son of Teleon; Phanos and Staphylos, sons
of Dionysos; Erginos, son of Poseidon; Periclymenos, son of
Neleus; Augeas, son of the Sun; Iphiclos, son of Thestios; Argos,
son of Phrixos; Euryalos, son of Mecisteus; Peneleos, son of
Hippalmos; Leitos, son of Alector; Iphitos, son of Naubolos;
Ascalaphos and Ialmenos, sons of Ares; Asterios, son of Com-
etes; and Polyphemos, son of Elatos.

The women of Lemnos; in the land of the Doliones

17 They set out to sea* with Jason in command, and called in
at Lemnos. It happened that there were no men at all in
Lemnos at that time, and the island was ruled by a queen,
Hypsipyle, daughter of Thoas. The reason was this. The
Lemnian women had failed to honour Aphrodite, and the goddess had afflicted them with an evil smell; as a result, their
husbands had taken women captive from the neighbouring land
of Thrace and slept with them instead. The Lemnian women
had responded to this slight by murdering their fathers and
husbands—Hypsipyle alone had saved her father, Thoas, by
hiding him away. So the Argonauts put in at Lemnos while
it was under female rule, and they had intercourse with the
women there. Hypsipyle slept with Jason and bore him two
sons, Euneos and Nebrophonos.

18 After Lemnos, they visited the land of the Doliones, who
were ruled by Cyzicos; and he offered them a friendly welcome. But as they were sailing from his land by night, they
met with contrary winds, and without realizing it, landed once
more amongst the Doliones. The Doliones for their part took
them for an army of Pelasgians—for it happened that they were
under constant attack from the Pelasgians—and joined battle
with them by night, each side failing to recognize the other.
The Argonauts killed many of their opponents, including
Cyzicos; but when day came, and they saw what had happened,
they lamented bitterly, cut off their hair, and offered Cyzicos
a splendid burial. After the funeral, they sailed on their way,
and put in at Mysia.

The loss of Hylas and abandonment of Heracles

19 There they abandoned Heracles and Polyphemos.* For Hylas, the son of Theiodamas and beloved of Heracles, had been sent to draw water, and was snatched away by nymphs* because of his beauty. Polyphemos heard him cry out, and drawing his sword, he set out after him, thinking that robbers were dragging him off. When he came across Heracles, he told him what had happened; and while the two of them were searching for Hylas, the ship put out to sea. Polyphemos founded the city of Cios in Mysia, and ruled there as king, while Heracles for his part returned to Argos. According to Herodoros, however, Heracles never set out on a voyage at all at that time, but was serving as a slave with Omphale; and Pherecydes says that he was left behind at Aphetai in Thessaly, because the *Argo* had spoken out to say that she was unable to bear his weight. But Demaratos has recorded that he sailed all the way to Colchis, while Dionysios goes so far as to call him the leader of the Argonauts.*

Polydeuces and Amycos; Phineus and the Harpies; the Clashing Rocks

20 They left Mysia for the land of the Bebryces, which was under the rule of Amycos, son of Poseidon and a Bithynian [nymph]. A man of spirit, he made strangers who landed there box with him, and in that way brought about their death. So he went up to the *Argo* on this occasion too, and challenged the best man present to a boxing match. Polydeuces agreed to take him on and killed him with a blow to the elbow; and when the Bebryces rushed forward to attack Polydeuces, the heroes snatched up their weapons and slaughtered many of them as they were fleeing.

21 From there they put out to sea again, and called in at Salmydessos in Thrace, the home of Phineus, a diviner who had lost the use of his eyes. Some call him a son of Agenor, others a son of Poseidon. According to some accounts, he was blinded by the gods for foretelling the future to the human race, or, according to others, by Boreas and the Argonauts

because he had blinded his own children at the urging of their stepmother,* or again, by Poseidon for having informed the children of Phrixos of the route from Colchis to Greece.

The gods had also sent the Harpies* against him. These were female creatures with wings, and when a table was laid in front of Phineus, they would fly down from the sky and snatch away most of the food, and even the little that they left behind stank so strongly that nobody could touch it. When the Argonauts wanted to consult Phineus about their route, he replied that he would advise them on their route if they would rid him of the Harpies. So they set a table of food in front of him, and the Harpies immediately swooped down with loud cries and snatched the food away. At the sight of this, Zetes and Calais, the sons of Boreas, who were themselves endowed with wings, drew their swords and chased the Harpies through the air. Now it was fated that the Harpies would die at the hands of the sons of Boreas, and equally that the sons of Boreas would die if they failed to catch those they pursued.* During the chase one of the Harpies dropped into the Tigres, a Peloponnesian river, which is now called the Harpys after her; this Harpy was called Nicothoe, or according to others, Aellopous. As for the other, called Ocypete, or, according to some accounts, Ocythoe (or Ocypode according to Hesiod*), she fled along the Propontis until she arrived at the Echinadian Islands, which are now called the *Strophades** because of her; for she *turned* in her flight on reaching them, and while she was over their shore fell down exhausted along with her pursuer. According to Apollonius, however, in the *Argonautica*,* the Harpies were pursued as far as the Strophades, but they came to no harm after they had sworn an oath that they would stop persecuting Phineus.

22 When he had been delivered from the Harpies, Phineus told the Argonauts what route to take, and advised them about the Symplegades [or Clashing Rocks], which lay before them in the sea. These were rocks of enormous size which were forced into collision by the power of the winds and closed the passage through the sea. Thick mist swirled over them, the crash was tremendous, and it was impossible even for birds to pass between them. So Phineus advised the Argonauts to release a

dove between the rocks, and if they saw it pass safely between them, to sail through in full confidence, but if it was destroyed, to make no attempt to force a passage. After hearing his advice, they put out to sea, and when they were close to the rocks, they released a dove from the prow; and as she flew, only the tip of her tail was snipped off as the rocks clashed together. So they waited until the rocks had drawn apart again, and with hard rowing and some assistance from Hera they made their way through, although the tip of the vessel's poop was shorn away. Ever afterwards, the Symplegades stood motionless; for it was fated that when a ship had passed through them, they would remain completely still.

23 The Argonauts arrived next at the land of the Mariandynians, where they received a friendly welcome from Lycos, their king. It was there that Idmon the diviner met his death, from a wound inflicted by a boar; Tiphys died there too, and Ancaios took over as steersman of the ship.

Jason, Medea, and the seizure of the fleece

They sailed past the River Thermodon and the Caucasos to arrive at the River Phasis, which lies in the land of Colchis. When the ship was moored, Jason visited Aietes, and explained what Pelias had told him to do and asked to be given the fleece. Aietes promised to hand it over if, without assistance, Jason yoked the bronze-footed bulls. These were two wild bulls that he owned, of exceptional size, a gift from Hephaistos; they had hooves of bronze and breathed fire from their mouths. And after he had yoked these bulls, Jason was to sow some dragon's teeth—for Aietes had received from Athene half of the dragon's teeth that Cadmos had sowed at Thebes.* When Jason was at his wit's end about how he could yoke the bulls, Medea fell in love with him. Now Medea, the daughter of Aietes and Eiduia, daughter of Oceanos, was a sorceress; and fearing that Jason might be killed by the bulls, she offered, in secret from her father, to help him yoke the bulls and obtain the fleece, if he would swear to accept her as his wife and take her with him when he sailed back to Greece. When he swore to do so, she gave him a potion,* and told him to rub it on to his shield and spear and his body when he set out to yoke the bulls, explaining that when he had been anointed with the potion, he would be invulnerable for a day to fire and steel alike. And she revealed to him that when the teeth were sown, armed men would spring up from the ground to attack him; and when he saw them gathered in a group, he should throw stones into their midst from a distance, which would cause them to fight amongst themselves, and he should then kill them. On hearing Medea's advice, Jason rubbed himself with the potion and made his way to the temple grove to search for the bulls; and although they charged him breathing flame, he put them under the yoke.* And then, after he had sowed the dragon's teeth, armed men sprang up from the ground. Where he saw a number of them together, he hurled stones at them, without revealing his presence; and as they were fighting amongst themselves, he went forward and killed them.

Although the bulls had been yoked, Aietes refused to surrender the fleece; and he wanted to set fire to the *Argo* and kill its crew. Before he could put his plan into effect, Medea guided Jason to the fleece by night and used her drugs to send the guardian dragon to sleep, and then, carrying the fleece with her, made her way back to the *Argo* with Jason. She was accompanied by her brother Apsyrtos too. And during the night, the Argonauts put out to sea with them.

The murder of Apsyrtos and journey to Circe

24 When Aietes discovered what Medea had dared to do, he set out in pursuit of the ship. But when Medea saw him drawing close, she murdered her brother,* cut him up, and threw the pieces into the sea; and as Aietes delayed to gather up the limbs of his child, he fell behind in the chase. So he turned his ship around, and buried what he had saved of his son's remains, naming the burial place *Tomoi*.* But he sent many of the Colchians in search of the *Argo*, threatening that if they failed to recover Medea, they themselves would undergo the punishment intended for her. So they separated and carried the search to many different areas.

The Argonauts had already passed the River Eridanos when Zeus, angered by the murder of Apsyrtos, sent a violent storm against them and drove them off course. And as they were sailing past the Apsyrtides Islands, the ship spoke out, saying that the anger of Zeus would not come to an end unless they travelled to Ausonia to be purified by Circe for the murder of Apsyrtos. So they sailed past the Ligurian and Celtic peoples,* crossed the Sardinian Sea, skirted Tyrrhenia, and arrived at Aiaie,* where they approached Circe as suppliants and were purified.

To the land of the Phaeacians

25 As they were sailing past the Sirens, Orpheus sang a song to counter their own,* thus holding the Argonauts back. Boutes alone tried to swim off towards them; but Aphrodite carried him off and settled him at Lilybaeum.

After the Sirens, Charybdis and Scylla awaited the ship, and then the Wandering Rocks, over which quantities of flame and smoke were seen to rise. But Thetis guided the ship through with the help of the Nereids, in response to a summons from Hera.

After skirting the island of Thrinacia, which held the cattle of the Sun, they came to the island of the Phaeacians,* Corcyra, which was ruled by Alcinoos. Now the Colchians had been unable to find the ship, and some of them went to settle in the Ceraunian mountains, while others travelled to Illyria and colonized the Apsyrtides islands. But some of them came to Phaeacia, and finding the *Argo* there, they asked Alcinoos to surrender Medea to them. He replied that if she had already slept with Jason, he would leave her with him, but if she were still a virgin, he would send her back to her father. But Arete, the wife of Alcinoos, took the initiative by marrying Medea to Jason; so the Colchians settled amongst the Phaeacians, and the Argonauts set out to sea with Medea.

Anaphe; Talos in Crete

26 As they were sailing along by night, they met with a violent storm;* but Apollo, taking position on the summit of the Melantian Rocks, shot an arrow into the sea, causing a flash

of lightning. They then beheld an island close at hand, where they cast anchor, naming it *Anaphe** because it had *appeared* to them against all expectation. They raised an altar there to Radiant Apollo, and when they had sacrificed, they settled down to feast. Now Medea had received as a gift from Arete twelve servant girls, who aimed playful jokes at the heroes; and that is why it is the custom even to this day for the women to make jokes* at the sacrifice.

After setting sail from Anaphe, they were prevented from coming ashore at Crete by Talos. It is said by some that he belonged to the race of bronze, while according to others, he had been given to Minos by Hephaistos; he was a man of bronze,* or, according to some accounts, a bull.* He had a single vein* which ran from his neck to his ankles, with a bronze nail driven into its end. Talos kept watch by running round the island three times a day, and so on this occasion too, when he saw the *Argo* approaching, he pelted it with stones. But Medea tricked him and caused his death. According to some, she drove him mad with her drugs, while according to others, she promised to make him immortal and pulled out the nail, causing him to die when all the ichor flowed away.* And there are some who say that Poias killed him, by shooting an arrow into his ankle.

The return to Iolcos and murder of Pelias

After remaining in Crete for a single night, they made Aegina their next port of call, to replenish their water; and a competition developed* between them as they fetched the water. From there they sailed between Euboea and Locris to arrive at Iolcos, completing the entire voyage in four months.

27 Pelias had abandoned any expectation of the Argonauts' return and wanted to put Aison to death.* Aison asked, however, that he should be allowed to take his own life, and while he was offering a sacrifice, he drank the bull's blood* without fear, and died. Jason's mother cursed Pelias and hanged herself, leaving an infant son, Promachos; but Pelias killed even the son whom she had left behind. When Jason arrived back, he delivered the fleece, and desiring vengeance for the wrongs

that he had suffered, he waited for a suitable occasion. For the present, he sailed to the Isthmus with the other heroes and dedicated the ship to Poseidon; but afterwards, he urged Medea to find a way to punish Pelias. So she went to the palace of Pelias and persuaded his daughters to chop their father into small pieces and boil him, promising to restore his youth with her drugs; and to gain their confidence, she cut up a ram and changed it into a lamb by boiling it. After that, they believed her, and chopped their father to pieces and boiled him.* Acastos buried his father with the help of the inhabitants of Iolcos, and banished Jason and Medea from the country.

The later history of Medea

28 They went to Corinth, where they lived happily for ten years, until Creon,* the king of Corinth, offered his daughter, Glauce, to Jason, who then put Medea aside and married her. So Medea, calling as her witnesses the gods whom Jason had sworn by, and after many a reproach to Jason for his ingratitude, sent his bride a robe steeped in poison. When Glauce put it on she was consumed by a raging fire,* as was her father when he tried to save her. And then, after killing Mermeros and Pheres, her children by Jason, Medea received from the Sun a chariot* drawn by winged dragons, and fled on it to Athens. According to another account, when Medea was fleeing, she abandoned her children, who were still very young, by seating them as suppliants on the altar of Hera Acraia; but the Corinthians forced them away* from the altar and inflicted fatal injuries on them.

So Medea went to Athens, where she married Aigeus,* and bore him a son, Medos.* Afterwards, however, when she tried to plot against Theseus, she was driven from Athens and went into exile with her son. Medos conquered many of the barbarians, and gave the name Media to the whole territory under his control. He died during an expedition against the Indians. Medea returned to Colchis without being recognized, and finding that Aietes had been deprived of his kingdom by his brother Perses, she killed Perses* and restored the throne to her father.

BOOK II

4. Early Argive mythology (the Inachids, Belid line)

The early descendants of Inachos

1 1 Now that we have given a full account of the family of
Deucalion, let us proceed to that of Inachos.

Oceanos and Tethys had a son, Inachos,* after whom the
River Inachos in Argos is named. To Inachos and Melia, daughter of Oceanos, two sons were born, Phoroneus and Aigialeus.*
Aigialeus died without offspring, and the whole country was
called Aigialeia; and Phoroneus, who reigned over the whole
of what would later be called the Peloponnese, fathered Apis
and Niobe by a nymph, Teledice.

Apis turned his power into a tyranny; a brutal tyrant, he
named the Peloponnese Apia after himself, and died childless
as the result of a plot by Thelxion and Telchis. He was reck-
oned to be a god and was called Sarapis.* Niobe, for her part,
had a son, Argos, by Zeus (she was the first mortal woman
with whom he had intercourse), and according to Acousilaos,
she had another son, Pelasgos,* and the inhabitants of the
Peloponnese were called the Pelasgians* after him. According to Hesiod, however, Pelasgos was born from the earth; 2
but we will return to him later. Argos took over the kingdom,
calling the Peloponnese Argos* after himself; and marrying
Evadne, daughter of Strymon and Neaira, he had four sons,
Ecbasos, Peiras, Epidauros, and Criasos, who succeeded to the
kingdom in his turn.

Ecbasos had a son, Agenor, and Agenor had a son, Argos,
the one who is known as Panoptes [or the All-Seeing]. He had
eyes all over his body,* and being endowed with exceptional
strength, he killed the bull that was bringing ruin to Arcadia
and clothed himself in its hide; and when a Satyr ill-treated
the Arcadians and robbed them of their cattle, he confronted
him and put him to death. And they say of Echidna* too, the

58

daughter of Tartaros and Ge who used to snatch away passers-
by, that Argos watched out until she was asleep and then killed
her. He also avenged the death of Apis by killing those who
were responsible.

The wanderings of Io, and division of the Inachid line

3 Argos and Ismene, daughter of Asopos, had a son, Iasos, who
is said to have been the father of Io. But Castor, the author of
the *Chronicles*, and many of the tragic poets claim that Io was
a daughter of Inachos; while Hesiod and Acousilaos say that
she was a daughter of Peiren.* Zeus seduced Io* while she
held the priesthood of Hera, but when Hera found him out,
he transformed the girl with a touch into a white cow and swore
that he had never made love with her; and for that reason,
according to Hesiod, oaths made for love attract no anger from
the gods. But Hera asked Zeus for the cow, and placed it under
the guard of Argos the All-Seeing. (Pherecydes says that this
Argos was a son of Arestor, Asclepiades that he was a son of
Inachos, and Cercops that he was a son of Argos and Ismene,
daughter of Asopos, while according to Acousilaos, he was
born from the earth.) Hera tethered the cow to the olive tree
which lay in the sacred grove of the Mycenaeans. Zeus ordered Hermes to steal the cow, but the plan was betrayed by
Hierax,* and since Hermes was now unable to steal the cow
without being seen, he *killed Argos* by throwing a stone at him;
and that is how he came to be called *Argeiphontes.** Hera sent
a gadfly after the cow; the animal went first to the *Ionian* Gulf,*
which bears that name because of her, and then, after travelling through Illyria and over Mount Haimos, she crossed what
was then called the Thracian Sound but is now called the
*Bosporos** because of her. From there she went to Scythia and
the land of the Cimmerians, wandering a great distance overland and swimming a great distance through the sea, in Europe
and Asia alike, until she finally arrived in Egypt, where she recovered her original form, and gave birth to a son, Epaphos,
by the banks of the River Nile. Hera asked the Curetes to steal
the child away, and they did so. When Zeus learned of it, he
killed the Curetes, and Io, for her part, went in search of her

child. She wandered through the whole of Syria (for it had been revealed to her that the wife of the king of Byblos was nursing her son there), and when she had discovered Epaphos,* she returned to Egypt and married Telegonos, who was king of the Egyptians at the time. She erected a statue of Demeter, whom the Egyptians called Isis; and they gave this name, Isis, to Io likewise.

4 When Epaphos became king of the Egyptians, he married Memphis, daughter of the Nile, founded the city of Memphis in her name, and fathered a daughter, Libya, after whom the land of Libya was named. By Poseidon, Libya had twin sons, Agenor and Belos. Agenor departed to Phoenicia, where he became king and the founder of a great line, and for that reason, we shall reserve our treatment of him until later.* But Belos* remained in Egypt, where he became king, and married Anchinoe, daughter of the Nile, who bore him twin sons, Aigyptos and Danaos (and according to Euripides, Cepheus and Phineus in addition).

Aigyptos, Danaos, and the Danaids

Belos established Danaos in Libya and Aigyptos in Arabia; but Aigyptos conquered the land of the Melampodes* too, and named it Egypt after himself. Both had children by many different women, Aigyptos fifty sons and Danaos fifty daughters. Later, they quarrelled over the throne, and Danaos, fearing the sons of Aigyptos, constructed a ship on the advice of Athene— he was the first man to do so*—and putting his daughters on board, he fled the country.

Calling in at Rhodes, he set up the statue of Lindian Athene; and from there he went to Argos, where Gelanor, who was king at the time, surrendered the throne to him.* [After he had taken control of the country, Danaos named its inhabitants the Danaans after himself.*] There was no water in the land, because Poseidon had caused even the springs to run dry in his anger against Inachos for having testified that the land belonged to Hera;* so Danaos sent his daughters in search of water. Now one of them, Amymone, during her search, threw a javelin at a deer and hit a sleeping Satyr, who leapt up and was eager to make love with her; but when Poseidon appeared, the Satyr fled, and Amymone slept with Poseidon, who then revealed the springs of Lerna* to her.

5 The sons of Aigyptos came to Argos, and they invited Danaos to call an end to his hostility and asked to marry his daughters. Although Danaos distrusted their protestations and bore them a grudge because of his exile, he agreed to the marriages and apportioned the girls by lot. Hypermnestra, the eldest, was selected to be the wife of Lynceus, and Gorgophone to be the wife of Proteus; for Lynceus and Proteus were borne to Aigyptos by a woman of royal blood, Argyphie. Of those who remained, Bousiris, Encelados, Lycos, and Daiphron obtained in the lot the daughters who were borne to Danaos by Europe, namely, Automate, Amymone, Agave, and Scaie. These were borne to Danaos by a woman of royal blood; Gorgophone and Hypermnestra, for their part, were borne to him by Elephantis. Istros obtained Hippodameia in the lot; Chalcodon, Rhodia; Agenor, Cleopatra; Chaitos, Asteria; Diocorystes, [Phylodameia]; Alces, Glauce; Alcmenor, Hippomedousa; Hippothoos, Gorge; Euchenor, Iphimedousa; and Hippolytos, Rhode. These ten sons were borne by an Arabian woman, and the daughters by hamadryad nymphs, some being daughters of Atlanteia, others of Phoebe. Agaptolemos obtained Peirene in the lot; Cercetes, Dorion; Eurydamas, Phartis; Aigios, Mnestra; Argios, Evippe; Archelaos, Anaxibia; and Menemachos, Nelo. These seven sons were borne by a Phoenician woman, and the daughters by an Ethiopian woman. The sons borne by Tyria obtained the daughters of Memphis as their wives, not through the lot, but because of the similarity of their names, Cleitos obtaining Cleite; Sthenelos, Sthenele; and Chrysippos, Chrysippe. The twelve sons of Aigyptos by the naiad nymph Caliadne cast lots for the daughters of Danaos by the naiad nymph Polyxo. The sons were Eurylochos, Phantes, Peristhenes, Hermos, Dryas, Potamon, Cisseus, Lixos, Imbros, Bromios, Polyctor, and Cthonios; the daughters were Autonoe, Theano, Electra, Cleopatra, Eurydice, Glaucippe, Antheleia, Cleodore, Evippe, Erato, Stygne, and Bryce. The sons of Aigyptos by Gorgo cast lots for the daughters of Danaos by Pieria. Periphas obtained Actaie; Oineus, Podarce; Aigyptos, Dioxippe; Menalces, Adite;

Lampos, Ocypete; and Idmon, Pylarge. To proceed to the youngest sons, Idas obtained Hippodice, and Daiphron Adiante (the mother of these two girls was Herse); Pandion obtained Callidice; Arbelos, Oime; Hyperbios, Celaino; and Hippocorystes, Hyperippe: these were sons of Hephaistine and daughters of Crino respectively.

When they had obtained their brides in the lot and the marriage feast had been celebrated, Danaos handed daggers to his daughters, and they killed their bridegrooms as they slept, except for Hypermnestra, who spared Lynceus* because he had allowed her to preserve her virginity. Danaos imprisoned her for this, and kept her under guard. The rest of his daughters buried the heads of their bridegrooms at Lerna and held funerals for their bodies in front of the city; and they were purified* by Athene and Hermes on the orders of Zeus. Danaos later reunited Hypermnestra to Lynceus, and gave his other daughters in marriage to the victors at an athletic contest.*

Amymone bore a son, Nauplios, to Poseidon. This Nauplios lived to a great age, sailing the seas, and using beacon fires to draw those who came across him to their death. And it turned out that he himself met his death in that very manner.* Before his death, he married Clymene, daughter of Catreus (according to the tragic poets, but according to the author of the *Returns*, Philyra, or according to Cercops, Hesione), and had three sons by her, Palamedes, Oiax, and Nausimedon.

Proitos and Acrisios divide the Argolid

2 ¹ Lynceus became king of Argos after Danaos, and had a son, Abas, by Hypermnestra; and Abas had twin sons, Acrisios and Proitos, by Aglaia, daughter of Mantineus. The twins quarrelled with one another even while they were still in the womb, and when they grew up, they went to war over the kingdom. (It was during this war that they became the first inventors of shields.) Acrisios gained the upper hand and drove Proitos from Argos. Arriving in Lycia at the court of Iobates, or according to some, of Amphianax, Proitos married the king's daughter, whom Homer calls Anteia,* and the tragic poets, Stheneboia.

His father-in-law, with a Lycian army, restored Proitos to his own land, and he took possession of Tiryns, which was fortified for him by the Cyclopes.* The brothers divided the whole of the Argolid between them, and made it their home, Acrisios ruling in Argos, and Proitos in Tiryns.

Bias, Melampous, and the daughters of Proitos

2 By Eurydice, daughter of Lacedaimon, Acrisios had a daughter, Danae, and Proitos had three daughters, Lysippe, Iphinoe, and Iphianassa, by Stheneboia. When the daughters of Proitos were fully grown, they went mad, because, according to Hesiod, they refused to accept the rites of Dionysos, or, according to Acousilaos, because they had disparaged the wooden image of Hera.* In their madness, they wandered through the whole of the Argolid, and then, after passing through Arcadia and the Peloponnese, rushed through the desert in a state of complete abandon. Melampous, the son of Amythaon and Eidomene, daughter of Abas, who was a diviner and the first man to discover that illnesses could be cured by drugs and purifications, promised to cure the girls if he was given a third of the kingdom in return. When Proitos refused to hand them over for treatment at such a high price, not only did the girls' madness grow worse, but the other women* went mad also; for they too deserted their houses, destroyed their own children, and wandered into the wilderness. The calamity had developed to such an extreme that Proitos now offered to pay the demanded fee; but Melampous would promise to undertake the cure only if his brother Bias received a share of the land equal to his own. Fearing that if the cure were delayed, a still greater fee would be demanded of him, Proitos agreed to the cure on these terms.* So Melampous took the most vigorous of the young men, and with loud cries and ecstatic dancing, they chased the women out of the mountains and into Sicyon. During the pursuit, the eldest of Proitos' daughters, Iphinoe, met her death; but the other two were duly purified, and recovered their reason. Proitos gave his daughters in marriage to Melampous and Bias, and later became the father of a son, Megapenthes.

Excursus: the story of Bellerophon

3 ¹ Bellerophon, the son of Glaucos and grandson of Sisyphos, had accidentally killed his brother* Deliades (or according to some, Peiren, or according to others, Alcimenes) and came to Proitos to be purified.* Stheneboia fell in love with him,* and sent word to him proposing an assignation; but when he refused, she told Proitos that Bellerophon had been sending her messages in the hope of seducing her. Proitos believed her, and gave Bellerophon a letter to deliver to Iobates,* which contained a message that he should put Bellerophon to death; so when Iobates had read it, he told him to kill the Chimaera, believing that he would be destroyed by the monster. For it was no easy prey for a multitude of men, let alone for one, seeing that it was a single creature which yet had the power of three, having the foreparts of a lion, the tail of a dragon, and a third head in the middle*—a goat's head, through which it breathed fire. The beast was devastating the land and destroying the cattle. It is said, furthermore, that this Chimaera was reared by Amisodaros,* as Homer has stated also, and was the offspring of Typhon and Echidna, as Hesiod records.* ² So Bellerophon climbed on to his winged horse, Pegasos,* the offspring of Medusa and Poseidon, and soaring high into the air, killed the Chimaera by shooting arrows at it from above. After his battle with the Chimaera, Iobates told him to fight against the Solymoi,* and when he had fulfilled that task also, ordered him to attack the Amazons. When he had killed these also, Iobates picked out the Lycians who were thought to excel at the time in youthful vigour,* and told them to mount an ambush and kill him. But when Bellerophon had killed all of these in addition, Iobates, marvelling at his strength, showed him the letter and urged him to remain at his court; and he gave him his daughter, Philonoe, in marriage, and left him the kingdom when he died.

Danae and the birth of Perseus

4 ¹ When Acrisios consulted the oracle about the birth of male children, the god replied that his daughter would give birth to a son who would kill him. For fear of this, Acrisios built a bronze chamber beneath the ground and kept Danae guarded within it. She was seduced none the less, some say by Proitos* (so giving rise to the quarrel between the brothers), while according to others, Zeus had intercourse with her by transforming himself into a shower of gold and pouring through the roof into Danae's lap. Later, when Acrisios learned* that a child, Perseus, had been born to her, he refused to believe that she had been seduced by Zeus, and put his daughter into a chest along with her child, and threw it into the sea. The chest was cast ashore at Seriphos, where Dictys recovered it, and raised the child.

Perseus fetches the Gorgon's head

2 Polydectes, the brother of Dictys,* who was king of Seriphos at the time, fell in love with Danae; and when he was unable to achieve his desire now that Perseus was a grown man, he summoned his friends together, with Perseus amongst them, and claimed that he was gathering contributions for a marriage-offering* to enable him to marry Hippodameia, the daughter of Oinomaos. When Perseus declared that he would not deny him even the Gorgon's head, Polydectes demanded horses from all the others, but did not take the horses of Perseus* and ordered him to fetch the Gorgon's head.

Guided by Hermes and Athene, he went to see the daughters of Phorcos:* Enyo, Pephredo, and Deino. Daughters of Phorcos by Ceto, they were sisters of the Gorgons, and had been old women from the time of their birth. The three of them had only a single eye and a single tooth, which they exchanged in turn between themselves. Perseus gained possession of the eye and tooth, and when they asked him to give them back, he said that he would surrender them if they showed him the way to the nymphs. These nymphs had in their possession some winged sandals,* and the *kibisis*, which is said to have been a kind of wallet.† They also had the cap [of Hades*]. When the daughters of Phorcos had told him the way, he returned the eye and tooth to them, and visited the nymphs and obtained what he desired. He slung the *kibisis* around his neck, tied the sandals to his ankles, and placed the cap on his head; as long as he wore it, he could see whomever he wished while remaining invisible to others. After he had received in addition an adamantine sickle from Hermes, he flew to the Ocean, and when he arrived there, he caught the Gorgons asleep.

Their names were Stheno, Euryale, and Medusa. Only Medusa was mortal, and for that reason it was her head that Perseus was sent to fetch. The Gorgons had heads with scaly serpents coiled around them, and large tusks like those of swine, and hands of bronze, and wings of gold which gave them the power of flight; and they turned all who beheld them to stone. So Perseus stood over them as they slept, and while Athene guided his hand, he turned aside, and looking into a bronze shield in which he could see the reflection of the Gorgon, he cut off her head. As her head was severed, Pegasos, the winged horse, and Chrysaor, the father of Geryon, sprang from the Gorgon's body. (She had conceived them previously by Poseidon.*) [3] So Perseus placed Medusa's head in the wallet, and as he was making his way back, the Gorgons started from their sleep and tried to pursue him, but they were unable to see him because of the cap, which hid him from their view.

Perseus and Andromeda

Arriving in Ethiopia, which was ruled by Cepheus, he found the king's daughter Andromeda exposed as prey to a sea monster; for Cassiepeia,* the wife of Cepheus, had claimed to rival the Nereids in beauty, boasting that she surpassed them all. The Nereids were enraged by this, and Poseidon, who shared their anger, sent a sea-flood and a monster against the land. Now Ammon* had prophesied deliverance from this calamity if Cepheus' daughter Andromeda were offered as prey to the monster, and compelled by the Ethiopians, Cepheus had done so and tied his daughter to a rock. As soon as Perseus saw her, he fell in love, and promised Cepheus that he would destroy the monster if he would give him the rescued girl as a wife. When oaths had been sworn to this effect, Perseus confronted the monster and killed it, and set Andromeda free. Phineus, however, who was a brother of Cepheus and had been promised Andromeda beforehand, plotted against Perseus; but when Perseus learned of the conspiracy, he showed the Gorgon to Phineus and his fellow plotters, turning them to stone on the spot.

The later history of Perseus

When he arrived back at Seriphos, he found that his mother and Dictys had sought·refuge at the altars to escape the violence of Polydectes. So he went into the palace, where Polydectes had assembled his friends, and turning his head aside, he displayed the Gorgon's head. All who beheld it were turned to stone, each in the position he happened to have assumed at the time. And then, after making Dictys king of Seriphos, he restored the sandals, wallet, and cap to Hermes, and gave the Gorgon's head to Athene. Hermes returned the aforesaid objects to the nymphs and Athene fixed the Gorgon's head to the centre of her shield. But there are some who say that Medusa lost her head because of Athene—for they say that the Gorgon had claimed to rival the goddess in beauty.*

4 Perseus, accompanied by Danae and Andromeda, hurried off to Argos to see Acrisios. But when Acrisios learned of this, he feared what the oracle had predicted,* and left Argos and travelled to the land of the Pelasgians. Now Teutamides, king of Larissa,* was holding an athletic contest in honour of his dead father, and Perseus came to take part. While competing in the pentathlon, he threw his discus and struck Acrisios on the foot, killing him* instantly. Realizing that the oracle had been fulfilled, he buried Acrisios outside the city, and then, because he was ashamed to go to Argos to claim the inheritance of one who had died at his own hand, he went to Megapenthes, son of Proitos, and arranged an exchange of kingdoms with him, placing Argos in his hands. So in this way Megapenthes became king of the Argives, and Perseus king of Tiryns; and Perseus fortified Midea and Mycenae* in addition.

The immediate descendants of Perseus

5 By Andromeda, Perseus had the following sons, first, before their arrival in Greece, Perses, whom he left behind with Cepheus (and from whom, they say, the kings of Persia are descended), and later, in Mycenae, Alcaios, Sthenelos, Heleios, Mestor, and Electryon; he also had a daughter, Gorgophone, who became the wife of Perieres.

Alcaios had a son, Amphitryon, and a daughter, Anaxo, by Astydameia, daughter of Pelops (or according to some, by Laonome, daughter of Gouneus, or according to others, by Hipponome, daughter of Menoiceus); and Mestor and Lysidice, daughter of Pelops, had a daughter, Hippothoe. Hippothoe was carried off by Poseidon, who took her to the Echinadian Islands, where he had intercourse with her, fathering Taphios, who colonized Taphos and called his people the *Teleboans* because he had *gone far** from the land of his birth. To Taphios a son, Pterelaos, was born, whom Poseidon made immortal by planting a golden hair in his head; and Pterelaos had six sons, Chromios, Tyrannos, Antiochos, Chersidamas, Mestor, and Everes.

Electryon married Anaxo, the daughter of Alcaios, and fathered a daughter, Alcmene, and nine sons, [Stratobates,] Gorgophonos, Phylonomos, Celaineus, Amphimachos, Lysinomos, Cheirimachos, Anactor, and Archelaos; and after these, he also had an illegitimate son, Licymnios, by a Phrygian woman, Mideia.

Sthenelos had Alcyone and Medusa, by Nicippe, daughter of Pelops, and afterwards he had a son, Eurystheus, who also ruled in Mycenae. For when Heracles was due to be born, Zeus declared before the gods that the descendant of Perseus who was then about to be born* would become king of Mycenae, and Hera, out of jealousy, persuaded the Eileithuiai* to delay Alcmene's delivery, and arranged that Eurystheus, the son of Sthenelos, should be born at seven months.

The exile of Amphitryon

6 While Electryon was ruling at Mycenae, the sons of Pterelaos came there with Taphios and claimed back the kingdom of [their

maternal grandfather]* Mestor; and when Electryon disregarded their claim, they drove his cattle away. The sons of Electryon tried to rescue them, and they challenged and killed one another. Of the sons of Electryon, only Licymnios survived, because he was still a child, and of the sons of Pterelaos only Everes, who was guarding the ships. Those of the Taphians who escaped sailed away taking the stolen cattle, which they left in the care of Polyxenos, king of the Eleans; but Amphitryon ransomed them from Polyxenos and brought them back to Mycenae. Wanting to avenge the death of his sons, Electryon planned an expedition against the Teleboans. He entrusted the kingdom to Amphitryon, together with his daughter Alcmene, making him swear an oath that he would respect her virginity until his return. As he was receiving his cows back, however, one of them rushed forward, and Amphitryon let fly at her with the club that he had in his hands, but it rebounded from her horns to hit Electryon on the head, striking him dead.* Sthenelos grasped this as a pretext to banish Amphitryon from the whole of Argos and seize power for himself in Mycenae and Tiryns; as for Midea, he summoned Atreus and Thyestes, the sons of Pelops, and entrusted the city to them.

5. Heracles, and the Heraclids

Amphitryon in Thebes, and the war against the Teleboans

Amphitryon went to Thebes with Alcmene and Licymnios and was purified by Creon, and he gave his sister, Perimede, to Licymnios as a wife. And since Alcmene said that she would marry him* when he had avenged the death of her brothers, he promised to do so, and, inviting Creon's assistance, he prepared to march against the Teleboans. Creon said that he would join the expedition if Amphitryon would first rid the Cadmeia of the vixen* (for the Cadmeia was being devastated by a savage vixen). But even if somebody engaged to do so, it was fated that nobody could catch her. 7 Such harm was being caused to the country that each month the Thebans exposed a son of one of their citizens to her, for she would otherwise have carried off a great number of them. So Amphitryon visited Cephalos, son of Deioneus,* in Athens, and in return for a share of the plunder from the Teleboans, he persuaded him to bring to the hunt the dog* that Procris had been given by Minos and brought over from Crete; for it was fated that this dog would catch whatever it chased. So it came about that as the vixen was being pursued by the dog, Zeus turned both of them to stone.*

With the help of his allies, Cephalos from Thoricos in Attica, Panopeus from Phocis, Heleios, son of Perseus, from Helos in the Argolid, and Creon from Thebes, Amphitryon sacked the islands of the Teleboans. Now as long as Pterelaos was still alive, Amphitryon was unable to capture Taphos; but when Comaitho, the daughter of Pterelaos, who had fallen in love with Amphitryon, plucked the golden hair from her father's head, he died, and Amphitryon gained control of all the islands. He then put Comaitho to death* and sailed to Thebes with the plunder, giving the islands to Heleios and Cephalos, who founded cities that bear their name and settled in them.

The birth and early life of Heracles

8 Before Amphitryon arrived back in Thebes, Zeus came to the city by night, and tripling the length of that single night, he assumed the likeness of Amphitryon and went to bed with Alcmene, telling her all that had happened in the war with the Teleboans. When Amphitryon arrived and saw that his wife was welcoming him with no great ardour, he asked her the reason; and when she replied that he had come the previous night and slept with her, he found out from Teiresias about her intercourse with Zeus.

Alcmene gave birth to two sons, Heracles,* who was the son of Zeus and the elder by a night, and Iphicles, whom she bore to Amphitryon.

When Heracles was eight months old, Hera, wanting to destroy the child, sent two huge serpents to his bed. Alcmene cried out for Amphitryon, but Heracles leapt up and killed the serpents* by strangling them, one in each hand. According to

Pherecydes, however, it was Amphitryon who placed the serpents in the bed, because he wanted to find out which of the
children was his own; and seeing that Iphicles fled while Heracles
stood his ground, he realized that Iphicles was his child.

9 Heracles was taught chariot-driving by Amphitryon, wrestling by Autolycos, archery by Eurytos, fencing by Castor, and
lyre-playing by Linos. This Linos was a brother of Orpheus, who
had arrived in Thebes and become a Theban citizen, but was
killed by Heracles with a blow from his lyre (for Linos had
struck him,* and Heracles lost his temper and killed him). When
a charge of murder was brought against Heracles, he cited a
law of Rhadamanthys* saying that if a person defends himself
against another who has initiated the violence, he should suffer no penalty. So Heracles was acquitted. And Amphitryon,
fearing that he might do something similar again, sent him to
his herds; and there he grew up, surpassing all others in size
and strength. The mere sight of him was enough to show that
he was a son of Zeus: for his body measured four cubits, a
fiery gleam shone from his eyes, and he never missed his mark
with his arrows or javelins.

While he was still with the herds, and was now eighteen, he
killed the lion of Cithairon, a beast that used to make incursions from Cithairon to destroy the cattle of Amphitryon and
Thespios. 10 This last was king of Thespiae, and Heracles visited him when he wanted to kill the lion. He was entertained
by him for fifty days, and each night after Heracles went out
to the hunt, Thespios arranged that one of his daughters
should go to bed with him. For he had fifty of them, borne to
him by Megamede, daughter of Arneos, and he was eager that
they should all conceive children by Heracles.* And Heracles,
in the belief that he was always sleeping with the same woman,
had intercourse with all of them. When he had overcome the
lion, he dressed in its skin,* and used its gaping mouth as a
helmet.

Heracles and the Minyans; his first marriage, and madness

11 As he was returning from the hunt, he was met by some
heralds who had been sent by Erginos to collect the tribute

from the Thebans. The Thebans were paying this tribute to Erginos for the following reason. Clymenos, king of the Minyans,* had been wounded in the sanctuary of Poseidon at Onchestos when he was struck by a stone thrown by a charioteer of Menoiceus,* a man called Perieres; and Clymenos was carried back to Orchomenos half-dead, and as he was dying, he ordered his son, Erginos, to avenge his death. So Erginos mounted an expedition against Thebes, killed no small number of the Thebans, and concluded a treaty with them, sealed by oaths, that they should send tribute to him of a hundred cattle each year for twenty years. When Heracles met with the heralds who were travelling to Thebes for the tribute, he subjected them to a shameful mutilation; for he cut off their ears, noses, and hands, and tying these to their necks with cords, he told them to take that as tribute to Erginos and the Minyans. Outraged by this action, Erginos marched against Thebes. Heracles, who had received arms from Athene, took command of the Thebans, killed Erginos, and put the Minyans to flight; and he forced them to pay tribute to the Thebans at twice the aforementioned rate.

It happened that during the battle, Amphitryon, fighting with courage, met his death. As a prize of valour, Heracles received from Creon his eldest daughter, Megara, who bore him three sons, Therimachos, Creontiades, and Deicoon. And Creon gave his younger daughter to Iphicles, who already had a son, Iolaos, by Automedousa, daughter of Alcathous. And Rhadamanthys, son of Zeus, married Alcmene after the death of Amphitryon, and settled as an exile at Ocaleai in Boeotia.

Heracles, who had been taught archery earlier by [Eurytos],* received a sword from Hermes, a bow and arrows from Apollo, a golden breastplate from Hephaistos, and a robe from Athene; and he cut a club for himself at Nemea.

12 After his battle with the Minyans, it came about that Heracles was struck by madness through the jealousy of Hera, and threw his own children, who had been borne to him by Megara, into the fire, together with two of Iphicles' children. Condemning himself to exile on this account, he was purified by Thespios and went to Delphi to ask the god where he should

72

settle. It was on this occasion that the Pythia* called him Heracles for the first time (for until then he had been called Alceides). She told him to settle in Tiryns while he served Eurystheus for twelve years, and to accomplish the [ten] labours* that would be imposed on him; and then, she said, after the labours had been accomplished, he would come to be immortal.*

First labour: the Nemean lion

5 ¹ On hearing this, Heracles went to Tiryns and fulfilled what Eurystheus demanded of him. Eurystheus began by ordering him to fetch the skin of the Nemean lion; this was an invulnerable beast fathered by Typhon.* As he was travelling to confront the lion, Heracles arrived at Cleonai and stayed with a labourer called Molorchos; and when Molorchos wanted to offer a victim in sacrifice, Heracles told him to wait for thirty days, and then, if he had returned safely from the hunt, to offer a sacrifice to Zeus the Saviour, but if he had died, to offer it to himself as a hero.* On reaching Nemea, he sought out the lion, and began by shooting arrows at it, but when he discovered that the beast was invulnerable, he raised his club and chased after it. When the lion took refuge in a cave which had two entrances, Heracles walled up one of them and went in through the other to attack the beast; and throwing his arm round its neck, he held it in a stranglehold until he had throttled it. And hoisting it on to his shoulders, he carried it back to Cleonai. Coming upon Molorchos on the last of the thirty days as he was about to sacrifice to him as a dead hero, Heracles sacrificed to Zeus the Saviour instead, and proceeded to Mycenae with the lion. Astounded by his bravery, Eurystheus refused him entry to the city from that day forth, and told him to exhibit his trophies in front of the gates. They say, furthermore, that in his alarm he had a bronze jar made for himself to hide in beneath the ground, and that he conveyed his commands for the labours through a herald, Copreus,* a son of Pelops the Elean. (Copreus had fled to Mycenae because he had killed Iphitos, and had settled there after he had been purified by Eurystheus.)

Second labour: the Lernaean hydra

2 As a second labour, Eurystheus ordered Heracles to kill the Lernaean hydra;* this creature had grown up in the swamp of Lerna, and used to make incursions into the plain and destroy the cattle and the countryside. The hydra had a body of enormous size, and nine heads,* of which eight were mortal, but the one in the centre immortal. So climbing on to a chariot driven by Iolaos, Heracles made his way to Lerna, and halting his horses there, he discovered the hydra on a hill by the springs of Amymone,* where it had its lair. By hurling flaming brands at it, he forced it to emerge, and as it came out, he seized it and grasped it firmly. But it twined itself round one of his legs, and clung to him. By striking the hydra's heads off with his club Heracles achieved nothing, for as soon as one was struck off, two grew up in its place; and a huge crab came to its assistance by biting Heracles on the foot. So he killed the crab, and summoned assistance on his own account by calling Iolaos,* who set fire to part of the neighbouring forest, and using brands from it, burned out the roots of the hydra's heads to prevent them from regrowing. And when, by this means, he had prevailed over the regenerating heads, he cut off the immortal head, buried it, and placed a heavy rock over it by the road that leads through Lerna to Elaious. As for the body of the hydra, he slit it open and dipped his arrows into its gall. Eurystheus declared, however, that this labour should not be counted among the ten, because Heracles had not overcome the hydra on his own, but only with the help of Iolaos.

Third labour: the Cerynitian hind

3 As a third labour, Eurystheus ordered him to bring the Cerynitian hind alive to Mycenae. This hind, which had golden horns, lived at Oinoe, and was sacred to Artemis;* so Heracles, wanting neither to kill it nor wound it, pursued it for a full year. When the hind, worn out by the chase, fled for refuge to the mountain known as Artemision, and from there towards the River Ladon, Heracles struck it with an arrow* as it was about to cross over the stream, and was thus able

to catch it; and then, settling it on his shoulder, he hurried through Arcadia. But he came across Artemis in the company of Apollo, and she wanted to take the hind away from him, accusing him of trying to kill an animal that was sacred to her. By pleading necessity, however, and saying that the person responsible was Eurystheus, he allayed the anger of the goddess and brought the animal alive to Mycenae.

Fourth labour: the Erymanthian boar

4 As a fourth labour, Eurystheus ordered him to bring the Erymanthian boar alive. This beast was causing havoc in Psophis, sallying forth from the mountain known as Erymanthos. While Heracles was passing through Pholoe, he was entertained as a guest by the Centaur Pholos, son of Seilenos and a Melian nymph. The Centaur served roasted meat to Heracles, but he himself ate it raw. When Heracles asked for wine, he said that he was afraid to open the jar that was the common property of the Centaurs;* but Heracles urged him to take courage, and opened it up. Not long afterwards, the Centaurs became aware of the smell, and appeared at Pholos' cave armed with rocks and fir trees. The first who dared to come inside, Anchios and Agrios, were put to flight by Heracles, who hurled flaming brands at them; and he pursued the others with arrows as far as Malea, where they took refuge with Cheiron (who had settled there after he had been driven from Mount Pelion by the Lapiths).* As the Centaurs clung to Cheiron for safety, Heracles shot an arrow at them, which passed through the arm of Elatos and lodged in Cheiron's knee. Distressed at this, Heracles ran up to him, pulled out the arrow, and applied a potion which Cheiron gave to him; but when the wound turned out to be incurable, Cheiron withdrew to his cave. He wanted to die, but was incapable of doing so because he was immortal. Only when Prometheus offered himself to Zeus to become immortal in his place was Cheiron able to die.* The rest of the Centaurs fled in all directions; some went to Malea, while Eurytion went to Pholoe, and Nessos to the River Evenos. The rest were received at Eleusis by Poseidon, who hid them under a mountain. Pholos, for his part, had pulled

an arrow from a corpse, marvelling that so small a thing could kill creatures of such a size; but the arrow slipped from his hand and landed on his foot, killing him instantly.* When Heracles returned to Pholoe and saw that Pholos was dead, he buried him and went out to hunt the boar. He chased the beast from the thicket with loud cries; and thrusting it exhausted into deep snow, he trapped it in a noose, and took it to Mycenae.

Fifth labour: the cattle of Augeias

5 As a fifth labour, Eurystheus ordered Heracles to remove the dung of the cattle of Augeias without assistance in a single day. Augeias was the king of Elis, and, according to some, he was a son of the Sun, or according to others, of Poseidon, or again, of Phorbas; and he owned many herds of cattle. Heracles went up to him, and without disclosing Eurystheus' order, said that he would remove the dung in a single day if Augeias would give him a tenth of his cattle. Augeias gave his word, not believing that he could do it. After he had engaged Phyleus, the son of Augeias, as a witness, Heracles made a breach in the foundations of [the wall surrounding] the cattle yard, and then, diverting the courses of the Alpheios and the Peneios which flowed nearby, he channelled their water into the yard, after first making an outlet through another breach. When Augeias discovered that the task had been accomplished on the order of Eurystheus, he refused to pay the reward,* and went so far as to deny that he had ever promised to pay a reward, saying that he was ready to submit to arbitration on the matter. When the judges had taken their seats, Phyleus was called by Heracles and testified against his father,* saying that he had agreed to pay a reward to Heracles. Augeias flew into a rage, and before the vote had been cast, ordered both Phyleus and Heracles to depart from Elis. So Phyleus went to Doulichion and settled there; and Heracles visited Dexamenos in Olenos. He caught him as he was about to give his daughter, Mnesimache, under compulsion to the Centaur Eurytion; and when he was asked to help, Heracles killed Eurytion as he arrived to claim his bride. Eurystheus would not accept this labour

either as one of the ten, saying that it had been accomplished for pay.

Sixth labour: the Stymphalian birds

6 As a sixth labour, Eurystheus ordered him to drive away the Stymphalian birds. At the city of Stymphalos in Arcadia there was a lake called Stymphalis, in the depths of a thick forest; and innumerable birds had sought refuge there, fearing to become the prey of wolves. So when Heracles was at a loss as to how he could drive the birds from the wood, Athene gave him some bronze castanets which she had received from Hephaistos. By rattling these from a certain mountain that lay beside the lake, he frightened the birds. Unable to endure the noise, they flew up in alarm, and in that way Heracles was able to shoot them down* with his arrows.

Seventh labour: the Cretan bull

7 As a seventh labour, Eurystheus ordered him to fetch the Cretan bull. According to Acousilaos, this was the bull that had carried Europa* across the sea for Zeus, but it is said by some that it was the bull that was sent up from the sea by Poseidon* when Minos had promised to sacrifice to him whatever appeared from the sea. And they say that when Minos saw the beauty of the bull, he sent it to join his herds and sacrificed another to Poseidon; and the god in his anger turned the bull wild. Heracles arrived in Crete to confront this bull, and when Minos replied to his request for assistance by telling him to fight and capture it on his own, he captured it and took it to Eurystheus; and after he had shown it to him, he set it free. It wandered to Sparta and throughout Arcadia, and crossing the Isthmus, it arrived at Marathon* in Attica and harassed the inhabitants.

Eighth labour: the mares of Diomedes

8 As an eighth labour, Eurystheus ordered him to bring the mares of Diomedes the Thracian to Mycenae. This Diomedes,

a son of Ares and Cyrene, was king of the Bistones, a highly belligerent people in Thrace, and owned man-eating mares.* So Heracles sailed there with a company of volunteers, over-powered the men who were in charge of the mangers, and led the mares towards the sea. When the Bistones came fully armed to the rescue, he passed the mares over to Abderos to guard. (This Abderos, a Locrian from Opous who was a son of Hermes and a beloved of Heracles, was torn apart by the horses and killed.) So Heracles fought against the Bistones, killed Diomedes, and put the rest to flight. After founding the city of Abdera by the grave of Abderos, who had met his death in the meantime, he took the horses to Eurystheus and handed them over to him. But Eurystheus released them, and they went to the mountain called Olympos, where they were killed by the wild beasts.

Ninth labour: the belt of Hippolyte

9 As a ninth labour, Eurystheus ordered him to fetch the belt of Hippolyte. She was queen of the Amazons, who lived by the River Thermodon* and were a people who excelled in war; for they cultivated manly qualities, and if they ever had inter-course with men and gave birth to children, they raised the girls. They pressed down* their right breasts to ensure that they would not be hindered from throwing their javelins, but retained their left breasts to allow them to suckle their children. Hippolyte had the belt of Ares* in her possession as a symbol of her supremacy over the others, and Heracles was sent to fetch the belt because Admete, the daughter of Eurystheus, wanted it for herself. So taking some volunteers to assist him, he set sail in a single ship, and called in at the island of Paros, where the sons of Minos were living, namely Eurymedon, Chryses, Nephalion, and Philolaos. It happened that two men from the ship who had gone ashore were killed by the sons of Minos; and in his fury at this, Heracles slew them on the spot, and kept the other islanders under close siege until they sent a delegation to invite him to take whatever pair of them he pleased in return for the men who had been mur-dered. So he lifted the siege, and taking on board Alcaios and

Sthenelos, the sons of Androgeos, son of Minos, he arrived in
Mysia, at the court of Lycos, son of Dascylos. He was entertained there by [Lycos, and when Lycos*] joined battle with
the king of the Bebrycians, Heracles came to his aid, and killed
many men, including King Mygdon, the brother of Amycos.
And he deprived the Bebrycians of a large amount of land and
gave it to Lycos, who called the whole territory Heracleia.

When he put in at the harbour of Themiscyra, Hippolyte
came to see him, and she asked him why he had come and
promised to give him the belt. But Hera assumed the likeness
of an Amazon and wandered around in the crowd saying that
the strangers who had just arrived were abducting the queen.
Seizing their arms, the Amazons hastened to the ships on
horseback; and when Heracles saw them there fully armed, he
thought that this must be the result of a plot, and he killed
Hippolyte and robbed her of the belt. And then, after fighting
the rest of the Amazons, he sailed away, and called in at Troy.

It happened that the city was in a desperate plight at that
time, through the wrath of Apollo and Poseidon; for wanting
to put Laomedon's arrogance to the test, they had taken on
human form and undertaken to fortify Pergamon* in return
for pay. But when they had constructed the wall, he refused
to pay them their fee. In response, Apollo sent a plague, and
Poseidon a sea-monster which was carried along on a flood
and used to snatch away the inhabitants of the plain. When
oracles declared that they would be delivered from these misfortunes if Laomedon offered his daughter, Hesione, as prey
to the monster, Laomedon offered her up, binding her to some
rocks by the sea. When Heracles saw her exposed there, he
promised to rescue her if he received in return the mares that
Zeus had presented [to Tros*] in compensation for the abduction of Ganymede. Laomedon said that he would hand them
over, and Heracles killed the monster and rescued Hesione.
But Laomedon refused to pay the agreed reward, and Heracles
put to sea threatening to make war on Troy at some future
time.*

He then called in at Ainos, where he was entertained
by Poltys. As he was sailing off, he shot and killed a man of
violence on the shore there, Sarpedon, a son of Poseidon

and brother of Poltys. Arriving in Thasos, he subjugated the Thracians who inhabited the island and gave it to the sons of Androgeos to settle in. From Thasos he set out for Torone, where he was challenged to a wrestling match by Polygonos and Telegonos, the sons of Proteus, son of Poseidon, and killed them during the contest. And taking the belt to Mycenae, he gave it to Eurystheus.

Tenth labour: the cattle of Geryon

10 As a tenth labour, he was ordered to fetch the cattle of Geryon from Erytheia. Erytheia was an island that lay near the Ocean and is now called Gadeira; it was inhabited by Geryon, son of Chrysaor and Callirrhoe, daughter of Oceanos. He had the body of three men joined into one;* these were united at the waist, but divided into three again from the hips and thighs downwards. He owned red cattle, which were herded by Eurytion and guarded by Orthos, a two-headed dog that Echidna had borne to Typhon. So travelling through Europe to fetch the cattle of Geryon, Heracles killed many savage beasts,* and then arrived in Libya. He made his way to Tartessos, where he erected two pillars* standing opposite one another at the boundaries of Europe and Libya, as memorials of his journey. In the course of his journey, he was overheated by the Sun, and aimed his bow against the god; and the Sun was so impressed by his bravery that he offered him a golden cup* which he used when crossing the Ocean. Arriving at Erytheia, Heracles set up camp on Mount Abas. His presence was detected by the dog Orthos, which rushed to attack him; but he struck it with his club and when the herdsman Eurytion came to the dog's assistance, he killed Eurytion too. Menoites, who was pasturing the cattle of Hades in the area, informed Geryon of what had happened; and Geryon caught Heracles driving the cattle away near the river Anthemous, and engaged him in battle, but was killed by an arrow. Heracles put the cattle into the cup, and after he had made the crossing to Tartessos, he returned it to the Sun.

He passed through Abderia and arrived in Liguria, where Ialebion and Dercynos, sons of Poseidon, tried to rob him of the cattle, but he killed them and travelled on through

Tyrrhenia. At *Rhegion*,* a bull *broke loose*, plunged swiftly into the sea, and swam across to Sicily, and then, after passing through the neighbouring land which was named *Italy* after it (because the Tyrrhenians called the bull *italus**), it arrived at the plain of Eryx, who was king of the Elymoi; and Eryx, a son of Poseidon, mixed the bull amongst his own herds. Entrusting the rest of the cattle to Hephaistos, Heracles hurried off in search of the bull; he discovered it in the herds of Eryx, and when Eryx declined to surrender it unless Heracles defeated him* in a wrestling match, he defeated Eryx three times in the course of the match and killed him. He then took the bull and drove it with the other cattle to the Ionian Sea.

When he reached the top of the gulf,* Hera sent a gadfly against the cattle and they dispersed among the foothills of the Thracian mountains. Heracles set out in pursuit, and recovering some of them, he drove them towards the Hellespont, but those that he left behind were wild from that time forth. Having had difficulty collecting his cattle together, he blamed the River Strymon, and although it had been navigable previously, he made it unnavigable by filling it with rocks. He took the cattle to Eurystheus, and handed them over; and Eurystheus offered them in sacrifice to Hera.

Eleventh labour: the apples of the Hesperides

11 When these labours had been accomplished in eight years and a month, Eurystheus, who would not acknowledge the labour of the cattle of Augeias or that of the hydra, ordered Heracles, as an eleventh labour, to fetch some golden apples from the Hesperides.* These apples were to be found, not in Libya, as some have claimed, but on Mount Atlas in the land of the Hyperboreans.* They had been presented to Zeus [by Ge] at the time of his marriage to Hera, and were guarded by an immortal dragon, the offspring of Typhon and Echidna, which had a hundred heads and could speak with all manner of different voices. And with this dragon, the Hesperides—Aigle, Erytheia, Hesperia, and Arethousa by name—also kept guard. So Heracles proceeded on his way, until he arrived at the River Echedoros, where Cycnos, the son of Ares and Pyrene,

challenged him to single combat [. . .] to avenge him, Ares too engaged him in single combat,* but a thunderbolt was hurled between the two combatants, bringing the fight to an end. Travelling through the land of the Illyrians, Heracles hurried to the River Eridanos, where he visited the nymphs who were daughters of Zeus and Themis; and they told him where he could find Nereus. Heracles seized hold of him while he was asleep, and although he transformed himself* into many different shapes, Heracles tied him up and refused to let him go until he had learned from him where the apples and the Hesperides were located. After he had acquired this information, he travelled through Libya, which was then ruled by Antaios,* a son of Poseidon, who compelled strangers to wrestle with him and killed them. When he too was compelled to wrestle with him, Heracles seized him in his arms, lifted him into the air, and crushed him until he was dead; for whenever he touched the earth, Antaios would always grow stronger (which is why some have called him a son of Ge).

Leaving Libya, he passed through Egypt, which was then under the rule of Bousiris, son of Poseidon and Lysianassa, daughter of Epaphos. Bousiris used to sacrifice strangers on an altar of Zeus, in accordance with an oracle; for barrenness had gripped the land of Egypt for nine years, and Phrasios, a skilled diviner who had come from Cyprus, said that the barrenness would come to an end if they slaughtered a male foreigner in honour of Zeus every year. Bousiris began by slaughtering the diviner himself, and continued to slaughter strangers who landed there. So Heracles was arrested and dragged to the altars, but he broke free of his bonds, and killed both Bousiris and his son Amphidamas.

After passing through Asia, he put in at Thermydrai, the harbour of the Lindians. And releasing one of the bullocks from the cart of a drover,* he sacrificed it and feasted on its flesh. The drover, unable to defend himself, stood on a certain mountain and cursed him; and because of that, even to this day, when they sacrifice to Heracles there, they do so to the accompaniment of curses.

Passing by Arabia, he killed Emathion* the son of Tithonos; and he travelled through Libya* to the outer sea, where he

received the cup from the Sun. He crossed over to the mainland opposite, and on the Caucasos he shot the eagle, born to
Echidna and Typhon, that fed on the liver of Prometheus. He
then set Prometheus free, taking the fetters of olive for himself, and presented Cheiron to Zeus as an immortal being who
was willing to die in Prometheus' place.*

When he reached Atlas in the land of the Hyperboreans,
Heracles followed the advice of Prometheus, who had told him
not to go for the apples himself but to take over the sky from
Atlas and send him instead. So Atlas took three apples from
the Hesperides and returned to Heracles; and not wishing to
hold up the heavens again, [he said that he himself would carry
the apples to Eurystheus, and asked Heracles to support the
sky in his place. Heracles promised that he would, but passed
it back to Atlas by means of a ruse. For Prometheus, when
offering his advice, had told him that he should ask Atlas to
take the sky back until*] he had prepared a pad for his head.
And when Atlas heard his request, he placed the apples on the
ground and took the sky back. In this way, Heracles was able
to pick up the apples and depart. (It is said by some, however, that he did not get the apples from Atlas, but plucked
them himself after killing the guardian snake.*) He brought
the apples back, and gave them to Eurystheus; but as soon as
he received them, he returned them to Heracles. Then Athene
took them from Heracles, and carried them back again; for it
was unholy* for them to be deposited anywhere else.

Twelfth labour: the capture of Cerberos

12 As a twelfth labour, he was ordered to fetch Cerberos* from
Hades. Cerberos had three dogs' heads, the tail of a dragon,
and on his back, the heads of all kinds of snakes. When Heracles was about to depart for Cerberos, he went to Eumolpos
in Eleusis with a view to being initiated;*† but since it was
impossible for him to behold the Mysteries unless he had been
purified from the murder of the Centaurs, he was purified
by Eumolpos* and initiated thereafter. He made his way to
Tainaron in Laconia, where the mouth of the descent to Hades
is located, and descended through it. When the souls caught

sight of him, they fled, except for Meleager and the Gorgon Medusa.* He drew his sword against the Gorgon as if she were still alive, but learned from Hermes that she was an empty phantom. As he drew close to the gates of Hades, he discovered Theseus there, and Peirithoos,* who had tried to gain Persephone as his bride, and had been imprisoned there for that reason. When they saw Heracles, they stretched their arms towards him, hoping that his strength would enable them to be raised from the dead. He took Theseus by the hand and raised him up, but when he wanted to raise Peirithoos, the earth shook and he let him go. He also rolled aside the stone of Ascalaphos.* Wanting to procure blood for the souls,* he slaughtered one of the cattle of Hades; but their herdsman, Menoites, son of Ceuthonymos, challenged him to a wrestling match. Heracles seized him round the middle and broke his ribs, but let him go when Persephone interceded. When he asked Pluto for Cerberos, Pluto told him to take the beast if he could overpower it without using any of the weapons that he was carrying. Discovering Cerberos by the gates of Acheron,* Heracles, sheathed in his breastplate and fully covered by his lion's skin, grasped its head between his arms and never relaxed his grip and stranglehold on the beast until he had broken its will, although he was bitten by the dragon in its tail. Then he carried it off and made his way back, ascending through Troezen. As for Ascalaphos, Demeter turned him into an owl.* After Heracles had shown Cerberos to Eurystheus, he returned the beast to Hades.

The murder of Iphitos and Heracles' enslavement to Omphale

6 ¹ After his labours, Heracles returned to Thebes. He gave Megara to Iolaos,* and wanting to remarry, he made enquiries and learned that Eurytos, king of Oichalia, had offered the hand of his daughter Iole as a prize to the man who could defeat himself and his sons at archery.* So he went to Oichalia and proved himself superior to them at archery, but even so, he failed to get his bride; for although Iphitos, the eldest of the sons, said that Iole should be given to Heracles, Eurytos and the others refused, saying that they were afraid that if he had children, he would kill his offspring once again. ² Not long afterwards, some cattle were stolen* from Euboea by Autolycos, and Eurytos thought that Heracles was responsible. Iphitos, however, did not believe it, and went to see Heracles. Meeting him as he was returning from Pherae after he had saved the dead Alcestis for Admetos, Iphitos asked him to help in the search for the cattle. Heracles promised to do so and entertained him as a guest; but then, in a fresh fit of madness,* he hurled him from the walls of Tiryns. Wanting to be purified of the murder he visited Neleus, who was king of the Pylians. When Neleus rejected him* because of his friendship with Eurytos, he then went to Amyclai and was purified by Deiphobos, son of Hippolytos.

He was struck by a terrible disease as the result of his murder of Iphitos, and went to Delphi to ask how he could be delivered from it. When the Pythia refused to grant him a response,* he wanted to plunder the temple and tried to carry off the tripod to found an oracle of his own. But Apollo joined battle with him, until Zeus hurled a thunderbolt between them. After they had been separated in this way, Heracles received a response from the oracle, which told him that he would be delivered from his illness if he was sold into slavery, served for three years, and gave the price paid for him to Eurytos as compensation for the murder. ³ Following the delivery of this oracle, Hermes put him up for sale, and he was purchased by Omphale, daughter of Iardanos, queen of Lydia, who had been left the kingdom by her husband, Tmolos, after his death. As for the money paid for him, Eurytos refused to accept it when it was brought to him.

While serving Omphale as a slave, Heracles captured and bound the Cercopes* at Ephesus, and at Aulis he killed Syleus —who compelled strangers to dig [in his vineyard*]—and also his daughter, Xenodoce, and burned his vines to their roots. Calling in at the island of Doliche, he saw the body of Icaros* cast ashore there, and buried it, calling the island Icaria instead of Doliche. In return, Daidalos made a statue at Pisa in the likeness of Heracles (who failed to recognize it one night, and threw a stone at it, taking it for a living person). It was during the time of his servitude to Omphale that the voyage to Colchis* is said to have taken place, and the hunt for the Calydonian boar, and that Theseus is said to have cleared the Isthmus as he travelled from Troezen.*

The first sack of Troy

4 After the completion of his servitude, when he was rid of his disease, he sailed against Ilion* with eighteen fifty-oared ships, and an army that he had assembled beforehand from heroes who had volunteered for the expedition. On his arrival at Ilion, he left Oicles behind to guard the ships while he and the other heroes set off to attack the city. Laomedon for his part marched against the ships with the greater part of his force and killed Oicles in the fighting, but he was driven back by the troops of Heracles and put under siege. After the siege was engaged, Telamon was the first to break through the wall and make his way into the city, with Heracles behind him. When Heracles saw that Telamon had entered first, he drew his sword and rushed to attack him, anxious that nobody should be thought a better man than himself. Seeing the situation, Telamon began to heap together some stones that lay at hand; and when Heracles asked him what he was doing, he said that he was building an altar to Heracles the Noble Victor.* Heracles praised him for this, and when he had taken the city and shot down Laomedon and all his sons except for Podarces, he gave Laomedon's daughter Hesione to Telamon as a prize, allowing her to take with her any person she wished from the captives. When she chose her brother Podarces, Heracles said that he must first become a slave, and that she should then offer something in payment for him so as to acquire him. So when he was sold, she removed the veil from her head and gave it in payment for him; and that was how Podarces came to be called *Priam.**

7   1 As Heracles was sailing back from Troy, Hera sent violent storms* against him, which so angered Zeus that he suspended her from Olympos.* Heracles wanted to sail in to Cos, but the Coans, taking him for the leader of a band of pirates, tried to prevent his approach by hurling stones. He turned to force and seized the island by night, killing its king, Eurypylos,

son of Astypalaia and Poseidon. In the course of the fighting, Heracles was wounded by Chalcodon, but Zeus snatched him away and he suffered no further harm. After ravaging Cos, he went to Phlegra at Athene's behest, and helped the gods to victory in their war against the Giants.*

Campaigns in the Peloponnese

2 Not long afterwards, he mounted an expedition against Augeias,* gathering together an Arcadian army and raising volunteers from the foremost men of Greece. When Augeias heard that Heracles was preparing to make war on him, he appointed as generals of the Eleans Eurytos and Cteatos,* who were two men joined into one, and were superior in strength to all others of their time. They were sons of Molione and Actor (who was a brother of Augeias), although their real father was said to be Poseidon. Now it happened that in the course of the expedition Heracles fell ill, and for that reason he arranged a truce with the Molionides; but later, when they came to learn of his illness, they attacked his army and killed many of his men. So at the time Heracles retreated; but afterwards, when the Isthmian Games were being celebrated for the third time and the Eleans sent the Molionides to take part in the sacrifices, Heracles set an ambush* for them at Cleonai and killed them. Then he marched against Elis and captured the city. After he had killed Augeias and his sons, he recalled Phyleus* and granted him the throne. He also established the Olympic Games, founded an altar of Pelops,* and raised six altars to the twelve gods.

3 After the capture of Elis, he marched against Pylos.* He took the city and killed Periclymenos, the bravest of Neleus' sons, who used to change shape as he fought. He killed Neleus too, and all his sons, except for Nestor, who was still a boy and was being brought up amongst the Gerenians. During the battle, he also wounded Hades, who came to the aid of the Pylians.*

After he had captured Pylos, he mounted an expedition against Lacedaimon, wanting to punish the sons of Hippocoon. He was angry with them because they had fought as allies of Neleus, and was even angrier when they killed the son of

Licymnios:* for while he was looking at the palace of Hippocoon, a Molossian hound ran out and dashed towards him, and when he threw a stone and struck the dog, the sons of Hippocoon rushed out and beat him to death with their cudgels. It was to avenge his death that Heracles assembled an army to attack the Lacedaimonians. Arriving in Arcadia, he asked Cepheus to join him as his ally, along with his sons, of whom he had twenty. Cepheus, fearing that the Argives would attack Tegea if he left it, refused to take part in the expedition; but Heracles, who had acquired from Athene a lock of the Gorgon's hair in a bronze jar, gave it to Cepheus' daughter, Sterope, saying that if an army attacked, she should hold up the lock three times from the ramparts without looking at it herself and the enemy would turn and flee. As a result, Cepheus joined the expedition with his sons, and in the course of the fighting, he and his sons were killed, together with Iphicles, the brother of Heracles. After he had killed Hippocoon and his sons and taken control of the city, Heracles recalled Tyndareus and entrusted the kingdom to him.

4 As he was passing by Tegea, Heracles raped Auge, without realizing that she was the daughter of Aleos.* She gave birth in secret and hid her baby in the sanctuary of Athene; but when the country was ravaged by a plague,* Aleos entered the sanctuary, conducted a search, and discovered his daughter's child. So he had the baby exposed on Mount Parthenion, but it was saved by an act of divine providence: for a *doe* that had just given birth offered her *teat* to it, and some shepherds took up the child and named it *Telephos*.* As for Auge, her father handed her over to Nauplios, son of Poseidon, to sell in foreign parts, and Nauplios gave her to Teuthras, king of Teuthrania, who made her his wife.

Marriage to Deianeira; Heracles in northern Greece

5 Arriving in Calydon, Heracles sought to win Deianeira, the daughter of Oineus,* as his wife. To gain her hand, he wrestled with Acheloos,* and when Acheloos assumed the form of a bull, Heracles broke off one of its horns. So Heracles married Deianeira, and Acheloos recovered his horn by offering

that of Amaltheia* in exchange. (Amaltheia was the daughter of Haimonios and she owned a bull's horn, which, according to Pherecydes, had the power to furnish as much meat or drink as one could wish for, in limitless supply.)

6 Heracles marched with the Calydonians against the Thesprotians, and after capturing the city of Ephyra,* which was ruled by Phylas, he had intercourse with the king's daughter, Astyoche, and became the father of Tlepolemos.* During his stay with them, he sent a message to Thespios telling him to retain seven of his sons,* but dispatch three of them to Thebes and send the remaining forty to the island of Sardinia to found a colony. Subsequently, as he was feasting with Oineus, he killed Eunomos,* son of Architeles, with a blow of his fist while the boy (who was a relative of Oineus) was pouring water over his hands. Because this had come about unintentionally, the father of the boy forgave Heracles, but he wanted to suffer exile in accordance with the law, and decided to depart to Ceux at Trachis.

Taking Deianeira with him, he arrived at the River Evenos. The Centaur Nessos had settled there,* and used to ferry travellers across the river for a fee, claiming that he had been granted the post of ferryman by the gods because of his honesty. Heracles for his own part crossed the river without assistance, but he entrusted Deianeira to Nessos and paid him the demanded fee to carry her across. But while Nessos was carrying her over, he tried to rape her; and Heracles heard her cries, and shot Nessos in the heart as he emerged from the water. On the point of death, Nessos called Deianeira to his side and said that if she wanted a love-potion* to use on Heracles, she should mix the semen that he had shed on the ground with the blood that had flowed from the wound made by the arrowhead. She did so, and kept the potion at hand.

7 While he was passing through the land of the Dryopes, Heracles was short of food, and when he came across Theiodamas* driving a pair of bullocks, he unyoked one of the bullocks, slaughtered it, and feasted on its flesh. When he reached Ceux* in Trachis, he was entertained by him, and then defeated the Dryopes in war.

Later he set out from Trachis to fight as an ally of Aigimios, king of the Dorians;* for the Lapiths, under the command of Coronos, had gone to war with Aigimios over the boundaries of the land, and finding himself besieged, he had summoned Heracles to his aid, offering a share of the land in exchange. So Heracles came to his assistance, killed Coronos and others too, and delivered the whole country to Aigimios without accepting any reward. He also killed Laogoras, king of the Dryopes, along with his children, as he was feasting in a sanctuary of Apollo; for Laogoras was a man of violence and an ally of the Lapiths. As he was passing Itonos, he was challenged to single combat by Cycnos,* son of Ares and Pelopia; so Heracles joined battle with him, and killed him too. When he arrived at Ormenion, its king, Amyntor, appearing under arms, would not allow him to pass through; so, prevented from passing on his way, Heracles killed Amyntor* also.

The sack of Oichalia; the death and apotheosis of Heracles

On his arrival at Trachis, he assembled an army to attack Oichalia, desiring vengeance on Eurytos.* With Arcadians, Melians from Trachis, and Epicnemidian Locrians as his allies, he killed Eurytos and his sons, and captured the city. After burying those of his comrades who had fallen, namely, Hippasos, son of Ceux, and Argeios and Melas, the sons of Licymnios, he plundered the city and took Iole captive. Bringing his ship to anchor at Cenaion, a headland of Euboea, he erected an altar to Cenaian Zeus; and proposing to offer a sacrifice, he sent [Lichas] the herald to Trachis to fetch fine clothing. But Deianeira, learning from Lichas how matters stood with regard to Iole,* was afraid that Heracles might be more in love with Iole than with herself, and thinking that the blood that had flowed from Nessos really was a love-potion, she rubbed it into the tunic. So Heracles put it on, and proceeded with the sacrifice. But as soon as the tunic grew warm, the poison from the hydra began to bite into his skin. In response, he lifted Lichas by the feet and hurled him [into the Euboean Sea*], and tried to tear off the tunic, which had become attached to his body; but his flesh was torn off along with the clothing. In this sorry plight, he was carried back to Trachis by ship; and when Deianeira learned what had happened, she hanged herself. After instructing Hyllos, his eldest son by Deianeira, to marry Iole when he came of age, Heracles made his way to Mount Oeta (which lies on Trachinian territory), and built a pyre there and climbed on to it, ordering that it should be set alight. When nobody was willing to do so, Poias,* who was passing by in search of his flocks, set it alight; and Heracles presented his bow and arrows to him. As the pyre blazed, a cloud is said to have passed beneath Heracles and raised him up to heaven* to the accompaniment of thunder. There he obtained immortality, and becoming reconciled with Hera, he married her daughter Hebe,* who bore him two sons, Alexiares and Anicetos.

The children of Heracles

8 He had the following sons by the daughters of Thespios.* By Procris, he had Antileon and Hippeus (for the eldest daughter gave birth to twins); by Panope, he had Threpsippas; by Lyse, he had Eumedes; by [. . .], he had Creon; by Epilais, he had Astyanax; by Certhe, he had Iobes; by Eurybia, he had Polylaos; by Patro, he had Archemachos; by Meline, he had Laomedon; by Clytippe, he had Eurycapys; he had Eurypylos by Eubote; by Aglaia, he had Antiades; by Chryseis, he had Onesippos; by Oreie, he had Laomenes; he had Teles by Lysidice; he had Entelides by Menippis; by Anthippe, he had Hippodromos; he had Teleutagoras by Eury [. . .]; he had Capylos by Hippo; by Euboia, he had Olympos; by Nice, he had Nicodromos; by Argele, he had Cleolaos; by Exole, he had Erythras; by Xanthis, he had Homolippos; by Stratonice, he had Atromos; he had Celeustanor by Iphis; by Laothoe, he had Antiphos; by Antiope, he had Alopios; he had Astybies by Calametis; by Phyleis, he had Tigasis; by Aischreis, he had Leucones; by Antheia, he had [. . .]; by Eurypyle, he had Archedicos; he had Dynastes by Erato; by Asopis, he had Mentor; by Eone, he had Amestrios; by Tiphyse, he had Lyncaios; he had Halocrates by Olympousa; by Heliconis, he had Phalias; by Hesiocheia, he had Oistrables; by Terpsicrate, he had Euryopes; by Elacheia, he had Bouleus; he had

Antimachos by Nicippe; he had Patroclos by Pyrippe; he had Nephos by Praxithea; by Lysippe, he had Erasippos; he had Lycourgos by Toxicrate; he had Boucolos by Marse; he had Leucippos by Eurytele; and by Hippocrate, he had Hippozygos. These were his sons by the daughters of Thespios.

And he had the following sons by other women. By Deianeira, daughter of Oineus, he had Hyllos, Ctesippos, Glenos, and Oneites; by Megara, daughter of Creon, he had Therimachos, Deicoon, and Creontiades; by Omphale, he had Agelaos, from whom the family of Croesus was descended; by Chalciope, daughter of Eurypylos, he had Thettalos; by Epicaste, daughter of Augeias, he had Thestalos; by Parthenope, daughter of Stymphalos, he had Everes; by Auge, daughter of Aleos, he had Telephos; by Astyoche, daughter of Phylas, he had Tlepolemos; by Astydameia, daughter of Amyntor, he had Ctesippos; and by Autonoe, daughter of Peireus, he had Palaimon.

The return of the Heraclids

8 1 After Heracles had been transported to the gods, his sons fled from Eurystheus and took refuge with Ceux; but when Eurystheus told him to surrender them and threatened war, they grew afraid, and withdrawing from Trachis, took flight through Greece. With Eurystheus in pursuit, they made their way to Athens, where they sat down on the altar of Pity* and asked for help. When the Athenians refused to hand them over, they became embroiled in a war with Eurystheus* and killed his sons, Alexander, Iphimedon, Eurybios, Mentor, and Perimedes. Eurystheus himself fled in a chariot, but Hyllos, who had set off in pursuit, killed him* as he was passing the Scironian Rocks, and cut off his head; and he gave it to Alcmene, who gouged out the eyes with weaving pins.

2 After the death of Eurystheus, the Heraclids attacked the Peloponnese and captured all its cities. But when a year had elapsed since their return,* the entire Peloponnese was gripped by a plague, and an oracle revealed that the Heraclids were to blame because they had returned before the proper time. Accordingly, they left the Peloponnese and withdrew to Marathon, where they settled.

Before their departure from the Peloponnese, Tlepolemos had accidentally killed Licymnios* (for he had been beating a servant with his stick, and Licymnios had run between them); so he went into exile at Rhodes with a good number of followers, and settled there.

Hyllos married Iole as his father had ordered, and sought to achieve the return of the Heraclids. So he went to Delphi and asked how they could return, and the god declared that they should await the third harvest and then return. Hyllos thought that the third harvest meant three years, and after waiting that length of time, he returned with his army* [. . .] of Heracles to attack the Peloponnese when Tisamenos, son of Orestes, was king of the Peloponnesians.* There was a further battle, which was won by the Peloponnesians, and Aristomachos was killed. When the sons of [Aristomachos*] came of age, they consulted the oracle about their return. The god gave the same response as before, and Temenos admonished him, saying that when they had obeyed this oracle, they had met with misfortune; but the god replied that they were responsible for their own misfortunes because they had failed to understand the oracles, for he meant by the third harvest not a harvest of the earth but of generations of men, and by the narrows, the broad-bellied sea* to the right of the Isthmus. On hearing this, Temenos prepared his army and *constructed ships* at the place in Locris which has come to be called *Naupactos** for that reason. While the army was there, Aristodemos* was struck dead by a thunderbolt, leaving twin sons, Eurysthenes and Procles, by Argeia, daughter of Autesion.

3 And it happened that in Naupactos, a disaster befell the army too. For there appeared amongst them a diviner delivering oracles in a state of inspired abandon, whom they took to be a sorcerer sent by the Peloponnesians to bring ruin to the army. So Hippotes, son of Phylas, son of Antiochos, son of Heracles, hurled a javelin at him, which struck and killed him. As a result, the naval force was destroyed with the loss of all the ships, and the land force was stricken by famine and the army disbanded. When Temenos consulted the oracle about this calamity, the god said that it had all come about because of the diviner,* and he ordered him to banish the

murderer for ten years and to take the Three-Eyed One as their guide. Accordingly, they banished Hippotes and searched for the Three-Eyed One; and they came across Oxylos,* son of Andraimon, seated on a one-eyed horse (for its other eye had been struck out by an arrow). He had fled into exile at Elis because of a murder, and was making his way back to Aetolia now that a year had passed. So gathering the meaning of the oracle, they made him their guide. And when they engaged the enemy in battle, they gained the upper hand by land and sea, and killed Tisamenos, son of Orestes. On their own side, Pamphylos and Dymas, the sons of Aigimios,* were killed in the fighting.

4 When they had gained control of the Peloponnese, they erected three altars to Paternal Zeus, offered sacrifices on them, and then drew lots for the cities. The first draw would be for Argos, the second for Lacedaimon, and the third for Messene; and they brought a jug of water and decided that each of them should cast a lot into it. Temenos, and Procles and Eurysthenes, the two sons of Aristodemos, threw pebbles into the jug, but Cresphontes, wanting to be allotted Messene, threw a clod of earth.* When this had dissolved in the water, the other two lots would of necessity be the ones that came to light. That of Temenos was drawn first, and that of the sons of Aristodemos second, and Cresphontes acquired Messene.

5 They discovered signs lying on the altars where they had made the sacrifices: a toad for those who had won Argos, a snake for those who had won Lacedaimon, and a fox for those who had won Messene. The diviners said of these signs that those who had found the toad would do best to stay in their city (for the creature lacks the strength to travel), whilst those who had found the serpent would be fearsome in attack, and those who had found the fox would be crafty.

Temenos spurned his sons, Agelaos, Eurypylos, and Callias, and relied instead on his daughter Hyrnetho and her husband Deiphontes.* As a result, his sons bribed some men from Titana*] to murder their father. After the murder had taken place, however, the army decided that the kingdom rightly belonged to Hyrnetho and Deiphontes.

Cresphontes had been ruling in Messene for only a short

time when he was assassinated* with two of his sons. Polyphontes, who was one of the Heraclids, succeeded him as king,
and forced Merope, the widow of the murdered king, to become his wife. But he too was killed; for Merope had a third
son, called Aipytos, whom she had given to her father to bring
up. When he reached manhood, he returned in secret and killed
Polyphontes, and so recovered his father's kingdom.

BOOK III

6. Cretan and Theban mythology
(the Inachids, Agenorid line)

The abduction of Europa to Crete,
and dispersal of the sons of Agenor

1 ¹ Having now reached the point in our account of the family of Inachos where we have covered the descendants of Belos as far as the Heraclids, we must proceed next to the line of Agenor. As we have said,* Libya had two sons by Poseidon named Belos and Agenor: Belos became king of Egypt and fathered the sons who were mentioned above, but Agenor went away to Phoenicia, where he married Telephassa and had a daughter, Europa, and three sons, Cadmos, Phoenix, and Cilix. (It is said by some,* however, that Europa was not Agenor's daughter, but a daughter of Phoenix.) Zeus fell in love with Europa, and taking the form of a docile bull whose breath smelled of roses,* he took her on his back and carried her across the sea to Crete. There he had intercourse with her, and she gave birth to Minos, Sarpedon, and Rhadamanthys (though according to Homer,* Sarpedon was a son of Zeus by Laodameia, daughter of Bellerophon).

When Europa disappeared, her father Agenor sent his sons in search of her, telling them not to return until they had found her. Her mother, Telephassa, joined them in the search, as did Thasos, son of Poseidon, or according to Pherecydes, of Cilix. But when they had searched high and low and were still unable to find her, they abandoned any thought of returning home, and each of them settled in a different place. Phoenix settled in Phoenicia, and Cilix in its vicinity, giving the name Cilicia to all the land that lay under his control near the River Pyramos. Cadmos and Telephassa went to live in Thrace, as did Thasos, who founded the city of Thasos in Thrace* and settled there.

Minos and his brothers

2 Europa became the wife of Asterios, ruler of the Cretans, who raised her children. When they grew up, they quarrelled with one another,* for they fell in love with the same boy, who was called Miletos and was a son of Apollo by Areia, daughter of Cleochos. When the boy responded more favourably to Sarpedon, Minos went to war and gained the upper hand. The others fled. Miletos landed in Caria* and founded a city there, naming it Miletos after himself; and in return for a share of the territory, Sarpedon became an ally of Cilix, who was at war with the Lycians, and he became king of Lycia. And Zeus granted him the privilege of living for three generations. According to some accounts, however, the brothers fell in love with Atymnios, son of Zeus and Cassiepeia, and it was over him that they quarrelled.

Rhadamanthys laid down laws for the islanders,* but later fled to Boeotia and married Alcmene;* and following his death, he sits as a judge with Minos in Hades.*

Minos lived in Crete, where he enacted laws, and married Pasiphae, daughter of the Sun and Perseis (though according to Asclepiades his wife was Crete, daughter of Asterios). His sons were Catreus, Deucalion, Glaucos, and Androgeos, and his daughters Acalle, Xenodice, Ariadne, and Phaedra. By a nymph, Pareia, he had Eurymedon, Nephalion, Chryses, and Philolaos, and by Dexithea, a son, Euxanthios.

Minos, Pasiphae, and the origin of the Minotaur

3 When Asterios died without offspring, Minos wanted to become king of Crete, but he encountered opposition. So he claimed that the kingdom had been granted to him by the gods, and to make people believe him, he said that whatever he prayed for would come to pass. And during a sacrifice to Poseidon, he prayed that a bull should appear from the deep, promising to sacrifice it when it appeared. When Poseidon responded by sending up a magnificent bull, Minos acquired the kingdom; but he sent the bull away to join his herds and sacrificed another.† 4 Poseidon, angry with Minos for having failed

to sacrifice the bull, turned it savage, and caused Pasiphae to conceive a desire for it. Becoming infatuated with the bull, Pasiphae enlisted the help of Daidalos, an architect who had been exiled from Athens for murder.* He built a wooden cow, mounted it on wheels, hollowed it out, sewed round it the hide from a cow that he had skinned, and placing it in the meadow where the bull habitually grazed, he made Pasiphae climb inside. The bull came up to it and had intercourse with it as if it were a genuine cow. As a result, she gave birth to Asterios, who was called the Minotaur;* he had the face of a bull, but the rest of his body was human. In obedience to some oracles, Minos kept him enclosed in the Labyrinth. This Labyrinth, which Daidalos had constructed, was a building 'that with a maze of winding ways confused the passage out'.* As for the tale of the Minotaur, and Androgeos, and Phaedra, and Ariadne, we will speak of that later* in our account of Theseus.

Catreus and Althaimenes

2 1 Catreus, son of Minos, had three daughters, Aerope, Clymene, and Apemosyne, and a son, Althaimenes. When he consulted the oracle* to discover how his life would come to an end, the god said that he would die at the hand of one of his children. He tried to keep the oracles secret, but Althaimenes came to hear of them, and fearing that he would become his father's murderer, he sailed away from Crete with his sister Apemosyne; and coming to land at a place in Rhodes, he took possession of it and named it Cretinia. After climbing the mountain known as Atabyrion,* he surveyed the surrounding islands; and catching sight of Crete also and remembering the gods of his fathers, he erected an altar to Atabyrian Zeus. Not long afterwards, he became the murderer of his sister. For Hermes had conceived a passion for her, but when she fled from him and he was unable to catch her because she was so much faster on her feet, he spread hides from freshly skinned animals across her path, and she slipped on them as she returned from the spring, and was raped by him; and she informed her brother of what had happened, but he took the god to be merely an excuse, and kicked her, causing her death.

² Catreus gave Aerope and Clymene to Nauplios,* to be sold in foreign lands. Pleisthenes married one of the sisters, Aerope,* and fathered two sons, Agamemnon and Menelaos, while Nauplios married Clymene and became the father of Oiax and Palamedes.

Later, when he was gripped by old age, Catreus was anxious to transfer the kingdom to his son Althaimenes, and travelled to Rhodes with that in mind. When he disembarked, however, with the Cretans at a desolate spot on the island, he was driven back by the cowherds, who thought that pirates had landed. When he tried to tell them the truth of the matter, they were unable to hear him because of the barking dogs, and as they were pelting him, Althaimenes arrived and killed him with a javelin throw, not realizing that he was Catreus. Afterwards, when he discovered what had happened, he was swallowed up by a chasm in answer to his prayer.

Polyidos and the revival of Glaucos

3 ¹ To Deucalion were born Idomeneus* and Crete, and an illegitimate son, Molos.

Now Glaucos,* when he was still a young child, fell into a jar of honey while he was chasing a mouse, and was drowned. After his disappearance, Minos conducted a thorough search and consulted diviners about how he could find him. The Curetes told him that in his herds he had a three-coloured cow, and that the person who could suggest the best image to describe its colours would also be able to return his son to him alive. When the diviners were assembled, Polyidos,* son of Coiranos, compared the cow's colouring to a blackberry,* and when he was made to search for the child, he discovered him by a certain kind of divination.* Minos declared, however, that he wanted him back alive, and Polyidos was shut in with the dead body. When he was at his wit's end, he saw a snake approach the body; and fearing that he himself would be killed if any harm came to the body, he threw a stone at the snake and killed it. But then another snake appeared, and seeing that the first one was dead, it went off and then came back again carrying a herb, which it applied to the whole body of its fellow. No sooner was the herb applied than the first snake came back to life. Viewing all this with wonderment, Polyidos applied the same herb to the body of Glaucos and brought him back to life. 2 Minos had now recovered his son, but all the same, he would not allow Polyidos to depart to Argos until he had taught Glaucos the art of divination. So under compulsion, Polyidos taught him; but as Polyidos was sailing off, he told Glaucos to spit into his mouth, and when Glaucos did so, he forgot all knowledge of divination. As regards the descendants of Europa, this is where we must call a halt.

Cadmos and the foundation of Thebes

4 1 When Telephassa died, Cadmos saw to her burial, and after receiving hospitality from the Thracians, went to Delphi to enquire about Europa. The god told him that he should not worry about Europa, but should take a cow to guide him, and found a city at the place where it fell down exhausted. After receiving this oracle, he travelled through Phocis, and coming across a cow from the herds of Pelagon,* he followed in its footsteps. It passed through Boeotia, and sank to the earth where the city of Thebes now lies. Wishing to sacrifice the cow to Athene, he sent some of his companions to draw water from the spring of Ares; but the spring was guarded by a dragon, which was said by some to be the offspring of Ares, and it killed most of those who were sent for the water. Angered by this, Cadmos killed the dragon, and then, following the advice of Athene, sowed its teeth. No sooner were they sown than fully armed men sprang up from the earth, who were called the *Spartoi*.* They killed one another, some entering into conflict deliberately,* and some out of ignorance. According to Pherecydes, however, when Cadmos saw fully armed men springing up from the earth, he hurled stones at them, and they, believing that they were being pelted by one another, fought amongst themselves. Five of them survived, namely, Echion, Oudaios, Chthonios, Hyperenor, and Peloros. 2 To atone for the killing, Cadmos served Ares as a labourer for an everlasting year* (for a year in those times lasted eight of our own).

After the completion of his servitude, Athene consigned the

kingdom to him, and Zeus gave him Harmonia, daughter of Aphrodite and Ares, as a wife. And all the gods left the sky to take part in the wedding feast on the Cadmeia* and join in the singing. Cadmos gave his wife a robe and the necklace fashioned by Hephaistos, which according to some accounts had been given to him by Hephaistos himself, though according to Pherecydes it was given to him by Europa, who had received it from Zeus. Cadmos had four daughters, Autonoe, Ino, Semele, and Agave, and a son, Polydoros. Ino became the wife of Athamas, Autonoe the wife of Aristaios, and Agave the wife of Echion.

Semele and Dionysos; the death of Actaion

3 As for Semele, Zeus fell in love with her, and slept with her in secret from Hera. Now Zeus had engaged to do whatever Semele asked, and as the result of a deception by Hera,* she asked him to come to her just as he had come when he was courting Hera. Unable to refuse, Zeus came to her bedchamber in a chariot to the accompaniment of lightning and thunder, and hurled a thunderbolt. Semele died of fright, but Zeus snatched her aborted sixth-month child from the fire, and sewed it into his thigh. (After Semele's death, the other daughters of Cadmos spread the tale that Semele had slept with a mortal but falsely laid the blame on Zeus, and that she had been struck down with a thunderbolt because of that.*) When the appropriate time arrived, Zeus brought Dionysos to birth by untying the stitches, and handed him over to Hermes, who took him to Ino and Athamas, and persuaded them to bring him up as a girl. But Hera in her fury drove them mad,* and Athamas hunted his eldest son Learchos in the belief he was a deer and killed him, while Ino threw Melicertes into a cauldron of boiling water, and carrying it with her dead child inside, leaped into the sea. She is known as Leucothea* and her son is known as Palaimon—these were the names given to them by mariners, who receive help from them when they are caught in storms. The Isthmian Games were founded in honour of Melicertes* on the orders of Sisyphos.

As for Dionysos, Zeus rescued him from the anger of Hera

by turning him into a kid; and Hermes gathered him up and took him to some nymphs who lived at Nysa in Asia, those whom Zeus later turned into a constellation, naming them the Hyades.*

4 Autonoe and Aristaios had a son, Actaion, who was brought up by Cheiron to be a hunter and was later devoured on Cithairon by his own dogs. According to Acousilaos, he met such a death because Zeus was angry with him for courting Semele, but most authors ascribe it to the fact that he saw Artemis bathing.* The goddess, they say, transformed him instantly into a deer and drove his pack of fifty dogs into a frenzy, causing them to devour him without recognizing who he was. Once he was dead, the dogs searched for their master, howling all the while, until their search brought them to the cave of Cheiron, who made an image of Actaion, which brought their grief to an end.†

5 1 After his discovery of the vine, Dionysos was driven mad by Hera* and roamed around Egypt and Syria. He was welcomed first by Proteus, king of the Egyptians, but then arrived at Cybela in Phrygia, and after he had been purified by Rhea and learned the rites of initiation,* and had received the [initiate's] robe from her, he hurried through Thrace to attack the Indians. Lycourgos,* son of Dryas, the ruler of the Edonians, who live by the River Strymon, was the first to insult and expel him. Dionysos sought refuge in the sea with Thetis, daughter of Nereus, while the Bacchai* were taken prisoner along with the crowd of Satyrs* who followed in his train. But later the Bacchai were suddenly set free, and Lycourgos was driven mad by Dionysos. During his madness, Lycourgos, believing that he was pruning a vine branch,* killed his son Dryas with blows from his axe and had cut off his limbs by the time he recovered his senses. When the land remained barren, the god declared in an oracle that it would become fruitful again if Lycourgos were put to death. On hearing this, the Edonians took him to Mount Pangaion and tied him up, and there he died through the will of Dionysos, killed by horses.

2 After travelling through Thrace and the whole of India, where he set up pillars,* he arrived in Thebes,* where he forced the women to desert their houses and abandon themselves to

Bacchic frenzy on Mount Cithairon. But Pentheus, a son of Echion by Agave, who had inherited the throne from Cadmos, tried to put an end to these practices, and when he went to Mount Cithairon to spy on the Bacchai, he was torn to pieces by his mother Agave, who, in her frenzy, took him for a wild beast. Having shown the Thebans that he was a god, he went to Argos, and there again, when they failed to honour him, he drove the women mad, and they carried their unweaned children into the mountains and feasted on their flesh.

3 Wanting to make the sea-passage from Icarios to Naxos, he chartered a pirate ship with a crew of Tyrrhenians. When they had him on board,* however, they sailed past Naxos and pressed on towards Asia hoping to sell him. But he changed the mast and oars into snakes and filled the craft with ivy and the sound of flutes; and the pirates went mad, and jumped into the sea, where they turned into dolphins.

In this way, men came to know that he was a god and paid due honour to him; and after he had brought his mother up from Hades and named her Thyone, he ascended to heaven in her company.

Successors and usurpers at Thebes

4 Cadmos left Thebes with Harmonia and went to the land of the Encheleans.* Now the Encheleans were being attacked by the Illyrians, and the god had revealed to them in an oracle that they would obtain victory over the Illyrians if they had Cadmos and Harmonia as their leaders. In obedience to the god, they engaged them as their leaders against the Illyrians, and gained the upper hand. Cadmos became king of the Illyrians and had a son, Illyrios. Later he was turned into a snake* together with Harmonia, and sent to the Elysian Fields by Zeus.

5 When Polydoros became king of Thebes, he married Nycteis, the daughter of Nycteus, [son of] Chthonios, and had a son, Labdacos, who lost his life after Pentheus because he thought in much the same way* as him. He left a one-year-old child, Laios, but Lycos, the brother of Nycteus, seized control of the government as long as Laios remained a child.* The

two brothers had fled [from Euboea] because they had killed Phlegyas, son of Ares and Dotis the Boeotian, and had settled at Hyria;* and [from there, they had moved to Thebes,*] where they became citizens as a result of their friendship with Pentheus. So it came to pass that Lycos, after being chosen as polemarch* by the Thebans, seized supreme power, and ruled for twenty years until he was murdered by Zethos and Amphion, for the following reason.

Antiope was a daughter of Nycteus; and Zeus had intercourse with her. When she turned out to be pregnant and her father threatened her, she ran away to Epopeus* in Sicyon, and became his wife. Nycteus was thrown into such despondency that he killed himself,* ordering Lycos to punish Epopeus and Antiope. So Lycos marched against Sicyon, killed Epopeus, and took Antiope prisoner. On the way back, she gave birth to two sons at Eleutherai in Boeotia. They were exposed, but a cowherd discovered them and brought them up, calling one of them Zethos and the other Amphion. Zethos devoted himself to cattle-rearing, while Amphion practised singing to the lyre (for he had been given a lyre by Hermes). As for Antiope, Lycos and his wife Dirce kept her in confinement and ill-treated her. One day, however, without her jailers knowing it, her bonds untied themselves of their own accord, and she made her way to her sons' farmhouse, hoping to find refuge with them. Recognizing her as their mother, they killed Lycos, and bound Dirce to a bull, and then, when she was dead, hurled her body into the spring that bears the name of Dirce on her account.

After taking power, they built a wall around the city (the stones followed the sound of Amphion's lyre*) and they expelled Laios. He went to live in the Peloponnese as a guest of Pelops; and while he was teaching Pelops' son Chrysippos how to drive a chariot, he fell in love with him and carried him off.

Amphion, Niobe, and their children

6 Zethos married Thebe, from whom the city of Thebes derives its name, and Amphion married Niobe, daughter of Tantalos, who bore him seven sons, Sipylos, Eupinytos, Ismenos, Damas-

ichthon, Agenor, Phaidimos, and Tantalos, and the same number of daughters, Ethodaia (or according to some, Neaira),
Cleodoxa, Astyoche, Phthia, Pelopia, Astycrateia, and Ogygia.
According to Hesiod, however, they had ten sons and ten daughters, while Herodoros says that they had two male and three
female children, and Homer* that they had six sons and six
daughters. Having so many children, Niobe said that she was
better blessed with children than Leto; and Leto was so
angered by this that she incited Artemis and Apollo against
them, and Artemis shot down the female children inside the
house, and Apollo all the male children as they were hunting
on Mount Cithairon. Of the males, Amphion alone survived,*
and of the females, only the eldest, Chloris,* who later became the wife of Neleus (though according to Telesilla, those
who survived were Amyclas and Meliboia, and Amphion was
amongst their victims). Niobe herself left Thebes and went to
stay with her father Tantalos at Sipylos; and there, in response
to her prayers to Zeus, she was transformed into a stone* that
streams with tears by night and day.

Laios and Oedipus

7 After the death of Amphion,* Laios took over the kingdom.
He married a daughter of Menoiceus whom some call Iocaste,
others Epicaste.* An oracle from the gods had warned him not
to have a child, for if he did, the son who would be born to
him would become his father's murderer; but while he was
drunk with wine, he had intercourse with his wife. When the
child was born, he pierced its ankles with buckle-pins and passed
it to a herdsman for exposure. But when he exposed it on Mount
Cithairon, the herdsmen of Polybos, king of Corinth, discovered the baby and brought it to the king's wife, Periboia.
She took him in and passed him off as her own son, and after
she had healed his ankles she called him *Oedipus*,* giving him
that name because of his *swollen feet*.

When the boy grew up and surpassed the others of his age
in strength, they grew jealous and poured scorn on him for
being a supposititious child.* He questioned Periboia but
could learn nothing from her, so he went to Delphi and asked

who his true parents were. The god told him not to return to his native land, for if he did, he would murder his father and sleep with his mother. Hearing this, and believing that he really was born from those who were said to be his parents, he kept away from Corinth. But as he was travelling through Phocis in his chariot, he came across Laios, also driving in a chariot, on a certain narrow track.* And when Polyphontes, the herald of Laios, told him to make way, and killed one of his horses because he refused to obey or was slow to do so, Oedipus was enraged and killed both Polyphontes and Laios; and he drove on to Thebes.

8 Laios was buried by Damasistratos, king of Plataea, and Creon, son of Menoiceus,* succeeded to the throne. During his reign, a disaster of no small proportion struck Thebes; for Hera sent the Sphinx.* The mother of the Sphinx was Echidna and her father Typhon, and she had the face of a woman, the chest, feet, and tail of a lion, and the wings of a bird. She had learned a riddle from the Muses, and seated on Mount Phicion, she posed it to the Thebans. The riddle ran as follows: what is it that has a single voice,* and has four feet, and then two feet, and then three feet? Now the Thebans possessed an oracle telling them that they would be freed from the Sphinx when they solved her riddle, so they gathered together repeatedly to seek the solution; but when they failed to discover it, the Sphinx would carry one of them off and devour him. When many had died in this way, including, ultimately, Creon's son Haimon, Creon proclaimed that he would give both the kingdom and the widow of Laios to the man who could solve the riddle. When Oedipus heard of this, he supplied the answer, saying that the riddle of the Sphinx referred to man; for he is four-footed as a baby when he crawls on all fours, two-footed as an adult, and takes on a third limb in old age in the form of a stick. So the Sphinx hurled herself from the Acropolis, and Oedipus took over the kingdom, and also, without realizing it, married his mother. He had two sons by her, Polyneices and Eteocles, and two daughters, Ismene and Antigone. There are some who say, however, that these children were born to him by Euryganeia,* daughter of Hyperphas.

9 Afterwards, when what was unknown was revealed, Iocaste

hanged herself in a noose, and Oedipus put out his eyes and was driven from Thebes, cursing his sons,* who watched him being expelled from the city without coming to his aid. Arriving with Antigone at Colonos* in Attica, where the sanctuary of the Eumenides* lies, he sat down there as a suppliant and received a friendly reception from Theseus, and died not long afterwards.

7. The Theban Wars

Eteocles and the exile of Polyneices to Argos

6 ¹ Eteocles and Polyneices came to an agreement over the throne, deciding that each of them should rule in alternate years. Some say that Polyneices was the first to rule, and that after a year he surrendered the throne to Eteocles; while according to others, Eteocles was the first to rule, and refused to give up the throne.* In any case, Polyneices was exiled from Thebes and arrived in Argos, bringing with him the necklace and robe [of Harmonia]. Argos was ruled at that time by Adrastos, son of Talaos;* and as Polyneices was approaching his palace by night, he became involved in a fight with Tydeus, son of Oineus, who had fled there from Calydon.* In response to the sudden outbreak of shouting, Adrastos came out and separated the pair; and calling to mind the advice of a diviner who told him to yoke his daughters to a boar and a lion, he chose the two of them as their husbands, because one of them had the front half of a boar on his shield and the other that of a lion.* So Tydeus married Deipyle and Polyneices, Argeia; and Adrastos promised to restore both of them to their native lands. He was eager to march against Thebes initially, and gathered together the leading warriors.

Prelude in Argos: Amphiaraos and Eriphyle

² But Amphiaraos, son of Oicles, who was a diviner and foresaw that all who took part in the expedition except for Adrastos were destined to be killed, was reluctant to join the

expedition himself and tried to dissuade the others. Polyneices went to Iphis,* son of Alector, and asked to be told how
Amphiaraos could be compelled to take part; and he replied
that this could be brought to pass if Eriphyle gained possession of the necklace. Although Eriphyle had been told by
Amphiaraos not to accept gifts from Polyneices, he gave her
the necklace and asked her to persuade Amphiaraos to join the
expedition. This lay within her power, because earlier, when
[a conflict had] arisen between Amphiaraos and Adrastos,*
Amphiaraos had sworn at its conclusion that if he had any future disagreements with Adrastos, he would allow Eriphyle to
decide* between them. So now, when there was to be a campaign against Thebes and it was supported by Adrastos but
opposed by Amphiaraos, Eriphyle, on receiving the necklace,
persuaded her husband to march with Adrastos. Joining the
expedition under compulsion, Amphiaraos left orders for his
sons telling them to kill their mother when they came of age
and mount a campaign against Thebes.

The advance against Thebes and stationing of the champions

3 When he had assembled [an army] under seven leaders,*
Adrastos hastened to war against Thebes. The leaders were the
following: Adrastos, son of Talaos; Amphiaraos, son of Oicles;
Capaneus, son of Hipponoos; Hippomedon, son of Aristo-
machos or according to some, of Talaos; all of these came from
Argos, but Polyneices, son of Oedipus, came from Thebes, while
Tydeus, son of Oineus, was an Aetolian, and Parthenopaios,
son of Melanion, an Arcadian. In some sources, however,
Tydeus and Polyneices are not counted amongst the seven, and
Eteoclos, son of Iphis, and Mecisteus are listed instead.

4 When they arrived at Nemea, which was then under
the rule of Lycourgos,* they went in search of water; and
Hypsipyle showed them the way to a spring, leaving behind
a young child, Opheltes. This was a son of Eurydice and
Lycourgos who was being reared by Hypsipyle; for when the
Lemnian women had discovered that [her father] Thoas had
been spared,* they had killed him and sold Hypsipyle abroad,
and for that reason she was serving with Lycourgos as a pur-

chased slave. As she was pointing the way to the spring, the child who had been left behind was killed by a snake; and when Adrastos and his companions reappeared, they killed the snake and buried the child. Amphiaraos told them that this was a sign foretelling what would happen in the future: so they named the child *Archemoros*.* And in his honour, they founded the Isthmian Games. The horse race was won by Adrastos, the foot-race by Eteoclos, the boxing by Tydeus, the jumping and discus-throwing by Amphiaraos, the javelin-throwing by Laodocos, the wrestling by Polyneices, and the archery by Parthenopaios.

5 On their arrival at Cithairon, they sent Tydeus ahead to give notice to Eteocles that he should surrender the kingdom to Polyneices in accordance with their agreement. When Eteocles paid no attention, Tydeus, wanting to test out the Thebans, challenged them to single combat and was victorious every time. The Thebans for their part armed fifty men and set an ambush for him on his departure; but he killed all of them, except for Maion, and made his way back to the camp.*

6 The Argives took up their arms and advanced towards the walls.* There were seven gates,* and Adrastos stationed himself in front of the Homoloidian Gate, Capaneus in front of the Ogygian, Amphiaraos in front of the Proitidian, Hippomedon in front of the Oncaidian, Polyneices in front of the Hypsistan, Parthenopaios in front of the Electran, and Tydeus in front of the Crenidian. Eteocles, on his side, armed the Thebans and appointed an equivalent number of leaders, stationing each of them opposite his counterpart. And he consulted the diviners to discover how they could prevail over the enemy.

Excursus: the earlier history of Teiresias

7 Now there lived amongst the Thebans a diviner, Teiresias, son of Everes and the nymph Chariclo. He was a descendant of Oudaios, one of the Spartoi, and had lost the use of his eyes; on how he came to be blind and gained his prophetic powers, conflicting stories are told. Some say that he was blinded by the gods because he divulged to the human race what they

wanted to keep concealed. Or according to Pherecydes, he was blinded by Athene; for Athene and Chariclo were close friends [and it came about that he] saw the goddess completely naked,* and she covered his eyes with her hands, depriving him of his sight. When Chariclo begged her to restore the use of his eyes, she lacked the power to do so, but purified his ears instead, giving him a complete understanding of the language of birds.* She also gave him a cornel-wood staff, thus enabling him, while he carried it, to walk like those who can see. Hesiod says,* however, that he caught sight of some snakes coupling near Mount Cyllene, and when he injured the snakes, he was changed from a man to a woman; but when he saw the same snakes coupling on a further occasion, he became a man again. And for this reason, when Zeus and Hera were having an argument as to whether men or women gain more pleasure from love-making, they consulted Teiresias. He said that judging the act of love on a scale of ten, men get one part of the pleasure and women nine parts.* On that account, Hera turned him blind, but Zeus granted him the gift of prophecy;† and he lived to a considerable age.*

The Theban victory and its aftermath

So when the Thebans consulted him, Teiresias told them that they would be victorious if Menoiceus, the son of Creon, offered himself as a sacrifice to Ares.* On hearing this prophecy, Menoiceus, son of Creon, slaughtered himself in front of the gates. In the ensuing battle, the Cadmeians were chased back to their walls, and Capaneus seized a ladder and was using it to climb the wall when Zeus struck him down* with a thunderbolt. 8 When this took place, the Argives turned and fled. Because so many had died, Eteocles and Polyneices, in accordance with the decision of both armies, fought for the throne in single combat and killed one another. Fierce fighting broke out once again, and the sons of Astacos performed deeds of valour, Ismaros killing Hippomedon, Leades killing Eteoclos, and Amphidicos killing Parthenopaios (though according to Euripides, Parthenopaios was killed by Periclymenos, son of Poseidon). And Melanippos, the last of the sons of Astacos, wounded Tydeus in the stomach. As he lay half dead, Athene asked Zeus for a remedy and brought it along, with the intention of applying it to make him immortal. But Amphiaraos realized what she intended, and in his hatred against Tydeus for persuading the Argives to march against Thebes in opposition to his own judgement, he cut off the head of Melanippos (for Tydeus, although wounded, had killed Melanippos*) and gave it to Tydeus, who split it open and gulped down the brains. At the sight of this, Athene was so revolted that she withheld her intended favour and refused to grant it. Amphiaraos fled beside the River Ismenos, and before Periclymenos could wound him in the back, Zeus hurled a thunderbolt to open a chasm in the earth. And Amphiaraos was swallowed up in it, together with his chariot and his charioteer Baton (or according to some, Elaton); and Zeus made him immortal.* Adrastos, the sole survivor, was saved by his horse Areion (which Demeter had borne to Poseidon after having intercourse with him in the likeness of a Fury*).

7   ¹ Creon, who then succeeded to the Theban throne,* caused the bodies of the Argive dead to be thrown out unburied, issued a proclamation that nobody should bury them, and posted guards. But Antigone, one of the daughters of Oedipus, stole the body of Polyneices and gave it a secret burial; and when she was caught in the act, she was buried alive in the grave by Creon himself.

Adrastos made his way to Athens, where he sought refuge at the altar of Pity, and placing a suppliant's bough* on the altar, he asked to be allowed to bury his dead. The Athenians marched against Thebes with Theseus, captured the city,* and gave the dead to their relatives for burial. As the pyre of Capaneus was blazing, his wife Evadne, daughter of Iphis, threw herself on to it and was burned with her husband.

The Epigoni and the Second Theban War

² Ten years later, the sons of the fallen, who were called the Epigoni,* decided to mount an expedition against Thebes because they wanted to avenge the death of their fathers. When they consulted the oracle, the god foretold victory if Alcmaion

was their leader. Although Alcmaion had no desire to lead the expedition before he had punished his mother, he went to war none the less; for Eriphyle, on receiving the robe [of Harmonia] from Polyneices' son Thersandros, persuaded her sons also to take part* in the expedition. So taking Alcmaion as their leader, the Epigoni went to war against Thebes. Those who took part in the expedition were the following: Alcmaion and Amphilochos, sons of Amphiaraos; Aigialeus, son of Adrastos; Diomedes, son of Tydeus; Promachos, son of Parthenopaios; Sthenelos, son of Capaneus; Thersandros, son of Polyneices; and Euryalos, son of Mecisteus.

3 They began by sacking the villages in the neighbourhood of Thebes, and then, when the Thebans under Laodamas, son of Eteocles, advanced against them, they fought with valour. Laodamas killed Aigialeus,* but was killed in his turn by Alcmaion, and after his death the Thebans fled inside their walls. Teiresias then advised them to send a herald to the Argives to talk about a truce while they themselves made their escape. So they sent a herald to the enemy, and in the meantime loaded their women and children on to the wagons and fled from the city. They arrived by night at a spring called Tilphoussa, and as Teiresias drank from it, his life came to an end. After travelling a great distance, the Thebans founded the city of Hestiaia* and settled there. 4 When the Argives eventually learned that the Thebans had fled, they entered the city, where they gathered together the plunder and pulled down the walls. They sent part of the plunder to Delphi as an offering to Apollo, and with it Manto, daughter of Teiresias; for they had made a vow that if they captured Thebes, they would dedicate the finest of the spoils to the god.

The later history of Alcmaion

5 After the capture of Thebes, when Alcmaion learned that his mother Eriphyle had accepted bribes to his detriment also, his outrage was all the greater, and in obedience to an oracle granted him by Apollo, he put his mother to death. Some say that he killed her with the help of his brother Amphilochos, others that he did so on his own. Alcmaion was pursued by

the Fury of his mother's murder,* and overcome by madness, he went first to Oicles in Arcadia and then to Phegeus in Psophis; and after he had been purified by Phegeus, he married his daughter Arsinoe, and gave her the necklace and the robe. But afterwards, as a result of his presence, the earth grew barren, and he was told by the god in an oracle to depart to Acheloos and receive from him [a land which had not yet been seen by the Sun*]. So he went first to Oineus in Calydon, who offered him hospitality, and then to the Thesprotians, who drove him from their country; but finally he arrived at the springs of Acheloos, and was purified by him, and received his daughter, Callirrhoe, in marriage. And on land that Acheloos had formed by laying down his silt, he founded a city and settled there.

Later, Callirrhoe wanted to acquire the necklace and the robe, and told Alcmaion that she would no longer live with him unless she obtained them; so he went back to Psophis and told Phegeus that he had been informed by an oracle* that he would be delivered from his madness when he had taken the robe and necklace to Delphi and dedicated them. Phegeus believed him and handed them over; but when a servant revealed that he was taking them to Callirrhoe, the sons of Phegeus, on their father's orders, set an ambush for Alcmaion and killed him. When Arsinoe rebuked them, the sons of Phegeus packed her into a chest and carried her to Tegea, where they gave her to Agapenor as a slave, on the false accusation that it was she who had murdered Alcmaion. 6 When Callirrhoe learned of Alcmaion's death, she asked Zeus (who had become her lover) to cause the sons whom she had borne to Alcmaion to become fully grown, and so enable them to avenge their father's murder. And all of a sudden her sons were adults, and they set off to avenge their father. It happened that Pronoos and Agenor, the sons of Phegeus, who were taking the necklace and robe to Delphi for dedication, called in at the house of Agapenor at just the same time as Amphoteros and Acarnan, the sons of Alcmaion; so the sons of Alcmaion killed their father's murderers, and then went on to Psophis, where they entered the palace and killed Phegeus and his wife. They were pursued as far as Tegea, but were saved by the Tegeans and some Argives, who came to their rescue and put the Psophidians to flight.

7 When they had informed their mother of what had happened, they went to Delphi, and dedicated the necklace and the robe, on the instructions of Acheloos. Then they travelled to Epirus, gathered together some settlers, and founded Acarnania.*

Euripides* says that during the time of his madness Alcmaion had two children by Manto, daughter of Teiresias, namely Amphilochos and a daughter, Tisiphone; and that he took the babies to Corinth and gave them to Creon, king of Corinth, to bring up; and because of her exceptional beauty, Tisiphone was sold into slavery by Creon's wife, who was afraid that Creon might take her as his wife, and she was purchased by Alcmaion, who kept her as a servant girl without realizing that she was his daughter; and when he returned to Corinth to reclaim his children, he recovered his son also; and Amphilochos, in obedience to oracles from Apollo, founded Amphilochian Argos.*

8. Arcadian mythology (the Pelasgids)

Lycaon and his sons

8 1 Let us return now to Pelasgos, who is described by Acousilaos as a son of Zeus and Niobe, as we observed above,* while Hesiod says that he was born from the earth. By Meliboia, daughter of Oceanos, or according to others, by a nymph, Cyllene, he had a son, Lycaon, who became king of the Arcadians, and by many different women fathered fifty sons:* Melaineus, Thesprotos, Helix, Nyctimos, Peucetios, Caucon, Mecisteus, Hopleus, Macareus, Macednos, Horos, Polichos, Acontes, Evaimon, Ancyor, Archebates, Carteron, Aigaion, Pallas, Eumon, Canethos, Prothoos, Linos, Corethon, Mainalos, Teleboas, Physios, Phassos, Phthios, Lycios, Halipheros, Genetor, Boucolion, Socleus, Phineus, Eumetes, Harpaleus, Portheus, Plato, Haimon, Cynaithos, Leon, Harpalycos, Heraieus, Titanas, Mantineus, Cleitor, Stymphalos, and Orchomenos. They outstripped all men in arrogance and impiety; and Zeus, wanting to test their impiety, visited them in the guise of a labourer. They invited him to share their hospital-

ity, and slaughtering a child from the local population, they mixed his entrails into the sacrifices* and served them up to him, at the instigation of the eldest brother, Mainalos. Zeus, in revulsion, overturned the *table* at the place which is now known as *Trapezous*,* and struck Lycaon and his sons with thunderbolts, with the exception of the youngest, Nyctimos, for Ge interceded beforehand by grasping the right hand of Zeus and calming his anger. 2 When Nyctimos succeeded to the throne, Deucalion's flood took place; some said that it had been brought about by the impiety of Lycaon's sons.

Callisto and the birth of Arcas; early Arcadian genealogies

According to Eumelos and some other sources, Lycaon had a daughter too, named Callisto (though Hesiod says that she was one of the nymphs,* Asios that she was a daughter of Nycteus, and Pherecydes that she was a daughter of Ceteus). A companion of Artemis in the hunt, she wore the same clothing, and had sworn to her that she would remain a virgin. But Zeus conceived a passion for her, and despite her unwillingness, had intercourse with her, taking on the form, some say, of Artemis, or according to others, of Apollo; and wanting Hera to remain ignorant of the matter, he turned her into a bear. Hera persuaded Artemis, however, to shoot her* down as a wild beast (though some say that Artemis shot her because she had failed to preserve her virginity). After Callisto's death, Zeus gathered up her baby son and gave him to Maia to bring up in Arcadia, naming him Arcas.* As for Callisto, he turned her into a constellation and called it the Bear.

9   1 Arcas had two sons,* Elatos and Apheidas, by Leaneira, daughter of Amyclas (or by Meganeira, daughter of Crocon, or according to Eumelos, by a nymph, Chrysopeleia). They divided the land between them, but Elatos held all the power. Elatos had two sons, Stymphalos and Pereus, by Laodice, daughter of Cinyras; and Apheidas had a son, Aleos, and a daughter, Stheneboia, who became the wife of Proitos. Aleos in turn had a daughter, Auge, and two sons, Cepheus and Lycourgos, by Neaira, daughter of Pereus.

Auge was raped by Heracles,* and hid her baby in the

sanctuary of Athene, whose priesthood she held. When the land became infertile and the oracles revealed that there was something sacrilegious in the sanctuary of Athene, she was found out, and delivered by her father to Nauplios to be put to death; but Nauplios passed her on to Teuthras, the ruler of the Mysians, who married her. Her baby was exposed on Mount Parthenion, where a *doe* offered him her *teat*, which is how he came to be called *Telephos*. After he had been reared by the herdsmen of Corythos, he went to Delphi in the hope of discovering his parents, and following the advice of the god, he made his way to Mysia, where he became the adopted son of Teuthras, and later, when Teuthras died, his successor as king.

Atalante

2 Lycourgos had four sons, Ancaios, Epochos, Amphidamas, and Iasos, by Cleophyle or Eurynome. Amphidamas had a son, Melanion, and a daughter, Antimache, who became the wife of Eurystheus. Iasos and Clymene, daughter of Minyas, had a daughter, Atalante.* She was exposed by her father, who desired male children, but a she-bear came along frequently to suckle her until she was discovered by some hunters, who brought her up amongst themselves. When she was fully grown, Atalante preserved her virginity, and spent her time hunting in the wilderness, arms in hand. The Centaurs Rhoicos and Hylaios tried to rape her, but she shot them down with her arrows and killed them. She was present, moreover, amongst the heroes at the hunt for the Calydonian boar,* and at the games held in honour of Pelias* she wrestled with Peleus and defeated him. Later she discovered her parents, and when her father tried to persuade her to marry, she went to a place which was well fitted to be a race-course, and halfway along it she placed a three-cubit stake. From this point, she caused her suitors to set out in advance of her in a race, which she would run fully armed; and if she caught up with any of the suitors, his penalty was death on the spot, and if she did not, his reward was marriage. When many suitors had already perished, Melanion fell in love with her and arrived to take part in the race. He brought with him some golden apples*

which he had acquired from Aphrodite, and as Atalante was chasing after him, he threw them down; and when Atalante delayed to pick them up, she was defeated in the race. So Melanion became her husband. And one day, so it is said, while they were out hunting, they entered the sanctuary of Zeus, and when they ventured to make love there, they were turned into lions.

According to Hesiod and some other sources, Atalante was a daughter not of Iasos, but of Schoineus, while according to Euripides, she was a daughter of Mainalos, and her husband was not Melanion, but Hippomenes. She bore to Melanion (or Ares) a son, Parthenopaios, who took part in the expedition against Thebes.

9. Laconian and Trojan mythology (the Atlantids)

The Pleiades

10 ¹ To Atlas and Pleione, daughter of Oceanos, seven daughters were born at Cyllene in Arcadia, who were known as the Pleiades,* namely, Alcyone, Merope, Celaino, Electra, Sterope, Taygete, and Maia. Of these, Sterope became the wife of Oinomaos, and Merope the wife of Sisyphos; and Poseidon had intercourse with two of them, first with Celaino, who bore him a son, Lycos, whom he settled in the Isles of the Blessed, and secondly with Alcyone, who bore him a daughter, Aithousa (who bore Eleuther to Apollo), and two sons, Hyrieus and Hyperenor. Hyrieus and a nymph, Clonie, had two sons, Nycteus and Lycos; and by Polyxo, Nycteus became the father of Antiope, who bore Zethos and Amphion to Zeus.

The birth and early exploits of Hermes

² Zeus had intercourse with the three remaining daughters of Atlas. After the eldest of them, Maia, had slept with him, she gave birth to Hermes* in a cave on Mount Cyllene. He was laid on a winnowing fan in his swaddling clothes, but freed

himself from them and made his way to Pieria,* where he stole the cattle which were being pastured there by Apollo. So as not to be given away by their tracks, he put shoes over their feet, and took them to Pylos, where he concealed them in a cave, except for two that he sacrificed. He nailed the skins of these to some rocks, and some of their flesh he boiled and ate, and some of it he burned; and he then returned swiftly to Cyllene. And in front of the cave there, he found a tortoise grazing. Clearing out the shell, he stretched across it some strings made from the guts of the sacrificed cattle; and after creating a lyre by this means, he also invented the plectrum.

As Apollo was searching for his cattle, he arrived in Pylos and questioned the inhabitants. They said that they had seen a boy driving the cattle away, but were unable to say where they had been driven, because they could find no tracks. Discovering the identity of the thief by divination, Apollo went to Maia in Cyllene and accused Hermes. She pointed to him in his swaddling clothes; and Apollo took him to Zeus, and demanded the return of his cattle. When Zeus ordered him to give them back, Hermes denied that he had them, but meeting with disbelief, he took Apollo to Pylos and handed the cattle back. On hearing his lyre, however, Apollo gave him the cattle in exchange for it; and while Hermes was pasturing them, he made a shepherd's pipe and played on that. Wanting to acquire the pipe as well, Apollo offered him the golden staff that he possessed as a herdsman. But as well as receiving this in exchange for the pipe, Hermes wanted to acquire the art of divination also. So he handed over the pipe, and learned from Apollo how to divine by the use of pebbles.* And Zeus made him his own herald and herald to the gods of the Underworld.*

Early Lacedaimonian genealogies; the story of Asclepios

3 Taygete bore to Zeus a son, Lacedaimon, from whom the land of Lacedaimon derives its name; and by Sparta, daughter of Eurotas (who was a son of Lelex,* who had been born from the earth, and of Cleochareia, a naiad nymph), Lacedaimon had a son, Amyclas, and a daughter, Eurydice, who

became the wife of Acrisios. Amyclas and Diomede, daughter of Lapithes, had two sons, Cynortas and Hyacinthos.* This last is said to have been the beloved of Apollo, who accidentally killed him when throwing a discus. Cynortas had a son, Perieres, who married Gorgophone, daughter of Perseus, according to Stesichoros, and fathered Tyndareus, Icarios, Aphareus, and Leucippos. Aphareus* and Arene, daughter of Oibalos, had three sons, Lynceus, Idas, and Peisos; but it is said by many that the father of Idas was in fact Poseidon. Lynceus was remarkable for the sharpness of his sight, which was so acute that he could even see what lay beneath the earth. Leucippos had two daughters, Hilaeira and Phoebe, who were carried off by the Dioscuri, and became their wives.

In addition to these, he had a third daughter, Arsinoe, who gave birth to Asclepios after Apollo had made love with her. Some say, however, that Asclepios was not the daughter of Arsinoe, daughter of Leucippos, but rather of Coronis,* daughter of Phlegyas in Thessaly; and they say that Apollo fell in love with her and immediately had intercourse with her, but that she, against her father's wishes, preferred Ischys, the brother of Caineus, and became his wife. Apollo cursed the crow that brought him this news, and turned it black, instead of white as it had been hitherto. Coronis he put to death; and as she was consigned to the flames, he seized her [unborn] baby from the pyre, and took him to Cheiron the Centaur, who brought him up and taught him the arts of medicine and hunting. Asclepios became a surgeon, and he developed the art to such a degree that he not only prevented some people from dying, but even raised them from the dead. For he had received from Athene blood that had flowed from the veins of the Gorgon; and he used the blood that had flowed from the veins on the left side* to put people to death, and that which had flowed from the right, to save them—and it was by this means that he raised the dead.†⁴ But Zeus, fearing that human beings would acquire the art of healing from him and be able to come to one another's rescue, struck him down* with a thunderbolt. Angered by this, Apollo killed the Cyclopes who had forged the thunderbolt* for Zeus. As Zeus was about to hurl him into Tartaros, Leto interceded on his behalf, and he ordered him instead to serve a man as a labourer for a year. So Apollo went to Admetos,* son of Pheres, at Pherae, and served him as a herdsman, causing all his cows to deliver twins at every birth.

Tyndareus, Leda, and their children

But there are those who say that Aphareus and Leucippos were born to Perieres, son of Aiolos, and that Perieres, son of Cynortas, was the father of Oibalos, who fathered Tyndareus, Hippocoon, and Icarios by a naiad nymph, Bateia.*

5 Hippocoon became father of the following sons: Dorycleus, Scaios, Enarophoros, Euteiches, Boucolos, Lycaithos, Tebros, Hippothoos, Eurytos, Hippocorystes, Alcinous, and Alcon. With the help of his sons, Hippocoon expelled Icarios and Tyndareus* from Lacedaimon. They took refuge with Thestios,* and joined him as allies in the war he was waging against his neighbours; and Tyndareus married Thestios' daughter, Leda. Afterwards, however, when Heracles had killed Hippocoon and his sons,* they returned to Lacedaimon and Tyndareus succeeded to the throne.

6 Icarios and a naiad nymph, Periboia, had five sons, Thoas, Damasippos, Imeusimos, Aletes, and Perileos, and a daughter, Penelope, who became the wife of Odysseus; Tyndareus and Leda had some daughters, namely, Timandra, who became the wife of Echemos, and Clytemnestra, who became the wife of Agamemnon, and also Phylonoe, who was made immortal by Artemis.

7 Taking the form of a swan, Zeus had intercourse with Leda, as did Tyndareus on the same night, and she bore Polydeuces and Helen to Zeus, and Castor* [and Clytemnestra*] to Tyndareus. According to some, however, Helen was a daughter of Zeus by Nemesis;* for when Nemesis tried to avoid intercourse with Zeus by changing herself into a goose, Zeus in turn took the form of a swan and had intercourse with her. As the fruit of their intercourse, she laid an egg, which was discovered in the woods by a shepherd, who took it to Leda and presented it to her. She placed it in a chest and kept it safe, and when

in due time Helen hatched out, Leda brought her up as her own daughter.

Helen and her suitors

Helen grew into a girl of such remarkable beauty that Theseus carried her off and took her to Aphidnai;* but while he was in Hades, Polydeuces and Castor marched against the city, captured it, and recovered Helen, and also took away Theseus' mother, Aithra, as a captive.

8 The kings of Greece came to Sparta to seek the hand of Helen. These were her suitors: Odysseus, son of Laertes; Diomedes, son of Tydeus; Antilochos, son of Nestor; Agapenor, son of Ancaios; Sthenelos, son of Capaneus; Amphimachos, son of Cteatos; Thalpios, son of Eurytos; Meges, son of Phyleus; Amphilochos, son of Amphiaraos; Menestheus, son of Peteos; Schedios [and] Epistrophos[, sons of Iphitos]; Polyxenos, son of Agasthenes; Peneleos[, son of Hippalcimos]; Leitos[, son of Alector]; Aias, son of Oileus; Ascalaphos and Ialmenos, sons of Ares; Elephenor, son of Chalcodon; Eumelos, son of Admetos; Polypoites, son of Peirithoos; Leonteus, son of Coronos; Podaleirios and Machaon, sons of Asclepios; Philoctetes, son of Poias; Eurypylos, son of Evaimon; Protesilaos, son of Iphiclos; Menelaos, son of Atreus; Aias and Teucros, sons of Telamon; and Patroclos, son of Menoitios.

9 When Tyndareus saw the throng of suitors, he was afraid that if he picked out one of them, the rest would turn to violence. Odysseus promised, however, that if Tyndareus would help him to gain the hand of Penelope, he would suggest a means by which all dissension could be averted; and when Tyndareus promised his help, Odysseus told him to make all the suitors swear an oath* that they would come to the aid of the chosen bridegroom if he were ever injured by another with regard to his marriage. On hearing this advice, Tyndareus made the suitors swear the oath, and while he himself chose Menelaos as a bridegroom for Helen, he asked Icarios to grant Penelope in marriage to Odysseus.

11   1 By Helen, Menelaos had a daughter, Hermione, and according to some accounts, a son, Nicostratos;* and by a slave-woman,

Pieris, of Aetolian descent (or according to Acousilaos, by Tereis), he had a son, Megapenthes, and by a nymph, Cnossia, he had, according to Eumelos, a son, Xenodamos.

The fate of the Dioscuri

2 Of the two sons born to Leda, Castor devoted himself to the arts of war, and Polydeuces to boxing; and because of their valour,* the pair were called the Dioscuri. Wishing to marry the daughters of Leucippos,* they abducted them from Messene and took them as their wives; and Polydeuces became the father of Mnesileos by Phoebe, and Castor the father of Anogon by Hilaeira. After driving some plundered cattle from Arcadia with the aid of Idas and Lynceus, sons of Aphareus, they entrusted them to Idas for division. Cutting a cow into four, he said that whoever ate his share first should have half of the plunder, and the one who ate his share second should have the remainder. And before the others had a chance, Idas swallowed down his own portion and then his brother's too, and with his brother's help, drove the plunder to Messene. The Dioscuri responded by marching against Messene and taking away the plundered cattle and much else besides; and they waited in ambush for Idas and Lynceus. But Lynceus caught sight of Castor* and revealed his presence to Idas, who killed him. Polydeuces chased after them, and killed Lynceus with a javelin throw, but as he was pursuing Idas, he was hit on the head by a stone that Idas had thrown, and fell unconscious. And Zeus struck Idas with a thunderbolt and carried Polydeuces up to heaven; and when Polydeuces was unwilling to accept immortality while Castor lay dead, Zeus granted that both of them should live alternate days amongst the gods and amongst mortals.* After the Dioscuri had been raised to the gods, Tyndareus summoned Menelaos to Sparta and transferred the kingdom to him.

Early Trojan mythology

12 1 Electra, daughter of Atlas, had two sons, Iasion and Dardanos, by Zeus. Iasion conceived a passion for Demeter

and was struck by a thunderbolt because he wanted to violate the goddess;* and Dardanos, stricken with grief at his
brother's death, left Samothrace and went to the mainland
opposite.* The king of that land was Teucros, son of the River
Scamander and a nymph, Idaia, and its inhabitants were called
the Teucrians after him. Dardanos was welcomed by the king,
and after receiving a share of the land and the king's daughter, Bateia, in marriage, he founded a city, Dardanos; and when
Teucros died, he called the whole country Dardania. 2 He
had two sons, Ilos and Erichthonios, one of whom, Ilos, died
without offspring, while the other, Erichthonios, inherited the
kingdom, married Astyoche, daughter of Simoeis, and became
the father of Tros. When Tros succeeded to the throne, he
named the country Troy* after himself, and taking Callirrhoe,
daughter of Scamander, as his wife, he had a daughter,
Cleopatra, and three sons, Ilos, Assaracos, and Ganymede. This
Ganymede* was so beautiful that Zeus used an eagle to carry
him off, and made him cupbearer to the gods in heaven.
Assaracos for his part had a son, Capys, by Hieromneme, daughter of Simoeis. And by Themiste, daughter of Ilos, Capys had
a son, Anchises, who aroused Aphrodite's amorous desire;* and
she slept with him, and gave birth to Aeneas, and to Lyros,
who died without offspring.

3 Ilos went to Phrygia, and finding that games were being
held there by the king, he became victor in the wrestling. As
a prize he received fifty boys and as many girls, and the king,
in obedience to an oracle, also gave him a dappled cow, telling
him to found a city at the place where the cow lay down.* So
he followed the cow, and when it arrived at a certain hill, called
the Hill of Phrygian Ate, it lay down; and there Ilos founded
a city, naming it Ilion. And he prayed to Zeus to reveal a sign
to him, and when day arrived, he saw the Palladion,* which
had fallen from the sky, lying outside his tent. It was three
cubits high; its feet were joined together, and in its right hand
it held a raised spear and in the other, a distaff and spindle.

This is the story that people tell about the Palladion. They
say that after her birth, Athene was brought up by Triton,*
who had a daughter, Pallas; and that both girls practised the
arts of war, and this led them into conflict one day. And when

Pallas was about to land a blow, Zeus grew alarmed and placed his aegis* in the way, causing Pallas to look upwards in fright and fall victim to a fatal wound from Athene. Greatly distressed at her loss, Athene fashioned a wooden statue in her likeness, and wrapping the aegis which had aroused her fear around its chest, she set it up by Zeus' side and paid honour to it. Subsequently, since Electra had sought refuge at the Palladion when she was raped,* Zeus threw the Palladion along with Ate* into the land of Ilion, where Ilos built a temple for it and honoured it. That is what people say about the Palladion.

Ilos married Eurydice, daughter of Adrastos, and became the father of Laomedon, who married Strymo, daughter of Scamander (though according to some, his wife was Placia, daughter of Otreus, or according to others, Leucippe). Laomedon had five sons, Tithonos, Lampos, Clytios, Hicetaon, and Podarces, and three daughters, Hesione, Cilla, and Astyoche; and by a nymph, Calybe, he had a son, Boucolion.

4 Dawn so loved Tithonos* that she carried him off and took him to Ethiopia, where she slept with him and gave birth to two sons, Emathion and Memnon.

Priam, Hecuba, and their children

5 After Ilion was captured by Heracles, as we mentioned* somewhat earlier, Podarces, afterwards known as Priam, became king there. He took as his first wife Arisbe, daughter of Merops, by whom he had a son, Aisacos, who married Asterope, daughter of Cebren, and so mourned for her when she died that he was turned into a bird.* Priam later gave Arisbe to Hyrtacos, and took as his second wife Hecuba, daughter of Dymas (or according to some, the daughter of Cisseus, or according to others, of the River Sangarios and Metope). The first child born to her was Hector; and when her second child was about to be born, Hecuba had a dream* in which she gave birth to a firebrand and the fire spread through the whole city and burned it down. When Priam learned of the dream from Hecuba, he sent for his son Aisacos, who could interpret dreams because he had been taught the art by his maternal grandfather

Merops. Aisacos said that the birth of the child meant the ruin of his country, and advised that the baby should be exposed. So when the baby was born, Priam gave it to a servant (Agelaos by name) to be taken to Mount Ida for exposure; and after it had been exposed by him, the baby was suckled for five days by a bear. When Agelaos found the child still alive, he picked him up and took him home to rear in the country as his own son, naming him Paris. When he grew up to be a young man, Paris, who was superior to many in beauty and strength, acquired the further name of *Alexander*, for warding off robbers and *protecting** the flocks. And not long afterwards he rediscovered his parents.*

After Paris, Hecuba gave birth to some daughters, Creousa, Laodice, Polyxene, and Cassandra. Apollo wanted to sleep with Cassandra and promised to teach her the art of prophecy;* but after she had learned it, she refused to sleep with him. In response, Apollo deprived her prophecies of all power to convince. Afterwards, Hecuba had eight sons, Deiphobos, Helenos, Pammon, Polites, Antiphos, Hipponoos, Polydoros, and Troilos—she is said to have borne this last to Apollo.

And by other women Priam had further sons, Melanippos, Gorgythion, Philaimon, Hippothoos, Glaucos, Agathon, Chersidamas, Evagoras, Hippodamas, Mestor, Atas, Doryclos, Lycaon, Dryops, Bias, Chromios, Astygonos, Telestas, Evandros, Cebriones, Mylios, Archemachos, Laodocos, Echephron, Idomeneus, Hyperion, Ascanios, Democoon, Aretos, Deiopites, Clonios, Echemmon, Hypeirochos, Aigeoneus, Lysithoos, and Polymedon, and also some daughters, Medusa, Medesicaste, Lysimache, and Aristodeme.

6 Hector married Andromache, daughter of Eetion, and Alexander married Oinone, daughter of the River Cebren. Oinone had learnt the art of prophecy from Rhea, and warned Alexander not to sail for Helen; but when she failed to convince him, she told him to come to her if he were ever wounded,* for she alone could cure him. When he had abducted Helen from Sparta and Troy was under attack, he was struck by an arrow that Philoctetes had shot from the bow of Heracles, and made his way back to Oinone on Mount Ida. But she was bitter at the wrong she had suffered and refused to cure him. So

Alexander was carried off to Troy, where he died; and when Oinone had a change of heart and brought the remedies for his cure, she found him already dead and hanged herself.

10. The Asopids

Aiacos in Aegina

The River Asopos was a son of Oceanos and Tethys, or, according to Acousilaos, of Pero and Poseidon, or, according to some accounts, of Zeus and Eurynome. Metope, who was herself a daughter of the River Ladon, married Asopos and bore him two sons, Ismenos and Pelagon, and twenty daughters, one of whom, Aegina, was carried off by Zeus. Asopos set out to find her, and arriving in Corinth, he learned from Sisyphos* that her abductor was Zeus. When Asopos tried to pursue him, Zeus sent him back to his own stream by hurling thunderbolts at him (and because of that, coals are collected to this very day from the waters of the Asopos). Zeus took Aegina away to the island that was then known as Oinone, but is now named Aegina after her, where he slept with her and had a son, Aiacos, by her. Because Aiacos was alone on the island, Zeus turned the ants into people* for him; and he married Endeis, daughter of Sceiron, who bore him two sons, Peleus and Telamon. Pherecydes says, however, that Telamon was a friend of Peleus rather than a brother, and that he was in fact a son of Actaios and Glauce, daughter of Cychreus. Afterwards Aiacos had intercourse with Psamathe, daughter of Nereus, who turned herself into a seal* in the hope of escaping his embraces, and he fathered a son, Phocos.

Of all men Aiacos was the most pious, and for that reason, when Greece was gripped by infertility because of Pelops (who had made war against Stymphalos, king of the Arcadians, and finding himself unable to conquer Arcadia, had feigned friendship with the king and then killed and dismembered him and scattered his limbs), oracles from the gods proclaimed that Greece would be delivered from its present afflictions if Aiacos offered prayers on its behalf; and when he offered the prayers,

Greece was delivered from its barrenness.* After his death, Aiacos is honoured in the realm of Pluto also and guards the keys of Hades.*

The exile of Peleus and Telamon

Because Phocos excelled in the games, his brothers, Peleus and Telamon, plotted against him; and when Telamon was selected in the lot, he killed his brother* by hurling a discus at his head while they were exercising together, and then, with the help of Peleus, he carried the body away and hid it in a wood. But the murder was discovered and they were exiled from Aegina by Aiacos.

7 Telamon went to the court of Cychreus in Salamis. Cychreus, the son of [Poseidon and] Salamis, daughter of Asopos, had gained the throne by killing a snake which was devastating the island; and when he died without offspring, he left the throne to Telamon. And Telamon married Periboia, daughter of Alcathous, son of Pelops; and because Heracles had prayed that he would have a male child and after his prayers an *eagle* had appeared, Telamon called the son who was born to him *Aias*.* He then accompanied Heracles on his expedition against Troy, and received as a prize Hesione, daughter of Laomedon, who bore him a son, Teucros.

Peleus in Phthia, Calydon, and Iolcos

13 1 Peleus for his part fled to Phthia, to the court of Eurytion, son of Actor, and was purified by him and received from him his daughter, Antigone, and a third of the country; and a daughter, Polydora, was born to him, who became the wife of Boros, son of Perieres. 2 From there he went with Eurytion to join the hunt for the Calydonian boar, but as he threw a javelin at the boar, he struck Eurytion instead, and accidentally killed him. So he went into exile again, leaving Phthia for Iolcos, where he arrived at the court of Acastos and was purified by him. 3 And he competed at the games held in honour of Pelias, wrestling with Atalante.

Astydameia, the wife of Acastos, fell in love with Peleus and sent him a message proposing an assignation. When she was unable to persuade him, she sent word to his wife saying that he was intending to marry Sterope, the daughter of Acastos; and when his wife heard this, she hanged herself. Astydameia also made false accusations to her husband against Peleus, claiming that he had tried to seduce her. When he heard this, Acastos, who was unwilling to kill a man whom he had purified, took him hunting on Mount Pelion. There they competed in the chase, and Peleus cut out the tongues of the animals caught by him and put them in his pouch, while Acastos and his companions picked up his prey and made fun of Peleus, alleging that he had failed to catch anything. He produced the tongues, however, and told them that he had killed as many beasts as he had tongues. When Peleus fell asleep on Mount Pelion, Acastos left him, concealing his sword* in a pile of cow dung, and returned home. On arising, Peleus tried to find his sword, and while he was doing so, he was caught by the Centaurs; and he would shortly have lost his life if he had not been saved by Cheiron, who also searched for his sword and restored it to him.

The marriage of Peleus and Thetis, and early life of Achilles

4 Peleus married Polydora, daughter of Perieres, who bore a son, Menesthios, nominally to Peleus, but in reality to the River Spercheios.* 5 Later he married Thetis, the daughter of Nereus. Zeus and Poseidon had competed for her hand, only to withdraw when Themis had prophesied that the son born to her would be more powerful than his father. It is said by some, however, that when Zeus was set on having intercourse with her, he was told by Prometheus* that the son she would bear to him would become the ruler of heaven; while according to others,* Thetis was unwilling to have intercourse with Zeus because she had been brought up by Hera, and in his anger at this, Zeus wanted to marry her to a mortal. Now Peleus had been advised by Cheiron to seize her and keep a firm grip on her; however, she changed her shape, so he lay in wait and caught hold of her, and though she changed now into fire, now

into water, now into a wild beast, he never loosened his grip until she had returned to her original form. And he married her on Mount Pelion, and the gods celebrated his wedding there with feasting and songs. Cheiron gave Peleus an ashwood spear, and Poseidon gave him two horses,* Balios and Xanthos, of immortal stock.

6 When Thetis gave birth to a child by Peleus, she wanted to make it immortal, and in secret from Peleus, she used to bury it in the fire by night to destroy the mortal element in its nature that came from its father, and rubbed it by day with ambrosia. But Peleus kept a watch on her, and shouted out when he saw the child squirming in the fire; and Thetis, frustrated in her purpose, abandoned her infant son and went back to the Nereids.* Peleus delivered the child to Cheiron, who took him in, and fed him on the entrails of lions and wild boars and the marrow of bears, and named him *Achilles*—his former name was Ligyron—because he had *not* applied his *lips** to a breast.

7 After this, Peleus sacked Iolcos with the help of Jason and the Dioscuri, and slaughtering Astydameia,* the wife of Acastos, he cut her body limb from limb and led his army into the city through her remains.

8 When Achilles was nine years old, Calchas declared that Troy could not be taken without him, but Thetis—who knew in advance that he was fated to be killed if he joined the expedition—disguised him in women's clothing and entrusted him to Lycomedes* in the semblance of a young girl. While he was growing up at his court, Achilles had intercourse with Deidameia, the daughter of Lycomedes, and a son, Pyrrhos, was born to him, who was later called Neoptolemos.* Achilles' whereabouts were betrayed, however, and Odysseus, searching for him at the court of Lycomedes, discovered him by causing a trumpet to be sounded.* And so it came about that Achilles went to Troy.

Phoenix, son of Amyntor, accompanied him. Phoenix had been blinded by his father when Phthia, his father's concubine, had falsely accused him of having seduced her;* but Peleus had taken him to Cheiron, who cured his eyes, and had made him king of the Dolopians.

Achilles was also accompanied by Patroclos, son of Menoitios and of Sthenele, daughter of Acastos, or of Periopis, daughter of Pheres, or according to Philocrates, of Polymele, daughter of Peleus. At Opous, during an argument over a game of knucklebones, Patroclos had killed a boy,* Cleitonymos, son of Amphidamas, and had fled with his father to live at the court of Peleus, where Achilles had become his lover.*

11. The kings of Athens

Cecrops and his descendants; the story of Adonis

14 1 Cecrops, who was born from the earth and had the body of a man and a serpent joined into one, was the first king of Athens, and he named the land, which was known as Acte in earlier days, Cecropia after himself. During his time, they say, the gods decided to take possession of cities where each of them would be honoured with his own special cult. So Poseidon was the first to come to Attica, and striking a blow with his trident on the middle of the Acropolis, he caused a sea to appear, which is now known as the Erechtheid Sea.* After Poseidon, Athene arrived; and taking Cecrops as her witness, she claimed possession by planting an olive tree, which is still shown to visitors in the Pandroseion.* When the two of them entered into conflict for possession of the land, Zeus separated them, and appointed as judges, not Cecrops and Cranaos as some have claimed, nor Erysichthon, but the twelve gods. In accordance with their decision, the country was awarded to Athene, because Cecrops had testified that it was she who had first planted the olive tree. So Athene named the city Athens after herself, while Poseidon, in a rage, flooded the Thriasian plain* and submerged Attica under the sea.

2 Cecrops married Agraulos, the daughter of Actaios,* and had a son, Erysichthon, who died without offspring, and three daughters, Agraulos, Herse, and Pandrosos. Agraulos in turn had a daughter, Alcippe, by Ares. When Halirrhothios, son of

Poseidon and a nymph, Euryte, tried to rape Alcippe, he was caught in the act by Ares and killed by him. Poseidon brought charges against Ares, who was tried on the Areiopagos* before the twelve gods, and was acquitted.

3 Herse had a son, Cephalos, by Hermes. Dawn fell in love with him and carried him off; and after having intercourse with him in Sicily, she bore him a son, Tithonos, who in turn had a son, Phaethon,* whose son Astynoos had a son, Sandocos, who left Syria for Cilicia, where he founded a city, Celenderis, and after marrying Pharnace, daughter of Megassares, king of Hyria, became the father of Cinyras. Arriving in Cyprus with some followers, Cinyras founded Paphos, where he married Metharme, daughter of Pygmalion, king of Cyprus, and became the father of Oxyporos and Adonis, and had three daughters in addition, Orsedice, Laogore, and Braisia. Victims of Aphrodite's wrath, his daughters slept with foreigners* and finished their lives in Egypt.

4 Through the anger of Artemis, Adonis died in a hunt while he was still a young boy, from a wound inflicted by a boar. According to Hesiod, however, he was a son [not of Cinyras but] of Phoenix and Alphesiboia, while according to Panyasis, he was a son of Theias,* king of Assyria, who had a daughter called Smyrna. And this Smyrna, through the wrath of Aphrodite (whom she had failed to honour), conceived a passion for her father, and enlisting the aid of her nurse, shared her father's bed for twelve nights before he realized who she was. But when he found out, he drew his sword and chased after her. As he caught up with her, she prayed to the gods to be made invisible; and the gods, taking pity on her, turned her into a tree of the kind known as a *smyrna* [or myrrh tree]. Ten months later the tree burst open and Adonis, as he is called, was brought to birth. Struck by his beauty, Aphrodite, in secret from the gods, hid him in a chest while he was still a little child, and entrusted him to Persephone. But when Persephone caught sight of him, she refused to give him back. The matter was submitted to the judgement of Zeus; and dividing the year into three parts, he decreed that Adonis should spend a third of the year by himself, a third with Persephone, and the

remaining third with Aphrodite (but Adonis assigned his own
share also to Aphrodite). Later, however, while he was hunting, Adonis was wounded by a boar and died.

Three early kings: Cranaos, Amphictyon, and Erichthonios

5 When Cecrops died, Cranaos [became king]. He was born
from the earth, and it was during his reign that Deucalion's
flood is said to have taken place. He married a woman from
Lacedaimon, Pedias, daughter of Mynes, who bore him Cranae,
Cranaichme, and Atthis. This Atthis died while still a young
girl, and Cranaos named the country Attica after her.

6 Cranaos was driven out by Amphictyon, who took over
the throne. Some call him a son of Deucalion, while others say
that he was born from the earth. When he had ruled for twelve
years, Erichthonios drove him out. Some say that Erichthonios
was a son of Hephaistos and Atthis, daughter of Cranaos, while
according to others, he was born to Hephaistos and Athene,*
in the following way. Athene visited Hephaistos, wanting to
fashion some arms. But Hephaistos, who had been deserted by
Aphrodite, yielded to his desire for Athene and began to chase
after her, while the goddess for her part tried to escape. When
he caught up with her at the expense of much effort (for he
was lame), he tried to make love with her. But she, being chaste
and a virgin, would not permit it, and he ejaculated over the
goddess's leg. In disgust, she wiped the semen away with a
piece of wool* and threw it to the ground. As she was fleeing,
Erichthonios came to birth from the seed that had fallen on
the earth. Athene reared the child in secret from the other gods,
wishing to make him immortal; and placing him in a chest,
she entrusted it to Pandrosos, the daughter of Cecrops, telling
her not to open it. Out of curiosity, however, the sisters of
Pandrosos opened it, and beheld a snake* lying coiled beside
the baby; and according to some, they were destroyed by the
snake itself, while according to others, they were driven mad
through the anger of Athene and hurled themselves from the
Acropolis. After Erichthonios had been brought up by Athene
herself within her sanctuary,* he expelled Amphictyon and became king of Athens. He erected the wooden image of Athene*

on the Acropolis, and founded the festival of the Panathenaia;*
and he married Praxithea, a naiad nymph, who bore him a son,
Pandion.

Pandion I and his children; Icarios and Erigone; Tereus, Procne, and Philomela

7 When Erichthonios died, he was buried in the same precinct
of Athene, and Pandion became king. It was during his reign
that Demeter and Dionysos came to Attica. But Demeter was
welcomed by Celeos at Eleusis,* and Dionysos by Icarios, who
received a vine-cutting from the god and learned the art of
wine-making. Wanting to pass the god's blessings on to mankind, Icarios visited some shepherds, who, after a taste of the
drink, enjoyed it so much that they drank it down in quantities without water, and then, imagining that they had been poisoned, killed Icarios. When day came and they were sober again,
they buried him. While his daughter, Erigone, was searching
for her father, a pet dog named Maira, which had accompanied
him, revealed his dead body to her; and in her grief for her
father, she hanged herself.

8 Pandion married his mother's sister, Zeuxippe, and
fathered two daughters, Procne and Philomela, and twin sons,
Erechtheus and Boutes. When war broke out with Labdacos*
over the boundaries of the land, he summoned Tereus, son of
Ares, to his assistance from Thrace, and after he had brought
the war to a successful conclusion with his help, he gave
Tereus his own daughter, Procne, in marriage. Tereus had a
son, Itys, by her, but he conceived a passion for Philomela also,
and raped her; and telling her that Procne was dead, he hid
her away in the country* and cut out her tongue. But she wove
characters into a robe and used these to reveal her sufferings
to Procne. After recovering her sister, Procne killed her son,
Itys, boiled him, and served him as a meal to her unknowing
husband; and then she fled in all haste with her sister. When
Tereus realized what had happened, he snatched up an axe
and set out in pursuit. Finding themselves overtaken as they
reached Daulis in Phocis,* the sisters prayed to the gods to be
turned into birds. Procne became a nightingale, and Philomela

a swallow;* and Tereus, who was also transformed into a bird, became a hoopoe.

15 ¹ When Pandion died, his sons divided the paternal inheritance between them, Erechtheus taking the kingdom, and Boutes the priesthood of Athene and Poseidon Erechtheus.* And Erechtheus married Praxithea, the daughter of Phrasimos and Diogeneia, daughter of Cephisos, and had three sons, Cecrops, Pandoros, and Metion, and four daughters, Procris, Creousa, Chthonia, and Oreithuia, who was carried off by Boreas.

Procris and Cephalos; Oreithuia and her children

Chthonia was married to Boutes, Creousa to Xouthos, and Procris to Cephalos, son of Deion. In return for a golden crown, Procris went to bed with Pteleon;* and when she was caught by Cephalos, she fled to Minos, who fell in love with her and urged her to have intercourse with him. Now if a woman had intercourse with Minos, it was impossible for her to come out alive; for Minos had been unfaithful with so many women that Pasiphae had put a spell on him, and whenever he slept with another woman, Minos discharged harmful beasts* into her genitals, and the women died as a result. But Minos had a fast-running dog* and a javelin that never missed its mark, and to obtain these, Procris gave him a drink from the Circaean root* to prevent him from causing her any harm, and then went to bed with him. Afterwards, however, through fear of Pasiphae, she returned to Athens. Becoming reconciled with Cephalos, she accompanied him when he went hunting (for she was herself a skilful hunter). But as she was chasing a beast in the thicket, Cephalos threw his javelin without realizing that she was there, and hit Procris, causing her death. He was tried for this in the Areiopagos and condemned to perpetual exile.

² While Oreithuia was playing by the River Ilissos, Boreas carried her off* and had intercourse with her; and she gave birth to two daughters, Cleopatra and Chione, and two winged sons, Zetes and Calais, who sailed with Jason and met their death while pursuing the Harpies* (or according to Acousilaos, were killed by Heracles* on Tenos). ³ Phineus married Cleopatra, and had two sons by her, Plexippos and Pandion. After hav-

ing these sons by Cleopatra, he married Idaia, daughter of Dardanos, and when she came to Phineus with false allegations that her stepsons had tried to seduce her, Phineus believed her and blinded them both. The Argonauts, as they sailed by with Boreas, punished him for this.*

Eumolpos, and the war with Eleusis; the exile of Pandion II

4 Chione had intercourse with Poseidon. In secret from her father, she gave birth to Eumolpos, and to escape discovery, threw the child into the sea. But Poseidon recovered him, and taking him to Ethiopia, entrusted him to Benthesicyme (a daughter of his by Amphitrite) to bring up. When he was of age, the husband of Benthesicyme gave him one of their two daughters as a wife; but he tried to rape his wife's sister, and for that reason, he was banished from the land. Accompanied by his son Ismaros, he went to Tegyrios, king of Thrace, who offered his daughter in marriage to Eumolpos' son. Later when he plotted against Tegyrios and was detected, he fled to the Eleusinians* and made friends with them. Subsequently, on the death of Ismaros, he was summoned back by Tegyrios, and on his return, he resolved their former differences, and succeeded him on the throne.

When war broke out between the Athenians and the Eleusinians, and the Eleusinians asked him to come to their aid, he fought as their ally with a large force of Thracians. Erechtheus consulted the oracle about how the Athenians could achieve victory, and the god declared that they would be successful in the war if he slaughtered one of his daughters. And when he slaughtered the youngest, the others killed themselves too; for they had sworn a pact, some people said, to die together. In the battle that followed the sacrifice, Erechtheus killed Eumolpos; 5 but Poseidon destroyed Erechtheus* and his house, and Cecrops, the eldest of the sons of Erechtheus, then became king. He married Metiadousa, daughter of Eupalamos, and fathered a son, Pandion. And Pandion ruled after Cecrops, but he was expelled by the sons of Metion in a revolt, and went to the court of Pylas in Megara, where he married the king's daughter, Pylia. Later he

was even made king of the city; for Pylas, after killing his father's
brother Bias, transferred the kingdom to Pandion,* while he
himself departed to the Peloponnese with some of his people
and founded the city of Pylos.*

Aigeus and the conception of Theseus

During his time in Megara, Pandion had the following sons,
Aigeus, Pallas, Nisos, and Lycos (though some claim that
Aigeus was a son of Scyrios, who was passed off by Pandion
as his own son). 6 After the death of Pandion, his sons marched
on Athens, expelled the sons of Metion, and divided the kingdom into four; but Aigeus held all the power. He married as
his first wife Meta, daughter of Hoples, and as his second,
Chalciope, daughter of Rhexenor. When he failed to have a
child, he grew afraid of his brothers, and went to Pytho* to
ask the oracle how he could have children. The god replied:

> The bulging mouth of the wineskin,* most excellent of men,
> Untie it not until you have arrived at the height of Athens.

7 Baffled by the oracle, he departed again for Athens, travelling by way of Troezen,* where he stayed with Pittheus, son
of Pelops; and Pittheus, grasping the sense of the oracle, made
Aigeus drunk and ensured that he went to bed with his daughter, Aithra. On the same night Poseidon slept with her too.*
Aigeus gave instructions to Aithra, telling her that if she gave
birth to a male child, she should bring him up without telling
him who his father was; and, leaving a sword and a pair of
sandals under a rock, he said that when her son could roll the
rock aside and recover them, she should send her son to him
bearing these tokens.

The war with Minos and the origin of the tribute to the
Minotaur

Aigeus himself returned to Athens, where he celebrated the
games of the Panathenaia. During these games, Androgeos, the
son of Minos, defeated all others, and Aigeus sent him to confront the bull of Marathon,* which killed him. According to

some accounts, however, as he was travelling to Thebes to take part in the games held in honour of Laios, he was ambushed by his fellow competitors, and murdered out of jealousy. Minos received the news of his death as he was sacrificing to the Graces in Paros. He cast the garland from his head and silenced the flutes, but completed the sacrifice none the less; that is why, even to this day, they sacrifice to the Graces in Paros without flutes and garlands. 8 Not long afterwards, being master of the sea, Minos attacked Athens with a fleet; and he captured Megara, which was then under the rule of Nisos, a son of Pandion, and killed Megareus,* son of Hippomenes, who had come from Onchestos to the aid of Nisos. Nisos met his death also, through the treachery of his daughter. For he had a purple hair on the middle of his head, and an oracle had declared that if it were pulled out, he would die; and his daughter Scylla, who had fallen in love with Minos, pulled the hair out. But when Minos had gained control of Megara, he tied the girl by her feet to the prow of a ship and drowned her.*

When the war dragged on and he was unable to capture Athens, Minos prayed to Zeus to grant him vengeance on the Athenians. The city was then afflicted by a famine and a plague. First, obeying an ancient oracle, the Athenians slaughtered the daughters of Hyacinthos, Antheis, Aigleis, Lytaia, and Orthaia, on the grave of Geraistos the Cyclops. (Their father, Hyacinthos,* had come from Lacedaimon to settle in Athens.) But when this had no effect, they asked the oracle how they could be rid of their troubles, and the god replied that they should offer Minos whatever satisfaction he chose. So they sent a deputation to Minos, and allowed him to claim a penalty at his own discretion; and Minos ordered them to send seven boys and seven girls, all unarmed, to serve as food for the Minotaur. Now the Minotaur was confined in a labyrinth,* and anyone who entered it found it impossible to escape, for its maze of winding ways ensured that the way out remained undiscoverable. It was constructed by Daidalos, son of Eupalamos, son of Metion and Alcippe. 9 For Daidalos was an excellent architect and the first man to invent statues, and he had fled from Athens because he had hurled Talos, the son of his sister Perdix, from the Acropolis. This Talos was his pupil, and he was so gifted that Daidalos was afraid that he would be outshone by him, since Talos, using a snake's jawbone* that he had found, had managed to saw through a thin piece of wood. After the corpse was discovered, Daidalos was tried in the Areiopagos, and when he was found guilty, went into exile at the court of Minos.†

The labours of Theseus, and his arrival at Athens

16 1 Aithra bore to Aigeus a son, Theseus.* When he was fully grown, he pushed back the rock, recovered the sandals and the sword,* and hurried on foot to Athens; and he cleared the road,* which was beset by evildoers. First, in Epidauros he killed Periphetes, son of Hephaistos and Anticleia, who was referred to as Corynetes* [or the Club-Man] because of the club that he carried; for being weak on his feet, he carried an iron club, and used it to kill passers-by. Theseus seized the club from Periphetes and carried it himself ever after. 2 Secondly, he killed Sinis, son of Polypemon and Sylea, daughter of Corinthos. Sinis was referred to as Pityocamptes [or the Pine-Bender]; for living on the Isthmus of Corinth, he forced passers-by to bend pine trees to the ground and hold them down, and when they were too weak to do so, they were hurled into the air* by the trees to meet with a miserable death. Theseus killed him in that very manner.

EPITOME

1 ¹ Thirdly, he killed at Crommyon the sow known as Phaia, which was named after the old woman who had reared it; some say that it was the offspring of Echidna and Typhon. ² Fourthly he killed Sceiron the Corinthian, a son of Pelops, or, according to some, of Poseidon. Sceiron occupied the rocks in the Megarid which are named the Sceironian Rocks because of him, and forced passers-by to wash his feet; and as they did so, he would kick them into the deep to become the prey of a giant turtle. ³ But Theseus grasped Sceiron by the feet and flung him [into the sea]. Fifthly, in Eleusis, he killed Cercyon, son of Branchos and a nymph, Argiope. Cercyon forced passers-by to wrestle with him, and killed them during the fight. Theseus raised him into the air and dashed him to the ground. ⁴ Sixthly, he killed Damastes, whom some call Polypemon.* He had a house by the roadside and made up two beds, one small and the other large. Offering hospitality to passers-by, he would place short men on the large bed and beat them out with hammers to make them the same length as the bed, but tall men he would place on the small bed, and saw off the parts of their bodies that projected beyond it.

So in this way, Theseus cleared the road, and arrived in Athens. ⁵ But Medea, who was married to Aigeus at the time, schemed against him* and persuaded Aigeus to beware of him, alleging that he was a conspirator. Aigeus, failing to recognize him as his son, was afraid, and sent him out against the bull of Marathon* in the expectation that he would be destroyed by it. ⁶ When Theseus had killed the beast, Aigeus offered him some poison that he had received from Medea that very day. But as Theseus was about to drink the potion, he presented the sword to his father, and when Aigeus recognized it, he knocked the cup out of his hands. After he had been recognized by his father and informed of the plot, Theseus drove Medea from the land.

Theseus, Ariadne, and the killing of the Minotaur

7 When the third tribute was sent to the Minotaur,* he was included on the list, or, according to some, he offered himself as a volunteer. As the ship had a black sail, Aigeus ordered his son to raise white sails on it if he came back alive. 8 When Theseus arrived in Crete, Ariadne, the daughter of Minos, fell in love with him and promised to assist him if he would agree to take her away to Athens and have her as his wife. When Theseus agreed on oath to do so, she asked Daidalos to reveal how it was possible to escape from the Labyrinth. 9 On his advice, she gave Theseus a thread as he entered. He attached it to the door and played it out as he went in; and discovering the Minotaur in the innermost part of the Labyrinth, he killed it with blows from his fists, and then made his way out again by pulling back on the thread. [On the journey back,] he arrived at Naxos by night with Ariadne and the children.* There Dionysos fell in love with Ariadne* and carried her off; and taking her to Lemnos, he had intercourse with her, fathering Thoas, Staphylos, Oinopion, and Peparethos.

10 In his grief for Ariadne, Theseus forgot to spread white sails on his ship as he put into port. And when Aigeus saw from the Acropolis that the ship had a black sail, he thought that Theseus had died, and threw himself down to his death. 11 Theseus then succeeded him as king of Athens, and killed the sons of Pallas,* who were fifty in number; and in the same way, all who tried to rebel were killed by him, and he held sole power.

Excursus: Daidalos and Icaros, and the death of Minos

12 When Minos learned that Theseus and his companions had escaped, he enclosed Daidalos—who was to blame for it—in the Labyrinth, together with his son Icaros (who had been borne to him by Naucrate, a slave of Minos). But Daidalos constructed wings for himself and his son; and as his son took flight, he warned him not to fly too high, for fear that the glue would be melted by the sun and the wings would come loose, nor to fly too close to the sea, for fear that they would come loose because of the moisture. 13 But Icaros disregarded his father's

instructions and in his elation soared higher and higher; and when the glue melted, he plunged into the sea which is named the Icarian Sea* because of him, and perished. [Daidalos for his part escaped safely to Camicos in Sicily.]

14 Minos went in pursuit of Daidalos, and to every land that he visited on his search, he brought a spiral shell and proclaimed that he would give a large reward to the man who could draw a thread through it, thinking that by this means he would be able to discover Daidalos. Arriving at Camicos in Sicily, he visited the court of Cocalos, with whom Daidalos was hiding, and displayed the shell. Cocalos took the shell, promising that he would thread it, and gave it to Daidalos. 15 Daidalos attached a thread to an ant, pierced a hole in the shell, and let the ant make its way through. When Minos received it back with the thread drawn through, he realized that Daidalos was staying with Cocalos and demanded at once that he be handed over. Cocalos promised to surrender him, and offered Minos his hospitality. But Minos was killed in his bath by the daughters of Cocalos; according to some, he died when boiling water was poured over him.

Theseus and the Amazons; Phaedra and Hippolytos

16 Theseus accompanied Heracles on his expedition against the Amazons,* and he abducted Antiope, or according to some, Melanippe, or according to Simonides, Hippolyte. It was for that reason that the Amazons marched against Athens* and after they had pitched camp by the Areiopagos,* they were defeated by Theseus and the Athenians. Although he had a son, Hippolytos, by the Amazon, 17 he afterwards accepted Phaedra, daughter of Minos, as a wife from Deucalion,* putting an end to their previous hostility. During the wedding celebrations, the Amazon who had been formerly married to him arrived fully armed with her fellow Amazons, and was on the point of killing the guests; but they closed the doors with all speed, and killed her. Or, according to some, she was killed in battle by Theseus.

18 After Phaedra had borne two children, Acamas and Demophon, to Theseus, she fell in love with Hippolytos, his

son by the Amazon, and asked him to sleep with her.* But he hated all women* and shunned her embraces. So Phaedra, fearing that he might accuse her to his father, broke down the doors of her bedroom, ripped her clothing, and falsely accused him of rape. 19 Theseus believed her and prayed to Poseidon for the destruction of Hippolytos. And when Hippolytos was riding in his chariot and drove it along the sea-shore,* Poseidon caused a bull to emerge from the breakers. The horses were panic-stricken and the chariot was dashed to pieces; and becoming entangled [in the reins], Hippolytos was dragged to his death. When Phaedra's passion came to light, she hanged herself.

Theseus and Peirithoos

20 Ixion* conceived a passion for Hera and tried to take her by force. Hera reported the matter to Zeus; and Zeus, wanting to know whether it was really the case, fashioned a cloud in Hera's likeness and laid it down beside Ixion. When Ixion boasted that he had slept with Hera, Zeus fastened him to a wheel on which, as a punishment, he is whirled through the air by the force of the winds. As for the cloud, it gave birth to Centauros, a child by Ixion.

21 [Theseus joined Peirithoos* as an ally when he went to war against the Centaurs. For when Peirithoos had married Hippodameia, he had invited the Centaurs to the wedding feast as relatives of the bride.* But they were unaccustomed to wine, and drank it down so copiously that they became drunk; and when the bride was brought in, they tried to rape her. So Peirithoos took up arms, and aided by Theseus, engaged them in battle. Theseus killed a good number of them.]

22 Caineus was originally a woman, but after Poseidon had intercourse with her, she asked to become a man and to be invulnerable. For that reason, he had no concern for wounds during the battle with the Centaurs, and killed a large number of them. The survivors, however, surrounded him, and hammered him with fir trees until he was buried in the earth.*

23 Theseus came to an agreement with Peirithoos that both would marry daughters of Zeus. With the aid of Peirithoos,

he abducted Helen (then aged twelve) from Sparta for himself, and then, in the hope of winning Persephone as a bride for Peirithoos, made his way down to Hades. [While he was there,] the Dioscuri, with the Lacedaimonians and Arcadians, captured Athens,* and recovered Helen; and with her, they took away Aithra,* the daughter of Pittheus, as a captive. But Demophon and Acamas escaped. The Dioscuri also brought Menestheus* back from exile and entrusted the throne of Athens to him. 24 When Theseus arrived in Hades with Peirithoos, he became the victim of a trick. For on the pretence that they were about to enjoy his hospitality as guests, Hades asked them to sit down first on the Chair of Forgetfulness; and they became stuck to it,* and were held down by coils of snakes. Peirithoos remained a prisoner in Hades ever after, but Heracles brought Theseus back to earth and sent him to Athens. He was driven from there by Menestheus, and went to Lycomedes,* who threw him into an abyss and killed him.

12. The Pelopids

Tantalos

2 1 The punishment suffered by Tantalos* in Hades is to have a stone suspended over him, and remain perpetually in a lake, seeing at either side of his shoulders fruit-laden trees growing by its bank; the water grazes his chin, but when he wants to drink from it, the water dries up, and when he wants to feed from the fruit, the trees and their fruits are raised by winds as high as the clouds. It is said by some that he suffers this punishment because he divulged the secrets of the gods to men and tried to share ambrosia with his friends.*

2 Broteas,* who was a hunter, failed to honour Artemis, and said that even fire could cause him no harm; so he went mad and threw himself into the fire.

Pelops and Hippodameia

3 Pelops, after being slaughtered and boiled at the banquet of the gods, was more beautiful than ever when he was brought

back to life again, and because of his remarkable beauty, he became the beloved of Poseidon, who gave him a winged chariot* which could run even across the sea without wetting its axles. 4 Now Oinomaos, the king of Pisa,* had a daughter, Hippodameia, and whether it was because he had a passion for her, as some people say, or because he had been warned by an oracle that he would die at the hand of the man who married her, nobody was able to win her as his wife, since her father could not persuade her to have intercourse with him, and her suitors were put to death by him. 5 For he possessed arms and horses given to him by Ares, and offered his daughter's hand to the suitors as the prize in a contest. Each suitor had to take Hippodameia on his own chariot and flee as far as the Isthmus of Corinth, and Oinomaos would immediately pursue him in full armour. If Oinomaos caught up with the suitor, he killed him, but if the suitor were not overtaken, he would win Hippodameia as his wife. In this way, he had killed numerous suitors (twelve according to some accounts). And he cut off the suitors' heads and nailed them to his house.

6 Pelops too arrived to seek her hand; and when Hippodameia saw how beautiful he was, she fell in love with him, and persuaded Myrtilos, son of Hermes, to come to his aid. (This Myrtilos was Oinomaos' charioteer.) 7 So Myrtilos, who loved her and wanted to please her, failed to insert the axlepins* into the wheel hubs, causing Oinomaos to be defeated in the race and to lose his life when he became entangled in the reins and was dragged to his death (though according to some, he was killed by Pelops). As he was dying, he cursed Myrtilos, recognizing his treachery, and prayed that he would perish at the hand of Pelops.

8 So in this way, Pelops won Hippodameia; and when he arrived at a certain place accompanied by Myrtilos, he went away some small distance to fetch water for his wife, who was thirsty; and during that time, Myrtilos tried to rape her. When she told Pelops of this, he threw Myrtilos into the Myrtoan Sea* that bears his name, at Cape Geraistos. As Myrtilos fell, he hurled curses at the house of Pelops.* 9 After he had made his way to the Ocean and been purified by Hephaistos, Pelops returned to Pisa in Elis and took over the kingdom of Oino-

maos, after first subjugating the land formerly known as Apia or Pelasgiotis,* which he now named the Peloponnese after himself.

Atreus and Thyestes

10 The sons of Pelops were Pittheus, Atreus, and Thyestes, amongst others. Now the wife of Atreus was Aerope, daughter of Catreus, and she was in love with Thyestes. And Atreus had once made a vow that he would sacrifice to Artemis the finest lamb born in his flock, but when a golden lamb appeared, they say that he failed to honour his vow, 11 and instead, he throttled it, and placed it in a chest* for safe keeping; and it was given to Thyestes by Aerope, who had been seduced by him. For the Mycenaeans had received an oracle telling them to choose a Pelopid as their king, and they had sent for Atreus and Thyestes;* and while they were discussing who should be king, Thyestes declared before the crowd that the man to gain the throne should be the one who possessed the golden lamb. And when Atreus agreed to this, Thyestes produced the lamb and so became king. 12 But Zeus sent Hermes to Atreus, telling him to reach an agreement with Thyestes that Atreus should become king if the Sun reversed his course, and when Thyestes had agreed, the Sun went down in the east. Since the deity had clearly attested that Thyestes was a usurper, Atreus took over the kingdom and banished Thyestes. 13 But later, when he learned of the adultery,* he sent a herald to Thyestes suggesting a reconciliation; and when Thyestes arrived, Atreus, pretending friendship all the while, slaughtered Aglaos, Callileon, and Orchomenos, the children whom Thyestes had fathered by a naiad nymph, although they had sat down as suppliants on the altar of Zeus. He then dismembered them, boiled them, and served them to Thyestes without the extremities. And after he had swallowed them down, Atreus showed him the extremities and expelled him from the land. 14 Seeking to gain revenge by any means, Thyestes went to consult the oracle on the matter and received this response, that he would gain his revenge if he fathered a son by intercourse with his own daughter.* So he did that very thing, and

by his daughter he fathered Aigisthos, who, when he reached manhood and learned that he was the son of Thyestes, killed Atreus and restored the kingdom to Thyestes.

Agamemnon and Menelaos

15 [But Agamemnon and Menelaos were taken by their nurse to Polypheides, king of Sicyon, and he in turn sent them to Oineus, the Aetolian. Not long afterwards, Tyndareus brought them back again; and they expelled Thyestes, exacting an oath from him, when he sought refuge* at the altar of Hera, that he would settle in Cythera. They for their part became the sons-in-law of Tyndareus by marrying his daughters.*]

16 Agamemnon became king of Mycenae and married Clytemnestra, after killing her former husband Tantalos, son of Thyestes, along with his child. A son, Orestes, was born to him, and three daughters, Chrysothemis, Electra, and Iphigeneia. Menelaos married Helen and became king of Sparta after Tyndareus had entrusted the kingdom to him.

13. The Trojan War

The judgement of Paris and abduction of Helen

3   1 Afterwards Alexander abducted Helen,* in accordance, some say, with the will of Zeus, so that his daughter would become famous for having brought Europe and Asia to war, or, as others have said, to ensure that the race of demigods* would be raised to glory. 2 For one of these reasons,* Eris threw an apple* in front of Hera, Athene, and Aphrodite as a prize for the most beautiful, and Zeus instructed Hermes to take them to Alexander on Mount Ida, to be judged by him for their beauty. They promised to give Alexander gifts; Hera promised him universal dominion if she were preferred above all other women, while Athene offered victory in war, and Aphrodite the hand of Helen. He decided in favour of Aphrodite, and sailed to Sparta with ships built by Phereclos.* 3 He was entertained for nine days by Menelaos, and on the tenth, when

Menelaos departed for Crete to celebrate the funeral of his maternal grandfather Catreus,* Alexander persuaded Helen to go away with him. She abandoned Hermione, who was nine years old at the time, and loading most of the treasures* on board, she set out to sea with him by night. 4 Hera sent a violent storm against them, which forced them to put in at Sidon;* and fearing that he might be pursued, Alexander delayed a long while in Phoenicia and Cyprus. When he thought that there was no further risk of pursuit, he went on to Troy with Helen. 5 It is said by some, however, that Helen was stolen by Hermes in obedience to the will of Zeus and taken to Egypt, where she was entrusted to Proteus, king of the Egyptians, for safe keeping, and Alexander went to Troy with a phantom of Helen* fashioned from clouds.

Agamemnon assembles the Greek army

6 When Menelaos heard of the abduction, he went to Agamemnon in Mycenae,* and asked him to assemble a force to attack Troy and to levy troops in Greece. So Agamemnon, sending a herald to each of the kings, reminded them of the oaths* that they had sworn, and warned each of them to look to the safety of his own wife, saying that this insult to Greece affected all of them equally and in common. When most were eager to take part in the expedition, envoys also visited Odysseus in Ithaca, 7 but he was unwilling to go, and pretended to be mad.* Palamedes, son of Nauplios, however, proved his madness to be a sham; for he followed Odysseus while he was making this pretence of madness, and snatching Telemachos from Penelope's lap, drew his sword* as if he were about to kill him. And Odysseus, fearing for his son's safety, confessed that his madness was merely a sham, and joined the expedition.

8 [Later, at Troy,] after capturing a Phrygian, Odysseus forced him to write a treasonable letter, supposedly addressed from Priam to Palamedes; and then, after burying some gold under Palamedes' tent, he dropped the letter in the camp. Agamemnon read it, discovered the gold, and delivered Palamedes to the allies to be stoned as a traitor.*

⁹ Menelaos went to Cyprus with Odysseus and Talthybios to persuade Cinyras to join the allies. He presented a breast-plate* to the absent Agamemnon and swore to send fifty ships; but in fact he sent a single ship, commanded by . . ., son of Mygdalion, and fashioned the rest from earthenware and sent those off to sea.

¹⁰ Elais, Spermo, and Oino,* the daughters of Anios, son of Apollo, are called the Wine-Growers. Dionysos granted them the power to draw oil, corn, and wine from the earth.

¹¹ The army assembled at Aulis. Those who took part* in the expedition against Troy were the following: of the Boeotians, ten leaders, who brought forty ships; of the Orchomenians, four, who brought thirty ships; of the Phocians, four, who brought forty ships; of the Locrians, Aias, son of Oileus, who brought forty ships; of the Euboeans, Elephenor, son of Chalcodon and Alcyone, who brought forty ships; of the Athenians, Menestheus, who brought fifty ships; of the Salaminians, Aias, son of Telamon, who brought twelve ships; ¹² of the Argives, Diomedes, son of Tydeus, and his companions, who brought eighty ships; of the Mycenaeans, Agamemnon, son of Atreus and Aerope, a hundred ships; of the Lacedaimonians, Menelaos, son of Atreus and Aerope, sixty ships; of the Pylians, Nestor, son of Neleus and Chloris, forty ships; of the Arcadians, Agapenor, seven ships; of the Eleans, Amphimachos and his companions, forty ships; of the Doulichians, Meges, son of Phyleus, forty ships; of the Cephallenians, Odysseus, son of Laertes and Anticleia, twelve ships; of the Aetolians, Thoas, son of Andraimon and Gorge, who brought forty ships; ¹³ of the Cretans, Idomeneus, son of Deucalion, forty ships; of the Rhodians, Tlepolemos, son of Heracles and Astyoche, nine ships; of the Symaeans, Nireus, son of Charopos, three ships; of the Coans, Pheidippos and Antiphos, the sons of Thessalos, thirty ships; ¹⁴ of the Myrmidons, Achilles, son of Peleus and Thetis, fifty ships; from Phylace, Protesilaos, son of Iphiclos, forty ships; of the Pheraeans, Eumelos, son of Admetos, eleven ships; of the Olizonians, Philoctetes, son of Poias, seven ships; of the Ainianians, Gouneus, son of Ocytos, twenty-two ships; of the Triccaeans, Podaleirios [and Machaon, sons of Asclepios], thirty ships; of the Ormenians,

Eurypylos [son of Evaimon], forty ships; of the Gyrtonians, Polypoites, son of Peirithoos, thirty ships; and of the Magnesians, Prothoos, son of Tenthredon, forty ships. So in all there were one thousand and thirteen ships, forty-three leaders, and thirty contingents.

15 While the army was at Aulis and a sacrifice was being offered to Apollo, a snake darted from the altar to a plane tree nearby, which contained a nest; and after swallowing down the eight sparrow chicks in the nest along with their mother, the snake turned to stone. Calchas said that this sign had been sent to them by the will of Zeus, and he concluded from the incident that Troy was destined to be taken after ten years.* And they made ready to set sail against Troy. 16 Agamemnon himself was commander of the whole force, while Achilles, at fifteen years of age, took command of the fleet.

The attack on Mysia; the Greeks assemble for a second time

17 Lacking any knowledge of the route to Troy, they landed in Mysia* and put it to the sack, in the belief that it was Troy. Now the king of the Mysians was Telephos, son of Heracles,* and when he saw his country being pillaged, he armed the Mysians and pursued the Greeks in a body to their ships, killing a large number of them, including Thersandros, son of Polyneices, who stood his ground. But when Achilles rushed to the attack, Telephos failed to hold firm and was put to flight; and during the pursuit, he became entangled in a vine branch* and suffered a wound in the thigh from a spear.

18 Leaving Mysia, the Greeks put out to sea, and when a violent storm set in, they became separated from one another and returned to land in their own countries. Because the Greeks turned back at this time, the war is said to have lasted twenty years;* for it was in the second year after the abduction of Helen that the Greeks, when they had completed their preparations, launched the expedition [for the first time], and following their withdrawal from Mysia to Greece, it was eight years before they returned to Argos and went back to Aulis.

19 When they had gathered again at Argos after this delay of eight years, they were in great perplexity about their route,

for want of a guide who could show them the way to Troy. 20
But Telephos (since his wound had failed to heal and Apollo
had told him that he would be cured when the man who had
inflicted the wound became his healer) arrived in Argos from
Mysia dressed in rags and begged Achilles to help him, promising that, in return, he would show them the route to Troy.
So Achilles healed him by scraping rust from his Pelian spear.*
Once he was cured, Telephos revealed the route, and Calchas,
by the use of his own powers of divination, confirmed the accuracy of his directions.

21 When, after sailing over from Argos, they arrived in Aulis
for the second time, the fleet was held back by adverse winds.
Calchas declared that they would be unable to sail unless the
most beautiful of Agamemnon's daughters was offered in
sacrifice to Artemis; for the goddess was angry with Agamemnon, because he had said when shooting a deer at a hunt on
Icarion, 'Not even Artemis* [could have shot as well as that],'
and because Atreus had failed to sacrifice the golden lamb to
her. 22 On hearing this oracle, Agamemnon sent Odysseus and
Talthybios to Clytemnestra to ask her for Iphigeneia, claiming that he had promised to give her in marriage to Achilles
as a reward for taking part in the expedition. So Clytemnestra
sent her off, and Agamemnon brought her to the altar and was
just about to slaughter her when Artemis carried her off to the
land of the Taurians and installed her there as her priestess,
substituting a deer for her at the altar.* According to some
accounts, Artemis made her immortal.

The Greeks call in at Tenedos

23 After putting out from Aulis, they called in at Tenedos,
which was ruled by Tenes, son of Cycnos and Procleia, or
according to some, of Apollo. He lived there because he had
been sent into exile by his father. 24 For after having this son
Tenes and a daughter, Hemithea, by Procleia, daughter of
Laomedon, Cycnos* had later married Philonome, daughter
of Tragasos; and she fell in love with Tenes, and when she was
unable to win him over, made false accusations against him,
telling Cycnos that he had tried to seduce her and producing

as her witness a flute player named Eumolpos. 25 Cycnos believed her, and put Tenes and his sister into a chest, which he threw into the sea. When the chest ran ashore on the island of Leucophrys, Tenes stepped out, and he settled on the island, calling it Tenedos after himself. Later, when Cycnos learned the truth, he had the flute player stoned and his wife buried alive in the earth.

26 So when Tenes saw the Greeks sailing in towards Tenedos, he tried to turn them away by pelting them with stones; but he was killed by Achilles with a sword blow to the breast, although Thetis had warned Achilles beforehand not to kill Tenes, for if he did, he himself would die at the hand of Apollo. 27 While the Greeks were offering a sacrifice to Apollo,* a water-snake advanced from the altar and bit Philoctetes. The wound failed to heal and began to stink, and because the army could not abide the stench, Odysseus, on the orders of Agamemnon, put Philoctetes ashore on Lemnos, together with the bow of Heracles* which was now in his possession; and he maintained himself in the wilderness by shooting birds with it.

The landing at Troy, and the first nine years of the war

28 Leaving Tenedos, the Greeks set sail for Troy, sending Odysseus and Menelaos* ahead to demand the return of Helen and the treasures. But the Trojans, after they had summoned an assembly, not only refused to return Helen, but even wanted to kill the envoys. 29 Antenor saved the envoys, but the Greeks, angered by the insolence of the barbarians, took up their arms and sailed to attack them. Achilles had been warned by Thetis not to be the first to disembark from the ships, because the first man ashore would be the first to die. When the barbarians learned that the fleet was sailing against them, they hurried to the sea under arms and tried to prevent the enemy from landing by pelting them with stones. 30 The first of the Greeks to disembark* from his ship was Protesilaos, who killed a good many of the barbarians, but died at the hand of Hector. His wife, Laodameia,* continued to love him even after his death, and making an image in his likeness, she lived with it as though

they were man and wife. The gods took pity on her, and Hermes brought Protesilaos up from Hades. Seeing her husband and thinking he had returned from Troy, Laodameia was overjoyed at the time, but later, when he was taken back to Hades, she took her own life.

31 After the death of Protesilaos, Achilles disembarked with the Myrmidons, and killed Cycnos by hurling a stone at his head.* When the barbarians saw that Cycnos was dead, they fled to the city, and the Greeks, leaping ashore from their ships, filled the plain with dead bodies; and when they had penned the Trojans in, they put them under siege, and hauled their ships from the water. 32 Since the courage of the barbarians had failed, Achilles laid an ambush for Troilos* in the sanctuary of Thymbrian Apollo and slew him, and raided the city by night and captured Lycaon.* And then, taking some of the foremost warriors with him, he laid waste to the land, and went to Mount Ida to rustle the cattle of Aeneas* [and] Priam. When Aeneas fled, Achilles killed the herdsmen and Mestor, son of Priam, and drove away the cattle. 33 He also captured Lesbos and Phocaia, then Colophon and Smyrna, and Clazomenai, and Cyme, and after these, Aigialos and Tenos [, the so-called Hundred Cities]; and then, successively, Adramytion and Side, and then Endion, Linaion, and Colone. He also captured Hypoplacian Thebes and Lyrnessos, and furthermore, [Ant]andros, and many other cities.

34 After nine years had passed, the following allies* arrived to help the Trojans. From the neighbouring cities came Aeneas, son of Anchises, and with him Archelochos and Acamas, sons of Antenor and Theano, leading the Dardanians. Of the Thracians, Acamas, son of Eusoros; of the Ciconians, Euphemos, son of Troizenos; of the Paeonians, Pyraichmes; of the Paphlagonians, Pylaimenes, son of Bilsates; 35 from Zelia, Pandaros, son of Lycaon; from Adrasteia, Adrastos and Amphios, sons of Merops; from Arisbe, Asios, son of Hyrtacos; from Larissa, Hippothoos, son of [Lethos] the Pelasgian; from Mysia, Chromios and Ennomos, sons of Arsinoos; of the Alizones, Odios and Epistrophos, sons of Mecisteus; of the Phrygians, Phorcys and Ascanios, sons of Aretaon; of the Maeonians, Mesthles and Antiphos, sons of

Talaimenes; of the Carians, Nastes and Amphimachos, sons of Nomion; of the Lycians, Sarpedon, son of Zeus, and Glaucos, son of Hippolochos.

The wrath of Achilles (a summary of the Iliad)

4 1 In his anger over Briseis, the daughter of Chryses the priest, Achilles would no longer go out to fight. As a result, the barbarians recovered their confidence and advanced outside the city. Alexander fought in single combat against Menelaos, but when Alexander faced defeat, Aphrodite snatched him away; and Pandaros broke the truce by shooting an arrow at Menelaos.

2 Diomedes performed deeds of valour* and wounded Aphrodite when she came to the aid of Aeneas; and when he encountered Glaucos, he remembered the friendship between their fathers and exchanged armour* with him. Hector challenged the bravest man present to single combat. Although many stepped forward, Aias was chosen by lot and engaged in combat; but the pair were separated at nightfall by the heralds.

3 To protect the anchorage, the Greeks constructed a wall and a ditch; and after a battle on the plain, the Trojans chased the Greeks to the safety of their wall. The Greeks dispatched Odysseus, Phoenix, and Aias as envoys to Achilles, to ask him to assist them in the fighting and promise him Briseis and other gifts. 4 At nightfall, they sent Odysseus and Diomedes on reconnaissance; and they killed Dolon, son of Eumelos, and Rhesos the Thracian (who had arrived the previous day as an ally of the Trojans, and because he had yet to enter battle, had set up camp at some distance from the Trojan force, and separately from Hector). They also killed the twelve men who were sleeping around Rhesos and took their horses to the ships. 5 The next day, a fierce battle developed. Agamemnon, Diomedes, Odysseus, Eurypylos, and Machaon were wounded, and the Greeks were put to flight; Hector breached the wall and passed inside, and after Aias had retreated, set fire to the ships.

6 When he saw the ship of Protesilaos in flames, Achilles sent out Patroclos with the Myrmidons, equipping him with

his own arms and lending him his horses. When the Trojans saw Patroclos, they took him for Achilles, and turned to flee. Patroclos pursued them up to the city wall, killing many of them, including Sarpedon, son of Zeus, but met his own death at the hand of Hector after first being wounded by Euphorbos. 7 In the fierce battle that developed for his corpse, Aias performed deeds of valour and, with difficulty, rescued the body. Achilles now put his anger aside, and recovered Briseis; and when a full set of arms was brought to him from Hephaistos, he put on the armour and went out to fight. He chased the Trojans in a mass as far as the Scamander, killing many of them including Asteropaios, son of Pelagon, son of the River Axios. The river rushed out at him in fury, 8 but Hephaistos turned its flooding waters dry, and pursued it [back to its bed] with a massive flame.* And Achilles killed Hector in single combat, and tying him by the ankles to his chariot, dragged him back to the ships. When he had buried Patroclos, he celebrated games in his honour, in the course of which Diomedes won the chariot race, Epeios the boxing, and Aias and Odysseus the wrestling. After the games, Priam visited Achilles, and ransomed Hector's body and buried it.

Penthesileia the Amazon; Memnon and the death of Achilles; the suicide of Aias

5 1 Penthesileia, daughter of Otrere and Ares, had accidentally killed Hippolyte* and had been purified by Priam. She killed many Greeks in battle, including Machaon, but later died at the hand of Achilles, who fell in love with the Amazon after her death, and killed Thersites* for abusing him. [2]†

3 Memnon,* the son of Tithonos and Dawn, arrived at Troy to fight the Greeks, accompanied by a large force of Ethiopians, and after killing many of the Greeks, including Antilochos, he met his own death at the hand of Achilles. When Achilles went in pursuit of the Trojans also, he was shot down in front of the Scaean Gates* by Alexander and Apollo, with an arrow in the ankle.* 4 In the fight for his body, Aias killed Glaucos, and asking someone else to carry Achilles' arms to the ships, he picked up the body, and surrounded by the enemy, carried

it away through a hail of missiles while Odysseus fought off the attackers.

5 At the death of Achilles, the army was filled with gloom. They buried him with Patroclos [on the White Island*], mixing the bones of the pair together. It is said that Achilles lives on after his death as the husband of Medea on the Isles of the Blessed.* The Greeks held games in his honour, in the course of which Eumelos won the chariot race and Diomedes the footrace, Aias the discus-throwing, and Teucros the archery. 6 When Achilles' armour was offered as a prize to the bravest, Aias and Odysseus entered the lists. With the Trojans acting as judges,* or according to some, the allies,* Odysseus was picked as the winner. Aias was so overcome by resentment that he planned a night attack on the army; but Athene drove him out of his wits and turned him against the cattle, sword in hand, and in his delusion, he slaughtered the cattle along with their herdsmen, supposing them to be the Achaeans.* 7 Afterwards, however, when he had recovered his wits, Aias killed himself.* Agamemnon ordered that his body should not be burned, so Aias alone of the men who fell at Ilion lies in a coffin. His grave is at Rhoiteion.

Philoctetes and the death of Paris; conditions for the fall of Troy

8 When the war had already lasted for ten years and the Greeks were losing heart, Calchas prophesied that Troy could not be taken unless they had the bow of Heracles* to help them. On hearing this prophecy, Odysseus made his way to Lemnos with Diomedes to see Philoctetes,* and gaining possession of his bow by a trick, he persuaded him to sail to Troy. So Philoctetes arrived there, and after he had been cured by Podaleirios,* killed Alexander with an arrow.

9 After the death of Alexander, Helenos and Deiphobos quarrelled over Helen's hand; and because Deiphobos was preferred, Helenos left Troy and went to live on Mount Ida. But when Calchas declared that Helenos had knowledge of the oracles that protected the city, Odysseus captured him in an ambush and brought him to the camp; 10 and Helenos was forced to

reveal* how Ilion could be captured. This could be achieved if, in the first place, the bones of Pelops* were brought to the Greeks, and then if Neoptolemos fought as their ally, and thirdly, if the Palladion (which had fallen from heaven) was stolen from Troy—for while it remained inside the walls, the city was impregnable.

11 When they heard this, the Greeks had the bones of Pelops brought over, and sent Odysseus and Phoenix to Lycomedes on Scyros to persuade him to allow Neoptolemos* to go to war. So Neoptolemos arrived in the camp, where he received his father's arms from Odysseus, who willingly surrendered them; and he killed a large number of the Trojans. 12 Eurypylos, the son of Telephos, later arrived as an ally of the Trojans, bringing with him a powerful force of Mysians. He performed deeds of valour, but died at the hand of Neoptolemos.*

13 Odysseus went up to the city with Diomedes by night. Leaving Diomedes waiting outside, he assumed a mean appearance and put on shabby clothing, and entered the city undetected in the guise of a beggar. He was recognized, however, by Helen, and with her assistance he stole the Palladion, and then, after killing many of the guards, he took it to the ships with the aid of Diomedes.*

The wooden horse

14 Odysseus later had the idea of constructing a wooden horse, and he suggested it to Epeios,* who was an architect. Using timber felled on Mount Ida, Epeios constructed a horse that was hollow within and opened up at the side. Odysseus urged fifty—or according to the author of the *Little Iliad*, three thousand*—of the bravest men to enter this horse; as for all the rest, they were to burn their tents when night fell and put out to sea, but then lie in wait off Tenedos, ready to sail back again the following night. 15 Persuaded by his plan, the Greeks put their bravest men inside the horse, making Odysseus their commander; and they carved an inscription on it reading, 'For their return home, a thank-offering to Athene from the Greeks.' The others burned their tents, and leaving Sinon in place to light

a beacon for them, they put out to sea at night and lay in wait off Tenedos.

16 When day came and the Trojans saw the Greek camp deserted, they thought that the Greeks had fled. Overjoyed, they hauled the horse to the city, stationed it beside the palace of Priam, and debated what they should do. 17 When Cassandra said that there was an armed force inside it and she received support from the seer Laocoon, some proposed that they should burn it, and others that they should throw it down a cliff; but the majority decided that they should spare it because it was an offering sacred to a deity, and they turned to sacrifice and feasting. 18 A sign was then sent to them by Apollo; for two serpents swam across the sea from the islands nearby and devoured the sons of Laocoon.* 19 When night fell and all were fast asleep, the Greeks sailed over from Tenedos, and Sinon lit a fire on the grave of Achilles to guide their way. And Helen walked around the horse and called out to the heroes within, imitating the voice of each of their wives; but when Anticlos wanted to answer, Odysseus covered his mouth.* 20 When they judged that their enemies were asleep, they opened up the horse and climbed out with their weapons. Echion, son of Portheus, the first to emerge, was killed by the leap, but the others lowered themselves on a rope, made their way to the wall, and opened the gates to let in the Greeks who had sailed back from Tenedos.

The sack of Troy

21 Advancing into the city fully armed, they entered the houses and killed the Trojans as they slept. Neoptolemos killed Priam, who had taken refuge at the altar of Zeus of the Courtyard. But when Odysseus and Menelaos recognized Glaucos, son of Antenor, fleeing to his house, they came to his rescue* arms in hand. Aeneas picked up his father Anchises and fled, and the Greeks allowed him to pass because of his piety.* 22 Menelaos killed Deiphobos and led Helen away to the ships. Aithra,* the mother of Theseus, was led away also by Demophon and Acamas, the sons of Theseus (for they say that the two of them had later arrived at Troy*). The Locrian

Aias saw Cassandra clinging to the wooden image of Athene and raped her; and for that reason, they say, the statue looks up towards the sky.*

23 After killing the Trojans, they set fire to the city and divided the spoils. When they had sacrificed to all the gods, they hurled Astyanax from the ramparts* and slaughtered Polyxene* on the grave of Achilles. 24 As a special honour, Agamemnon received Cassandra, and Neoptolemos received Andromache, and Odysseus Hecuba. According to some accounts, however, Hecuba was awarded to Helenos, who crossed over to the Chersonese with her, where she turned into a bitch and was buried by him at the place now called the Bitch's Tomb.* 25 As for Laodice, the most beautiful of Priam's daughters,* the earth swallowed her up in chasm in full view of everyone. As the Greeks were about to sail off after sacking Troy, they were held back by Calchas, who said that Athene was angry with them because of the impiety of Aias. And they intended to kill him, but he took refuge by the altar* and they let him be.

14. The returns

Menelaos and Agamemnon quarrel; Calchas and Mopsos

6 1 After these events, the Greeks gathered together in assembly, and Agamemnon and Menelaos quarrelled, Menelaos advising that they should sail away and Agamemnon urging that they should remain and sacrifice to Athene.* Diomedes, Nestor, and Menelaos set out to sea together, and the first two had a favourable passage, but Menelaos ran into a storm, and losing the rest of his vessels, arrived in Egypt with only five ships.*

2 Amphilochos, Calchas, Leonteus, Podaleirios, and Polypoites left their ships at Ilion and travelled on foot to Colophon, where they buried Calchas the diviner; for he had been told in an oracle that he would die if he met a better diviner than himself. 3 Now they were received at Colophon by the diviner Mopsos, who was a son of Apollo and Manto,* and this Mopsos

challenged Calchas to a contest in the art of divination. There was a wild fig tree growing there, and when Calchas asked, 'How many figs is it carrying?', Mopsos replied, 'Ten thousand, or a bushel with one fig left over,' which was discovered to be the case. 4 Mopsos then questioned Calchas about a pregnant sow, asking, 'How many piglets is she carrying in her womb?' When Calchas replied, 'Eight,' Mopsos smiled and said, 'The divination of Calchas is anything but exact, but I, who am a son of Apollo and Manto, am richly provided with the clarity of vision that arises from exact divination, and I maintain that there are not eight piglets, as Calchas says, but nine piglets in her womb; and I can say, furthermore, that all of them are males and will be born tomorrow at the sixth hour without a doubt.'* When this all turned out to be true, Calchas was so dejected that he died. He was buried at Notion.

Agamemnon sails with the main fleet; the storm at Tenos, and Nauplios the wrecker

5 Agamemnon put to sea when he had offered his sacrifice, and called in at Tenedos. Neoptolemos was visited by Thetis,* who persuaded him to remain for two days and then offer a sacrifice; so he remained. But the others sailed off and were caught in a storm at Tenos (for Athene had appealed to Zeus to send a storm against the Greeks). And many ships were sunk.

6 Athene hurled a thunderbolt at the ship of Aias, but when the ship broke up, Aias escaped to safety on a rock and proclaimed that he had saved himself against the goddess's will. But Poseidon split the rock with a blow from his trident, and Aias fell into the sea and was killed.* His body was washed ashore and buried by Thetis at Myconos.

7 When the others were driven towards Euboea by night, Nauplios* lit a beacon on Mount Caphereus, and the Greeks, thinking that it came from some comrades who had escaped, sailed towards it, only to have their vessels wrecked on the Capherian Rocks, with the loss of many lives.

8 Now Palamedes, the son of Nauplios by Clymene, daughter of Catreus, had been stoned to death as a result of the intrigues of Odysseus.* And when Nauplios had come to hear

of it, he had sailed to the Greeks and demanded restitution for the death of his son; 9 but turning back with nothing achieved (because all the Greeks had wanted to gratify King Agamemnon, who had been involved with Odysseus in the murder of Palamedes), he had sailed along the coast of Greece contriving that the wives of the Greeks should be unfaithful to their husbands, Clytemnestra with Aigisthos, Aigialeia* with Cometes, son of Sthenelos, and Meda, wife of Idomeneus,* with Leucos. 10 But Leucos killed Meda along with her daughter, Cleisithyra, who had taken refuge in a temple; and he then arranged the defection of ten Cretan cities and became their tyrant. And when Idomeneus landed in Crete after the Trojan War, Leucos drove him out. 11 These, then, were the earlier machinations of Nauplios, and later, when he learned that the Greeks were returning home to their countries, he lit the beacon on Mount Caphereus, which is now called Xylophagos.* It was there that the Greeks approached the shore, supposing it to be a harbour, and met their deaths.

The fate of Neoptolemos; various wanderings and returns

12 After he had remained in Tenedos for two days as Thetis had advised, Neoptolemos travelled by land to the country of the Molossians,* accompanied by Helenos. Along the way, Phoenix died, and Neoptolemos buried him. He became king of the Molossians after defeating them in battle, and had a son, Molossos, by Andromache. 13 Helenos founded a city in Molossia, where he settled, and Neoptolemos gave him his mother, Deidameia, as a wife. When Peleus was expelled from Phthia by the sons of Acastos, and died, Neoptolemos recovered his father's kingdom.*

14 And when Orestes went mad,* Neoptolemos abducted his wife, Hermione, who had been promised to him previously at Troy,* and he was killed for that reason by Orestes at Delphi. But some say that he went to Delphi to demand reparation from Apollo for the death of his father,* and that he plundered the votive offerings and set fire to the temple, and was killed on that account by Machaireus* the Phocian.

15 After their wanderings, the Greeks landed in different

countries and settled there, some in Libya, some in Italy, others in Sicily, others again in the islands near Iberia, or along the River Sangarios; and there were some who settled in Cyprus too.

Agapenor settled in Cyprus. [Gouneus went to Libya, and leaving his ships behind, he made his way to the River Cinyps, where he settled. Meges and Prothoos were killed with many others at Caphereus in Euboea . . . and after Prothoos had been shipwrecked at Caphereus, the Magnesians with him were cast ashore on Crete and settled there.*]

[After the sack of Ilion, Menestheus, Pheidippos, and Antiphos, and the companions of Elephenor, and Philoctetes sailed together as far as Mimas. Then Menestheus went to Melos, where he became king because the previous king, Polyanax, had died. Antiphos, son of Thessalos, went to the land of the Pelasgians, and after seizing control of it, named it Thessaly. Pheidippos was driven to Andros with the Coans, and then to Cyprus, where he settled. Elephenor had died at Troy, but his companions were carried to the Ionian Gulf and settled at Apollonia in Epirus. The companions of Tlepolemos called in at Crete, and were then driven by the winds to the Iberian Islands, where they settled. The companions of Protesilaos were cast up on the [peninsula of] Pallene near the plain of Canastron. Philoctetes was driven to the land of the Campanians in Italy, and after a war against [the Lucanians], he settled at Crimissa, near Croton and [Thourioi]. Now that his wanderings had reached an end, he founded a sanctuary of Apollo the Wanderer, to whom, according to Euphorion, he dedicated his bow.]

[The Navaithos, a river in Italy, bears that name (according to Apollodorus and the rest) because after the capture of Ilion, the daughters of Laomedon and sisters of Priam, Aithylla, Astyoche, and Medesicaste, arrived in that part of Italy with the other captives, and fearing that they might become slaves in Greece, *set fire* to the *ships*. As a result, the river was called *Navaithos*, and the women the *Nauprestides*.* And the Greeks who were with them settled there after the loss of their ships.]

16 Demophon* called in at the land of the Thracian Bisaltians with a small number of ships. Phyllis, the king's daughter,

fell in love with him, and her father offered her in marriage to Demophon with the kingdom for her dowry; but he wanted to leave for his own country, and after much pleading, and swearing to come back again, he departed. Phyllis accompanied him as far as the place known as Nine Ways,* and she gave him a basket, telling him that it contained an object sacred to Mother Rhea, and that he was not to open it unless he had abandoned all hope of returning to he. 17 Demophon went to Cyprus and settled there. When the appointed time had elapsed, Phyllis called down curses on Demophon and killed herself. Demophon opened the basket, and terror-struck,* he jumped on to his horse and rode it at such a reckless pace that he lost his life; for the horse stumbled, and Demophon was thrown off and fell on his sword. His companions settled in Cyprus.

18 Podaleirios arrived in Delphi and asked the god where he should settle; and he received an oracle that he should settle in the city where he would suffer no harm if the surrounding heavens fell in. So he settled at a place in the Carian Chersonese which is girded by mountains on every side.

19 Amphilochos, son of Alcmaion, who, according to some accounts, had later arrived at Troy, was driven by a storm to the land of King Mopsos; and according to some accounts, they fought in single combat for the kingdom and killed one another.*

20 The Locrians with some difficulty made their way back to their own land; and when, three years later, Locris was struck by a plague,* they received an oracle telling them to propitiate Trojan Athene and to send her two maidens as suppliants for the next thousand years. The first to be picked out by the lot were Periboia and Cleopatra. 21 On their arrival at Troy, they were pursued by the inhabitants and fled to the sanctuary. Without ever approaching the goddess, they swept and sprinkled her sanctuary; and they never went outside the temple, and kept their heads shorn and wore only a single tunic without any shoes. 22 When the first suppliants died, the Locrians sent others. They entered the city by night to ensure that they would not be seen outside the sacred precinct and be put to death. Later, however, they sent them as babies with

their nurses; and after the Phocian War,* when the thousand years had elapsed, they stopped sending the suppliants.

The later history of the Pelopids

23 When Agamemnon arrived back at Mycenae with Cassandra, he was killed by Aigisthos and Clytemnestra;* for she gave him a tunic without sleeves or a neck, and he was struck down as he tried to put it on. Aigisthos became king of Mycenae, and they killed Cassandra too.* 24 But Electra, one of the daughters of Agamemnon, stole away her brother Orestes, and entrusted him to Strophios the Phocian to rear; and he brought him up with his own son, Pylades. On reaching manhood, Orestes went to Delphi to ask the god whether he should take vengeance on his father's murderers. 25 When this was authorized by the god, he left Mycenae in secret, accompanied by Pylades, and killed his mother and Aigisthos.* Not long afterwards, he was struck by madness, and pursued by the Furies, he went to Athens, where he was put on trial in the Areiopagos. According to some, he was indicted by the Furies, or according to others, by Tyndareus, or again, by Erigone, the daughter of Aigisthos and Clytemnestra, and when the votes at his trial were evenly divided, he was acquitted.*

26 When Orestes asked the oracle how he could be delivered from his affliction, the god replied that this would be achieved if he fetched the wooden statue that lay in the land of the Taurians.* Now the Taurians are part of the Scythian race, who murder strangers and cast their bodies into the sacred fire. The fire lay in the sanctuary and rose up from Hades through a certain rock. 27 So when Orestes arrived with Pylades in the land of the Taurians, they were discovered, captured, and taken in chains to Thoas, the king, who dispatched the pair of them to the priestess. But Orestes was recognized by his sister, who was performing the rites amongst the Taurians, and he fled with her, taking the wooden statue with him. It was brought to Athens, where it is now called the Tauropolos Statue; but it is said by some that Orestes was driven by a storm to the island of Rhodes, [where the statue remained] and was dedicated in a defensive wall in obedience

to an oracle. [28] Returning to Mycenae, he united his sister Electra to Pylades, while he himself married Hermione, or according to some, Erigone, and became the father of Tisamenos.* He died from a snake-bite at Oresteion in Arcadia.

[29] Menelaos, with a total of five ships under his command, put in at Sounion, a headland of Attica; and when he was driven away from there by the winds towards Crete, he was carried a great distance, and wandered along the coasts of Libya, Phoenicia, Cyprus, and Egypt collecting a wealth of treasure.* [30] According to some accounts, he discovered Helen at the court of Proteus, king of Egypt; for until that time, Menelaos had possessed only a phantom* of her, fashioned from clouds. After wandering for eight years, he sailed back to Mycenae, where he found Orestes, who was there after avenging his father's murder. From there, he went to Sparta and recovered his own kingdom; and after he had been made immortal by Hera, he went to the Elysian Fields with Helen.*

The return of Odysseus (a summary of the Odyssey)

7 [1] Odysseus, according to some accounts, wandered to Libya, or according to others, to Sicily, or again around the Ocean and the Tyrrhenian Sea.

[2] After putting to sea from Ilion, he called in at Ismaros, a city of the Ciconians, and seized it by force of arms and pillaged it, sparing only Maron, who was a priest of Apollo. When the Ciconians who lived on the mainland came to hear of this, they armed themselves and advanced against him. Losing six men from each ship, he put to sea and fled.

[3] Landing at the country of the Lotos-Eaters, he sent some of his men to discover who the inhabitants were. But they tasted the lotos and remained where they were; for in that land, there grew a delicious fruit called the lotos, which caused those who tasted it to forget all else. When Odysseus learned of this, he kept the others back, and dragged the men who had tasted the lotos back to the ships by force. And he set sail for the land of the Cyclopes and approached its shore.

[4] Leaving the rest of his ships at the neighbouring island, he approached the land of the Cyclopes with only a single ship,

and disembarked with twelve companions. Close to the sea there was a cave, which he entered, taking with him the wineskin that Maron had given him. This cave was owned by Polyphemos, who was a son of Poseidon and the nymph Thoosa; he was a man of enormous size, a savage man-eater with a single eye on his forehead. 5 Lighting a fire, Odysseus and his companions sacrificed some of the kids and began to feast; but the Cyclops arrived, and after he had driven his flocks into the cave and placed a huge stone at its entrance, he caught sight of the men and devoured some of them. 6 Odysseus gave him some of Maron's wine to drink. He drank it down and asked for more, and then, when he had drunk for a second time, he asked Odysseus to tell him his name. Odysseus replied that he was called Nobody, and the Cyclops promised that he would kill Nobody last and the others before him: such was the gift of friendship that he promised him in return for the wine. And overcome by drunkenness he fell asleep.

7 Odysseus found a club lying in the cave, and helped by four of his comrades, he sharpened its point, and then, after heating it in the fire, blinded the Cyclops with it. Polyphemos cried out to the neighbouring Cyclopes and they came to help; but when they asked who was hurting him, and he replied, 'Nobody,' they went away again, believing him to mean that he was being injured by nobody. 8 When the flocks sought to leave for their usual pasture, he opened up the cave, and standing at the entrance, stretched out his hands to feel the sheep [as they passed]. But Odysseus tied three rams together and slipping beneath the largest of them, he hid under its belly and left with the sheep; and then, after releasing his companions from their sheep, he drove the animals to the ships, and as he was sailing away, shouted to the Cyclops that he was Odysseus and had escaped from his hands. 9 Now the Cyclops had been warned by a diviner that he would be blinded by Odysseus, and when he heard the name, he tore rocks from the ground and hurled them into the sea; and the ship only just escaped them. It was these events that gave rise to Poseidon's anger against Odysseus.

10 Sailing to sea with all [his ships], he came to the island of Aiolia, where Aiolos was king. He had been appointed

controller of the winds by Zeus, with power both to calm them and send them forth. After entertaining Odysseus as his guest, he gave him an oxhide bag in which he had imprisoned the winds, and when he had shown him which he should use on the voyage, he attached the bag securely to the ship. By making use of the appropriate winds, Odysseus had a successful passage, but when he drew close to Ithaca and could already see the smoke rising from the town, he fell asleep; 11 and his companions, thinking that he was carrying gold in the bag, untied it, and released the winds. Swept away by the winds, they travelled back the way they had come. Odysseus went to Aiolos and asked him for a favourable wind, but Aiolos drove him from the island, saying that he was unable to save a man if the gods were working against him.

12 So he sailed on until he arrived at the land of the Laistrygonians, [where he put in,] mooring his own ship last in the line. The Laistrygonians were cannibals and their king was Antiphates. Wanting to learn about the inhabitants, Odysseus sent some of his men to investigate; and the king's daughter met with them and took them to her father. 13 He grasped hold of one of them and swallowed him down, but the others fled, and he chased after them, shouting out to summon the rest of the Laistrygonians. And the Laistrygonians rushed down to the sea, where they broke up the vessels by hurling rocks at them, and devoured the men. Odysseus cut the cable of his ship and made his way out to sea, but all the other ships were lost together with their crews.

14 Left with a single ship, he put in at the island of Aiaie, the home of Circe, a daughter of the Sun and Perse and sister of Aietes, who had knowledge of all manner of drugs. Separating his comrades into two groups, he himself remained by the ship in accordance with the lot, while Eurylochos went to visit Circe with twenty-two companions. 15 At her invitation, all except Eurylochos went inside, and she offered each of them a cup that she had filled with cheese, honey, barley-meal, and wine, with a drug mixed in. And when they had drunk, she touched them with her wand and transformed them, turning some of them into wolves, and others into pigs, or asses, or lions.* 16 Eurylochos saw everything and went to

tell Odysseus. Obtaining some moly* from Hermes, Odysseus went to Circe and sprinkled it into her potions, so that when he drank from them, he alone escaped her enchantments. He drew his sword, with the intention of killing her, but Circe allayed his anger, and restored his comrades to their original form. After he had received an oath from her that she would cause him no harm, Odysseus went to bed with her, and she bore him a son, Telegonos.*

17 After delaying there for a year, he sailed on the Ocean, and then, after offering sacrifices to the souls [of the dead], he consulted the diviner Teiresias as Circe had advised, and beheld the souls of heroes and heroines alike. He also saw his mother Anticleia, and Elpenor, who had died from a fall in Circe's house.

18 He then went back to Circe, who sent him on his way again; and putting out to sea, he sailed past the island of the Sirens. The Sirens* were daughters of Acheloos by Melpomene, one of the Muses, and their names were Peisinoe, Aglaope, and Thelxiepeia. One of them played the lyre, another sang, and the third played the flute, and by these means they caused passing sailors to want to remain with them. 19 From the thighs down, they were shaped like birds. Now Odysseus wanted to hear their song as he sailed by; so following Circe's advice, he plugged the ears of his comrades with wax, and ordered that he himself should be bound to the mast. And when the Sirens prevailed on him to want to stay with them, he pleaded to be released, but his men bound him all the more firmly, and in this way he sailed by. There was a prophecy that if a ship sailed past the Sirens, they themselves would die; so they duly perished.

20 After this, Odysseus arrived at a point where he had a choice of two different routes. On one side were the Wandering Rocks, and on the other, two enormous cliffs. On one of these cliffs was Scylla, a daughter of Crataiis and Trienos or Phorcos, who had the face and chest of a woman, but from her flanks down, six heads and twelve dogs' feet; 21 and on the other was Charybdis, who sucked in the water and spewed it out again three times a day. On Circe's instructions, he avoided the passage around the Wandering Rocks, and sailed past the

cliff of Scylla, standing fully armed at the stern. Scylla appeared, snatched up six of his comrades, and devoured them.

22 From there he went to Thrinacia, an island of the Sun, where cattle* were grazing; and held back by unfavourable weather, he remained there. When his companions slaughtered some of the cattle and feasted on them for want of food, the Sun reported the matter to Zeus; and when they set sail again, Zeus struck them with a thunderbolt. 23 As the ship broke up, Odysseus clung to the mast and was carried towards Charybdis. But when Charybdis sucked down the mast, he seized hold of an overhanging fig tree and waited; and when he saw the mast rise up again, he threw himself on to it and was carried across the sea to the island of Ogygia.

24 He was welcomed there by Calypso, daughter of Atlas, who went to bed with him, and bore him a son, Latinos.* He remained with her for five years,* and then built a raft and sailed away. It was broken up at sea, however, through the wrath of Poseidon, and he was cast ashore naked on the land of the Phaeacians. 25 Nausicaa, the daughter of King Alcinoos, was washing clothes there, and when Odysseus approached her as a suppliant, she took him to Alcinoos, who welcomed him as a guest. And then, after presenting him with gifts, he sent him away to his native land accompanied by an escort. In his anger against the Phaeacians, Poseidon turned the escorting ship to stone and surrounded their city with a mountain.

26 When Odysseus arrived in his native land, he found that his house had been ruined; for believing that he was dead, suitors* were courting Penelope. From Doulichion came fifty-seven: 27 Amphinomos, Thoas, Demoptolemos, Amphimachos, Euryalos, Paralos, Evenorides, Clytios, Agenor, Eurypylos, Pylaimenes, Acamas, Thersilochos, Hagios, Clymenos, Philodemos, Meneptolemos, Damastor, Bias, Telmios, Polyidos, Astylochos, Schedios, Antigonos, Marpsios, Iphidamas, Argeios, Glaucos, Calydoneus, Echion, Lamas, Andraimon, Agerochos, Medon, Agrios, Promos, Ctesios, Acarnan, Cycnos, Pseras, Hellanicos, Periphron, Megasthenes, Thrasymedes, Ormenios, Diopithes, Mecisteus, Antimachos, Ptolemaios, Lestorides, Nicomachos, Polypoites, and Ceraos. 28 From Same came

twenty-three: Agelaos, Peisandros, Elatos, Ctesippos, Hippo-
dochos, Eurystratos, Archemolos, Ithacos, Peisenor, Hyperenor,
Pheroites, Antisthenes, Cerberos, Perimedes, Cynnos, Thriasos,
Eteoneus, Clytios, Prothoos, Lycaithos, Eumelos, Itanos, and
Lyammos. 29 From Zacynthos came forty-four: Eurylochos,
Laomedes, Molebos, Phrenios, Indios, Minis, Leiocritos, Pro-
nomos, Nisas, Daemon, Archestratos, Hippo[machos, Euryalos,
Periallos, Evenorides, Clytios, Agenor], Polybos, Polydoros,
Thadytios, Stratios, [Phrenios, Indios,] Daisenor, Laome-
don, Laodicos, Halios, Magnes, Oloitrochos, Barthas, Theo-
phron, Nissaios, Alcarops, Periclymenos, Antenor, Pellas, Celtos,
Periphas, Ormenos, [Polybos,] and Andromedes. 30 And from
Ithaca itself, there were twelve suitors: Antinoos, Pronoos,
Leiodes, Eurynomos, Amphimachos, Amphialos, Promachos,
Amphimedon, Aristratos, Helenos, Doulichieus, and Ctesippos.

31 These suitors had travelled to the palace and consumed
the herds of Odysseus at their feasts. Penelope had been forced
to promise that she would consent to marry when the shroud
of Laertes was finished, and she worked at it for three years,
weaving it by day and unravelling it by night. In this way, the
suitors were fooled by Penelope, until the day came when
she was caught in the act. 32 When Odysseus learned of the
situation in his household, he visited his servant Eumaios
disguised as a beggar. And then, after making himself known
to Telemachos, he went to the city with him. Melanthios the
goatherd, a mere servant, met them on the way and abused
them. On arriving at the palace, Odysseus begged food from
the suitors, and discovering a beggar there called Iros, he wrestled with him.* He revealed his identity to Eumaios and Philoitios, and together with them and Telemachos, he devised a
plot against the suitors. 33 Penelope gave the suitors the bow
of Odysseus (which he had received from Iphitos in earlier days),
and said that she would marry the one who could flex the bow.
When none of them succeeded, Odysseus took it and shot down
the suitors, helped by Eumaios, Philoitios, and Telemachos.
He also killed Melanthios, and the maidservants who had been
sleeping with the suitors; and he revealed his identity to his
wife and father.

The later history of Odysseus

34 After sacrificing to Hades, Persephone, and Teiresias, he travelled on foot through Epirus, and arrived in the land of the Thesprotians,* where he propitiated Poseidon* by offering the sacrifices that Teiresias had advised in his prophecy.* Callidice, who was queen of the Thesprotians at the time, asked him to remain and offered him the throne; 35 and she slept with him and bore him a son, Polypoites. After he had married Callidice, he became king of the Thesprotians, and defeated in battle the neighbouring peoples who attacked them. When Callidice died, he transferred the throne to his son and returned to Ithaca, where he discovered that Penelope had borne him a son, Poliporthes.

36 When Telegonos learned from Circe that he was a son of Odysseus, he sailed away in search of him. Arriving at the island of Ithaca, he plundered some of the cattle,* and when Odysseus came to their rescue, Telegonos wounded him with the spear that he was carrying, which was tipped with the needle [from a stingray*]; and Odysseus died. 37 When Telegonos discovered his identity, he lamented bitterly, and took his corpse, and Penelope too, to the land of Circe, where he married Penelope;* and Circe sent the pair of them to the Isles of the Blessed.

38 It is said by some, however, that Penelope was seduced by Antinoos* and sent away by Odysseus to her father Icarios, and that when she reached Mantineia in Arcadia, she gave birth to Pan, as a son of Hermes.* 39 Others say that she was killed by Odysseus himself because of Amphinomos;* for they claim that she had been seduced by him. 40 And there are some who say that when the relatives of the men killed by Odysseus made accusations against him, he took as his judge Neoptolemos,* who ruled the islands off Epirus; and Neoptolemos, thinking he would gain possession of Cephallenia if Odysseus were out of the way, condemned him to exile. And Odysseus went to Thoas,* son of Andraimon, in Aetolia, where he married the daughter of Thoas, and died at a great age leaving behind a son by her, Leontophonos.

APPENDIX

SOME INTERPOLATIONS AND AN UNRELIABLE PASSAGE FROM THE EPITOME

Indicated by a dagger (†) in the text

1. 2. 4. 2 (p. 65)

Pindar and Hesiod in the *Shield* say of Perseus: 'The whole of his back was covered by [the head of] a fearsome monster, [the Gorgon,] which was enclosed in a *kibisis*.' The *kibisis* bears that name because clothes and food are placed in it.

2. 2. 5. 12 (p. 83)

It was unlawful at that time for foreigners to be initiated, for Heracles was initiated only after he had become the adopted son of Pylios.

3. 3. 1. 4 (p. 97)

He was the first to become master of the sea, and extended his rule to almost all of the islands.

4. 3. 4. 4 (p. 102)

The names of Actaion's dogs in the . . . were these:

Now surrounding his beautiful body, as though it were that of a beast,
His powerful dogs tore it apart. Beside it, Arcena first,
[. . .] after her, her valiant offspring,
Lynceus, and Balios the finely footed, and Amarynthos [. . .]—
And those that singled out by name are listed thus:
[. . .] and they then killed Actaios, at the instigation of Zeus,
For the first who drank the black blood of their master
Were Spartos, and Omargos, and Bores swift on the scent.
These were the first to devour Actaios and lap his blood.
And after these, the others rushed on him in a frenzy [. . .]
To be a remedy for the grievous sorrows of men.

5. 3. 6. 7 (p. 110)

What was said by Teiresias to Zeus and Hera:

Of the ten parts, a man enjoys only one,
But a woman in her heart enjoys all ten in full.

6. 3. 10. 3 (p. 119)

I have found some who are said to have been raised by him, namely, Capaneus and Lycourgos, according to Stesichoros in the *Eriphyle*; and Hippolytos, according to the author of the *Naupactica*, and Tyndareus, according to Panyasis, and Hymenaios, according to the Orphics, and finally, Glaucos, the son of Minos, according to Melesagoras.

7. 3. 15. 8 (p. 138)

And there, after Pasiphae had conceived a passion for the bull of Poseidon, he assisted her by constructing a wooden cow, and he built the Labyrinth, to which the Athenians sent seven boys and as many girls every year to serve as food for the Minotaur.

8. Epitome 5. 2 (p. 154)

Hippolyte was the mother of Hippolytos; she is also called Glauce and Melanippe. When Phaedra's marriage was being celebrated, Hippolyte arrived under arms with her fellow Amazons and said that she would kill those who were sharing the hospitality of Theseus. So a battle took place, and she was killed, whether accidentally by her ally Penthesileia, or by Theseus, or because the companions of Theseus, seeing the onset of the Amazons, closed the door with all speed catching her inside, and killed her.

Comments

1. A further explanation of the *kibisis* or wallet referred to in the sentence preceding the interpolation. The verse quotation, from Hes. *Shield* 223–4, is incomplete and has been corrected by two additions from the surviving text of the poem. There is no reference to the *kibisis* in the surviving works and fragments of Pindar. The *Shield* goes on to say that the *kibisis* was wondrous to behold and was made of silver with golden tassels; it would need to be strong to carry the Gorgon's head and prevent it from exercising its powers of petrifaction. The etymology for *kibisis*, a weak effort even by the usual standards, seems to appeal to the *kei* and *sthe* sounds in *keisthai ekei estheta*, 'clothes placed there'.

2. It is said that Heracles and later the Dioscuri were the first non-citizens to be initiated into the Eleusinian Mysteries (Xenophon *Hellenica* 6. 3. 6); each had to be adopted beforehand by a local citizen, Heracles by Pylios, and the Dioscuri by Aphidnas (Plut. *Thes.* 33).

3. Although it is present in the Epitome also, this sentence interrupts the narrative. The thought is a commonplace; compare in particular Thucydides 1. 4.

Appendix

4. This passage contains two verse citations (or possibly three, depending on whether the isolated line at the end forms part of the second), apparently of different origin, for different names are given for the first dogs to attack Actaion's body. In saying that the attack was instigated by Zeus the second passage follows the tradition reported for Acousilaos in 3. 4. 4 that Zeus was angry with Actaion for courting Semele. It is now known that this was the account offered in the Hesiodic *Catalogue* (fr. 217a in Hesiod OCT, 1983 edn.), and some have argued that the second passage at least comes from the *Catalogue* (but it is not included by Merkelbach and West). The more familiar story that Actaion died because he saw Artemis naked was of later origin; see p. 102 and note. The remedy for human sorrows in the final line is presumably wine, as bestowed by Dionysos, Semele's son by Zeus. The verses are cited for the information that they offer on the names of Actaion's dogs, a matter of some interest to later authors, as witnessed by the catalogues in Collectanea Alexandrina 71–2, Ov. *Met.* 3. 155 ff., and Hyg. *Fab.* 181. (The passage is poorly preserved; Wagner's text, which is somewhat different from that of Frazer, has been followed in the translation. In the second citation, Actaion's name appears in an alternative and presumably early form as Actaios.)

5. A citation from the *Melampodeia*, an early epic devoted primarily to the seer Melampous and his family. The ancients ascribed the poem to Hesiod (other testimonies relating to the present passage can be found under Hes. fr. 275). This is Teiresias' judgement on the relative pleasure that men and women derive from love-making (see p. 110). It should be noted that Teiresias' verdict in these lines from the *Melampodeia* is not the same as that ascribed to him in Apollodorus' text; for here he says that a man enjoys one part and a woman *ten* (on the same scale of ten), while in the text he is reported to have said that a man enjoys one part and a woman *nine* (as if there were ten available 'points' to be divided between them). The nine-to-one division can also be found in a collection of Wonders by Phlegon (cited under Hes. fr. 275), an author of the second century AD, whose account of the episode is certainly not derived from Apollodorus. (As it happens, the manuscripts give Apollodorus' ratio as nine to ten rather than nine to one; but this is improbable in itself, and it is generally accepted that it can be corrected on the evidence of Tzetz. sc. Lycophr. 638 and the passage from Phlegon.)

6. The fact that this passage is introduced in the first person, which is unparalleled in the *Library*, confirms that it is a later gloss. It contains a standard list, recorded in four other sources (Philodemus *On Piety* 45b, Gomperz 1865: Sextus Empiricus *Adv. Math.* 1. 260–2; sc. Eur. *Alc.* 1; sc. Pind. *Pyth.* 3, 96); and because it was cited by Philodemus, who wrote in the first century BC, we can be sure that the author of the *Library* was not responsible for its compilation. The first two names are of Argive leaders who fell in the First Theban War (for Capaneus, see p. 110; the present Lycourgos would be the son of Pronax, and nephew of Adrastos, mentioned on p. 47, who is said to have fought with Amphiaraos during the war, Paus. 3. 18. 12, although he is not included in any surviving list of the seven champions). For the death of Hippolytos, see p. 142; this becomes the prime example in the literature on the mythology of the constellations (to explain how Asclepios came to die and be transferred to the sky as the constellation Ophiouchos or the Serpent-Holder, *Catast.* 6, cf. Hyg. *Astr.* 2. 14). The most likely occasion for the death and revival of Tyndareus was Heracles' campaign against Hippocoon, pp. 87 f. Hymenaios was a god of marriage, specially associated with the wedding procession and hymns. For this account of the revival of Glaucos, cf. Hyg. *Astr.* 2. 14; Apollodorus offers a conflicting account on pp. 99 f.

7. This merely repeats matter from 3. 1. 4 and shortly before in the same paragraph.

8. According to Epitome 5. 1, Penthesileia, the Amazon, came to Troy to be purified after accidentally killing Hippolyte. The present paragraph (5. 2, found only in the Vatican epitome) offers an explanation of who this Hippolyte was, and how Penthesileia came to kill her. This, we are told, was the Hippolyte abducted by Theseus, and Penthesileia killed her—or may have killed her—when the Amazons invaded Attica after Theseus had put Hippolyte aside in favour of Phaedra (see p. 141). But this attempt to explain an event that took place in the final year of the Trojan War by an incident at Theseus' wedding involves a gross anachronism (for it was universally agreed from Homer onwards that Menestheus was king of the Athenians during the Trojan War and that Theseus must have died some time before it began). So can this paragraph be accepted as a reliable report on Apollodorus' text? Even a brief comparison with 1. 17 (in the Sabbaitic epitome only), which is largely the same, will suggest that it cannot. It seems, rather, that the Vatican epitomist wrongly assumed that the present Hippolyte could be identified with the Amazon of that name associated with Theseus, and reworked material from earlier in the *Library* to put over the point; and crucially, the phrase stating that Theseus' Hippolyte may have been killed 'accidentally by her ally Penthesileia' is almost certainly the epitomist's own contribution. For this is not stated as one of the alternatives in 1. 17, and there is a marked awkwardness in the way in which the text (as summarized above) has been rearranged to allow for its insertion.

The alternative names for Hippolyte in 5. 2 do not correspond with those in the Sabbaitic epitome at 1. 16 (as translated in the main text). The corresponding passage in the Vatican epitome mentions the names Glauce and Melanippe (though not, as it happens, Hippolyte).

Although it is not explicitly attested in Proclus' summary or elsewhere, it can be reasonably assumed that in reporting that the accidental killing accounted for Penthesileia's presence at Troy (5. 1), Apollodorus was following the *Aethiopis* in the epic cycle. It is surely probable that the incident would have taken place in her native land within Asia Minor to the east of Troy, as indicated in the surviving accounts in Diodorus 2. 46. 5 and Quintus of Smyrna 1. 21 ff. Diodorus is vague, merely stating that she killed her (unnamed) sister and had to leave her native land, but according to Quintus, she killed Hippolyte when throwing her spear at a stag (which may well be the early tradition).

EXPLANATORY NOTES

References: these are included either to suggest passages for comparison and further reading in ancient works which are readily accessible in translation, or to state the source of specific information given within the note. In the latter case, the references are selective, and refer if necessary to untranslated works.

The following *abbreviations* are used:

Aesch.   Aeschylus (tragic poet, 525/4–456 BC).

[Aesch.] *PV*   *Prometheus Enchained*, a play transmitted under Aeschylus' name but of uncertain authorship.

AL   Antoninus Liberalis, *Metamorphoses* (compendium of transformation myths, *circa* second century AD; for translation see Select Bibliography).

Ap.   Apollodorus, the author of the *Library*.

AR   Apollonius of Rhodes, *Argonautica* (epic, third century BC).

Bacch.   Bacchylides (lyric poet, flourished fifth century BC; the numbering follows Snell's Teubner edition).

Catast.   Pseudo-Eratosthenes, *Catasterisms* (compendium of constellation myths; in *Mythographi Graeci*, Leipsig, vol. 3).

DS   Diodorus of Sicily, *Library* (a world history, first century BC, translated in the Loeb series).

Eur.   Euripides (tragic poet, fifth century BC).

fr.   fragment.

Hdt.   Herodotus, *History* (fifth century BC).

Hes.   Hesiod. (For translations of the Hesiodic works, and of some of the testimonies and fragments, see the Hesiod volume in the Loeb series; the references for the fragments are to the standard edition by Merkelbach and West, Oxford, 1967.)

Hes. *Cat.*   *Catalogue of Women* (a sixth-century genealogical epic, not by the author of the *Theogony*; see Introduction and Select Bibliography).

Hes. *WD*   Hesiod, *Works and Days*.

HH   *Homeric Hymns* (post-Homeric, of varying date up to sixth century BC or later, translated in *Hesiod and the Homeric Hymns*, Loeb series).

Hyg.	Hyginus, *Fabulae* (mythological compendium; for translation see Select Bibliography).
Hyg. *PA*	Hyginus, *Poetic Astronomy* (Book II of the *Astronomy*; see Select Bibliography).
Il.	Homer's *Iliad*.
Od.	Homer's *Odyssey*.
Ov. *Met.*	Ovid's *Metamorphoses*.
P.	Pausanias, *Description of Greece* (second century AD, translated in the Loeb series and Penguin).
Parthen.	Parthenius of Nicaea, *Love Stories* (first century BC; in *Mythographi Graeci*, Leipsig, vol. 2).
Pind.	Pindar (lyric poet, 518–438 BC). *Isth.*: *Isthmian Odes*; *Nem.*: *Nemean Odes*; *Ol.*: *Olympian Odes*; *Pyth.*: *Pythian Odes*.
Plut. *Thes.*	Plutarch (first–second century AD), *Life of Theseus*.
Procl.	Proclus (of uncertain date, author of summaries of the early epics in the Trojan cycle; translated in *Hesiod and the Homeric Hymns*, Loeb series).
QS	Quintus of Smyrna, *Posthomerica* (epic poem on the fall of Troy, fourth century AD; translated in the Loeb series).
sc.	scholion. (The scholia were marginal notes by ancient and medieval scholars, which often preserve material from lost mythographical works. French translations of some of the scholia relevant to the text of the *Library* can be found in the notes to Carrière's edition; see Select Bibliography.) NB. In references to scholia conventional abbreviations have been used.
Theog.	Hesiod's *Theogony*.
Thuc.	Thucydides, *History of the Peloponnesian War* (fifth century BC).
Tzetz.	Johannes Tzetzes (Byzantine scholar, twelfth-century AD).
VM	The Vatican Mythographers (ed. G. H. Bode, *Scriptores Rerum Mythicarum Latini Tres*, Celle, 1834; late Latin compendia).

Dates: all are BC unless otherwise indicated.

Cross-references: these are selective, and the Index should also be consulted.

Textual matters: notes on these, and on points of language, have been kept to a bare minimum, except with regard to dubious passages and interpolations (marked by square brackets in the text) and to etymologies, which depend on wordplay in the original Greek (indicated by italics in the text).

Homer and Hesiod: it is convenient to refer to 'Homer', but this implies no judgement as to whether the *Iliad* and the *Odyssey* were composed by the same author, or on the extent to which each poem can be regarded as the work of a single poet. There is disagreement on whether the Hesiodic *Theogony* and *Works and Days* were written by the same author; and other works attributed to Hesiod by the ancients, notably the *Catalogue of Women* and the *Shield*, were certainly written at a later period.

Modern authors: all references are to editors or translators of the *Library* (see Select Bibliography).

Pherecydes, Acousilaos, and Hellanicos: for these early mythographer-historians, who are important sources for Apollodorus, see the Introduction.

27 *Ouranos . . . Ge*: respectively the Sky and the Earth (who was also referred to as Gaia, the form preferred by Hesiod). For the early history of the universe, cf. *Theog.* 116 ff., but the present account sometimes diverges significantly (perhaps following a theogony from the epic cycle, summarized by Proclus in Photius 319A). In *Theog.*, Chaos—representing a yawning gap rather than disorder—comes into being first, followed by Gaia, Tartaros, and Eros (116 ff.), and Gaia gives birth to Ouranos from herself (126 f.).

the Cyclopes: cf. *Theog.* 139 ff.; named the 'Round-Eyed' because of their single round eye. Their individual names were suggested by their prime function, as the beings who armed Zeus with his thunder (see p. 28): *(a)sterope* means lightning, *bronte*, thunder, and *arges* refers to the brightness associated with the thunderbolt. For other kinds of Cyclops, see p. 63 and note and pp. 164 f.

in Hades: here used in a loose sense to refer to the Underworld as a whole. In the early tradition at least, a clear distinction was drawn between Hades (where the souls of dead mortals dwell) and Tartaros, a dungeon for gods and monsters that lay far beneath it (cf. *Theog.* 720–819, *Il.* 8. 13 ff.).

who had been thrown into Tartaros: only the Cyclopes and Hundred-Handers; Hesiod's account, in which Ouranos also hides away their Titan children (*Theog.* 154 ff.), diverges significantly.

adamantine: made of adamant, a mythical metal of extreme hardness.

from the drops of blood that flowed out: from those that fell on Ge, the Earth, causing her to conceive the Furies, and the Giants whom

179

she will bring to birth later (p. 34); cf. *Theog.* 183 ff. (In Ap.'s theogony the severed genitals play no part in the birth of Aphrodite, see p. 29 and note.)

28 *Mount Dicte*: in most sources Mount Ida, in *Theog.* 484, Aigaion; Dicte only in Hellenistic and later sources, e.g. AR 1. 509. Although Dicte was associated with the cult of Zeus, there was no cave there.

Curetes: Cretan semi-divinities associated with fertility; estimates of their number vary from two to ten.

Amaltheia: either a nymph with a she-goat (see p. 89 and note) or the goat itself, as here (cf. Callim. *Hymn* 1. 47 f.).

Metis: personifies practical or cunning intelligence. In *Theog.* 494 ff., where the stratagem is not explained, the advice is offered by Gaia.

a helmet: this leather helmet or cap makes its wearer invisible. It will be used by Perseus, see pp. 65 f. and note. In *Theog.* 501 ff. the Cyclopes arm Zeus alone, in gratitude for their release.

they shared power: following *Il.* 15. 187 ff.

Pluto over the halls of Hades: Pluto, 'the Wealthy One', was a ritual title for Hades, god of the Underworld; his name is also applied to his realm (although in classical Greek a genitive form was used in such cases, to indicate that the 'halls of' Hades were being referred to rather than the god himself).

Oceanides: the daughters of Oceanos and Tethys, who were nymphs of springs and groves. Hes. names forty-one of the 'eldest' daughters (*Theog.* 346 ff.), but remarks that there were three thousand (364); Ap. only gives the names of those who will be mentioned in the following genealogies. For Hesiod, Amphitrite was a Nereid (243). The sons of Oceanos and Tethys were the rivers of the earth (337 ff.). *Theog.* should be consulted for further details on all these divine genealogies (although Ap. sometimes chooses variants from other sources).

29 *Nice, Cratos, Zelos, and Bia*: abstractions signifying Victory, Power, Emulation, and Force (all needed by Zeus for his victory against the Titans). See *Theog.* 383 ff.

oaths: specifically the oaths of the gods.

Pontos: a personification of the Sea. Ap. offers no genealogy; in *Theog.* 132 ff. he is borne by Gaia without prior intercourse. An ancestor of marine beings, and also of monstrous beings not easily associable with Zeus' immediate family, see *Theog.* 233–336.

Nereids: beautiful sea nymphs, usually said to be fifty in number, who lived with their father in a cave at the bottom of the sea (*Il.* 18. 37 ff., *Theog.* 240 ff.). Most of their names were suggested by aspects of the sea.

Hebe, Eileithuia, and Ares: respectively, the personification of youth (who performed household duties for the gods, notably as cup-bearer, and later married Heracles, p. 91), the goddess of child-birth, and the god of war. For the genealogies in 3. 1 to 4. 6, cf. *Theog.* 886–933.

Eirene, Eunomia, and Dice: the Horai, Seasons, were associated with the seasons of growth in particular; these Hesiodic names (*Theog.* 901 f.)—Peace, Good Order, and Justice—point to the social conditions favouring successful agriculture.

by Dione he had Aphrodite: as in *Il.* 5. 370 f.; but in *Theog.* 188 ff. Aphrodite grows from the sea-foam (*aphros*) that surrounds the severed genitals of Ouranos when they are cast into the sea. Described above as a Titanid (but in *Theog.* 353, a daughter of Oceanos and Tethys), Dione was honoured at Dodona as the consort of Zeus, but otherwise she was of little importance in either cult or myth.

30 *by Styx, Persephone*: the river encircling Hades is a suitable mother for a goddess closely associated with the Underworld; but Persephone is usually regarded as Zeus' daughter by Demeter, as in *Theog.* 912 f. and *HH to Demeter* 2–3 (and below on p. 33).

Linos: see p. 71, a musician like his brother Orpheus.

persuaded Pluto: he is said to have enchanted Persephone and/or Pluto with his singing (DS 4. 25. 4, Conon 45).

Maenads: women possessed by Bacchic frenzy (see pp. 102 f.); in most accounts they are angered by the scorn that Orpheus showed for other women after he had lost Eurydice, e.g. Ov. *Met.* 11. 1 ff.

Cleio . . . Adonis: when Cleio mocked Aphrodite for falling in love with a mortal, Aphrodite caused her to become subject to a similar passion. Love for a mortal was acceptable for gods, but considered demeaning for goddesses (see Calypso's observations in *Od.* 5. 118 ff.).

the first man to love other males: Laios, p. 104, and Minos, p. 97, are other contenders for this title.

But Hyacinthos . . . a discus: it was sometimes said that the West (or North) Wind also sought his favour, and when he favoured Apollo, blew the discus at Apollo's head (Lucian *Dialogues of the*

Gods 14; see also P. 3. 19. 5, Ov. *Met.* 10. 162 ff.). Traditions vary on his birth, see also p. 119.

30 *challenged the Muses*: cf. *Il.* 2. 594 ff.

Rhesos . . . at Troy: see *Il.* 10. 435 ff. and [Eur.] *Rhesos*.

Corybantes: semi-divine beings who attended deities with orgiastic rites, associated primarily with the Phrygian goddess Cybele, but also with Rhea and Dionysos.

31 *Hera . . . by Zeus*: Hera calls him a son of Zeus in *Il.* 14. 338 f.; but in Hesiod's account, *Theog.* 924 ff., Hera is so angered when Zeus gives birth to Athene from his head that she decides to have a child of her own without prior intercourse with her spouse, and gives birth to Hephaistos.

Zeus threw him down . . . to his rescue: in *Il.* 1. 590 ff., Hephaistos is said to have been thrown from heaven by Zeus for coming to the aid of Hera (for her suspension, see *Il.* 5. 18 ff.), but in *Il.* 18. 394 ff., by Hera, because she was ashamed of his lameness; in the latter account he was rescued by Thetis and Eurynome, daughter of Oceanos, and taken to the cave of the Nereids beneath the sea.

Ge: inserted by Heyne; without this addition, the text would indicate that Metis herself gave the warning (placing her own safety at grave risk). Ge is the prime oracle in early mythical history. In *Theog.* 886 ff., Zeus takes this action on the advice of Ge and Ouranos.

near the River Triton: see p. 123 and note.

a city . . . called Delos: i.e. the island of Delos; its previous name is also given as Ortygia, after *ortyx*, a quail (e.g. Hyg. 140). In Pind. *Paean* 5. 42 (cf. Callimachus *Hymn* 4. 36–8), the holy island on which her sister Leto will give birth to Artemis and Apollo is formed from Asteria's metamorphosed body.

Themis: a personification of law and the right; on the presiding figures at Delphi before Apollo, see also Aesch. *Eumenides* 1 ff. and P. 10. 5. 3.

chasm: said to be the source of exhalations which inspired the Delphic priestesses to prophecy, although there is no sign of such a chasm on the modern site.

32 *Pytho*: Delphi.

Tityos suffers punishment: cf. *Od.* 11. 576 ff. On his death, cf. Pind. *Pyth.* 4. 90 ff.

disfigured her face: according to Hyg. 165, Hera and Aphrodite made fun of her when she played her flute at a banquet of the gods because it puffed her cheeks out, which she found to be true when she viewed herself in a spring on Mount Ida.

to do the same: as a wind instrument, his flute must be blown from the right end. On Marsyas, a Phrygian, see also Hdt. 7. 26.

blinded him: according to the fuller story in Parthen. 20 and *Catast.* 32, Orion cleared the island of wild beasts, but when Oinopion was reluctant to accept such a being as his son-in-law, he became impatient and raped Merope while he was drunk. This would explain Oinopion's extreme behaviour.

of Hephaistos: added by Heyne (but Ap. may have assumed that the reader would understand that without explicit statement). It lay on Lemnos; Orion could find his way there by following the sound. In *Catast.* 32 Hephaistos takes pity on him and offers him one of his helpers, Cedalion, as a guide.

with Ares: Aphrodite's lover, hence her anger.

shot by Artemis: in *Od.* 5. 121 ff. Artemis killed him because she and the other gods were angry that Dawn had fallen in love with a mortal. The later tradition is complex, but it was commonly said that he tried to rape Artemis herself, and that Artemis either shot him (Hyg. *PA* 34, referring to Callimachus) or sent a scorpion against him (Aratus 635 ff. with sc. to 636, thus explaining the origin of the two constellations); or Ge sent the scorpion because he boasted that he would kill all the beasts on earth (*Catast.* 32).

Opis: Opis (or Upis), and Arge, another representative of this legendary northern race, came to Delos after the birth of Artemis and Apollo bringing a thank-offering, which had been vowed to Eileithuia, the goddess of childbirth, in return for an easy labour for Leto, see Hdt. 4. 35.

33 *Rhode*: a personification of the island of Rhodes, where there was a notable cult of the Sun; also as Rhodos (again a feminine form). See Pind. *Ol.* 7. 54 ff.

abducted her: see Ap.'s main source, the *Homeric Hymn to Demeter*, for further details on all the following. There (16 ff.) she is abducted from the Nysian plain (of uncertain location; but in later writers, from Sicily, a land famed for its fertility). The abduction is in accordance with the plans of Zeus, but he plays no active part in it (ibid. 9; 30; and 77 ff.).

bearing torches: these played a significant role in the ritual associated with the Eleusinian Mysteries, and were emblematic of Demeter and her rites (ibid. 48).

33 *Hermion*: not in the *Hymn*, but appropriate because there was said to be a chasm there that communicated with the Underworld (P. 2. 35. 7).

Thesmophoria: an autumn festival celebrated by women in honour of Demeter to ensure fertility of the crops. The jokes were of an obscene nature.

Praxithea: presumably Demophon's nurse. In the *Hymn* (242 ff.) Metaneira keeps watch, and the child is not killed; Demeter merely places him on the ground and renounces her plan to make him immortal.

revealed her identity: and promised to teach the Eleusinians her rites (*HH Dem.* 273–4), which ensured the initiates a better lot in the afterlife.

she gave him wheat: knowledge of agriculture was revealed by Demeter at Eleusis and spread by Triptolemos throughout the inhabited world; a favourite theme in Athenian propaganda.

Kore: 'the Maiden', a cultic title for Persephone as worshipped in conjunction with her mother.

a pomegranate seed to eat: a visitor who takes food in the other world is obliged to stay there. Pomegranates were associated with blood and death.

Ascalaphos . . . bore witness against her: not in the *Hymn*, where Persephone herself tells Demeter that she has eaten in Hades (411 ff.) and the consequences follow necessarily from the action. On Ascalaphos see further p. 84 and note.

34 *a third of every year*: cf. *HH Dem.* 398 ff. The agricultural significance is evident: she departs in autumn and returns in spring. In later sources the year is commonly divided into equal parts (e.g. Hyg. 146, Ov. *Met.* 5. 564 ff.).

conceived by Ouranos: from the blood that dripped from his severed genitals, see p. 27 and note. Homer and Hesiod never refer to a battle between the gods and Giants; the earliest surviving references are in connection with Heracles' involvement in it (Pind. *Nem.* 1. 67 ff., ps.-Hes. *Shield* 28, cf. *Theog.* 954, part of a later addition to Hesiod's text). The battle appears in vase-paintings by the end of the seventh century, and it may have been covered in an early epic, the *Titanomachy*.

thyrsos: a staff with a fir-cone ornament at the head, carried by Dionysos and others who engaged in his rites.

35 *Nisyron*: this explains the origin of Nisyros, a small island south of Cos; it was part of Cos until Poseidon broke it off with his trident (cf. Strabo 10. 5. 16).

Gration: probably corrupt, but the proposed corrections are uncertain; perhaps Aigaion.

Typhon: Hesiod offers a rather different account of his struggle with Zeus, in *Theog.* 820 ff.

a hundred dragons' heads: following *Theog.* 824 ff., but in a confused manner, for there 'a hundred heads of a serpent' grow from his shoulders in place of a human head. The serpents' coils beneath his thighs are derived from the standard depiction of him in the visual arts.

took flight to Egypt: the following story, first attested for Pindar (fr. 81 Bowra), explains why the Egyptians had gods in animal form. In the earliest full account (AL 28, following Nicander) Hermes, for example, turns into an ibis, and Artemis into a cat, identifying them with Thoth and Bast respectively.

36 *Aigipan*: 'Goat-Pan'; some saw him as Pan himself in his quality as a goat, others as a separate figure.

ephemeral fruits: nothing further is known of them, but their effect is clearly the opposite of what the Fates suggested.

blood: *haima* in Greek, hence the name of Mount Haimos.

eruptions of fire: cf. Pind. *Pyth.* 1. 15 ff., [Aesch.] *PV* 363 ff., and later, Ov. *Met.* 5. 352 ff.; in all these sources Typhon himself is responsible for the eruptions.

fashioned men: not attested before the fourth century; in earlier sources, Prometheus is a benefactor of the human race, but not its creator (Hes. *Theog.* 510 ff. and *WD* 48 ff., cf. [Aesch.] *PV*). It was commonly assumed at an early period that the first men sprang directly from the earth, and different areas would have their own 'first man', e.g. Phoroneus in Argos, see p. 58 and note.

fennel: the narthex or giant fennel (a relative of the British cow-parsley), whose stalks contain a slow-burning white pith; cf. Hes. *Theog.* 565 ff., *WD* 50 ff.

as we will show: see p. 83.

37 *Pandora . . . the first woman*: described by Hesiod as a 'beautiful evil' (*Theog.* 585), she was moulded by Hephaistos on the orders of Zeus, as the price men would have to pay for having gained possession of fire (*Theog.* 569 ff. and *WD* 60 ff.). Epimetheus

Explanatory Notes

('Afterthought'), the brother of Prometheus, was foolish enough to accept her (*WD* 83 ff., *Theog.* 511 ff.).

37 *the race of bronze*: see Hes. *WD* 143 ff., where the members of this violent primordial race are responsible for their own destruction; there is no mention of the flood there (or in *Theog.*). This is the best mythographical account; for an imaginative portrayal, see Ov. *Met.* 1. 260 ff. For another explanation of its cause, see p. 115.

laoi . . . a stone: the same etymology is implied in Pind. *Ol.* 9. 44–6; the two words were of separate origin. The story originally accounted for the origin of the local people only (the Locrian Leleges, Hes. *Cat.* fr. 234; the stone-throwing took place at Opous in east Locris, Pind. *Ol.* 9. 43 ff.; but in Latin sources from Ovid onwards it is often suggested that Deucalion and Pyrrha were the only human beings to survive a universal flood). Here 'metaphor' means simply a transference of meaning (as often in Greek usage).

the Graicoi he named Hellenes: here the Hellenes are a Greek people who lived in southern Thessaly, as in the *Iliad* (2. 683, cf. 9. 395, although their name was later applied to the Greek race as a whole), and the Graicoi, a tribe who lived to the west of them in Epirus. For the present story, cf. Aristotle *Meteorology* 352a32 ff. The Graicoi remained prominent in the west, and the Romans used their name as a general term for the Hellenes.

opposite the Peloponnese: i.e. north of the Corinthian Gulf; specifically the small region known as Doris, north-west of Mount Parnassos (Strabo 8. 7. 1), which the Peloponnesian Dorians regarded as their original home. In myth, this was the area ruled by Doros' son, Aigimios (see p. 90 and note); the movement of the Dorians to the Peloponnese occurs very late in mythological history, see pp. 92 f.

38 *halcyon*: a fabulous bird that nests by, or on, the sea during the halcyon days of winter.

sea-swallow: or tern, for the *ceux*, a poetical bird of uncertain identity. Ap.'s version of this story is probably derived from Hes. *Cat.* (cf. frs. 15 and 16); in another version, Ceux is killed in a shipwreck and Alcyone throws herself into the sea for love of him, arousing the pity of the gods, who transform them into halcyons (Ov. *Met.* 11. 410 ff., Hyg. 65).

known as the Aloads: 'sons of Aloeus' (for Aloeus was their putative father as the husband of Iphimedeia). For their story, cf. *Od.* 11. 305 ff.

a cubit . . . a fathom: the English equivalents for the ancient measurements representing the lengths of a man's forearm and of his outstretched arms (*fæthm* in Old English). These measured about eighteen inches and six feet respectively.

Ossa . . . Olympos . . . Pelion: tall mountains in the coastal region of Thessaly. This story gave rise to the proverbial phrase, 'piling Pelion on Ossa'.

imprisoned Ares: in a bronze jar, for thirteen months, and he would have died if the Aloads' stepmother had not informed Hermes (*Il.* 5. 385 ff.).

met their death on Naxos: according to *Od.* 11. 318 they were killed by Apollo, for trying to climb to heaven (cf. Hyg. 28); here their failure in that enterprise is left unexplained, and Artemis causes their death on another occasion because of their designs on herself. It is said elsewhere that they set out to rape Artemis (Hyg. 28, cf. sc. Pind. *Pyth.* 4. 156) and that Apollo (Hyg.) or Artemis (sc. *Il.* 5. 385) sent a deer between them. Pindar knew a version of this story (*Pyth.* 4. 88 f., cf. P. 9. 22. 5).

39 *killed Apis, son of Phoroneus*: according to P. 5. 1. 8, this Apis was an Arcadian and a son of Jason (not the famous one); and Aitolos drove over him accidentally at the funeral games for Azan, son of Arcas, an Arcadian king. The son of Phoroneus, an Argive, died in another way, see p. 58.

the land of the Curetes: these Curetes, the aboriginal inhabitants of Aetolia (and Acarnania), in the south-western part of mainland Greece to the north of the Corinthian Gulf, should not be confused with the Cretan demigods on p. 28; on the Curetes in general, see Strabo 10. 3.

Evenos had a daughter . . . chasing after him: Homer mentions that Idas drew his bow against Apollo for the sake of a girl (*Il.* 9. 559 f.). According to the scholion on ibid. 557, Evenos (like Oinomaos, p. 144) challenged his daughter's suitors to a chariot race; if they won, they would gain her hand, but when they were overtaken by Evenos, he nailed their heads to the walls of his house. It is possible that the present passage refers to such a race rather than a simple pursuit after an abduction. See also Bacch. 20.

Messene: the land of Messenia, in the south-western Peloponnese, lying to the west of Laconia (rather than the city of Messene, which was of late foundation). Idas' father Aphareus was a Messenian king, see p. 119 and note.

40 *Sterope . . . to Acheloos*: probably following Hes. *Cat.*; later authors tended to give the Sirens a Muse as a mother (cf. p. 167, and AR 4. 895 f.), befitting their qualities as singers.

the first to receive a vine plant from Dionysos: a story in Hyg. 129 would explain this. When Dionysos fell in love with Althaia, Oineus tactfully absented himself by pretending that he had some rites to perform; and Dionysos slept with his wife, fathering Deianeira (a tradition mentioned by Ap. below), and afterwards presented the vine to Oineus, naming its product *oinos*, wine, after him.

for jumping over the ditch: an allusion to a lost story. (Some point to the death of Remus in Livy 1. 7. 2, but the comparison is of doubtful relevance.)

placed it in a chest: Bacchylides in the fifth century (5. 140 ff.) is the earliest surviving source for this story.

To hunt this boar: on Meleager and the boar see also *Il.* 9. 529 ff. (without any mention of Atalante), Bacch. 5. 96 ff. (the earliest surviving source for the story of the log, 136 ff.), DS 4. 34, and Ov. *Met.* 8. 270 ff. This was the first of the great adventures which brought together major heroes from all parts of Greece; for other catalogues of the participants see Ov. *Met.* 8. 299 ff. and Hyg. 173.

41 *with a woman*: on Atalante see also p. 116 and note.

the sons of Thestios: see p. 39 for their names. Thestios, the brother of Meleager's mother Aithra, was king of Pleuron in Aetolia.

said by some: this alternative account is largely based on *Il.* 9. 547 ff. (although Homer does not say that Meleager was killed).

transformed into birds: a later element in the story, often thought to be of Hellenistic origin (though Sophocles may have known of the transformation, see Pliny *Nat. Hist.* 37. 40). According to Nicander (AL 2), they were transformed by Artemis with a touch of her wand, to become guinea fowl (*meleagrides*), and transferred to the island of Leros; Deianeira (who had to survive to become Heracles' wife) and her sister Gorge were saved by the intervention of Dionysos.

42 *sent her . . . to Oineus*: cf. DS 4. 35. 1 f.

the sons of Melas: Melas was another brother of Oineus, p. 39.

killed his own brother: according to Pherecydes (sc. *Il.* 14. 120) Tydeus attacked the sons of Agrios (another brother of Oineus) for plotting against Oineus, and accidentally killed his brother (or his uncle Melas, in sc. *Il.* 14. 114), who happened to be present. For his subsequent history, see pp. 109–11.

Diomedes: the son of Tydeus remained in Argos, became one of the Epigoni, p. 112, and succeeded to the throne of his father-in-law Adrastos, to become ruler of Argos and Tiryns, and leader of the Argives at Troy, p. 148.

Thersites: familiar from the *Iliad*, 2. 212 ff. (but in Homer he is not of noble birth); and see p. 154.

43 *parch the wheat-grain*: roast it over a fire, killing the seed.

together with . . . Helle: the eponym of the Hellespont ('the Sea of Helle', see below; cf. Aesch. *Persians* 68); late sources (e.g. P. 9. 34. 4) explain that she was due to be sacrificed with Phrixos.

the wrath of Hera: because Athamas and Ino (who was also driven mad) had taken in the young Dionysos, her husband's child by another woman, see p. 101. Pausanias (1. 44. 11) cites an alternative tradition that the deaths resulted from Athamas' anger when he discovered how Ino had deceived him.

44 *Athamantia*: a plain in southern Thessaly (cf. AR 2. 514).

Ephyra, now known as Corinth: the exact location of Ephyra—the home of Sisyphos that lay 'in a corner of horse-rearing Argos', *Il.* 6. 152 f.—is unknown, but its identification with Corinth (which is referred to separately in the *Iliad* as one of the towns ruled by Agamemnon, 2. 570) is altogether dubious. It seems that when the Corinthians (notably the early epic poet Eumelos) found themselves short of significant local myth, they annexed the material from Ephyra, which had declined into obscurity.

who killed the . . . Chimaera: see p. 64; the full story is deferred because he was exiled to Argos.

punishment in Hades: Homer describes it, *Od.* 11. 593 ff., but does not explain the reason. For the present explanation, cf. P. 2. 5. 1; for the abduction of Aegina, see p. 126.

Dawn . . . carried him off: for Cephalos and Procris, see p. 134; the Cephalos associated with Dawn is described below as a son of Hermes, see p. 131 and note.

but of Cynortas: to give the father of Tyndareus (an important figure in the Laconian genealogies) a purely Laconian descent, see p. 119, and p. 120 and note.

Seriphos: a rocky island in the south-eastern Aegean, later of proverbial insignificance, but important in myth for the involvement of these sons of Magnes with Perseus and Danae, see p. 65.

45 *founded a city*: called Salmone (Strabo 7. 3. 31); Elis was in the north-west Peloponnese. On Salmoneus, see also Virgil *Aen.* 6. 585 ff.

45 *Poseidon had intercourse with her*: see *Od.* 11. 235 ff.

Pelias: so called because he had been left with a livid or black-and-blue mark (*pelion ti*), resembling a bruise (or a birthmark).

Sidero: see DS 4. 68. 2, she married Salmoneus after the death of Tyro's mother, Alcidice, and treated Tyro harshly 'as a stepmother would'; it seems that no further explanation is required. Her name suggests that she had an *iron* nature.

in Messene, he founded Pylos: Nestor's 'sandy Pylos' (*Il.* 9. 295 etc.) lay in the south-western Peloponnese, but it has been disputed since ancient times whether it should be identified with the Messenian Pylos near Sphacteria (as assumed here) or with the Pylos that lay further north in the west-central province of Triphylia. The archaeological evidence suggests that the former was the city behind the legend (although there are elements in Homer's accounts, notably in *Il.* 11. 711 ff., which favour the more northerly location). Strabo argued for the Triphylian location (8. 3. 7).

46 *he was killed by Heracles*: for his attack on Pylos, see p. 87. The story of Periclymenos' death was told in Hes. *Cat.* (fr. 33b): Athene told him who the bee was, and Heracles killed it with an arrow. In the later tradition Heracles is also said to have shot him as an eagle (Ov. *Met.* 12. 549 ff., Hyg. 10) or swatted him as a fly (sc. AR 1. 156). He was granted his powers of transformation by his grandfather Poseidon (Hes. *Cat.* fr. 33a. 13 ff.).

purified his ears: snakes, as chthonic creatures, are naturally associated with prophecy, and other seers (e.g. Cassandra and Helenos, according to one tradition, Tzetz. Arg. Lyc.) are said to have acquired their prophetic powers in this way.

could understand . . . the birds flying overhead: the interpretation of bird-flights was an important aspect of technical divination, but this takes us into the realm of magic.

Phylacos: for his birth, see p. 44; Phylace lay in south-eastern Thessaly.

Melampous promised his assistance: the basic elements of the following story can be found in Homer, *Od.* 11. 287 ff., without the name of the seer, or, predictably, the talking woodworms; we are simply told that Iphicles released Melampous in return for the oracles that he had delivered for him (ibid. 297 f., cf. P. 4. 36. 3).

47 *gelding lambs . . . took fright*: in Pherecydes' version (sc. *Od.* 11, 287), his father pursued him with his knife because he saw him doing something improper (masturbating presumably) and there is no men-

tion of the gelding; but the original story may have included both elements. This caused Iphicles to become impotent.

scraped off the rust . . . in a drink: because the rust comes from the instrument that inflicted the harm, it will also cure it, following a basic principle of sympathetic magic (compare the cure of Telephos on p. 150).

the women of Argos mad: see p. 63 (where this story is combined with the story of the cure of Proitos' daughters) and note.

48 *Apollo was serving him*: for the circumstances, see pp. 119–20. Apollo performs the following favours in gratitude for the kind treatment that he has received from Admetos (cf. Hyg. 50).

coils of snakes: as creatures of the earth, they are portents of death; hence the favour that Apollo asks of the Fates.

Kore sent her back: out of pity and admiration for her self-sacrifice (cf. Plato *Symposium* 179c). Kore is a name for Persephone (see p. 33 and note).

Heracles fought with Hades for her: as in Eur. *Alcestis* (although the theme goes back to Phrynichos, an early Athenian tragedian); after blundering into Admetos' house at the time of Alcestis' funeral, Heracles rescued her out of gratitude for Admetos' hospitality and remorse for his own tactless behaviour. In the play, he wrestled not with Hades personally, but with Death (Thanatos) when he came up for his prey.

Pelias . . . succeeded Cretheus: Jason's father, Aison, might have been expected to succeed his father Cretheus on the Iolcian throne, so the position of Pelias (the son of Tyro by Poseidon and thus Aison's half-brother) was at least dubious. Ap. is uninformative on the background; in Hes. *Cat.* fr. 40, and Pind. *Pyth.* 4. 102 ff. (where Pelias is definitely a usurper), Jason was reared in the country by the Centaur Cheiron.

49 *the wrath of Hera*: for its cause, see p. 45; Medea will return from Colchis with Jason and cause Pelias' death, p. 57.

the golden fleece: for its origins see p. 43.

Colchis: a land south of the Caucasus at the eastern end of the Black Sea; a remote area for the early Greeks.

the Argo after its builder: it is likely that its name was originally derived from the adjective *argos*, meaning swift (mentioned in DS 4. 41. 3, as an alternative etymology).

Dodona: an ancient oracle of Zeus at Epirus in north-western Greece (known to Homer, *Il.* 16. 233–5). The great oak, whose rustling leaves were supposed to reveal the will of Zeus, was a suitable source for the speaking (and oracular) timber.

50 *they set out to sea*: for further details on all the following, see Ap.'s main source, the *Argonautica* of Apollonius of Rhodes; this is a relatively late epic dating from the third century BC, but it draws extensively on early sources. Significant divergences will be noted.

51 *Polyphemos*: a Lapith from Thessaly, who is said by Homer, *Il.* 1. 264 ff., to have played a heroic role in the war between the Lapiths and the Centaurs (see p. 142): he was married to Heracles' sister Laonome (sc. AR 1. 1241a).

snatched away by nymphs: Hylas was drawn into the spring by a water-nymph (AR 1. 1228 ff.) or nymphs (three in Theocritus *Idyll* 13. 43 ff.), and was never seen again; in AR 1. 1310 ff. the prophetic sea-god Glaucos appears to the Argonauts and tells them that a nymph has made him her husband.

There they abandoned Heracles . . . leader of the Argonauts: the initial narrative follows AR 1. 1207 ff. Views on Heracles' involvement in the expedition vary greatly. Some deny that he ever joined the expedition (e.g. Herodoros, mentioned here, a fifth–fourth-century mythographer, and Ephoros, the fourth-century historian, and doubtless the earliest tradition). According to the sixth-century Hesiodic *Marriage of Ceux* he was left behind accidentally at Aphetai when sent for water (sc. AR 1. 1289); but the Hylas story, probably of later origin (fifth century?), is most favoured by later authors. Only in late novelistic accounts (e.g. by Dionysios 'the leather-armed', second/first century, cited here) does he travel all the way to Colchis and, inevitably, overshadow Jason.

52 *by Boreas . . . their stepmother*: see p. 135 and note.

the Harpies: for their parentage see p. 29, cf. *Theog.* 265 ff. The meaning of their name, 'Snatchers', is reflected in their characteristic action of swooping down and snatching away people (or here, Phineus' food).

failed to catch those they pursued: so here both of them die, because the Harpies fall down exhausted before they can catch them; for the birth of the Boreads, and another account of their death, see p. 134 and notes. Boreas was the North Wind, so it is natural that his sons should be swift-moving and winged.

Ocypode according to Hesiod: not in *Theog.* 267, where the Harpies are called Aello and *Ocypete* (meaning swift flier as against Ocypode, swift of foot), but this may be a reference to Hes. *Cat.* (which contained an account of the pursuit, frs. 150–7).

Strophades: these islands, which lie to the west of the Peloponnese opposite Messenia, mark the point where she 'turned' (*estraphe*). Ap. is wrong to suggest that this name was given to the Echinadian Islands (which were known under that name in historical times, and lie further north, near the entrance to the Corinthian Gulf facing Acarnania); according to AR 2. 297, the islands thus renamed were formerly known as the Plotai or 'Floating Islands'.

in the Argonautica: see 2. 284 ff. Iris (who was the messenger of the gods, but was acting on her own initiative here, presumably as a sister of the Harpies, *Theog.* 266 f.) intervened to say that the Harpies were simply performing their duties as the 'hounds of Zeus' and it was unlawful to destroy them. AR is misreported on the oath, for it is Iris who swore that the Harpies would never approach Phineus again. They departed to their den in Crete.

53 *that Cadmos had sowed at Thebes*: see p. 100; not of course the same teeth, but half of the teeth from the Theban dragon that Athene (or Athene and Ares, sc. Pind. *Isth.* 4. 13, citing Pherecydes) had held back and given to Aietes, cf. AR 3. 1183 f. This is a secondary motif, directly modelled on the Theban story.

a potion: see AR 3. 844 ff.; extracted from the Colchicum, or autumn crocus, which came into existence when the blood from the tormented Prometheus, p. 36, fell to the earth. The drug from its seed, used until modern times for treating rheumatism and gout, is here endowed with magical properties.

54 *he put them under the yoke*: on the bulls and their yoking by Jason, see also Pind. *Pyth.* 4. 224–41.

murdered her brother: Ap. prefers an earlier and more primitive version of this story to that in AR 4. 303 ff. where Apsyrtos is of military age and is sent in pursuit of Jason and Medea by his father, and is treacherously killed by Jason in a temple of Artemis on an island at the mouth of the Danube. Ap.'s version is similar to that in Pherecydes (sc. AR 4. 223 and 226), but there Medea takes the infant child from his bed in Colchis on Jason's instructions, and Jason participates in the killing and dismemberment. In the earlier tradition and AR alike the murder is of central importance as the cause of the Argonauts' diversion to the western Mediterranean.

Tomoi: meaning 'Pieces'; on the western shore of the Black Sea.

55 *past the Ligurian and Celtic peoples*: cf. AR 4. 646 f. In AR (592 ff.) they sail from the Adriatic up the Eridanos (or Po), down the Rhone, and then towards Italy and along its coast. The Ligurians lived in

north-western Italy and the eastern Riviera, and the Celts to the west and north of that; the vagueness of the language here may be deliberate, reflecting the author's awareness that the river voyage is geographically impossible.

55 *Aiaie*: a mythical island, cf. *Od*. 10. 135 ff. Although Homer placed her island in the remote east (in *Od*. 12. 3–4, it is described as the home of Dawn and associated with the rising Sun), the fabulous realms familiar from the *Odyssey* are now located firmly in the west.

to counter their own: as the finest of singers himself, p. 30, Orpheus could reasonably expect to outcharm the Sirens (cf. Hyg. 14); in AR 4. 905 ff. it is largely a matter of volume.

the island of the Phaeacians: see *Od*. 6–8; here identified with Corcyra, now Corfu.

a violent storm: the Argonauts encounter a storm in AR also when they leave Phaeacia, but it drives them to the coast of Africa (4. 1232 ff.). It is surprising that Ap. should omit all mention of the traditions connecting the Argonauts with Libya, for the theme is of early origin. The occasion for their visit varies. In one version, they return from Colchis by an eastward route along the River Phasis to the Ocean and thence the Red Sea, and then carry the *Argo* from there to Libya (sc. AR 4. 259 and 282, cf. Pind. *Pyth*. 4. 25 ff.); in Hdt. 4. 179 ff. they are driven there by a storm on the voyage out, but in DS 4. 56. 6 on their return as in AR.

56 *Anaphe*: its name is traced to the way in which it 'appeared' (from *anaphainein*) before the Argonauts. One of the southernmost Aegean islands, next to Thera (Santorini); but it is north of Crete, and in AR (4. 1717) they came to Anaphe after their encounter with Talos in Crete, on their voyage north from Africa.

make jokes: see AR 4. 1720 ff.; the story explains why the local women directed obscene jokes at the men when sacrifices were made to Apollo on Anaphe.

a man of bronze: to be understood literally, cf. AR 4. 1638 ff.; and it is thus natural that Hephaistos, famed as a creator of automata (see *Il*. 18. 373 ff. and 417 ff.), should have constructed him. That some (e.g. AR 4. 1641 f.) should have associated him with Hesiod's race of bronze (see Hes. *WD* 143 ff.) is understandable, but Hesiod was speaking metaphorically when he named his sequence of races after different metals.

a bull: otherwise unattested, but not unduly surprising in the Cretan context (cf. pp. 97 f.).

a single vein: AR speaks of a vein at his ankle covered by a thin layer of skin (4. 1646 ff.), but there is no mention of the bronze nail which acts as a stopper, an appealingly archaic element preserved here. Talos would be invulnerable if it were not for this vein.

the ichor flowed away: the fluid of life (originally a term for the fluid that takes the place of blood in the gods, *Il.* 5. 339 ff., but later used in a more general sense for animal serum). In AR 4. 1665 ff., Medea invokes the Keres, spirits of death, with songs and prayers, and when Talos tries to hurl boulders to repel them, he grazes his ankle on a rock, causing the ichor to pour out like molten lead. The alternative in which Poias (the father of Philoctetes who lit Heracles' pyre, p. 91) shoots him in the ankle implies the same cause of death.

a competition developed: again explaining a local custom, see AR 4. 1765 ff. (cf. Callimachus fr. 198; Hellenistic scholars, and scholar-poets, were much interested in local material of this kind).

put Aison to death: if Jason is dead, Pelias can safely consolidate his rule by eliminating Jason's father Aison, who has a legitimate claim to the throne as the son of Cretheus.

bull's blood: the Greeks believed that bull's blood was dangerous to drink because its rapid coagulation would cause the drinker to choke; there was a famous tale that Themistocles committed suicide by drinking it (see Plut. *Them.* 31).

57 *So she went to the palace . . . boiled him*: cf. P. 8. 11. 2 f. and Ov. *Met.* 7. 297 ff.; Medea had power enough as a magician to rejuvenate Pelias if she wished, but in his case she failed to put the necessary potions into the cauldron. She is said to have made Jason young again by boiling him (Arg. Eur. *Med.*, reporting Simonides and Pherecydes).

Creon: the son of Lycaithos, and his successor as king of Corinth; not to be confused with Creon, son of Menoiceus, the king or regent of Thebes, p. 111. His father ruled Corinth at the time of Bellerophon's departure (sc. Eur. *Med.* 19). According to an earlier tradition, ascribed to the Corinthian epic poet Eumelos, who was probably the inventor of the genealogical scheme underlying it, Medea was invited to Corinth to become queen in her own right (sc. Eur. *Med.* 19, quoting Simonides to the same effect).

a raging fire: see Eur. *Medea* 1167 ff. She is said to have thrown herself into a fountain named after her in Corinth (P. 2. 3. 6).

received from the Sun a chariot: following Eur. *Medea* (1317 ff., with Arg.; and for the murder of her two children, 1236 ff.). It should be remembered that her father Aietes was a son of the Sun, p. 43.

57 *the Corinthians forced them away*: the local Corinthian tradition, see P. 2. 3. 6; they stoned the children because they had carried the fatal gifts to Glauce, but as a result of this murder the young children of Corinth began to die. The Corinthians were ordered by the oracle to offer sacrifices in their honour each year (which were continued until the city was destroyed by the Romans in 146 BC) and to raise an altar to Fear.

she married Aigeus: Aigeus had difficulty fathering children, p. 136, and he is said to have married Medea when she promised to cure the problem by her spells (Plut. *Thes.* 12). For her expulsion see p. 139.

a son, Medos: either directly (P. 2. 3. 7) or through her son, she becomes the eponym of the Medes, whose empire south-west of the Caspian Sea was later absorbed into the Persian Empire. According to another tradition, Medea bore Medos to an Asian king after her expulsion from Athens, DS 4. 55. 7, and he then succeeded to his father's kingdom.

she killed Perses: or Medos killed him and conquered Media thereafter (DS 4. 56. 1, cf. Hyg. 27).

58 *Inachos*: as one of the most prominent features in the landscape, rivers often appear at an early stage in local genealogies. The statement that the river was named after him presents the matter in a rationalized form; Inachos would originally have been the river itself, which, in myth, can function as a person at the same time, cf. Acheloos on p. 113.

Phoroneus and Aigialeus: in the mythology of their particular areas each would be seen as the local earth-born 'first man', Phoroneus in Argos, and Aigialeus in Aigialeia to the north of Argos (in the region of Sicyon; compare his position in the local genealogies as reported by P. 2. 5. 5). Here they are absorbed into a broader genealogical scheme.

was called Sarapis: the cult of Sarapis, which was encouraged by the Hellenistic kings of Egypt, developed from the cult of Apis, the sacred bull worshipped at Memphis. The Argive Apis is here identified with the Egyptian Apis, and thence with Sarapis, who became the chief god in the cult of the Egyptian gods as celebrated outside Egypt.

Pelasgos: the 'first man' in Arcadia, in the central Peloponnese; that he was born from the earth was the local tradition. Ap. will return to Pelasgos and the mythology of Arcadia on p. 114.

Pelasgians: also used in a more general sense to refer to the aboriginal inhabitants of various parts of Greece, notably Thessaly.

calling the Peloponnese Argos: this continues a pattern in which regional names are said to have originated as names for the whole Peloponnese. (According to the context, the name Argos can refer either to the Argolid, as a region in the north-east Peloponnese, or to Argos, as the main city within it.)

eyes all over his body: as with the hydra's heads, the numbers vary according to the fancy of the author. That he had eyes 'all over' may have been wrongly inferred from his title Panoptes. In Pherecydes (sc. Eur. *Phoen.* 1116) he had only a single extra eye, on the back of his head, granted to him by Hera, who also made him sleepless.

Echidna: a fearsome monster and progenitor of monsters, who lived in a cave in a hollow of the earth and feasted on raw flesh, see *Theog.* 295 ff.

59 *Peiren*: a son of the first Argos and Evadne; he can be identified with Peiras two paragraphs previously.

Zeus seduced Io: for all the following, cf. Aesch. *Suppliants* 291 ff.; there Io is transformed by Hera. See also [Aesch.] *PV* 561 ff. and Ov. *Met.* 1. 583 ff.

betrayed by Hierax: otherwise unknown. Since *hierax* means a hawk, perhaps associated with a transformation story (as with another Hierax in AL 3).

Argeiphontes: an ancient title (e.g. *Od.* 8. 338) of uncertain origin, here interpreted as meaning 'Argos-slayer'.

Ionian Gulf: the Adriatic; for this explanation of its name, cf. [Aesch.] *PV* 836 ff.

Bosporos: 'the cow's strait', or 'ox ford'; a valid etymology.

60 *Hera asked the Curetes . . . discovered Epaphos*: as Ap. remarks, the Greeks identified Io with the Egyptian goddess Isis, and the present story is based on the tale of Isis' search for the lost Osiris; for a Greek account of the latter, see Plutarch's *Isis and Osiris* 355 ff. Osiris was washed ashore at Byblos. In view of the Curetes' previous services to him, p. 28, it seems ungrateful of Zeus to kill them.

until later: see pp. 96 ff. for Agenor and the Cretan/Theban line.

Belos: the name is derived from the Phoenician Baal, strictly a god, but often taken by the Greeks to be an early eastern king.

60 *Melampodes*: 'Blackfeet', an epithet for the Egyptians found in late authors only.

the first man to do so: but the *Argo*, p. 49, was more commonly regarded as the first ship (which is why it was turned into a constellation by Athene, *Catast.* 35). In either case, the ship was built with Athene's help.

Gelanor . . . surrendered the throne to him: according to P. 2. 16. 1, Gelanor, son of Sthenelas, was a great-grandson of Agenor, Io's uncle (or on p. 58, her great-grandfather); and Danaos too had a legitimate claim as a descendant of Io. Pausanias gives the local tradition (P. 2. 19. 3 f.). The Argives found their claims so evenly balanced that they deferred the decision until the following day; and early the next morning, a wolf attacked a herd of cattle grazing outside the walls and killed the bull. So the Argives ceded the throne to Danaos, taking this to be a sign from the gods (with the wolf representing Danaos, the outsider). And Danaos, believing that Apollo had sent the wolf, founded the most important cult in the city of Argos, that of Apollo Lycaios ('Wolfish' Apollo).

After he . . . Danaans after himself: included with the preceding lines in sc. *Il.* 1. 42, as part of a citation from the second book of Apollodorus; not accepted by all editors.

Poseidon . . . belonged to Hera: see p. 130 for a similar dispute at Athens; these were in effect contests for special cultic honours from the inhabitants. For further details, see P. 2. 15. 5; this explains why the Argive rivers (including the Inachos) run dry in summer, except at Lerna.

61 *Lerna*: there was a stream there called Amymone, p. 74, cf. P. 2. 37. 1. Lerna has more sinister associations as the home of the hydra, p. 74.

62 *Hypermnestra . . . spared Lynceus*: they will be the ancestors of the Argive royal line thereafter. See also P. 2. 25. 4 and 2. 19. 6.

they were purified: but in late sources the Danaids are listed amongst those who suffer punishment in Hades (e.g. Ov. *Met.* 4. 462, Horace *Odes* 3. 11. 28 ff.), where they attempt endlessly to fill perforated vessels with water.

at an athletic contest: see Pind. *Pyth.* 9. 112 ff.

Amymone bore . . . in that very manner: Nauplios was conceived at Lerna, p. 61. Since Nauplios' activities as a wrecker took place so much later (after the Trojan War, see p. 159), this would mean that he lived to an improbable age; some resolved the problem by claiming that the wrecker was a descendant of the Nauplios born to Amymone (in AR 1. 134 ff., he is a great-great-great-grandson). Seneca records that he was cast into the deep (*Medea* 658 f.), but nothing is known of the exact circumstances.

Homer calls Anteia: in *Il.* 6. 160; on Stheneboia see also p. 64, and p. 115 where she is said to have been the daughter of Apheidas, an Arcadian.

63 *fortified . . . by the Cyclopes*: imagining that the monumental architecture of the Mycenaeans was beyond the power of man, the Greeks supposed that the fortifications of Tiryns and their like must be the work of giants or 'Cyclopes' (cf. P. 2. 25. 7). In view of the popular origin of this tradition, there is little point in asking exactly who these Cyclopes were, but the ancient mythographers (e.g. sc. *Theog.* 139) thought that they should be distinguished from the primordial Hesiodic Cyclopes on p. 27, and also from the primitive pastoral Cyclopes of Homer, p. 165.

Acousilaos . . . Hera: the anger of Hera was generally regarded as the cause of their madness. According to Bacch. 2. 47 ff., they were sent mad for boasting in the precinct of Hera that their father was wealthier than the goddess; the present story that they mocked her primitive cultic image (*xoanon*) is probably of somewhat later origin. In Bacch. (2. 95 ff.) they were cured by Artemis after their father prayed to her and vowed twenty oxen, but in Hes. *Cat.* by Melampous (frs. 131 ff., cf. fr. 37).

the other women: the women of Argos, cf. p. 47, where the madness was attributed to Dionysos; the story was doubtless of separate origin from that of the daughters of Proitos. Herodotus (9. 34) is the only other source for the raising of the fee (but there the daughters of Proitos are not involved). Some date the madness of the Argive women to a later period, when Anaxagoras, a grandson of Proitos, was on the throne (DS 4. 68. 4; P. 2. 18. 4).

agreed to the cure on these terms: this introduces a further complexity into the pattern of rule in the Argolid. There are separate lines within the Inachid royal family, relating to a division of the territory between Tiryns and Argos, pp. 62 f. (and later, Mycenae); and now an additional Deucalionid royal family is inserted (which will be the most important at the time of the Theban Wars, see p. 107 and note). These complexities are the result of the mythographers' efforts to impose a modicum of order on an inherited mass of largely irreconcilable myth. The threefold division of Argos does not reflect a peculiarity in Argive institutions comparable to the dual monarchy in Sparta; and one soon finds that it is impossible to trace clear lines of descent linking each of the main centres to each family or branch of a family.

64 *killed his brother*: or a Corinthian nobleman named Belleros (sc. Lycophr. 17, sc. *Il.* 6. 155), hence his name Bellerophon (or 'Belleros-slayer', cf. Hermes 'Argeiphontes' on p. 59).

to be purified: this is a recurring pattern in these myths. A person who spills another's blood becomes polluted, and thus a danger to his native community (because he is liable to become the cause of barrenness, plague, and the like). He must therefore go into exile and be purified. That he is purified by a king rather than a priest reflects in part the sacral character of early kingship, and in part the social function of purification in enabling the polluted man to be integrated into the community of the king who purifies him.

Stheneboia fell in love with him: the following accords with *Il.* 6. 154 ff. (except that Homer calls her Anteia, as remarked above).

to Iobates: Proitos' father-in-law, see above, who lived in Lycia, in the south-western corner of Asia Minor.

a third head in the middle: we are to understand that the dragon's tail has a head at the end, cf. *Theog.* 321 ff., and that this middle head is on a neck that grows from the monster's back.

Amisodaros: see *Il.* 16. 328 ff. A Lycian like Iobates (who is not named by Homer), and the father of two sons in Sarpedon's company.

as Hesiod records: *Theog.* 319 f. (but Hesiod's text is ambiguous and he may have meant that the Lernaean hydra was its mother).

climbed on to . . . Pegasos: as in *Theog.* 325 and Hes. *Cat.* fr. 43a, 84 ff.; there is no mention of him in Homer's account, *Il.* 6. 179 ff. For the story of his birth, see p. 66 and *Theog.* 278 ff. He was given to Bellerophon by Poseidon (sc. *Il.* 6. 155), or by Athene, who had tamed and bridled him with her own hands (P. 2. 4. 1); or according to Pind. *Ol.* 13. 63 ff., Bellerophon bridled Pegasos himself after obtaining advice from a seer on how to obtain divine favour for the enterprise. It was said that Bellerophon was killed when he tried to fly to Olympos on Pegasos, Pind. *Isth.* 7. 44 ff.

the Solymoi: they lived in southern Asia Minor to the west of Lycia (see Strabo 14. 3. 9).

in youthful vigour: following Zenobius 2. 87; the text is problematic.

65 *some say by Proitos*: although this variant (apparently derived from Pindar, sc. *Il.* 14. 319) is cited first, it was generally accepted that Perseus was a son of Zeus; for the quarrel between the twins, see pp. 62 f.

when Acrisios learned: according to Pherecydes (sc. AR 4. 1091) he heard the voice of the child while he was at play at three or four years of age, and had Danae brought up from the chamber with the child's nurse, whom he killed.

Polydectes . . . Dictys: for their birth and origin, see p. 44.

a marriage-offering: as in Homer, the bride would be purchased from her father with a bride-gift, *hedna*, which was often substantial (e.g. *Il.* 11. 243 ff.). For Hippodameia, see p. 144.

did not take the horses of Perseus: this seems to be Ap.'s meaning (rather than that he failed to receive any horses from him, as in Frazer's translation), as in the clearer account reported from Pherecydes (in sc. AR. 4. 1515a; when Dictys asks him for a horse, Perseus replies hyperbolically that he would give him the Gorgon's head, and the following day, he refuses to accept Perseus' horse alone, holding him instead to his 'promise').

the daughters of Phorcos: the Graiai (Old Women). In *Theog.* 270 ff., there are only two, and although they were grey-haired from birth, they are said to be fair-cheeked and beautifully robed. The shared eye and tooth first appear in Pherecydes sc. AR 4. 1515a and [Aesch.] *PV* 795 f.

winged sandals: belonging to Hermes, which Perseus needs to reach the Gorgons, and then escape from them (the tradition that he escaped on Pegasos, e.g. Ov. *Amatoria* 3. 12. 24, found little favour in antiquity). On the *kibisis*, see Appendix, 1 and note.

of Hades: inserted by Heyne, but not necessarily in the original, as the reader could be expected to know (as in P. 3. 17. 3). The leather helmet or cap belongs to Hades because his name suggests invisibility (*a-ides*). The notion that he was 'armed' with it by the Cyclopes, p. 28, is a fancy from a relatively late period.

66 *conceived them previously by Poseidon*: she had slept with him in a spring meadow, see *Theog.* 278 ff.

Cassiepeia: the form Cassiopeia, familiar from the constellation, never appears in ancient writings; it seems to have originated as a hybrid between this and the ancient variant Cassiope (Ov. *Met.* 4. 738 etc.).

Ammon: he had an oracle at the oasis of Siwa in Egypt, which was regarded by the Greeks as an oracle of Zeus.

67 *claimed to rival the goddess in beauty*: this may seem surprising, but we have seen that she was once attractive to Poseidon; according to Ov. *Met.* 4. 798 ff., Athene transformed her into her familiar

Explanatory Notes

Gorgonic form because she had slept with Poseidon in the goddess' sanctuary.

67 *what the oracle had predicted*: that he would be killed by his daughter's son, pp. 64 f.

king of Larissa: this lay in the land of the (Thessalian) Pelasgians, and we should understand that Acrisios went to stay with Teutamides. In Pherecydes' account (sc. AR 4. 1091) Perseus went there specifically to find Acrisios, and became involved in the games by chance.

on the foot, killing him: this seems odd—the incident on p. 76, which involves a poisoned arrow, is not comparable—but it accords with Pherecydes' account in sc. AR 4. 1091. In Hyg. 63, the wind blows the discus from his hand at Acrisios' head, so fulfilling the will of the gods. Some said that Perseus himself invented the discus, and was using the occasion to demonstrate his skill with it (P. 2. 16. 2).

fortified . . . Mycenae: Perseus was commonly seen as its founder (cf. P. 2. 16. 3). Henceforth it will be one of the three great centres in the Argolid with Argos and Tiryns.

68 *gone far: telou ebe*, hence Teleboans. The etymology is forced; the name probably means 'those whose (war-)*cries* can be heard from *afar*'.

descendant of Perseus . . . about to be born: Zeus means Heracles (see p. 70), his own son by Alcmene, the wife of Amphitryon, grandson of Perseus; but Hera's stratagem will ensure that Eurystheus, a grandson of Perseus, will be born before Heracles, and thus rule at Mycenae in accordance with this declaration by Zeus. Hera is always jealous of Zeus' children by other women. (As is usual in mythical history, Heracles' divine parentage does not exclude him from the lineage of his putative mortal father; he is also descended from Perseus through his mother.)

the Eileithuiai: there was a goddess Eileithuia specifically associated with childbirth, cf. p. 29, but the name was also used in the plural as a generic term to refer to other divine beings in so far as they helped (or hindered) childbirth. The story is told by Homer, *Il.* 19. 96 ff.; compare P. 9. 11. 2 and Ov. *Met.* 9. 292 ff. for later developments. In Homer, Hera merely restrains the Eileithuiai (*Il.* 19. 119) from helping Alcmene, but in the later tradition they actively hinder the birth.

69 *of their maternal grandfather*: the text is confused. For the basis of their claim, see p. 68; the succession runs: Perseus—Mestor—

Hippothoe—Taphios—Pterelaos—the sons of Pterelaos. Earlier in the sentence I have kept the manuscript reading 'with Taphios' (cf. Tzetz. sc. Lycophr. 932; as against 'with some Taphians' following Heyne's emendation); the fact that the sons of Pterelaos are seeking to regain the kingdom of the maternal grandfather of *Taphios* could well explain the original meaning of the text, or the proper reference of the problematic phrase if it is a gloss. Note that Electryon, a son of Perseus, is involved in a dispute with the great-great-great-grandsons of Perseus! The islands of the Teleboans lay opposite Acarnania near the entrance to the Corinthian Gulf.

striking him dead: by accident, but there is also an early tradition that they argued over the cattle and Amphitryon killed him in a fit of anger (see Hes. *Shield* 11 f. and 82). This gives Sthenelos a pretext to take power in Mycenae, and Hera's stratagem will ensure that his son Eurystheus rules there after him; and the expulsion of Amphitryon and Alcmene explains why Heracles will start his life in exile at Thebes.

she would marry him: this corresponds with the account attributed to Pherecydes in sc. *Il.* 14. 323 and sc. *Od.* 11. 266, but in Hes. *Shield* 14 ff. (in lines taken from Hes. *Cat.*) they were already married (as one might well infer from the previous paragraph) and she makes the *consummation* of the marriage conditional on the vengeance. (Without a small emendation by Wagner, the passage would read, 'she would marry the person who avenged . . .')

the vixen: the Teumessian fox, which had its lair on Mount Teumessos in Boeotia; Dionysos is said to have sent it (P. 9. 19. 1) but we are not told why. (Perhaps because he was rejected by Pentheus, p. 103.) Here the Cadmeia clearly means the territory of Thebes (rather than just the citadel).

70 *Cephalos, son of Deioneus*: for his birth, see p. 44 (Deioneus can be identified with Deion).

the dog: its name was Lailaps, 'Hurricane' (e.g. Hyg. 189); for how Cephalos came to possess it, see also p. 134.

Zeus turned . . . them to stone: this divine intervention was needed to resolve, or at least remove, the intolerable contradiction which arose when a beast that was fated to catch its prey was set in pursuit of a beast that was fated never to be caught. In astral mythology Zeus turns the dog into a constellation (Canis Major, *Catast.* 33).

put Comaitho to death: he is unwilling to accept the love of one who has betrayed her father and city; compare the story of Scylla on p. 137.

70 *Heracles*: the only other complete life history to survive from antiquity is that of Diodorus of Sicily (4. 8–39), which follows a similar pattern, and should be consulted on all the following.

killed the serpents: cf. Pind. *Nem.* 1. 39 ff.

71 *Linos had struck him*: after losing patience at his 'sluggishness of soul', DS 3. 67. 2. Surviving accounts are late, although the episode is depicted in fifth-century vase-paintings.

Rhadamanthys: the Cretan lawmaker who became a judge in Hades, see p. 97.

should all conceive children by Heracles: he is impressed by his extraordinary strength and expects him to father fine children, cf. DS 4. 29. 3. According to the temple legend at Thespiai, P. 9. 27. 5, he slept with all but one, who became his priestess at the temple, and did so in a single night.

dressed in its skin: but according to some, it was the Nemean lion, p. 73, who provided the skin (e.g. Theocritus 25. 163 ff.; as the skin of an invulnerable beast, it had the advantage of being impenetrable—Heracles had to use the lion's own claws to cut it).

72 *the Minyans*: here the inhabitants of Orchomenos in northwestern Boeotia (cf. *Il.* 2. 511).

charioteer of Menoiceus: his master, a grandson of Pentheus, was a member of the Theban royal family; the killing was also attributed to a group of Thebans (P. 9. 37. 1 f.).

by Eurytos: in the manuscripts, *autou*, 'by him', referring to Rhadamanthys. Because this seems unlikely in itself, and Ap. said above that Heracles was taught archery by Eurytos, most editors favour the present emendation; but it is possible that there is a more extensive corruption. In DS 4. 14. 3 he is taught archery by Apollo.

73 *the Pythia*: the priestess who delivered the oracles at Delphi.

ten labours: corrected from twelve in the manuscripts (Hercher). According to the following account, Heracles was due to perform ten labours, but he has to perform two extra labours (making up the canonic twelve) because Eurystheus refuses to accept the second and fifth.

be immortal: referring to his apotheosis, which takes place some time after the completion of the labours, and is a relatively late element in the tradition, see p. 91 and note.

invulnerable beast fathered by Typhon: in *Theog.* 326 f., the son of Orthos, son of Typhon and Echidna; it was reared by Hera. There is another tradition, also of early origin, that it grew up on the Moon, who shook it down to earth (Epimenides, fr. 2 DK, cf. Hyg. 30). In these mythical contexts, invulnerability means quite literally insusceptibility to wounds; if such a being can be killed by a means that does not entail the piercing of its body, it is not immune to death (hence the strangling). Pindar is the earliest author to refer to its invulnerability (*Isth.* 6. 47 f.; Bacch. 13. 50 ff. is more explicit).

sacrifice . . . as a hero: exceptional men, legendary but also historical, who were thought to exercise power after their death, were worshipped in a special cult; sacrifices to the gods above and those to the heroized dead were performed according to a different ritual (which is reflected in the use of different words here, *thuein* and *enagizein* respectively).

Copreus: cf. *Il.* 15. 639 f. His name is suggestive of *kopros*, dung.

74 *the Lernaean hydra*: see *Theog.* 313 ff., a child of Echidna and Typhon, raised by Hera to be an adversary for Heracles; hydra, meaning a water-serpent, is not a proper name (although the Lernaean hydra came to be thought of as 'the' hydra).

nine heads: Hesiod, ibid., does not say that the hydra has more than one head. Although Pausanias, 2. 37. 4, claims that Peisandros, the seventh–sixth-century author of an epic poem on Heracles, was the first to give the hydra many heads, the artistic evidence shows that he was not the inventor of the theme, for such representations can be traced to about 700. The number of heads varies according to the fancy of the poet or artist; already in early lyric, Alcaeus gives it nine heads, and Simonides fifty (sc. Hes. *Theog.* 313). The immortality of the middle head is unattested elsewhere.

of Amymone: see p. 61.

Iolaos: the son of Heracles' half-brother Iphicles, p. 72; he accompanied Heracles on several of his adventures, acting as his charioteer.

sacred to Artemis: when Zeus wanted to rape Taygete, daughter of Atlas, Artemis rescued her by turning her into a deer; on returning to human form she dedicated the present deer to Artemis, and attached an inscription to it stating this (Pind. *Ol.* 3. 29 f., with sc. to 53).

struck it with an arrow: to bring it down without harming it. According to other accounts he used nets to trap it, or overpowered it when it was asleep or exhausted (DS 4. 13. 1).

75 *the common property of the Centaurs*: according to another tradition, Dionysos left the jar with Pholos to be opened when Heracles arrived four generations later, and the local Centaurs were driven into a frenzy by the scent of the wine (DS 4. 12. 3 f.).

Cheiron . . . by the Lapiths: he was driven out of Thessaly with the other Centaurs by this Thessalian people under the command of their king, Peirithoos (see also p. 142). Malea was a promontory at the south-east corner of the Peloponnese, far to the south of Pholoe in Arcadia.

Only when Prometheus . . . able to die: see p. 83 with note.

76 *killing him instantly*: it will be remembered that Heracles dipped his arrows in the hydra's gall; the virulence of the poison explains both their effect on the Centaurs and why Cheiron's wound is incurable.

he refused to pay the reward: thus far he had some justification, as he could reasonably claim that he had been deceived when he was asked to pay for a task that Heracles had to perform anyhow as an unpaid service to Eurystheus.

Phyleus . . . testified against his father: cf. P. 5. 1. 10, where Phyleus is exiled for admonishing his father (and there is no mention of the arbitration). Homer remarks that Phyleus went into exile in anger at his father, but gives no details (*Il.* 2. 628 ff.).

77 *shoot them down*: Heracles was not ordered to kill them, and in some accounts he merely scares them off (P. 8. 22. 4, referring to Peisandros, DS 4. 13. 2). It would seem that the birds were a problem only because of their numbers (DS is more explicit on this); Pausanias' suggestion (P. 8. 22. 4 ff.) that they may have been man-eaters is based on a later tradition in which they were identified with a fabulous race of Arabian birds.

Acousilaos . . . bull that had carried Europa: the earliest author known to have referred to this labour, but the identification he offered for the bull cannot be reconciled with the usual tradition that Europa's bull was Zeus himself in animal form (p. 96, cf. Hes. fr. 140).

sent up from the sea by Poseidon: see also p. 97; the identification favoured by DS (4. 13. 4) and Pausanias (1. 27. 9).

arrived at Marathon: where it is conveniently available for Theseus to kill, p. 139; Theseus' exploits as a killer of beasts and malefactors were modelled on those of Heracles.

Explanatory Notes

78 *man-eating mares*: cf. Eur. *Alcestis* 481 ff.; in DS 4. 15. 3 f. he captures the mares after he has satisfied their hunger by feeding them on Diomedes himself.

by the River Thermodon: in north-eastern Asia Minor.

pressed down: exethlibon, suggesting compression rather than removal. According to the Hippocratic treatise *Airs, Waters, Places*, 17, an Amazon mother would apply a hot iron to her daughter's breast while she was still a child to prevent it from growing; similarly DS 2. 45. 3 (who cites the common etymology that they are called Amazons because they are 'without a breast', *a-mazos*).

the belt of Ares: this *zoster*—which came from the god of war— would be a heavy warrior's belt, not a woman's girdle (*zone*), although it sometimes seems to have been taken as such in the later tradition (as Admete's desire to possess it may imply). In AR 2. 966 ff. Heracles captures Melanippe, the queen's sister, in an ambush and obtains the belt as a ransom; or he captures Melanippe, their commander, after killing many Amazons in battle, and then ransoms her for the belt, DS 4. 16. 1 ff.

79 *Lycos, and when Lycos*: added to fill a short gap in the text; his kingdom lay in the north-western corner of Asia Minor, and the land of his enemies the Bebryces (later Bithynia) to the north-west of that. On Amycos, see also p. 51.

undertaken to fortify Pergamon: see *Il.* 7. 452 ff. and 21. 441 ff. (in the latter Apollo serves as a herdsman). They were acting on the bidding of Zeus, 21. 444, apparently as a punishment for their attempted revolt against Zeus (see *Il.* 1. 398 ff., where Apollo is not mentioned; cf. sc. *Il.* 21. 444). In *Il.* 21. 453 ff., not only does Laomedon refuse to pay, but he threatens to tie them up, sell them into slavery, and cut off their ears.

to Tros: added for clarity, cf. *Il.* 5. 265 ff.; he was Laomedon's grandfather. On Ganymede see p. 123.

at some future time: for his attack on Troy, see p. 86.

80 *three men joined into one*: in *Theog.* 287 he is merely three-headed; but in Aesch. *Agamemnon* 870 he is three-bodied, and in Stesichorus (mid-sixth century, as reported by sc. *Theog.* 287) he is six-handed and six-footed (and winged).

killed many savage beasts: the killing of wild beasts, and of foreigners who are hostile to strangers, is an important part of Heracles' activity as a furtherer of civilization (or as a hero who made the world safe for Greek colonization). Diodorus is much more informative on this aspect of Heracles (see DS 4. 17. 3 ff. for the taming of Crete and Libya).

80 *two pillars*: these marked the boundaries of the inhabited world, *oikoumene*, to the west, as did those of Dionysos, p. 102, to the east; commonly identified with Gibraltar and Ceuta on either side of the entry to the Mediterranean.

a golden cup: the Sun passed from east to west across the sky, from sunrise to sunset, in a fiery chariot, and sailed back again in this golden cup by way of the Ocean (which encircles the earth). We are to imagine that Erytheia, the Red Isle, lies in the Ocean beyond Spain. Hdt. 4. 8 placed it near Cadiz, and it was later identified with Cadiz (Gadeira) as Ap. remarks above.

81 *Rhegion*: or Rhegium, now Reggio, at the toe of Italy, was a Greek colony, although its name was not of Greek origin. Here it is said to owe its name to the fact that the bull *aporrhegnusi*, breaks free there (from amongst Geryon's cattle). DS 4. 21–4 includes a mass of Italian and Sicilian material which Ap. characteristically ignores.

called the bull italus: Heracles asked the local people if they had seen the calf anywhere, and when he heard them talking about it in their own language, he gave the name Italy to the country that it had passed through, after *vitulus*, the Latin for a calf (Dionysius of Halicarnassus *Ant. Rom.* 1. 35, following Hellanicos).

unless Heracles defeated him: or they fought on the terms that if Heracles was victorious, he would take the land, but if Eryx was, he would take all the cattle of Geryon (DS 4. 23. 2, P. 3. 16. 4 f.). In the early fifth century, Dorieus, a member of the Spartan royal family which was supposedly descended from Heracles, went to Sicily and laid claim to the land on these grounds (P. 3. 16. 4, cf. Hdt. 5. 41 ff.).

the gulf: the Adriatic.

golden apples from the Hesperides: according to Pherecydes, Ge gave apple trees bearing golden fruit to Hera as a wedding present, and Hera ordered that they should be planted in the garden of the gods near Mount Atlas (sc. AR 4. 1396, Hyg. *PA* 3). In *Theog.* (213 ff.) the Hesperides, the nymphs of the evening who helped guard the fruit, were daughters of Night (but subsequent accounts vary).

in the land of the Hyperboreans: a mythical people who lived in the far north. Although Ap. rejects the tradition that the Hesperides lay in the west, that was certainly their original location; their name alone is sufficient to associate them with the evening, and thus the sunset and the west, and Atlas too was commonly associated with the western end of North Africa. In the present version (cf. DS 4. 26. 2 ff.) Heracles' journey takes him to all points of the compass; he passes through Italy to Libya and the west, then east again to Egypt, and south to Arabia, and finally north on the eastern Ocean to the Caucasus and beyond.

82 *to avenge him . . . engaged him in single combat*: interpreting the phrase *Areos de touton ekdikountos kai sunistantos monomachia* in a different sense, Frazer translates, 'Ares championed the cause of Cycnos and marshalled the combat,' which would allow us to assume that the text is complete, but in the present translation I have followed the example of Carrière, who argues that there is a short gap beforehand and that Ap.'s account originally accorded with that in Hyg. 31; there Heracles kills Cycnos in single combat, but when Ares is about to attack him to avenge the death of his son, Zeus hurls a thunderbolt to separate Heracles and *Ares*. Frazer's version raises serious problems; in all other accounts of the story (including Ap.'s second version of it on p. 90), Heracles kills Cycnos (cf. Hes. *Shield* 416 ff. and Stesichorus in sc. Pind. *Ol.* 10. 19), and the story seems altogether pointless if he does not. And it is hard to see why Zeus should intervene to protect Cycnos. (A discussion of the points of language can be found in Carrière's note.) It should be mentioned, however, that there is some evidence from sixth-century vase-paintings that there may have been a tradition in which Zeus restrained the combatants.

Nereus . . . transformed himself: for Nereus, see p. 29; sea-gods, as inhabitants of a formless medium, are naturally shape-shifters. Nereus appears in no other mythical narrative; the present story was probably suggested by Homer's account of Menelaos' encounter with Proteus, another old man of the sea (*Od.* 4. 382 ff.).

Antaios: he roofed Poseidon's temple with travellers' skulls, Pind. *Isth.* 4. 54. His peculiar relationship with the Earth is first recorded in Roman sources (Ov. *Met.* 9. 183 f., Lucan 4. 593 ff.), but the motif is surely of earlier origin.

a drover: in other versions, a ploughman (e.g. Conon 11). For a similar incident see p. 89 and note.

he killed Emathion: for his birth, see p. 124 and *Theog.* 984 f. The only indication of the reason for the killing is the remark in DS 4. 27. 3 that after Heracles had sailed up the Nile Emathion attacked him without provocation in Ethiopia. Perhaps the significance of the episode lay in the fact that it marked the southernmost stage of his journey.

83 *through Libya*: this may be an error; but it is unlikely that Ap. had a clear conception of the geographical connections here.

He then . . . in Prometheus' place: for the cause of Prometheus' punishment, see p. 36. There was an ancient tradition that crowns and garlands are symbolic of the shackles worn by Prometheus as a result of his services to the human race (Athenaeus 672e ff.); so presumably Heracles dons an olive crown as a symbolic substitute for Prometheus' fetters. (The wild olive was especially associated with Heracles, and he is said to have brought it to Greece from the land of the Hyperboreans, P. 5. 7. 7.) The meaning of Cheiron's exchange has been much disputed, and only a tentative suggestion can be offered here. We know that Cheiron wants to die because he is suffering from a painful and incurable wound, p. 75. Since Prometheus is immortal by nature, there can be no question of Cheiron simply exchanging his immortality for the mortality of Prometheus and thus becoming able to die (as might be inferred from the phrase on p. 75). It would seem, on the contrary, that this is another symbolic exchange; by passing below, Cheiron assumes the sufferings of Prometheus. The fact that Heracles presents him to Zeus suggests that by giving himself up to die, Cheiron is fulfilling a prior condition set by Zeus. A passage in [Aesch.] *PV* 1026 ff. may be relevant here, in which Hermes tells Prometheus that there will be no end to his sufferings unless a god shows himself ready to succeed to them and offers to descend to Hades. This would be a dire fate for an immortal being; but because of Cheiron's special circumstances, the seemingly impossible condition mentioned in *PV* could be fulfilled.

he said that . . . the sky back until: a passage from sc. AR 4. 1396 is inserted to fill a gap in the text; it is based on Pherecydes, Ap.'s main source here.

It is said . . . guardian snake: cf. Soph. *Trachiniae* 1099 f., and Eur. *Hercules Furens*, 394 ff.

unholy: these apples and the trees that bore them belonged to Hera or Zeus (see p. 81 and note), and it is thus unholy for them to be removed permanently from their appointed home.

to fetch Cerberos: Homer knew of this feat, *Il.* 8. 367 f., *Od.* 11. 623 ff.; see also Bacch. 5. 56 ff.

with a view to being initiated: into the Eleusinian Mysteries, which ensured a better fate for initiates in the Underworld after their death, and could thus prepare Heracles for his premature journey to Hades.

purified by Eumolpos: the legendary founder of the Mysteries, see also p. 135 and note. There was another tradition that Demeter founded the Lesser Mysteries (the preparatory rites at Agrai, near Athens) to purify Heracles (DS 4. 14. 3). In historical times, all who spoke Greek could be initiated, with the exception of murderers.

84 *the souls . . . Meleager . . . Medusa*: the souls are the shades of the dead. For the encounter with Meleager, see Bacch. 5. 71 ff. Medusa, the only mortal Gorgon, was killed by Perseus, p. 66; the present encounter was doubtless suggested by *Od.* 11. 633 ff., where Odysseus hurries from the world of the dead in a panic, afraid that Persephone may send some monstrous apparition like the Gorgon's head.

Theseus there, and Peirithoos: see p. 143.

stone of Ascalaphos: see p. 33.

to procure blood for the souls: the souls are flimsy and witless; a drink of blood increases their materiality and raises their level of consciousness, making it possible for them to communicate with outsiders, see *Od.* 11. 23 ff.

gates of Acheron: Acheron was strictly a river in the Underworld, but its name was also used by later authors for Hades itself; these are the gates of Hades mentioned above, symbolizing the boundary between the lands of the living and the dead. This frontier was guarded by Cerberos, who fawned on those who entered the realm of Hades, but attacked anyone who tried to escape through its gates, *Theog.* 770 ff.

into an owl: as a screech-owl (which is moreover a bird of ill omen) he will still be confined to the dark; Demeter will not permit him to escape punishment for his betrayal of her daughter. For another version of this transformation, see Ov. *Met.* 5. 538 ff.

gave Megara to Iolaos: after his madness and murder of their children, p. 72, there is no future in Heracles' marriage with Megara; for the gods are clearly against it. So he gives her to his nephew Iolaos as a reward for his help in the labours (here in overcoming the hydra, p. 74, but in other sources he is said to have assisted in the labours of the lion, boar, and cattle of Geryoneus also).

at archery: Eurytos was Heracles' own teacher in the art, p. 71. Eurytos died when he challenged Apollo himself to an archery contest, *Od.* 8. 226 ff.; the bow that Odysseus used to kill the suitors originally belonged to him, *Od.* 21. 13 ff.

85 *cattle were stolen*: in all other sources, mares, cf. *Od.* 21. 22 ff.

in a fresh fit of madness: other accounts are less favourable to Heracles. In the *Odyssey*, ibid., he treacherously killed Iphitos after entertaining him as his guest, and then took the mares; in Pherecydes (sc. *Od.* 21. 22) he killed Iphitos in anger at having been denied Iole; in DS 4. 31. 2 f., Heracles himself stole the mares for revenge, and when Iphitos came to Tiryns to seek for them, Heracles took him to the battlements and asked him if he could see them—and when he could not, Heracles claimed to have been falsely accused, and hurled him down.

Neleus rejected him: this is the reason for his later attack on Pylos, p. 87.

refused . . . a response: because he was defiled by the murder, see further P. 10. 13. 4.

the Cercopes: two brothers who robbed passers-by; for details we have to rely on late sources. According to Zenobius 5. 10, they had been warned by their mother to beware of the 'Black-Bottomed One' (*Melampygos*). When they tried to rob Heracles, he hung them by their feet from either end of a pole, and they saw too late that his bottom, where it was not covered by the lion's skin, was black because of the thickness of the hair. They laughed, and when Heracles asked why and he learned the reason, he was amused and released them.

in his vineyard: added for clarity, cf. DS 4. 31. 7; he killed Syleus with his own mattock.

the body of Icaros: see pp. 140 f.

86 *the voyage to Colchis*: the voyage of the Argonauts; for the tradition on Heracles' involvement, see p. 51 and note.

the hunt . . . from Troezen: since Meleager was killed after the hunt, p. 41, this is irreconcilable with the tradition that Heracles met him in Hades during his final labour, p. 84; and likewise, if Heracles brought Theseus up from Hades, Theseus could hardly have performed his earliest feat (of clearing the Isthmus of male-factors, see pp. 138 f.) at this later period.

he sailed against Ilion: known to Homer, *Il.* 5. 640 ff. (where he remarks on the small size of the expedition, with only six ships; although it is three times larger here, it is still far smaller than the later expedition, cf. p. 148). For the reason for Heracles' attack, see p. 79.

to Heracles the Noble Victor: *Kallinikos*, thus explaining a cultic title of Heracles as a hero who could overcome and avert evil.

Explanatory Notes

Priam: according to this etymology, the name of the king of Troy during the great Trojan War was derived from *priamai*, to buy.

Hera sent violent storms: see *Il.* 14. 249 ff. and 15. 24 ff.

suspended her from Olympos: with two anvils hanging from her feet, and her hands tied with a golden band, *Il.* 15. 18–20. See also p. 31 and note.

87 *war against the Giants*: see pp. 34 f.

against Augeias: who had refused to pay the agreed fee when Heracles cleared his stables, p. 76. Heracles now embarks on a series of campaigns in the Peloponnese, before his final campaigns in northern Greece.

Eurytos and Cteatos: at *Il.* 2. 621, Homer gives their names, and calls them the Actoriones after their father, but at 11. 709, the two Moliones, apparently after their mother. At *Il.* 23. 641 they are said to be twins, but there is no indication that they are joined together. See also Pind. *Ol.* 10. 26 ff. (where they are separate). Their depiction as 'Siamese' twins may have its origin in Hes. *Cat.* (see fr. 18).

set an ambush: a highly dubious action because they were protected by a religious truce at such a time (cf. P. 5. 2. 1 f., where we are told that the Eleans demanded satisfaction, and when none was offered, boycotted the Isthmian Games ever afterwards).

recalled Phyleus: the son of Augeias who had been exiled for supporting Heracles, p. 76.

an altar of Pelops: this seems inappropriate, because Pelops was a hero rather than a god; in P. 5. 13. 1 ff., the sanctuary of Pelops is said to have contained not an altar but a pit, into which annual sacrifices of a black ram were made, in the rite befitting the heroized dead.

marched against Pylos: on sandy Pylos and Periclymenos, see p. 45 and notes; for the cause of the war, p. 85 and note. The story explains why Nestor alone represented the sons of Neleus at Troy, cf. *Il.* 11. 690 ff.

Hades, who came to the aid of the Pylians: but see *Il.* 5. 395–7, Heracles struck him 'amongst the dead'; he was thus collecting the dead, cf. Pind. *Ol.* 9. 33 ff., rather than fighting in the battle. Ap.'s account reflects a later misunderstanding. Heracles is said to have wounded Hera also (*Il.* 5. 392; and Ares in Hes. *Shield* 357 ff.).

88 *the son of Licymnios*: Oionos (P. 3. 15. 4 f.), said to have been the first Olympic victor in the foot-race (Pind. *Ol.* 10. 64 ff.).

213

Licymnios, who went into exile with Amphitryon, p. 69, was the half-brother of Heracles' mother, so Heracles was bound to avenge the murder of his son. This campaign is important dynastically because it caused Tyndareus to be restored to the Spartan throne. According to Pausanias, Heracles attacked at once in a fury, but was wounded and withdrew (3. 15. 5), and returned later with an army after he had been cured by Asclepios (3. 19. 7).

88 *raped Auge . . . the daughter of Aleos*: Aleos was king of Tegea, and founder of the temple of Athene Alea (P. 8. 4. 8). The tradition is complex and contradictory; Ap. follows the Tegean temple legend, in which Heracles raped Auge by a fountain north of the temple, P. 8. 47. 4, as against the tradition in which he fathered the child in Asia Minor on the way to Troy (e.g. Hes. *Cat.* fr. 165). In another version of the Tegean story, the birth of Telephos resulted from a love affair (P. 8. 4. 8 f., after Hecataeus) rather than a rape.

by a plague: because of Auge's sacrilegious use of the sacred precinct. When Ap. refers to this episode again on p. 116, he says that the sacrilege caused the land to become barren; Wagner's suggestion that the original reading here was *limoi*, by a famine, rather than *loimoi*, by a plague, is quite plausible.

Telephos: the name is explained as a combination of *thele* (teat) and *elaphos* (deer).

Deianeira, the daughter of Oineus: see also p. 40; she was the sister of Meleager, who is said to have suggested the marriage to Heracles when they met in Hades (Bacch. 5. 165 ff., cf. sc. *Il.* 21. 194).

wrestled with Acheloos: strictly a river (the largest in Greece, flowing along the Acarnanian frontier of Aetolia for part of its course, and thus no great distance from Calydon), but river gods were thought to manifest themselves in the form of a bull. See also p. 113 and note.

89 *that of Amaltheia*: the cornucopia. Here Amaltheia is the nymph who fed the infant Zeus on milk from her goat (as against the goat itself on p. 28, cf. Hyg. *PA* 13 for both versions). According to Zenobius, 2. 48, Zeus turned the goat into a constellation in gratitude, but gave one of its horns to the nymphs who had cared for him, endowing it with the power to produce whatever they wished; in that case, Amaltheia's horn would not be a bull's horn as stated here. DS 4. 35. 4 offers a rationalized account identifying it with the horn broken from Acheloos.

Ephyra: in Epirus, on the mainland in the north-west, not the Ephyra identified with Corinth.

Tlepolemos: see p. 93. For this episode, cf. DS 4. 36. 1.

of his sons: by the fifty daughters of Thespios, see p. 71; he made Iolaos the leader of the forty who colonized Sardinia (see further DS 4. 29. 3 ff. with P. 7. 2. 2 and 9. 23. 1).

killed Eunomos: he hit him harder than he had intended, cf. DS 4. 36. 2; according to P. 2. 13. 8, he was angry because the boy, there named Cyathos, had used water from the foot-bath.

Nessos had settled there: for how he came to be there, see p. 75.

if she wanted a love-potion: in reality it would be a dangerous poison because the blood from his wound was tainted by the hydra's poison from Heracles' arrows, see p. 90.

Theiodamas: compare the story on p. 82. In the present case, Theiodamas is not a simple herdsman (as might be inferred), but the king of the Dryopes (cf. AR 1. 1213 ff. with the sc. on 1212, reporting Pherecydes). AR remarks that Heracles took the ox to provoke a war with the Dryopes; and according to Pherecydes, he returned to his city after Heracles took his ox, and mounted an expedition against him, but he was eventually killed by Heracles, who captured his son Hylas (see p. 51) and transferred the Dryopes from the north to the frontiers of Phocis. See also DS 4. 37. 1 f., where the king is named Phylas.

Ceux: a son of one of Amphitryon's brothers, and thus a relative of Heracles (sc. Soph. *Trach.* 40; not the son of Heosphoros on p. 38, etc.); he later sheltered the sons of Heracles, p. 92. Heracles appeared in the *Marriage of Ceux*, a lost epic that the ancients attributed to Hesiod.

90 *as an ally of Aigimios, king of the Dorians*: during Heracles' lifetime, the Dorians were still in their early home north of the Corinthian Gulf (see p. 37 and note), but the Heraclids (his sons and descendants) would maintain this alliance with the Dorians, and lead them in an invasion of the Peloponnese, to displace the last Pelopid and become rulers in the main centres (pp. 92 ff.). As Perseids they had a legitimate claim to Argos (and possibly to Laconia and Messenia also, as Heracles had settled the succession there during his campaigns). It was in fact the case that the Dorian inhabitants of the Peloponnese had entered it from the north at a relatively late period; and it was believed that their supposed involvement with the Heraclids gave legitimacy to their occupation of

the land. For the present war with the Lapiths, another Thessalian people, see also DS 4. 37. 3.

90 *Cycnos*: see the battle with Cycnos, son of Ares, on p. 82, and note. Although different names are given for Cycnos' mother, it can be assumed that both accounts refer to the same event.

killed Amyntor: in DS 4. 37. 4 Heracles attacks and kills the king (there called Ormenios) because he refuses to surrender his daughter, Astydameia (and afterwards fathers Ctesippos by her, who is mentioned as his son by the daughter of Amyntor on p. 92).

vengeance on Eurytos: for refusing to give him Iole after he had won the contest for her hand, p. 84. This episode was treated in an early epic, the *Sack of Oichalia*. There was disagreement on the location of Oichalia (cf. P. 4. 2. 3), but Euboea was the most favoured locality, which is consistent with the indications here (notably the remark on p. 85 that Eurytos' cattle were stolen from Euboea).

how matters stood with regard to Iole: DS 4. 38. 1 states explicitly that she learned from Lichas that Heracles loved Iole; we are probably meant to assume that here. For the tunic, see p. 89.

into the Euboean Sea: following Ov. *Met.* 9. 218 (cf. *Ibis* 492, and VM 1. 58 and 2. 165), to replace 'from Boeotia' in the manuscripts, which is evidently corrupt because he was at Cenaion, the northwestern promontory of Euboea.

91 *Poias*: the Argonaut, p. 50, and father of Philoctetes, p. 121. Although it was more commonly said that Philoctetes lit the pyre and was given Heracles' bow in return (e.g. Soph. *Philoctetes* 801 ff., DS 4. 38. 4), this may well be the earlier tradition.

raised him up to heaven: the apotheosis of Heracles is a relatively late element in the tradition. He is clearly regarded as mortal in *Il.* 18. 117 ff.; in the *Odyssey*, Odysseus meets Heracles in Hades, 11. 601-27 (although there is an awkward interpolation after the first line, stating that the Heracles in Hades was only a phantom, *eidolon*, and the real Heracles was in heaven with Hebe, 602-4; a similar passage in *Theog.*, 950 ff., that refers to his marriage in Olympos is also regarded as a later interpolation). The evidence from the visual arts suggests that the story of his apotheosis originated at the end of the seventh century. Before this promotion he was worshipped solely as a hero.

married . . . Hebe: there is no myth associated with Heracles as a god beyond this marriage to Hebe, the personification of youth (cf. Pind. *Nem.* 1. 69 ff. and 10. 17 f., *Isth.* 4. 55 ff.). The names for their children, otherwise unattested, are derived from Heracles' cultic titles as *Alexikakos* (Averter of Evil) and *Kallinikos* (the Noble Victor, see p. 86).

the daughters of Thespios: see p. 91.

92 *the altar of Pity*: or Mercy, in the marketplace, see P. 1. 17. 1; an unusual cult in Greece.

the Athenians . . . in a war with Eurystheus: under Theseus (P. 1. 32. 5) or Demophon, son of Theseus (AL 33, following Pherecydes, cf. Eur. *Heraclidae* 111 ff.).

Hyllos . . . killed him: or Iolaos did, Pind. *Pyth.* 9. 79 ff., P. 1. 44. 14.

their return: a return, *kathodos*, because the Heraclids were Perseids from Argos, and were claiming their legitimate rights. After the death of Eurystheus, it was the will of the gods that the Pelopids should rule the main Peloponnesian centres, in Mycenae (see p. 145 and note) and Sparta (see pp. 122 and 146 and note), and that they should not be displaced until after the Trojan War (fifty years after, it was usually said, when Tisamenos was killed, see p. 94 with p. 164 and note; this was regarded as the last episode in mythological history).

93 *Tlepolemos . . . killed Licymnios*: cf. *Il.* 2. 653 ff., Pind. *Ol.* 7. 27 ff., where the killing is not accidental as here; and see Strabo 14. 8. 6 ff. for the place of Tlepolemos in Rhodian mythology. On Licymnios, Alcmene's brother, see p. 69; the incident took place at Argos, where his grave was shown (P. 2. 22. 8).

with his army: the narrative is now interrupted by a gap in the text. Hyllos must certainly have been defeated and killed. It was generally accepted that he challenged the Peloponnesians to settle the matter by single combat; and that when Echemos, king of Tegea, took up the challenge and killed Hyllos, the Heraclids withdrew in accordance with the agreed terms (Hdt. 9. 26. cf. DS 4. 58. 2–4, and P. 8. 5. 1; but we cannot be sure that Ap. told the story in this way, because he talks of a 'further battle' in the next invasion). And then, according to Eusebius (*Prep. Evang.* 5. 20), Aristomachos, the son of Cleodaios and grandson of Hyllos, consulted the oracle about how they should invade the Peloponnese, and was told that they would be victorious if they travelled by the narrow route. So he invaded by the Isthmus of Corinth, only to be defeated and killed (as Ap. reports when the text resumes). This oracle, so disastrously misinterpreted by Aristomachos, must have been mentioned in the missing passage because it is referred to without explanation shortly below.

93 *Tisamenos . . . was king of the Peloponnesians*: as the last Pelopid, ruling both Argos and Lacedaimon, Tisamenos was the most important king in the Peloponnese, but by no means the only king (cf. P. 2. 18. 7).

Aristomachos: in the manuscripts, Cleolaos, a mistake for Cleodaios, the son of Hyllos and father of Aristomachos, but Cleodaios was killed during Hyllos' invasion and Aristomachos during the next, so the final return will be led by the sons of Aristomachos, Temenos and Cresphontes (Aristodemos, his other son, being killed beforehand), as we will see below. There must surely have been an account of the Heraclid line from Hyllos onwards in the missing passage just above.

by the narrows, the broad-bellied sea: this is not as perverse as it sounds. They had thought that the oracle meant a narrow stretch of land, the Isthmus of Corinth, but it really meant the Gulf of Corinth (which is to the right of the Isthmus from the perspective of Delphi, to the north of it), which stretches a great distance from east to west (and is in that sense broad-bellied) but is very narrow if one is crossing from its northern shore to the Peloponnese at the south.

Naupactos: the name is said to be derived from *naus epexato* (cf. P. 10. 38. 5). Naupactos lies in western Locris, where the Corinthian Gulf is at its narrowest before it widens again at the entrance.

Aristodemos: one of the three sons of Aristomachos; for another account of his death, see P. 3. 1. 6. According to the Lacedaimonian tradition he survived to lead the conquest of Sparta (Hdt. 6. 52, Xenophon *Agesilaos* 8. 7).

because of the diviner: these disasters were caused by the anger of Apollo, who had inspired the seer (named by Pausanias as Carnos, an Acarnanian) with his gift of prophecy (P. 3. 13. 4).

94 *Oxylos*: compare P. 5. 3. 5 ff., where he is said to have been the son of Haimon, son of Thoas, son of Andraimon; he had accidentally killed his brother Thermios (or a certain Alcidocos, son of Scopios) when throwing a discus.

Pamphylos and Dymas, the sons of Aigimios: see pp. 89–90. The Heraclids were leading a Dorian army together with the descendants of their king Aigimios (himself the son of Doros, eponym of the Dorians). These sons of Aigimios (now allies of the great-great-grandsons of Heracles!) were the eponymous ancestors of the Pamphyloi and Dymanes, two of the three tribes into which the

Dorians were divided in most of their communities, the third, the Hylleis, being named after Hyllos (regarded as an adopted son of Aigimios).

a clod of earth: cf. P. 4. 3. 4 f., essentially the same story, although the stratagem is slightly different. There was rich agricultural land in Messenia (which was conquered in the eighth to seventh centuries by the Spartans, who reduced its inhabitants to serfdom).

Temenos spurned . . . Deiphontes: see P. 2. 19. 1 and 2. 28. 3 ff.

some men from Titana: reading *Titanious* for *titanas*; Titana lay near Sicyon. Or perhaps simply *tinas*, 'some men'.

95 *Cresphontes . . . was assassinated*: presumably Polyphontes is responsible, as in Hyg. 137; but in P. 4. 3. 7, where there is no mention of Polyphontes, he is killed by the men of property because he has been ruling in the interest of the common people, and Aipytos, the son of Cresphontes who escaped, is placed on the throne by the Arcadians and other Dorian kings when he grows up.

96 *As we have said*: see p. 60.

It is said by some: including Homer, *Il.* 14. 321 f. There was much disagreement on these genealogies.

whose breath smelled of roses: reading *rhodou apopneon* (*apopleon* in the manuscripts). This may seem strange, but Hes. *Cat.* fr. 140 refers to an odour of saffron coming from the bull's mouth. Carrière points to Eustathius on *Il.* 14. 321, where it is further stated that Europa came to love the bull because it smelt of roses.

according to Homer: see *Il.* 6. 198 f.; but Homer's Sarpedon lived at a much later period, for he commanded the Lycians during the Trojan War. Ap. claims below that the present Sarpedon was granted an exceptionally long life by Zeus, while according to DS (5. 78. 3), the Sarpedon at Troy was a separate figure, the grandson of the present Sarpedon (who will settle in Lycia, see below); such were the alternative ways in which the mythographers resolved chronological problems of this kind.

the city of Thasos in Thrace: the island of Thasos, which contained a city of the same name, lay off the coast of Thrace; this is poorly expressed, if not corrupt. Thasos is said to have founded the original settlement on the island with Phoenician followers (cf. Hdt. 6. 46 f. and P. 5. 25. 12, where Thasos is described as a son of Phoenix and of Agenor respectively).

97 *they quarrelled with one another*: not all three of them, for it appears from the following narrative that the conflict over Miletos involved

Minos and Sarpedon alone (which is consistent with the account in AL 30, following Nicander, where there is no mention of Rhadamanthys). The present story is probably of Hellenistic origin; Herodotus (1. 173) speaks merely of a fight for the throne, in which Minos gained the upper hand and expelled Sarpedon and his followers.

97 *Miletos landed in Caria*: in the south-west corner of Asia Minor; Lycia lay south-east of it, and Cilicia to the east of that. For the foundation of Miletos, cf. P. 7. 2. 3.

for the islanders: although somewhat ambiguous, this is probably a reference to the tradition that he laid down laws for the Aegean islanders (cf. DS 5. 79). The Cretan constitution (which bore some resemblance to that of Sparta and was highly regarded) was attributed either to Rhadamanthys (DS 4. 60, Strabo 10. 4. 8) or to Minos (e.g. DS 4. 78).

married Alcmene: Heracles' mother, see p. 72. The reason for his flight is unclear.

sits as a judge with Minos in Hades: first attested by Plato in the fourth century (*Apol.* 41a, probably referring to an earlier tradition, associated with the Eleusinian Mysteries); in Homer, Minos judges in Hades, continuing his earthly function amongst the shades (*Od.* 11. 568 ff.), while Rhadamanthys lives for ever in Elysium (*Od.* 4. 563 f.) on the earth's surface. See also Pind. *Ol.* 2. 75 ff.

98 *exiled from Athens for murder*: see p. 138.

the Minotaur: the 'Minos-bull'. See also DS 4. 77.

with a maze . . . passage out: a verse fragment of unknown origin (Tr. Adesp. 34 Nauck).

we will speak of that later: see p. 140.

he consulted the oracle: according to the other main source, DS 5. 59. 1 ff., the oracle was revealed to Althaimenes himself when he was enquiring about other things; this would make Catreus' subsequent search for him more intelligible.

Atabyrion: the tallest mountain in Rhodes, over 4,000 feet; the cult there was very ancient, perhaps of Phoenician origin. Cf. DS 5. 59. 2.

99 *Nauplios*: see p. 62 and note; a great traveller who is enlisted elsewhere to perform such services, see p. 88.

Pleisthenes married . . . Aerope: following Hes. *Cat.* (fr. 194–5, where Pleisthenes is the son of Atreus); Agamemnon and Menelaos were more generally regarded as her children by Atreus, see also p. 146 and note.

Idomeneus: he succeeded Catreus as king of Crete, was one of Helen's suitors, p. 121, and led the Cretans in the Trojan War. Traditions vary as to whether he recovered his throne after the war (as *Od.* 3. 191 seems to suggest) or was expelled by Leucos, p. 160.

Glaucos: a son of Minos and Pasiphae, see p. 97.

Polyidos: a descendant of the seer Melampous (either a great-grandson or a great-great-grandson, P. 1. 43. 5 and sc. *Il.* 13. 63 respectively); he is particularly associated with Corinth (*Il.* 13. 663, cf. Pind. *Ol.* 13. 75).

compared the cow's colouring to a blackberry: according to Hyg. 136, the cow was not dappled, as one might suppose, but changed colour three times a day, and the colours were white, red, and black; a blackberry passes through that sequence of colours as it ripens.

by a certain kind of divination: Hyg., ibid., reports that while Polyidos was observing omens, he saw an owl (*glaux*, suggesting Glaucos) sitting over the wine-cellar and putting bees (suggesting honey) to flight.

100 *a cow from the herds of Pelagon*: according to the oracle as reported by sc. Eur. *Phoen.* 638, he was told to seek for this herdsman. This was no ordinary cow; on each flank it had a white mark like the full moon (P. 9. 12. 1).

Spartoi: 'Sown Men'.

deliberately: the reading in the Epitome, *hekousian*, is surely preferable to *akousian*, 'involuntarily', in the manuscripts. Otherwise the antithesis is lost.

for an everlasting year: to atone for the killing of Ares' dragon (not the death of the Spartoi); the text may well be corrupt here, because Hellanicos, who is almost certainly Ap.'s source for this story, says that Cadmos served Ares for a (normal) year (sc. *Il.* 2. 494, where we are also told that Ares initially wanted to kill him, but Zeus prevented it). The phrase explaining what an everlasting or 'great' year means seems to be a gloss.

101 *the Cadmeia*: the eminence dominating Thebes and site of the citadel.

a deception by Hera: Hera assumed the form of her nurse, Beroe, and appealed to her vanity: if Zeus really loved her, she should ask him to come to her as he would to a goddess (Hyg. 179, VM 2. 79; see also Ov. *Met.* 3. 259 ff., this would also serve as a test that he is not merely pretending to be a god).

101 *daughters of Cadmos . . . because of that*: see Eur. *Bacchae* 23 ff. and
242 ff.; the slander is central to the plot of the *Bacchae*, because it
is this that provokes Dionysos to demonstrate his powers in
Thebes and drive the women mad, as described below, p. 102.

Hera . . . drove them mad: see also p. 43 and note.

Leucothea: she became the 'White Goddess', who had a general
Mediterranean cult as a deity who protected seafarers. It was she
who saved Odysseus when Poseidon sent a storm against him after
he had left Calypso, *Od.* 5. 333 ff.

Isthmian Games . . . in honour of Melicertes: his body was cast
ashore on the Isthmus of Corinth; he is often said to have been
carried there by a dolphin, see P. 1. 44. 11. These games were held
at Corinth. For Sisyphos, king of Ephyra/Corinth, see p. 44. His
hero-cult as Palaimon was centred in this area (see e.g. P. 2. 2. 3).

102 *the Hyades*: seven stars in the constellation Taurus, outlining the
face of the bull; it was commonly said that Zeus placed them there
for delivering Dionysos safely to Ino (ascribed to Pherecydes in
Hyg. *PA* 21).

saw Artemis bathing: this story, which first appears in Callimachus
(*Hymn* 5. 107 ff.; cf. Hyg. 181), is generally accepted in the later
tradition; hunting on a hot day on Mount Cithairon in Boeotia, he
fell asleep by a spring, and awoke to see Artemis bathing. It dis-
places the earlier tradition, as represented in Hes. *Cat.* (see note
on Appendix, 4) and Stesichorus (P. 9. 2. 3) that the anger of Zeus
led to his death. Or according to Eur. *Bacchae* 339 ff., she killed
him because he boasted that he was a better hunter.

driven mad by Hera: because he was a son of Zeus by another woman.

learned the rites of initiation: the rites of Cybele, the great mother-
goddess of Phrygia, who was worshipped with ecstatic rites and
mountain wandering, came to be identified with those of Rhea in
Crete. Accordingly, Dionysos is taught his ecstatic rites by Rhea
at Cybele's home in north-western Asia Minor.

Lycourgos: for his hostility and the flight of Dionysos, cf. *Il.* 6.
130 ff.; the land of the Edonians lay in north-eastern Macedonia,
bordering Thrace.

Bacchai: the women seized by Bacchic frenzy.

Satyrs: daemons who attended Dionysos. They had a thick tail like
that of a horse, and in many depictions, the lower half of their
body is like that of a goat or a horse and they are ithyphallic. The
behaviour of the Satyr on pp. 60–1 is characteristic.

believing that he was pruning a vine branch: he was trying to eliminate the vines as a source of intoxication associated with Dionysos;
it is also said that he mutilated himself (Hyg. 132, VM 1. 122;
Carrière suggests a slight alteration in the text to give that meaning here).

and the whole of India . . . pillars: marking the eastern limits of the
inhabited world, corresponding to the pillars of Heracles in the
west, see p. 80 and note. Some regard this phrase as an interpolation.

he arrived in Thebes: the following is a summary of Eur. *Bacchae*,
which contains much of interest on Dionysos.

103 *When they had him on board*: see the fuller version of the following story in the first *Homeric Hymn to Dionysos*; there he frightened the sailors by causing a bear to appear and turning himself
into a lion (and it is not stated that the oars and mast were changed
into snakes). See also Ov. *Met.* 3. 605 ff.

Cadmos left Thebes . . . the Encheleans: resigning the throne to
Pentheus; the reason for his departure is unclear. The Encheleans,
like the Illyrians, lived in the western Balkans, north of Epirus.

into a snake: in hero-cult, a snake would often symbolize the hero
or represent the form in which he supposedly manifested himself;
but in late sources (e.g. Hyg. 6, cf. Ov. *Met.* 4. 562 ff.) it was suggested that the metamorphosis was a punishment for the murder
of Ares' dragon.

thought in much the same way: with regard to the Bacchants, presumably; but there is no record of that elsewhere. Polydoros
became king after Pentheus was killed in the way described above,
and he was succeeded by Labdacos. According to P. 9. 5. 2,
Labdacos was a child when he came to the throne, and was placed
under the guardianship of Nycteus and then of Lycos, but ruled
briefly in his own right when he came of age (no reason is given
for his death); and Lycos then became guardian of the young Laios.

as long as Laios remained a child: but Lycos never restored the throne
to Laios, and the suggestion of a guardianship conflicts with the
previous statement (confirmed below) that Lycos usurped the
throne; perhaps a clumsy way of saying that Lycos initially took
power as Laios' guardian.

104 *from Euboea . . . settled at Hyria*: a problematic passage. Ap. gives
two genealogies for Lycos and Nycteus. The present story is irreconcilable with that given just above, for if they were sons of
Chthonios, a 'Sown Man' (see p. 100), they would be native-born

Explanatory Notes

Thebans and their presence in Thebes would need no explanation. But if they were sons of Hyrieus (as on p. 117, of Atlantid descent), they would have been born in Hyria (near Aulis in Boeotia) because their father was the eponymous king of the city, and would not have come there from elsewhere. Furthermore, since Phlegyas, whom they are said to have killed, was king of Orchomenos (P. 9. 36. 1), which lies on the mainland in Boeotia, and the brothers themselves had no known connection with Euboea, it is not clear why their killing of Phlegyas should have made them flee from *Euboea*. (Perhaps in the original story this explained why they left their native Hyria. There is a Euboean Lycos in Eur. *Heracles*.)

104 *from there . . . to Thebes*: following a suggestion by Heyne to fill a short gap in the text.

polemarch: military commander.

to Epopeus: a son of Aiolos' daughter, Canace, p. 38, who left Thessaly for Sicyon (in the north-eastern Peloponnese near the Isthmus of Corinth), where he became king when the previous ruler died without children, see P. 2. 6. 1 ff.

killed himself: or according to P. 2. 6. 2, he himself attacked Epopeus, but was wounded, and gave the following orders before he died.

the stones followed . . . Amphion's lyre: cf. AR 1. 735 ff. and P. 9. 5. 3 f. Homer tells of their fortification of Thebes, *Od.* 11. 260 ff., but not of the power of Amphion's music; similar stories were told of Orpheus' music, p. 30. These were the famous walls with the seven gates.

105 *Homer*: he gives the essentials of the following story in *Il.* 24. 602 ff., although the details vary greatly within the subsequent tradition.

Amphion alone survived: presumably the father of the children rather than a Niobid not mentioned above.

Chloris: see P. 2. 21. 10 (where this Chloris is identified with Meliboia below; her name was changed to Chloris, 'pale', because she went pale with fear and remained so ever afterwards). Ap. wrongly identifies this Chloris, the daughter of Amphion of Thebes, with the daughter of Amphion of Orchomenos who married Neleus (see *Od.* 11. 281 ff., P. 10. 29. 2).

transformed into a stone: Homer records that she became a stone (*Il.* 24. 614 ff.) without explaining how. The rock, on Mount Sipylos (in Lydia, Asia Minor), bore no resemblance to a woman when viewed close at hand, but if the visitor drew back, he could make out the image of a weeping woman bowed in grief (according to Pausanias, who claims to have seen it, 1. 21. 5, cf. QS 1. 299 ff.).

the death of Amphion: he is said to have reacted to the death of his children by killing himself (Ov. *Met.* 6. 271), or by trying to storm the temple of Apollo, provoking the god to shoot him (Hyg. 9). For the death of Zethos, see P. 9. 5. 5.

others Epicaste: as in *Od.* 11. 271, when Odysseus meets her in Hades; but Iocaste (Jocasta) is general in later writers.

called him Oedipus: the name Oidipous is derived from *oidein*, to swell, and *pous*, a foot (a valid etymology); but the familiar Latinized form of his name is used in the translation. For further details on all the following see Ap.'s main sources, Sophocles' *Oedipus the King* and *Oedipus at Colonos*.

supposititious child: i.e. as one who was not the child of his supposed parents, but is passed off as being their child.

106 *a certain narrow track*: the 'Cleft Way', a mountain track leading to Delphi, see P. 10. 5. 1 ff.

Creon, son of Menoiceus: and thus the great-grandson of Pentheus, and a member of the Theban royal line. He was the brother of Iocaste and uncle of Oedipus.

Hera sent the Sphinx: in *Theog.* 326, the daughter of Orthos and Chimaira. In the absence of a settled tradition, different sources point to various episodes in Theban history that might have caused a deity to send her. Ap. may be referring to the tradition that Hera sent her in anger at Laios' abduction of Chrysippos, p. 104 (sc. Eur. *Phoen.* 1760); but it was also said that Ares sent her, still angry at the murder of his dragon, p. 100 (Arg. Eur. *Phoen.*), or Dionysos (sc. *Theog.* 326), angry at his rejection by Pentheus, p. 103.

a single voice: an obscure indication that the same being is involved in each case.

by Euryganeia: according to Pherecydes (sc. Eur. *Phoen.* 53), he first married Iocaste, who bore him two sons, Phrastos and Leonytos, but he put her aside after his descent was revealed and married Euryganeia, who bore him the sons ascribed elsewhere to Iocaste. She was the mother of his children in the *Oedipodia*, an early epic (P. 9. 5. 5).

107 *cursing his sons*: it was also said that he cursed them for setting the silver table and golden goblet of Cadmos before him, so reminding him of his birth (Athenaeus 465e f.), and for serving him meat

from the haunch, considered a less honourable portion, rather than the shoulder (sc. Soph. *Oed. Col.* 1375, both quoting the *Thebais*, an early epic).

107 *Arriving . . . at Colonos*: following Sophocles' *Oedipus at Colonos*. In early sources, he continued to rule in Thebes (*Od.* 11. 274 ff., cf. *Il.* 23. 678 ff., Hes. *Cat.* fr. 192); this is also implied in the traditions from early epic mentioned in the previous two notes. Colonos (Sophocles' birthplace) lay a mile north of Athens.

the Eumenides: 'the gracious ones', a euphemism for the Erinyes (Furies). On their sanctuary, see Soph. *Oed. Col.* 36 ff.; they had another by the Areiopagos (P. 1. 28. 6).

Eteocles . . . refused to give up the throne: cf. Eur. *Phoenissae* 67 ff.; this is the dominant tradition in later sources, but the names of the brothers suggest that Polyneices, 'the man of many quarrels' (cf. Aesch. *Seven against Thebes* 658), rather than Eteocles ('true glory'), was originally the guilty party. Pherecydes and Hellanicos offered conflicting accounts (sc. Eur. *Phoen.* 71), the one saying that Polyneices was expelled by force, and the other that Polyneices was offered a choice between the throne and the Cadmeian treasures and chose the latter, but then tried to seize the throne as well.

Adrastos, son of Talaos: and thus a grandson of Bias, p. 47, while Amphiaraos is a descendant of the seer Melampous (cf. *Od.* 15. 223 ff.).

Tydeus . . . had fled there from Calydon: see p. 42 and note.

a boar . . . a lion: the emblem on Tydeus' shield refers to the Calydonian boar, and that on Polyneices' to the lion-faced Sphinx expelled by his father Oedipus (according to sc. Eur. *Phoen.* 409). On this episode see also Eur. *Phoenissae* 408 ff. and *Suppliants* 132 ff.

108 *went to Iphis*: an Argive king descended from Proitos. Polyneices may have wanted the benefit of his local knowledge; or perhaps this is connected with the tradition that Eriphyle was the daughter of Iphis (sc. *Il.* 11. 326).

conflict . . . between Amphiaraos and Adrastos: they had quarrelled over the kingship, and Adrastos had been expelled for a time (see DS 4. 65. 6, with Pind. *Nem.* 9. 13 f.); he went to Sicyon, and ruled there after the previous king had died (P. 2. 6. 3).

allow Eriphyle to decide: as the sister of Adrastos and wife of Amphiaraos, she might be expected to be even-handed. Homer alludes to her betrayal of her husband (*Od.* 11. 326 f.) without telling the story.

seven leaders: corresponding to the seven gates in the walls of Thebes, see below.

Lycourgos: son of Pheres, see p. 48; Nemea was on the northern border of the Argolid.

Thoas had been spared: when the Lemnian women killed their menfolk, Hypsipyle, their queen, spared her father, see p. 50.

109 *Archemoros*: meaning the beginning of death, or first to die; cf. Bacch. 9. 14, 'an omen of the coming slaughter'.

sent Tydeus ahead . . . to the camp: cf. *Il.* 4. 382 ff.; portents from the gods caused him to release Maion (ibid. 398).

advanced towards the walls: the attack on Thebes was recounted in an early epic, the *Thebais*, and became a favourite theme in tragedy, see Aesch. *Seven against Thebes*, and Eur. *Phoenissae*.

seven gates: see P. 9. 8. 4 ff. (who offers some explanation of the names). Hypsistan means 'highest'; the name of the Crenidian suggests that it was by a spring.

110 *saw the goddess completely naked*: preceded by a short gap in the text. For the story, see Callimachus *Hymn* 5. 57 ff. (probably following Pherecydes). While Athene and Chariclo, the mother of Amphiaraos, were bathing at noon in the Hippocrene, a spring on Mount Helicon in Boeotia, Teiresias, who was out with his dogs, happened to approach the waters, and caught sight of them.

purified his ears . . . the language of birds: compare the story of Melampous on p. 46 and see notes.

Hesiod says: in the *Melampodeia* (Hes. fr. 275), see also Appendix, **4** and note. The following story is reported somewhat differently in sc. *Od.* 10. 494. There he kills the female snake on the first occasion, and becomes a man again when he kills the male snake on the second; this has a certain logic, but we cannot tell whether it is closer to the version in the *Melampodeia* in the absence of any relevant quotation. It should be noted, however, that in all other versions, he is said to have wounded or killed one snake or both on the second occasion also (e.g. AL 17, Ov. *Met.* 3. 316 ff., Hyg. 75). Cyllene lay in Arcadia.

one part . . . nine parts: apparently a misinterpretation of the *Melampodeia*, see Appendix, **5** and note.

to a considerable age: on the same occasion Zeus granted him the privilege of living for seven generations (Phlegon under Hes. fr. 275).

Explanatory Notes

110 *Menoiceus . . . as a sacrifice to Ares*: see Eur. *Phoenissae* 930 ff.; to gain the favour of Ares, a descendant of one of the Sown Men must offer his life to atone for the murder of Ares' dragon (see p. 100).

Zeus struck him down: as retribution for his impious arrogance, for Capaneus boasted that he would sack the town whether Zeus wished it or not, and said that the thunder and lightning of Zeus were no worse than the midday sun (Aesch. *Seven against Thebes* 427 ff., cf. Eur. *Suppl.* 496 ff.). Or he climbed the ladder with two torches, saying that one was thunder and the other lightning (sc. Eur. *Phoen.* 1173), behaving rather like Salmoneus on p. 45. A descendant of Proitos, Capaneus was a member of the native royal line in Argos.

111 *for Tydeus . . . killed Melanippos*: in all other sources, Amphiaraos himself killed him (e.g. sc. *Il.* 5. 126, referring to Pherecydes). This may well be an interpolation.

Zeus made him immortal: he was worshipped as a healer god and had an oracle at Oropos (latterly in Attica, but previously in Boeotia). See P. 1. 34. 2 (and, for the site of his disappearance, 9. 8. 2).

after having intercourse with him in the likeness of a Fury: but see P. 8. 25. 4 ff. Poseidon wanted to have intercourse with her while she was searching for her daughter; she turned herself into a mare, but Poseidon responded by turning himself into a stallion, and so achieved his desire; and she received the title of Fury (Erinys) because of her anger afterwards (hence the cult of Demeter Erinys at Thelpusa). It was this intercourse in horse-form that led Demeter to give birth to Adrastos' horse, Areion. On Areion see also *Il.* 23. 346 f.

Creon . . . to the Theban throne: thus in Sophocles' *Antigone*, Ap.'s source for the following; but the tradition that he was acting as regent until Eteocles' son Laodamas came of age (P. 1. 39. 2 and 9. 10. 3) is easier to reconcile with other elements in the mythology of this period. It will be seen that Laodamas was king of the Thebans when the Epigoni invaded (and there was indeed a tradition that it was he who caused the death of Antigone, and her sister Ismene too, Arg. Soph. *Ant.*).

suppliant's bough: an olive bough, placed on an altar as a symbolic gesture when claiming divine protection. For the present altar, see p. 92 and note.

captured the city: it may be doubted that Theseus was ever said to have captured the city, in the strict sense. He either forced the Thebans to surrender the bodies by defeating them in a battle, or persuaded them to do so by negotiation (see Plut. *Thes.* 29, P. 1. 39. 2, and cf. Eur. *Suppliants* 653 ff.).

the Epigoni: 'the afterborn', used as a proper name when referring to these sons of the Argive leaders who mounted a second, and now successful, expedition against Thebes.

112 *Eriphyle . . . persuaded her sons also to take part*: a reduplication of the story of Eriphyle and Amphiaraos on p. 108; but it should be noted that she does not have the same hold on her sons as she had on her husband, and far from being fated to die, her sons will survive as leading figures in a successful expedition. Amphiaraos had indeed ordered them to mount such an expedition, p. 108. The story of the Second Theban War was told in an early epic, the *Alcmaionis*; and there (sc. *Od.* 11. 326) Alcmaion kills his mother before departing, leaving no place for the present story.

killed Aigialeus: just as Adrastos was the only leader to survive on the first expedition, his son Aigialeus is the only leader to be killed on the second (thus giving his life in place of his father, as Hyg. 71 explicitly states).

Hestiaia: in Thessaly; but they are also said to have travelled further north, to Illyria (Hdt. 5. 61; P. 9. 5. 7).

113 *the Fury of his mother's murder*: those who shed blood, especially within their own family, were liable to be pursued by an Erinys, or avenging spirit.

a land . . . by the Sun: since the text is hopelessly corrupt at this point, I follow Carrière's example and simply give the content of the oracle as reported by Thucydides (2. 102). He must seek a land that did not exist when the pollution was incurred (cf. P. 8. 24. 8). From Aetolia, he travels to the Thesprotians in Epirus in north-western Greece, and thence to the springs of the River Acheloos (also in Epirus) but founds his city much further south at its mouth, by the entrance to the Corinthian Gulf (at Oiniadai in Acarnania, Thuc. 2. 102). Acheloos functions both as a person and a river. On Acheloos see also p. 88 and note.

had been informed by an oracle: although one might infer from the present narrative that Alcmaion is inventing this, he is said to have received such an oracle (Athenaeus 232d ff. tells how it supposedly ran).

Explanatory Notes

114 *founded Acarnania*: to the west of Aetolia facing the Ionian Sea; see also P. 8. 24. 9.

Euripides: in his lost tragedy *Alcmaion in Corinth*.

founded Amphilochian Argos: Thucydides' report (2. 68) that it was founded by his uncle Amphilochos, son of Amphiaraos, on his return from Troy reflects the older tradition; the present Amphilochos was apparently invented by Euripides, and his late entry into the family causes nothing but confusion, cf. p. 162 and note.

as we observed above: see p. 58 and note. Pelasgos, the Arcadian 'first man', becomes the father of Lycaon, the founder of the common cult of the Arcadian communities, that of Zeus Lycaios on Mount Lycaion.

fifty sons: for the most part eponymous founders of Arcadian towns. See also P. 8. 3. The list is one name short.

115 *a child . . . into the sacrifices*: according to a similar account by Nicolaus of Damascus, first century BC (see Frazer i. 390 n. 1 for a translation), the pious Lycaon warned his subjects that Zeus made constant visits to inspect their behaviour; and one day, when he offered a sacrifice saying that the god was about to visit, some of his sons performed the present action to check whether the god really did come (for if he did, he would surely recognize what they had done). There is a conflicting version of this story in which Lycaon himself (angered by Zeus' seduction of Callisto, see below) served his grandson Arcas to Zeus, who reacted by overturning the table and transforming Lycaon into a wolf (see under Hes. *Cat.* fr. 163, and Hyg. *PA* 4). See also P. 8. 2. 1 ff. for the local tradition, and Ovid's portrait of a wicked Lycaon in *Met.* 1. 196 ff.

Trapezous: from *trapeza*, a table; but the town is also said to have been named after one of Lycaon's sons (P. 8. 3. 3).

Hesiod . . . one of the nymphs: according to *Catast.* 1, Hesiod called her a daughter of Lycaon; but Ap. may be reporting the *Catalogue*, and *Catast.* the Hesiodic *Astronomy*.

Hera persuaded Artemis . . . to shoot her: after discovering what had happened, and leaving Artemis ignorant of the bear's identity; in a somewhat different version, Callisto sleeps willingly with Zeus and Hera herself transforms her (P. 8. 3. 6 f.; attested for Callimachus in sc. *Il.* 18. 487). But in the story attributed to Hesiod in *Catast.* 1, it is Artemis who transforms her, angered to see that her companion is pregnant when she is taking a bath. See also Ov. *Met.* 2. 409 ff.

naming him Arcas: in Greek there is a similarity in sound between *arktos*, a bear (his mother's present form), and *Arcas*. He gave his name to Arcadia (cf. P. 8. 4. 1, formerly named Pelasgia).

Arcas had two sons: for a fuller account of the sons of Arcas and their descendants, see P. 8. 4. 2 ff.

Auge was raped by Heracles: see also p. 88 and note.

116 *Iasos and Clymene . . . had a daughter, Atalante*: this genealogy (cf. Theognis 1287 ff., where her father is called Iasion, and Hyg. 99) connects Atalante with Arcadia; but in the main alternative cited below (that she is a daughter of Schoineus, as in Hes. *Cat.* fr. 72), she is connected with Boeotia. Some details in the stories associated with her vary according to the tradition (for instance, the husband of the Boeotian Atalante is not Melanion, who is clearly an Arcadian, cf. P. 3. 12. 9, but Hippomenes, son of Megareus, a Boeotian), but the stories themselves are substantially the same, and there is no reason to assume that there were two separate Atalantes, one Arcadian and one Boeotian.

the hunt for the Calydonian boar: where her presence as the only woman had important repercussions, see p. 41.

games held in honour of Pelias: for the death of Pelias, see p. 57; the games were held by his son Acastos (see p. 127, which also explains Peleus' presence there; and cf. Hyg. 273).

golden apples: from the Hesperides, see p. 81 and note (e.g. VM 1. 39), or according to Ovid (*Met*. 10. 644 ff.) from the sanctuary of Aphrodite at Tamasos in Cyprus.

117 *the Pleiades*: familiar as the cluster of stars in the constellation Taurus. According to the usual story, Orion pursued them (and their mother) through Boeotia, and the gods, or Zeus, taking pity on them, transferred them to the heavens (Hyg. *PA* 21; the story was known to Pindar, see *Nem*. 2. 10 ff.).

gave birth to Hermes: most of the following derives from the fuller account in the *Homeric Hymn to Hermes*, q.v. (but the present narrative differs on certain details).

118 *Cyllene . . . Pieria*: Hermes' birthplace was in Arcadia; Pieria lay north of Mount Olympos in Thessaly.

pebbles: *thriai*, or divining pebbles, which were used none the less in a subordinate role at Apollo's oracle at Delphi. It is not known exactly how they were employed.

herald to the gods of the Underworld: he conducted the souls of the dead between this world and Hades (cf. *Od*. 24. 1 ff. and p. 152).

118 *Lelex*: the local 'first man', and eponym of the Leleges, the aboriginal inhabitants; comparable to Pelasgos and the Pelasgians in Arcadia, p. 58 and notes. His son Eurotas represents the main Lacedaimonian river, and his granddaughter Sparta the main Lacedaimonian town. See also P. 3. 1. 1 ff.

119 *Hyacinthos*: see p. 30 and note.

Aphareus: a Messenian king, see also P. 4. 2. 4 ff.

but rather of Coronis: as in Hes. *Cat.* fr. 60. This Thessalian descent is consistent with the tradition that Asclepios was reared by Cheiron (on Mount Pelion in Thessaly). We know Apollo's own view on this matter because an Arcadian asked the Delphic oracle, and it declared in favour of Coronis (P. 2. 26. 6). For the story of Asclepios' birth to Coronis, see also Pind. *Pyth.* 3. 8 ff. (where there is as yet no mention of the crow).

on the left side: as always, the side of ill omen.

Zeus . . . struck him down: the story was told in Hes. *Cat.* (fr. 51). In Pind. *Pyth.* 3. 54 ff., he raises a single man in return for a handsome bribe; a number of names are cited from early sources in an interpolation here, see Appendix, 6. The theme becomes exaggerated in the later tradition and we find Hades complaining to Zeus about a serious diminution of the dead (DS 4. 71. 2); but to raise a single man is to transgress mortal bounds, meriting this response from Zeus. Asclepios was worshipped initially as a hero, and then as a healing god with an important cult at Epidaurus.

who had forged the thunderbolt: see p. 28.

120 *Apollo went to Admetos*: see also p. 48.

there are those . . . Bateia: Perieres was first introduced to us as a Deucalionid king of Messenia, p. 44; but Tyndareus is a figure of such importance in the Laconian genealogies that it was natural that others preferred to regard him as being of purely Laconian descent, and this was the tradition followed by Ap. in the preceding genealogies. Here we are told that some tried to reconcile the conflicting traditions on his birth by claiming that there were two Perieres, one the Messenian son of Aiolos, who fathered Aphareus and Leucippos, two Messenian rulers, and the other the Laconian son of Cynortas, who became the father of Tyndareus.

Hippocoon expelled Icarios and Tyndareus: Hippocoon (and his sons) and Tyndareus disputed the throne after the death of the previous king, Oibalos (cf. P. 3. 1. 4). There are conflicting traditions on the position of the third brother, for Icarios is also said to have assisted Hippocoon in the expulsion of Tyndareus (P. 3. 1. 4, sc.

Eur. *Orest.* 457; apparently the Lacedaimonian version). Some claim that Hippocoon was an illegitimate son (e.g. sc. Eur. *Orest.* 457, where his mother is a certain Nicostrate).

Thestios: an Aetolian, see p. 39, the king of Pleuron; see also P. 3. 13. 8.

Heracles had killed Hippocoon and his sons: see pp. 87 f.

Polydeuces . . . Helen . . . Castor: that Helen was a daughter of Zeus was agreed from Homer onwards, but with regard to the Dioscuri —Polydeuces (or under his Latin name, Pollux) and Castor— there was disagreement as to whether Castor was a mortal son of Tyndareus or a son of Zeus like Polydeuces. Although Pindar agrees with the present account in *Nem.* 10 (see 73 ff., though not in *Pyth.* 4. 171 f.) and Castor was mortal in the *Cypria* (Clem. Al. *Protr.* 2. 30), there was also an early tradition that both were sons of Zeus, as the name Dioscuri implies (Hes. *Cat.* fr. 24, cf. *HH to the Dioscuri*).

and Clytemnestra: most editors favour this addition; but since Clytemnestra has been mentioned already with Timandra and Phylonoe as one of Tyndareus' children by Leda, it cannot be assumed that Ap. must have listed her as one of the children conceived *on this occasion* (and Carrière remarks that she is not always included in comparable lists, e.g. VM 2. 132).

a daughter of Zeus by Nemesis: they had intercourse at Rhamnos in Attica (*Catast.* 25), where there was a sanctuary of Nemesis (P. 1. 33. 2); according to the local legend, Nemesis was her mother, but Leda suckled and reared her (P. 1. 33. 7). The story goes back to early epic (the *Cypria*, see Athenaeus 334b ff., with a quotation). Leda too is said to have laid an egg after her intercourse in bird form (it was shown to visitors in Sparta, P. 3. 16. 1).

121 *to Aphidnai*: in Attica; see also p. 143 and note.

swear an oath: if they are to be eligible. This will be important later because when Helen is abducted by Paris, all her previous suitors will be obliged to go to war to help Menelaos recover her, p. 147.

a son, Nicostratos: in Homer, Hermione is her only child (*Od.* 4. 12 ff., cf. *Il.* 3. 175). Nicostratos would have been born after the Trojan War, as his name, 'Victorious Army', indicates. According to P. 2. 18. 5, he was an illegitimate son of Menelaos by a slave-woman, like Megapenthes below (who is mentioned in *Od.* 4. 11); in any case, Menelaos was succeeded by Orestes, son of Agamemnon, which would indicate that he had no legitimate male heirs at the time of his death.

Explanatory Notes

122 *because of their valour*: the name of the *Dioskouroi* (*kouros* means a boy, *Dios* is the genitive of Zeus) suggests that they are sons of Zeus, but here Castor has been described as the son of Tyndareus, so some explanation of their name is required, and it is claimed that they owed it to their personal qualities rather than their joint birth. Their part in two great adventures has already been mentioned, pp. 40 and 49; Ap. now tells of their later life, in particular the incident that leads to their death, thus explaining why they are not present at Troy, and why Menelaos, a Pelopid, is ruling in Lacedaimon at that time. Tyndareus has no other male descendants.

the daughters of Leucippos: a Messenian king (see p. 44, cf. P. 4. 2. 4). There was a tradition that Hilaeira and Phoebe were betrothed to Idas and Lynceus, the sons of his brother Aphareus, and that this abduction (rather than the following incident) was the cause of the quarrel that led to the death of the Dioscuri (e.g. Hyg. 80).

Lynceus caught sight of Castor: on the fate of the Dioscuri Ap., and Pindar in his more detailed account in *Nem*. 10. 55 ff., largely follow the early epic the *Cypria* (judging by Proclus' summary); there Lynceus saw both brothers hiding inside a hollow oak (sc. Pind. *Nem*. 10. 114).

amongst mortals: strictly, amongst the dead; on their shared immortality, cf. *Od*. 11. 303–4. The story rests on the assumption that Castor was a son of Tyndareus, and thus of wholly mortal birth.

123 *he wanted to violate the goddess*: she is commonly said to have actually slept with him, and willingly; according to *Od*. 5. 125 ff. on a thrice-ploughed field, causing Zeus to strike him dead afterwards when he came to hear of it. Demeter for her part gave birth to Ploutos (Wealth, here as related to successful harvests) in Crete (*Theog*. 969 ff.). See also DS 5. 77. 1 f.

went to the mainland opposite: his departure from Samothrace is often associated with a great flood sent by Zeus (sometimes identified with Deucalion's flood, p. 37), and he is said to have used inflated skins to cross the waters (e.g. Lycophron 72 ff, with scholia, and sc. *Il*. 20. 215).

named the country Troy: although we commonly refer to the city as Troy (as does Homer on occasion), this was strictly the name of the Trojans' *land* (Troia, or Troas, the Troad). The city was Ilios or Ilion (or in its Latin form, Ilium).

Ganymede: cf. *Il.* 20. 232 ff., *HH to Aphrodite* 202 ff., without as yet the eagle (general in late accounts, e.g. Verg. *Aen.* 5. 253) or any suggestion that he became the beloved of Zeus (first recorded in Eur. *Orestes* 1392, cf. Plato *Phdr.* 255c).

aroused Aphrodite's amorous desire: the central theme of *HH to Aphrodite*, cf. *Il.* 2. 819 ff.

found a city . . . where the cow lay down: this story, which is not in Homer, is clearly modelled on the Theban foundation myth, p. 100. Homer never expressly states that Ilos was the founder of Ilion, although he refers several times to his tomb on the plain (e.g. *Il.* 11. 166). In *Il.* 20. 231 ff., he is the son of Tros, but in the passing references in 11 (166 and 372), the son of Dardanos, which is probably the older tradition. Homer notes a movement from the mountains (for the kingdom of Dardanos lay on the slopes of Mount Ida, *Il.* 20. 215–18) to a more civilized and prosperous life on the rich farmland of the plains (ibid. 219 ff.).

the Palladion: a talismanic image which protected the city, see p. 156.

Triton: a sea-god (p. 33, *Theog.* 931 f.), here as the god of the River Triton in Libya (see Hdt. 4. 179 ff.; P. 9. 33. 5 claims that Athene was reared by a small river of that name in Boeotia). The myth explains Athene's title Tritogeneia (which is very ancient, and probably of quite different origin).

124 *aegis*: the 'goatskin', an attribute of Zeus depicted as a short cloak or a shield; see *Il.* 5. 733 ff.

Electra . . . raped: the daughter of Atlas, by Zeus (see p. 122, but it is not recorded there, or anywhere else, that she was *raped* by him).

with Ate: reading *met'Ates* for *met'autes* ('with her', i.e. with Electra). This explains the name of the Hill of Ate mentioned above; that she fell to earth at Ilion and the hill was named after her is confirmed by sc. *Il.* 19. 131. Ate is the personification of delusion; when Zeus was deceived by Hera over his plans for Heracles, p. 68, Zeus threw her down to earth (see *Il.* 19. 91 ff.), where her actions are clear to see.

Dawn so loved Tithonos: see *Theog.* 984 ff. and *HH to Aphrodite*, 218 ff. On Emathion see p. 82 and note; Memnon will be an important ally of the Trojans, p. 154.

as we mentioned: see p. 86.

Aisacos . . . was turned into a bird: the only other account, Ov. *Met.* 11. 749 ff., is quite different. Aisacos fell in love with the nymph

Hesperia, who was bitten by a viper while he was pursuing her; and when he threw himself into the sea in grief at her death, Tethys transformed him into a bird (there a *mergus*, or diver, but the identification depends upon a purely Latin etymology).

124 *Hecuba had a dream*: cf. Pind. *Paean* 8 (rather different), Eur. *Troades* 920 ff., Cicero *On Divination* 1. 21. 42; not in Homer.

125 *protecting: alexesas*; Alexander (strictly, Alexandros) was thus the man (*aner, andros*) who *protected* or defended.

he rediscovered his parents: Hyg. 91 gives the full story. Priam's servant came to fetch a bull for games that were to be held in honour of Priam's lost son (i.e. Paris himself). Paris went to the city and took part in the games, defeating his brothers; and when one of them, Deiphobos, drew his sword on him, he took refuge at the altar of Zeus Herceios. When Cassandra declared prophetically that he was her brother, Priam accepted him as his son.

Apollo . . . art of prophecy: cf. Aesch. *Ag.* 1202 ff.; there was another story that serpents licked the ears (cf. p. 46) of Cassandra and her brother Helenos when they were left overnight as children in the sanctuary of Thymbraean Apollo (sc. *Il.* 7. 44).

if he were ever wounded: we should probably assume that she knows by her prophetic powers that he will be wounded if he abducts Helen (as explicitly stated in Parthen. 4); a pathetic tale that appealed to later sentiment (Hellanicos in the fifth century is the earliest recorded source, Parthen. 4).

126 *learned from Sisyphos*: see also p. 44 and note.

turned the ants into people: suggested by the etymological fancy that the ancestors of the Myrmidons (the people commanded by Aiacos' grandson Achilles at Troy) were created from ants, *myrmekes*.

into a seal: she conceived *Phocos*, the eponym of the Phocians, while she was in the form of a seal, *phoke*.

127 *when Greece was gripped . . . delivered from its barrenness*: see further DS 4. 61. 1 ff., P. 2. 29. 6.

guards the keys of Hades: see also Plato *Apol.* 41a, where he judges the dead, and Isocrates *Evagoras* 15, where he is said to sit beside Pluto and Kore, and enjoy the highest honours.

Telamon . . . killed his brother: there is a varied tradition. In the earliest recorded source, the *Alcmaionis*, an early epic, both strike him (sc. Eur. *Andr.* 687). Peleus is often said to deal the deathblow (e.g. P. 2. 29. 7, where they are said to have killed him to please their mother, who would have been angry that Phocos was born to another woman). In DS 4. 72. 6 the death is accidental.

because Heracles . . . Aias: for the full story see Pind. *Isth.* 6. 35 ff. The appearance of an eagle, the bird of Zeus, indicates that Zeus will respond positively to the prayer; the son is called Aias after the *aietos* (eagle). Ajax is the Latinized form of his name. For Telamon at Troy, see p. 86.

128 *concealing his sword*: a magic sword made by Hephaistos; Acastos expects that Peleus will be killed by the Centaurs who live on Mount Helicon while he is searching for it (cf. Hes. *Cat.* fr. 209). But he is saved by the good Centaur Cheiron.

Polydora . . . River Spercheios: she is the mother of Menesthios by this river in *Il.* 16. 173; but there she is the *daughter* of Peleus and wife of Boros, son of Perieres, as on p. 127. This report that Peleus married Polydora is unattested elsewhere, and may be an error.

was told by Prometheus: alluded to in [Aesch.] *PV* 907 ff.; cf. Hyg. *PA* 15.

according to others: see Pind. *Isth.* 8. 27 ff., AR 4. 783 ff.

129 *an ashwood spear . . . horses*: later passed on to Achilles, see *Il.* 16. 140 ff. and 19. 400 ff.

When Thetis gave birth . . . went back to the Nereids: following AR 4. 869 ff. Ambrosia, the food of the gods, would foster what was immortal in the child's nature. For the use of fire to burn away what is mortal in the body, cf. p. 33. In some sources, Thetis is said to have killed several children born before Achilles while trying to immortalize them (sc. Aristoph. *Clouds* 1068a), or test whether they were mortal (sc. AR 4. 816). The passages in the *Iliad* where Homer refers to Thetis in her home under the sea at the time of the Trojan War (e.g. *Il.* 1. 358) seem to assume her departure; but in other passages there is talk of her welcoming Achilles home to the house of Peleus (e.g. 18. 441, cf. 332).

not . . . lips: privative *a* (implied rather than directly stated) and *cheile*, hence Achilles! By feeding on the flesh and marrow of powerful and courageous animals, Achilles would come to share their qualities.

slaughtering Astydameia: she had falsely accused him to her husband, p. 128.

Lycomedes: he ruled the island of Scyros, off Euboea.

Pyrrhos . . . later called Neoptolemos: because he was young, *neos*, when he went to war, *polemos*, at Troy (see p. 156), or because his

Explanatory Notes

father was (P. 10. 26. 1, reporting the *Cypria*). His previous name was explained by his red, *pyrrhos*, hair (Serv. on *Aen.* 2. 469). Achilles refers to his son on Scyros in *Il.* 19. 326 f.

129 *causing a trumpet to be sounded*: this is explained by Hyg. 96. Odysseus placed women's finery in the courtyard of the palace with a shield and spear amongst it. He then had a trumpet sounded, accompanied by shouts and the clashing of arms. Thinking that they were under attack, Achilles took off his women's clothing and seized the shield and spear. Or more simply, when women's finery with arms mixed amongst it was placed before Achilles and his female companions, he instinctively seized the arms (sc. *Il.* 19. 326). In Homer's account, *Il.* 11. 769 ff., Achilles remained with Peleus, and was eager to go when Nestor and Odysseus came to fetch him and Patroclos; and the present story was absent from the *Cypria* also (for Achilles came to Scyros and married Deidameia after the Greek attack on Mysia, Procl., cf. sc. *Il.* 19. 326 on the *Little Iliad*). Because Achilles was too young to be one of Helen's suitors, he was not bound by oath to join the expedition (and subsequently, when Agamemnon offended him, he could threaten to go home, *Il.* 1. 169 ff., etc.).

Phoenix had been blinded . . . seduced her: in Homer's account, *Il.* 9. 447 ff., he actually sleeps with her, at the instigation of his mother (who is jealous of the concubine); he has to go into exile, but is not blinded.

130 *Patroclos had killed a boy*: cf. *Il.* 23. 84 ff.

Achilles had become his lover: this is never stated by Homer; see also Plato *Symp.* 180a. Patroclos was older than Achilles (*Il.* 11. 787).

the Erechtheid Sea: not a sea in the literal sense, but a sea-water well in the Erechtheum on the Acropolis, from which the sound of waves could be heard to rise when the south wind was blowing (see P. 1. 26. 6, with Hdt. 8. 55). This symbolic sea, and the mark of his trident in the rock (which can still be seen), were the evidence that Poseidon produced to support his claim (P. 1. 26. 6).

the Pandroseion: an enclosure near the Erechtheum. The olive tree survived until Roman times (after miraculously regrowing when the Persians set fire to Athens, P. 1. 27. 2, Hdt. 8. 55).

flooded the Thriasian plain: to the north-west of the city. Not a permanent flood (although he wanted it to be, until Zeus sent Hermes to forbid it, Hyg. 164).

Agraulos, the daughter of Actaios: her name appears in the form Aglauros elsewhere. Actaios was presumably invented to explain

238

why Attica was previously called Acte (see above); Pausanias (1. 2. 6) records a tradition that he was the first king of Attica and that Cecrops succeeded to the throne by marrying his daughter.

131 *was tried on the Areiopagos*: the Areiopagos, the traditional Athenian high court which dealt especially with cases involving blood-guilt, met on the place of that name to the north-west of the Acropolis. The present story explains its name (the 'Hill of Ares') and its prime function. Because his victim was trying to rape a close relative, and was caught in the act, Ares' defence would have been acceptable in classical Athens.

Herse . . . Phaethon: in *Theog.* 984 ff., Dawn bears Memnon and Emathion to Tithonos (as on p. 124), and Phaethon to Cephalos. On p. 44 this Cephalos was said to be a son of Deion; but it seems likely that Cephalos son of Deion, the hunter and husband of Procris, p. 134, was originally not the same figure as the son of Hermes associated with Dawn. In *Theog.* 986 ff. this Phaethon is abducted by Aphrodite and made guardian of one of her temples; he should not be identified with the more famous son of the Sun who borrowed his father's chariot and was struck by Zeus with a thunderbolt when he was unable to control the horses and almost set the earth on fire, DS 5. 23, Ov. *Met.* 2. 19 ff.

slept with foreigners: presumably a reference to temple prostitution in connection with the cult of Aphrodite–Astarte. The cause of Aphrodite's anger (perhaps neglect of her cult) is not recorded. Cinyras was associated with the cult of Paphian Aphrodite in Cyprus (Pind. *Pyth.* 2. 15 ff., Tacitus *Hist.* 2. 3).

a son of Theias: the following story of incest between father and daughter is most generally favoured to explain Adonis' birth, whether the king in question is called Theias (cf. AL 34) or Cinyras (e.g. Hyg. 58, where Cinyras is described as the king of the Assyrians; cf. Ov. *Met.* 10. 298 ff.). As we see in Ovid, his daughter is sometimes called Myrrha (in Greek, *smyrna* was an alternative word for myrrh).

132 *born to Hephaistos and Athene*: it will be seen that this is a loose expression, as he is born from the earth as a son of Hephaistos. The following story allows him to be earthborn (in a peculiar way) and yet have a special connection with Athene although she is a virgin goddess.

with a piece of wool: this was introduced into the story for etymological reasons, to explain Erichthonios' name by his birth from the ground, *chthon*, when the wool, *erion*, fell on it (as in *Et.*

Magn.; others pointed to the struggle, *eris*, between Athene and Hephaistos, e.g. Hyg. 166).

132 *a snake*: placed there by Athene to guard him (cf. Eur. *Ion.* 21–3, where there are two snakes, and VM 2. 37); but the serpent is sometimes identified with the earthborn Erichthonios himself (Hyg. *PA* 13; in Hyg. 166, he is half serpent like Cecrops).

her sanctuary: the Erechtheum on the Acropolis.

the wooden image of Athene: a primitive olive-wood statue (*xoanon*), comparable to the Palladion at Troy, p. 123 (and said by some to have fallen from the sky as the Palladion did, P. 1. 26. 7).

133 *Panathenaia*: the great summer festival celebrated in honour of Athene as patroness of the city. There was a procession to the Parthenon (as depicted in its frieze), bulls were sacrificed, and a new robe was offered to the enormous statue of Athene in the temple.

Demeter . . . at Eleusis: see p. 33. Eleusis was independent until the seventh century. Demeter introduced corn, Dionysos wine.

Labdacos: king of Thebes, see p. 103, in Boeotia, which lay on Attica's northern border; this is the only mythical tale associated with his brief reign.

hid her away in the country: this is followed by a problematic phrase omitted in the translation, 'and then, after marrying Philomela, he went to bed with her'. There is no suggestion in any surviving source that Tereus married Philomela, nor is it implied elsewhere in the present account. On the contrary, he sleeps with her *secretly*, and Procne remains his wife. It was said that Tereus had travelled to Athens to fetch Philomela because her sister wanted to see her, and he raped her on the journey back (e.g. VM 1. 8).

reached Daulis in Phocis: Phocis lay to the west of Boeotia and Attica. Tereus was commonly said to have been king of Daulis (Thuc. 2. 29, P. 1. 41. 8, etc.), but here he lives far to the north in Thrace (as in Hyg. 45) and pursues the sisters to Daulis. It was generally accepted that he was of Thracian descent.

134 *Philomela a swallow*: her lack of a tongue explains the swallow's inarticulate cries; her identification with the nightingale in medieval and modern poetry is the result of a confusion in the Latin tradition (see Hyg. 45).

Poseidon Erechtheus: following Heyne's emendation (from *Erichthoniou*); a cult of this name is well attested for Athens.

went to bed with Pteleon: in all other versions, Cephalos tests her virtue, causing her to flee when found wanting. He returns in disguise after travelling abroad for eight years, and offers her some finery to sleep with him (Pherecydes in sc. *Od*. 11. 321), or he tells a servant to offer her gold (AL 41), or Dawn changes his form to allow him to test her (Hyg. 189). It is possible that this Pteleon, who is otherwise unknown but is presumably the eponym of the Attic deme of Ptelea, may have been acting for Cephalos like the servant in AL. See also Ov. *Met*. 7. 690 ff.

harmful beasts: snakes, scorpions, and millipedes, according to AL 41; Pasiphae was his wife.

a fast-running dog: for its subsequent fate, see p. 70, and note.

the Circaean root: this came from a plant of the milkweed family, but here it is clearly viewed as a magical charm rather than a herbal remedy. In AL 41 she finds a mechanical solution, by ensuring that the beasts are discharged into a goat's bladder before Minos has intercourse with her.

by the River Ilissos, Boreas carried her off: not far from Athens, see Plato *Phdr*. 229a ff., where there is a vivid description of the locality (and Socrates makes some shrewd comments on the rationalization of such myths), and AR 1. 211 ff. There was an alternative tradition that she was abducted from the Acropolis and conveyed to Thrace to become his wife (sc. *Od*. 14. 533). Boreas was the North Wind.

while pursuing the Harpies: see p. 52 and note.

killed by Heracles: for persuading the Argonauts not to return for him when he was left behind in Mysia (AR 1. 1298 ff; for Heracles' abandonment, see p. 51).

135 *married Idaia . . . punished him for this*: this version of the story, in which Idaia brings a false accusation against her adult stepsons, follows Sophocles' lost *Phineus* (sc. AR 2. 178); in another version, she blinds them herself while they are still young with a weaving pin (see Soph. *Antigone* 970 ff.). Boreas' presence with the Argonauts is unusual, but DS (4. 44. 4, cf. Serv. on *Aen*. 3. 209) records that according to some mythographers (presumably following the *Phineus*) Phineus blinded his sons and was blinded in turn by Boreas (as the father of Phineus' first wife, Cleopatra). For another version again, see DS 4. 43. 3 ff. (cf. sc. AR 2. 207).

fled to the Eleusinians: and became closely associated with the Mysteries. He was the eponymous ancestor of the priestly family of the Eumolpidai, which provided the hierophant who presided over the rites and revealed the mysteries to the initiates.

135 *Poseidon destroyed Erechtheus*: because the Athenians under Erechtheus had killed Eumolpos, his son (cf. Eur. *Ion* 281 f.). The story is presumably connected with the origin of the Poseidon–Erechtheus cult, p. 136, in which the god and the heroized Erechtheus shared the same shrine (P. 1. 26. 6).

136 *transferred the kingdom to Pandion*: see also P. 1. 5. 3 and 1. 39. 4; Pandion's tomb could be seen in Megara.

founded ... Pylos: the Elian Pylos in the north-western Peloponnese. See also P. 6. 22. 5 and 4. 36. 1.

Pytho: Delphi.

mouth of the wineskin: the wineskin stands for his stomach, and its mouth or neck for his penis (cf. sc. Eur. *Med.* 679, which reports that the Greek word for the mouth of a wineskin, *podeon*, was often used in such a sense); if he sleeps with another woman before he returns to the height of Athens, meaning the Acropolis, he will have a male child by her rather than by his wife.

by way of Troezen: south of the Isthmus in the Argolid, and thus well out of his way; Plut. *Thes.* 2 suggests that he went there to consult Pittheus about the oracle. For the place of Pittheus in Troezenian mythology, see P. 2. 30. 5 ff.; he later adopts Theseus' son Hippolytos, see p. 142 and note.

Poseidon slept with her too: this paternity is associated with a specific story told in Bacch. 17. 33 ff. (cf. P. 1. 17. 3). When Minos wanted to sleep with one of the Athenian girls from the tribute (see p. 137), Theseus withstood him, claiming to be the son of Poseidon; and to prove this, he leapt into the sea and recovered a golden ring thrown there by Minos, and was also given a magnificent crown by Poseidon's wife Amphitrite (which later became a constellation, Hyg. *PA* 5).

the bull of Marathon: for its origins, see p. 77 and note. Theseus will kill it, p. 139. Here Androgeos is sent to almost certain death; or he was treacherously murdered (cf. Plut. *Thes.* 15, and DS 4. 60. 5, where Aigeus fears Androgeos' friendship with his enemies, the sons of Pallas). The following story of the ambush, which absolves Aigeus from blame, was probably of relatively late origin. See also P. 1. 27. 10.

137 *Megareus*: he came with an army of Boeotians, was buried where he was killed, and the city, formerly called Nisa, was named

Megara after him (see P. 1. 39. 5; this was a Boeotian tradition, apparently followed here); he was often said to be a son of Poseidon. Megara lay on the Isthmus of Corinth, bordering Attica.

drowned her: because he was shocked by her betrayal of her father and city (cf. P. 2. 34. 7, and the similar story on p. 70). In Aesch. *Choephoroi* 612 ff., Minos is said to have bribed Scylla with bracelets of Cretan gold.

Their father, Hyacinthos: not the famous Hyacinthos who was loved by Apollo, p. 119.

labyrinth: see p. 98.

138 *a snake's jawbone*: cf. DS 4. 76. 5 f., this led to the invention of the iron saw.

Theseus: see Plutarch's life of Theseus for a fuller account of all the following, with many variants. Theseus was said to have founded the Attic state by incorporating the communities outside the city of Athens (Thuc. 2. 15; Plut. *Thes.* 24).

the sandals and the sword: the tokens of his birth, see p. 136.

cleared the road: a series of labours, emulating those of Heracles (cf. DS 4. 59. 1), which establishes his heroic status. For the earliest account, see Bacch. 18. 16 ff.

was referred to as Corynetes: a descriptive surname or nickname (as with Pityocamptes below) rather than a proper name; it was doubtless suggested by *Il.* 7. 138. It seems fitting that a son of the lame god Hephaistos should have weak feet, although this is otherwise unattested.

hurled into the air: or he attached the extremities of his victims to two trees, causing them to be torn apart when the trees were released (P. 2. 1. 4, DS 4. 59. 3; in Hyg. 38 Sinis helps them to bend a tree back and they are thrown up when he lets go).

139 *Polypemon*: as in Bacch. 18. 27, but he is more familiar as Procroustes (e.g. P. 1. 38. 5; this may have been mentioned in the full text as a descriptive surname like those above, meaning 'he who beats out'). In DS 4. 59. 5 the travellers are adjusted to fit a single bed. In Hyg. 38, he stretches the legs of the short men by hanging anvils from them.

Medea . . . schemed against him: to protect her position and that of her son by Aigeus; see also p. 57.

the bull of Marathon: see p. 77 and note.

140 *tribute . . . to the Minotaur*: for the tribute, see p. 137; for the Minotaur, p. 98.

140 *the children*: the boys and girls saved from the tribute.

Dionysos fell in love with Ariadne: in *Od.* 11. 321 ff., she was killed there by Artemis at the urging of Dionysos. For the varied tradition thereafter, see Plut. *Thes.* 20; she was often said to have been deserted by Theseus (either for another woman or accidentally).

the sons of Pallas: Pallas was the brother of Aigeus; he and his sons disputed the succession, alleging that Aigeus was not a true son of Pandion (Plut. *Thes.* 13; Ap. points to a tradition that Aigeus was a supposititious child on p. 136).

141 *Icarian Sea*: in the south-eastern Aegean, in the region of Icaria and Samos.

accompanied Heracles . . . against the Amazons: this was generally regarded as a separate and later expedition, made by Theseus alone, or in conjunction with Peirithoos (see Plut. *Thes.* 26).

Amazons marched against Athens: see also DS 4. 28, Plut. *Thes.* 27.

by the Areiopagos: see Aesch. *Eumenides* 685 ff., where it is said that the hill gained its name because they offered sacrifices there to Ares (as god of war); but see also p. 131 and note.

Deucalion: the son of Minos and a successor as king of Crete, see pp. 97 and 99.

142 *Phaedra . . . asked him to sleep with her*: Ap. gives the traditional version of her story (cf. Ov. *Met.* 15. 497 ff., and Seneca's *Phaedra*). Euripides' surviving *Hippolytos* (his second play on the theme) is more sympathetic to Phaedra, presenting her as an unwilling victim of Aphrodite who refuses to declare her love and kills herself when her nurse betrays it to Hippolytos.

hated all women: he was a devotee of the virgin goddess Artemis.

along the sea-shore: at Troezen in the Argolid, where Hippolytos was the adopted heir of its king, Pittheus (the grandfather of Theseus, see p. 136). Historically there was a cult of Hippolytos there; girls made offerings of their hair to him at marriage (P. 2. 32. 1).

Ixion: his story is relevant to the subsequent account of Theseus' association with Peirithoos (king of the Lapiths in Thessaly) and their battle with the Centaurs, because Ixion was both the father of Peirithoos and the ancestor of the Centaurs (through his son Centauros, who fathered them by mating with mares near Mount Pelion, Pind. *Pyth.* 2. 44 ff., except for the 'good' Centaurs Cheiron and Pholos, who were of different birth, see pp. 29 and 75). Ixion's behaviour towards Hera was particularly reprehensible because Zeus had purified Ixion after he had murdered his father-in-law, and welcomed him in heaven (DS 4. 69. 4); for a fuller portrayal of his transgression and punishment, see Pind. *Pyth.* 2. 21 ff.

Theseus joined Peirithoos: this paragraph is inserted from Zenobius 5. 33. Surviving accounts of the banquet are late (e.g. DS 4. 70. 3 f., Plut. *Thes.* 30), although the prowess of Peirithoos, Theseus, and Caineus in fighting the Centaurs is referred to by Homer (*Il.* 1. 262 ff.).

as relatives of the bride: thus Zenobius, but this is probably a mistake, because they were certainly relatives of the *bridegroom* (cf. VM 1. 162, where they are invited as Peirithoos' neighbours and relatives), and this connection would surely have been explained in the preceding section on Ixion.

buried in the earth: the gods are said to have incited the Centaurs against Caineus because of his violence and his presumption in wanting to be honoured as a god (e.g. sc. *Il.* 1. 264). On the limits of invulnerability, see p. 73 on the Nemean lion and note.

143 *captured Athens*: according to the usual account, followed on p. 121, she was hidden at Aphidnai, to the north-east of Athens, and was recovered when the Dioscuri captured that city (cf. Plut. *Thes.* 32–3, where it is said that they were received into Athens afterwards without a fight). It is reported, however, that in a poem in the epic cycle they plundered Athens after taking Aphidnai (sc. *Il.* 3. 242; cf. P. 5. 19. 3 on the Cypselos chest). The Epitome may misrepresent the original text here.

took away Aithra: she became Helen's servant and was taken to Troy (see Plut. *Thes.* 34, and *Il.* 3. 143 f.); and when it fell, she was recovered by these two sons of Theseus, Demophon and Acamas, see p. 157.

Menestheus: a great-grandson of Erechtheus, and thus in the royal line; the leader of the Athenians in the Trojan War, p. 148, *Il.* 2. 552.

became stuck to it: the rock grew to their flesh (P. 10. 29. 9, referring to Panyasis and contrasting this with the tradition that they were pinioned to the chair; it seems that two versions from different sources are combined here). The name of the chair suggests that it affected the mind also (see Horace *Odes* 4. 7. 27 f.).

Lycomedes: he ruled in Scyros, off Euboea, and either feared Theseus' influence over his subjects or wanted to gratify Menestheus (see Plut. *Thes.* 35, P. 1. 17. 6). See also p. 129.

143 *Tantalos*: son of Zeus and Pluto, daughter of Cronos (or according to some, the son of Tmolos). A wealthy king in Lydia, in Asia
Minor, he is introduced here as the ancestor of the Pelopids, the
Peloponnesian line which provided the kings of Mycenae and
Sparta at the time of the Trojan War. For his punishment, cf. *Od.*
11. 582 ff. (without any mention of the stone, but Archilochus knew
of it in the seventh century, sc. Pind. *Ol.* 1. 97).

share ambrosia with his friends: after he had been welcomed at the
table of the gods and made immortal with ambrosia, the food of
the gods, he wanted to share it with other mortals, Pind. *Ol.* 1. 59
ff. For the betrayal of divine secrets, cf. DS 4. 74. 2. The darker
story that he served his son Pelops at a banquet of the gods (which
Pindar refused to believe, *Ol.* 1. 26 ff.) must have been mentioned
in the full text, as it is referred to just below.

Broteas: the son of Tantalos; see also Ovid *Ibis.* 517 ff. and P. 3.
22. 4.

144 *a winged chariot*: since Pindar talks of a golden chariot drawn by
horses with unwearying wings (*Ol.* 1. 87), and Pelops' horses were
portrayed with wings on the sixth-century chest of Cypselos (P.
5. 17. 7), the 'winged chariot' of the Epitome may be misleading.
In Pindar's account, this gift from Poseidon is sufficient to ensure
victory for Pelops (and probably elsewhere in the earlier tradition;
Pherecydes, in the fifth century, is the earliest author known to
have referred to Myrtilos in this connection, sc. AR 1. 752).

Pisa: in Elis, the north-western province of the Peloponnese.

failed to insert the axle-pins: or according to Pherecydes (ibid.) he
inserted axle-pins made of wax.

the Myrtoan Sea: lying to the east of the Peloponnese and south
of Attica; Geraistos was the southernmost cape of Euboea. It was
also said that Pelops had promised Myrtilos that he could spend
a night with Hippodameia, and pitched him overboard when he
reminded him of this (P. 8. 14. 11).

curses at the house of Pelops: amply fulfilled; it was said by some
that this caused Hermes, the father of Myrtilos, to send the
golden lamb that causes such trouble below (Eur. *Orest.* 989 ff.
with sc. to 990; but below it is sent by Artemis as a sign to con-
firm Atreus' kingship).

145 *Apia or Pelasgiotis*: for Apia as a previous name of the Peloponnese,
see p. 58; Pelasgiotis must likewise be a previous name, when it
was named after Pelasgos (cf. ibid., although we would expect the
form Pelasgia). It now gains its definitive name (as the 'island' of

Pelops; but it should be noted that the story of Pelops' sons and grandsons indicates that the main centres outside Elis could not have been ruled by him at this time).

placed it in a chest: i.e. its fleece.

the Mycenaeans . . . had sent for Atreus and Thyestes: they are already outside their father's kingdom of Pisa in Elis because they were summoned by Sthenelos, the father of Eurystheus, to Midea in Argos when he banished Amphitryon, p. 69. In the meantime, Sthenelos has died and Eurystheus has been killed by Hyllos, p. 92, but the Perseid heirs, the Heraclids, have been told by the oracle that they are not to return to the Peloponnese until later, ibid. Correspondingly, it is the divine will that the Pelopids should rule Mycenae in the intervening period; according to sc. Eur. *Orest.* 4, this was revealed in the oracle received by the Heraclids. It was also said that Pelops had expelled Atreus and Thyestes for murdering his illegitimate son Chrysippos (ibid.).

the adultery: between his wife Aerope and Thyestes.

intercourse with his own daughter: her name was Pelopia. In one version of this story, she submitted to the incest out of duty (e.g. Hyg. 254), in another, Thyestes raped her unknowingly at Sicyon during nocturnal rites (Hyg. 88). Here we can assume the former; Thyestes is acting in direct obedience to the oracle.

146 *sought refuge*: i.e. from Agamemnon and Menelaos, when they came of age.

But Agamemnon . . . marrying his daughters: the gap in the text is filled by an extract from Tzetzes, *Chiliades* 1. 456–62, which is based on Ap. It explains how Agamemnon and Menelaos escaped to safety after the murder of Atreus. Although they were described above, p. 99, as sons of Pleisthenes (and thus grandsons of Atreus), they are surely sons of Atreus here. Tyndareus fled to Aetolia after he was expelled from Sparta by Hippocoon and his sons, see p. 120 and note. After Heracles had killed them, Tyndareus was able to return (see p. 88), bringing Agamemnon and Menelaos with him. Later Agamemnon expelled Thyestes and became king in Mycenae, and Menelaos became king in Sparta after the death of the Dioscuri deprived Tyndareus of his heirs, p. 122.

Alexander abducted Helen: we now pass to the events leading up to the Trojan War. Ap.'s main source henceforth will be the poems in the epic cycle that gave an account of the events not covered by Homer; but he also introduces material from later sources. For all the following, compare the summaries of these epic poems by Proclus (English translations of these can be found, with other relevant material, in *Hesiod and the Homeric Hymns* in the Loeb series). Events prior to the *Iliad* were covered in a single epic, the *Cypria*.

146 *demigods*: a term sometimes applied to the heroes of the Trojan War and earlier adventures (see Hes. *WD* 159 ff., cf. *Il.* 12. 23); it need not imply divine parentage.

For one of these reasons: Homer remarks enigmatically in *Il.* 1. 5 that the war fulfilled the will of Zeus, but offers no explanation. Elsewhere two main reasons are adduced (which need not be exclusive), one, as here, that it was to be a source of glory for those involved, and another that Zeus wanted to lighten the burden on the Earth, which was weighed down by an excessive number of mortals (thus the *Cypria* as quoted in sc. *Il.* 1. 5; some included the Theban War as part of the plan, sc. Eur. *Orest.* 1641).

Eris threw an apple: Eris, discord personified, now sets in motion the chain of events that will lead to the Trojan War. This takes place at the marriage of Peleus and Thetis (Procl.; for the marriage see p. 129). The apple is first mentioned in late sources (e.g. Hyg. 92) but the theme could well be early; it is inscribed 'to the fairest', or Eris says that the fairest should take it. On Eris, see also *Il.* 4. 440 ff. The judgement of Paris is mentioned by Homer, *Il.* 24. 25 ff.

with ships built by Phereclos: on Phereclos, see *Il.* 5. 59 ff. The fleet was suggested by Aphrodite, and she told Aeneas to sail with Paris (Procl.).

147 *the funeral of his maternal grandfather Catreus*: after he had been killed by his son Althaimenes, p. 99; Menelaos was his grandson through Aerope.

the treasures: from the palace of Menelaos; this became an issue in the war, see *Il.* 3. 70 ff. and 285 ff.

put in at Sidon: Homer alludes to his stay there in *Il.* 6. 289 ff.; in the *Cypria*, he captured the city (Procl.).

a phantom of Helen: a theme invented by the lyric poet Stesichorus (late seventh to early sixth century). According to a later (and doubtless apocryphal) story, he was struck blind after he had spoken badly of Helen in one of his poems, and this caused him to write a recantation saying that only her phantom was present at Troy (thus absolving her from blame for the war); see Plato *Phaed.* 243a f., with the verses quoted there. See also Eur. *Helen* (31 ff. and *passim*) and Hdt. 2. 112 ff.

to Agamemnon in Mycenae: as king of Mycenae he was the richest and most powerful king in Greece, and undisputed leader of the expedition. According to the Homeric catalogue he ruled the north-eastern corner of the Peloponnese in an area also embracing Corinth and Sicyon (*Il.* 2. 569 ff., while Diomedes ruled Argos, Tiryns, and much of the Argolid, ibid. 559 ff.); but there are also suggestions that he held wider authority (e.g. ibid. 107 ff.).

the oaths: most of the Greek kings had been suitors for Helen's hand, and had sworn to help the one who was chosen as her husband if he should be wronged with regard to his marriage, see p. 121.

pretended to be mad: he is said to have yoked an ox with a horse (Hyg. 95), and sown the land with salt (VM 1. 35).

drew his sword: or he placed the child in front of Odysseus' plough (Tzetz. sc. Lycophr. 818). Procl. is vague: he picked up the child 'to punish it'.

after capturing . . . as a traitor: this is Odysseus' later revenge for his ignominious exposure. It was also said that Odysseus killed Palamedes because he was envious of his cleverness (Xen. *Mem.* 4. 2. 33), or that Odysseus, Agamemnon, and Diomedes plotted against him because they were jealous of his popularity with the army for his inventions etc. (sc. Eur. *Orest.* 432). In the *Cypria*, Odysseus and Diomedes drowned him while he was fishing (P. 10. 31. 1).

148 *a breastplate*: in the manuscripts, 'breastplates', but this is surely a reference to the magnificent breastplate described in *Il.* 11. 19 ff., a personal gift from one king to another rather than a practical contribution to the expedition. The ruse of the earthenware ships, absent from Homer, may go back to the *Cypria* (although Procl. makes no mention of it). For Cinyras, see p. 131.

Elais, Spermo, and Oino: their names refer to the oil, grain, and wine elicited by them. They lived with their father, Anios, on Delos. Ap.'s account in the original text was probably comparable with that in Dictys of Crete, *Trojan War* 1. 23, where they send provisions to the Greeks at Aulis. It was also said that Anios, who knew that Troy could not be taken until the tenth year, offered to maintain the Greek army at Delos for the intervening period, using his daughters to feed them (Tzetz. sc. Lycophr. 570, reporting the *Cypria* and Pherecydes), or that his daughters came to help the Greeks when they were suffering from hunger at Troy (ibid. 580, reporting Callimachus).

148 *Those who took part:* compare Homer's catalogue, *Il.* 2. 494 ff.; some of the names and numbers diverge.

149 *a snake . . . after ten years:* cf. *Il.* 2. 308 ff. The nine birds eaten by the snake represent nine years of war; Troy will be captured in the tenth.

Mysia: in the north-western corner of Asia Minor; historically the Troad lay within the province of that name.

Telephos, son of Heracles: see pp. 88 and 116.

entangled in a vine branch: through the anger of Dionysos, because Telephos had deprived him of his cult (sc. *Il.* 1. 59); hence the vine, which is emblematic of the god.

lasted twenty years: this is clearly problematic, as the war would then end twenty (rather than ten) years after the portent of the sparrows (which is said to have been revealed at the *first* muster by both Ap. above and Procl.). But there are indications that this was not a fancy of late origin. In the *Cypria* (Procl.) and *Little Iliad* (sc. *Il.* 19. 326) Achilles married Deidameia (and thus fathered Neoptolemos) on his way back from Mysia, and Neoptolemos must have had time to grow to fighting age before joining the Greeks in the final year of the war (see p. 156); and there is the anomalous statement by Helen in *Il.* 24. 765 f., where she says that it is the twentieth year since she left her homeland.

150 *scraping rust from his Pelian spear:* following the principle of sympathetic magic noted for Iphiclos' knife on p. 47, that what inflicts harm can cure it. The Pelian spear was the ashwood spear cut on Mount Pelion by Cheiron as a wedding present for Peleus, see p. 129 with *Il.* 16. 143 f.

Not even Artemis: following the Vatican epitome, where the meaning of this is left to the reader's understanding; I have completed the sentence following sc. *Il.* 1. 108 (cf. sc. Eur. *Orest.* 658). The reading in the Sabbaitic epitome, 'it could not escape alive even if Artemis wanted it to,' is surely a misinterpretation of the statement in its abbreviated form.

Agamemnon brought her . . . at the altar: as in the *Cypria* (Procl.). See also Euripides' *Iphigeneia in Aulis* and the introductory speech of his *Iphigeneia in Tauris.*

Cycnos: not the adversary of Heracles (pp. 82, 90) but a son of Poseidon who ruled at Colonai in the Troad (cf. P. 10. 14. 1 ff.). Tenedos was a small island lying off the coast of the Troad.

151 *While . . . offering a sacrifice to Apollo:* on Tenedos, following the *Cypria* (Procl.). Homer mentions the water-snake, *hydros,* as the

cause of his wound, *Il.* 2. 723. The later tradition varies; in Soph. *Philoct.* 1327 f., he is bitten on Chryse, an island near Lemnos, by a serpent guarding the local temple of Athene; or he is bitten where his comrades abandon him, on Lemnos (e.g. Hyg. 102).

the bow of Heracles: Heracles gave it to his father Poias (or to Philoctetes himself) for lighting his pyre, see p. 91 and note.

sending Odysseus and Menelaos: cf. *Il.* 3. 205 ff.

first . . . to disembark: cf. *Il.* 2. 701 f., where his killer is a nameless Dardanian (as against Hectōr in the *Cypria*, see Procl.); that Protesilaos would be the first to enter battle is suggested in his name.

Laodameia: there seems to have been some coverage of her story in the *Cypria* (P. 4. 2. 7; there she was described as Polydora, daughter of Meleager, but the present name is general in later authors). The pathetic tale appealed to later sentiment and was much developed and varied. Protesilaos was to be released from Hades for a limited period only. (See also Ovid *Heroides* 18. and Hyg. 103 and 104. In Hyg. 103, Laodameia prays to be allowed three hours with him, and is unable to endure the sorrow when he dies for a second time.)

152 *by hurling a stone at his head*: Cycnos (the father of Tenes, see above) was said to be invulnerable except in his head (sc. Lycophr. 232). There was another tradition that he was wholly invulnerable and Achilles had to strangle him as Heracles strangled the Nemean lion (e.g. Ov. *Met.* 12. 144, with the thong of his helmet).

Troilos: a son of Priam (or Apollo, p. 125) and Hecuba (*Il.* 24. 257). There was a tradition that Troy could not be taken if he remained alive (Plautus *Bacchides* 953 f., or if he lived to the age of twenty, VM 1. 210).

captured Lycaon: see *Il.* 21. 34 ff. for the full story. Lycaon was sold into slavery in Lemnos (also Procl.), but was ransomed, and came up against Achilles on the twelfth day after his return, giving rise to the memorable scene in which he entreats the pitiless Achilles to spare him.

rustle the cattle of Aeneas: cf. *Il.* 20. 90 ff. and 188 ff.

the following allies: for the Trojan allies cf. Homer's catalogue, *Il.* 2. 819 ff.

153 *performed deeds of valour*: for *aristeuein*; the *aristeiai* of the various heroes, episodes in which an individual comes to the fore and remains the centre of attention while he performs exceptional feats, formed set-pieces in the epic narrative.

Explanatory Notes

153 *exchanged armour*: in Homer's account, Glaucos exchanged 'gold
for bronze' (the phrase became proverbial), provoking the poet to
observe, in a rare personal comment, that Zeus must have deprived
him of his wits (*Il*. 6. 234 ff.).

154 *The river rushed out . . . massive flame*: this is rather unsatisfactory
as a summary of *Il*. 21. 211 ff.

accidentally killed Hippolyte: her sister, whom she killed with her
lance while aiming at a deer, according to QS 1. 21 ff.; see also
Appendix, 8 and note. The tradition that she came there to win
glory to enable her to marry (Tzetz. Posthom. 14, referring to
Hellanicos and others) reflects later ethnographical interests (see
Hdt. 4. 117).

Thersites: he abused Achilles 'for his alleged passion' (Procl.) for
the Amazon, apparently an accusation of necrophilia (Eustath. on
Il. 2. 219), and gouged out her eyes with his spear-point (Tzetz.
sc. Lycophr. 999). The *Aethiopis* (Procl.) went on to say that
Achilles sailed to Lesbos, sacrificed to Apollo, and was purified
from the murder of Thersites by Odysseus (the first known reference to such a purification in Greek literature, for none is mentioned in Homer). On Thersites, see also p. 42 and *Il*. 2. 211 ff.

Memnon: to provide a suitable opponent for Achilles, a warrior who
resembles him in being the son of a goddess and having a set of
arms made by Hephaistos (Procl.; cf. Achilles' arms in *Il*. 18. 457
ff.). Proclus further reports that Thetis told her son Achilles of
the fate in store for Memnon, and that Dawn asked Zeus to grant
him immortality.

shot down . . . Scaean Gates: as foretold in *Il*. 22. 359 f.

in the ankle: it is said in late sources at least that his mother Thetis
held Achilles by the ankle when dipping him into the Styx, or the
fire (cf. p. 129), to make him immortal (e.g. Serv. on *Aen*. 6. 57).

155 *on the White Island*: in the *Aethiopis* (Procl.) Thetis, with the Muses
and her sisters, snatched Achilles' body from the fire and conveyed
it to the White Island (Leuke, in the Black Sea). But the present
passage surely refers to the Homeric account in *Od*. 24. 43 ff., where
the Greeks mix the bones in a golden urn for burial in a mound
by the Hellespont; as Wagner observed, the phrase must have originated as a gloss on the Isles of the Blessed in the next sentence.

on the Isles of the Blessed: a home at the ends of the earth for those
whom the gods absolved from death, see Hes. *WD* 167 ff. In
Homer, Achilles descends to Hades, where he complains to
Odysseus of his fate as king of the shades, *Od*. 11. 473 ff., but in

the *Aethiopis*, it can be inferred from Proclus' summary that Thetis would have revived him and made him immortal after taking him to the White Island. In Pind. *Ol.* 2. 79 ff., she conveyed him to the Isles of the Blessed. Ibycus, a sixth-century lyric poet, and Simonides are said to have placed him in Elysium (which was much the same) with Medea (sc. AR 4. 816).

the Trojans acting as judges: in *Od.* 11. 542 ff., the Trojans and Athene are said to be the judges. In the *Little Iliad* (sc. Aristophanes. *Eq.* 1056) spies are sent to listen under the walls of Troy, and they hear two girls discussing the matter; when one says that Aias must have been the bravest because he carried off the body of Achilles, the other counters that Odysseus was even braver because he covered their retreat. There was also a tradition that they simply asked the Trojan prisoners (sc. *Od.* 11. 547).

the allies: cf. Pind. *Nem.* 8. 26, where the Greeks decide the matter by secret ballot.

the Achaeans: the Greeks (as in Homeric usage).

Aias killed himself: see Sophocles' *Ajax*.

Calchas prophesied . . . bow of Heracles: in the *Little Iliad* (Procl.) this was revealed by the Trojan Helenos, see below, and it seems to have been his only prophecy; in the later tradition the prophecies multiply, and are shared between Calchas and Helenos (to whom three different prophecies are attributed below). For a fuller account of the following see QS 9. 325 ff., which follows the same pattern. For the bow of Heracles, now owned by Philoctetes, see p. 151 and note. It was needed to kill Paris.

Odysseus . . . to see Philoctetes: cf. QS 9. 333 ff. In the *Little Iliad* (Procl.) he was fetched by Diomedes alone.

cured by Podaleirios: as sons of Asclepios, he and his brother, Machaon, performed valuable services as healers while serving with the Greeks (cf. *Il.* 2. 731 f.). In the *Little Iliad* he was healed by Machaon (Procl.), here as in QS 9. 461 ff.

156 *Helenos . . . to reveal*: a son of Priam and Hecuba, p. 125, whose qualities as a diviner are mentioned by Homer (*Il.* 6. 76, cf. 7. 44 ff.).

bones of Pelops: see also P. 5. 13. 4 ff.

Neoptolemos: the son of Achilles by Deidameia, the daughter of Lycomedes (see p. 129); he is still on Scyros, the island off Euboea where he was born. For Odysseus' journey, cf. *Od.* 11. 506 ff. (where there is no mention of Phoenix).

Explanatory Notes

156 *Eurypylos . . . at the hand of Neoptolemos*: cf. *Od.* 11. 519 ff., he was killed with many others, 'for the sake of a woman's gifts'; for Priam had bribed his mother, Astyoche, to send him by offering her a golden vine made by Hephaistos (sc. *Od.* 11. 520, following Acousilaos).

Odysseus went . . . aid of Diomedes: in the *Little Iliad* (Procl.), these were two separate expeditions. In the first, in which Diomedes played no part, Odysseus disguised himself to enter the city as a spy, where he was recognized by Helen (compare Helen's own account in *Od.* 4. 242 ff.); in the second, he stole the Palladion with the help of Diomedes.

Odysseus . . . suggested it to Epeios: in the *Little Iliad*, Epeios acted on Athene's advice (Procl.; cf. *Od.* 8. 493). It is understandable that the idea should also have been attributed to the crafty Odysseus.

three thousand: the text is surely defective here. Stesichorus said that there were a hundred (Eustathius 1698), and later authors give lower figures. Their function was merely to open the city to the main army.

157 *devoured the sons of Laocoon*: in the *Sack of Troy* (Procl.) in the epic cycle, Laocoon was killed with one of his two sons; the portent signified that Troy would be destroyed along with the senior branch of the Trojan royal family, and understanding its meaning, Aeneas, who belonged to the junior branch, withdrew to Mount Ida. Although later authors disagreed on the cause and significance of the episode, it can be assumed here that the snakes are sent by Apollo as a sign of the coming destruction.

Helen . . . Odysseus covered his mouth: see *Od.* 4. 274 ff.

came to his rescue: because his father Antenor had offered them his hospitality and protection when they visited the city as ambassadors before the Greek landing, see p. 151 and *Il.* 3. 205 ff.

Aeneas . . . his piety: cf. Xen. *On Hunting* 1. 15 (where he takes the household gods also); this is the tradition developed by Virgil *Aen.* 2. 699 ff. For the ancients, respect and care for parents was a religious duty (cf. Plato *Laws* 930e ff.). In the *Sack of Troy* (Procl.) Aeneas left before the sack, while in the *Iliad* (20. 307 ff.), Poseidon prophesied that he and his descendants would rule in Troy after the destruction of Priam's family.

Aithra: she was taken captive by the Dioscuri when they were recovering Helen from Attica, p. 143, and became Helen's maid and went to Troy with her (*Il.* 3. 143 f., Plut. *Thes.* 34).

254

had later arrived at Troy: i.e. after the period covered by the *Iliad*; a similar phrase is used of Amphilochos on p. 162, another figure not mentioned by Homer.

158 *Locrian Aias . . . towards the sky*: 'lesser' Aias (cf. *Il.* 2. 527 ff.), not to be confused with the more famous son of Telamon (who killed himself before the sack, p. 155). In early epic, Aias merely dragged her away, pulling the statue over as he did so (Procl., cf. P. 5. 19. 5); the rape and the statue's shocked response are Hellenistic developments (first attested for Callimachus in the third century, sc. *Il.* 13. 66). An important episode, because it gives rise to the wrath of Athene, which plays such an important part in the story of the return voyages.

they hurled Astyanax from the ramparts: as in Proclus' summary of the *Sack of Troy*, the killing of Hector's son (and slaughter of Polyxena) take place after the burning of Troy; Proclus states that in the epic Odysseus killed him, but the full story may have accorded with Eur. *Troades* 721 ff., where it is said that Odysseus argued for his death before the assembly and the Greeks carried out the sentence. In the *Little Iliad*, Neoptolemos hurled him down *during* the sack, after seizing him from his nurse (quotation in Tzetz. sc. Lycophr. 1268). His fate was predicted in the *Iliad* (24. 734 ff.).

slaughtered Polyxene: a daughter of Priam and Hecuba not mentioned by Homer. This episode was portrayed in the *Sack of Troy* (Procl.); according to Euripides *Hecuba* 37 ff., the ghost of Achilles appeared above his grave and claimed her as his prize of honour. His son Neoptolemos slaughtered her (Ibycus, in sc. Eur. *Hec.* 40, presumably following early epic).

Hecuba was awarded . . . Bitch's Tomb: this curious story is referred to in Eur. *Hecuba* 1260 ff. and in a lyric fragment of earlier date (PMG fr. 965) and is thus no late invention. In Euripides it is prophesied that she will turn into a dog, disappear into the sea, and her grave, Cynossema (the dog's tomb), will become a landmark for sailors. It lay at the entrance to the Hellespont on the Thracian bank (Strabo 13. 1. 28, cf. Thuc. 8. 104). Others say that she was stoned rather than drowned (e.g. Ov. *Met.* 13. 565 ff.). There was an alternative tradition that she was conveyed to Lycia by Apollo (P. 10. 27. 2, reporting Stesichorus).

the most beautiful of Priam's daughters: cf. *Il.* 3. 122 ff., where she is the wife of Antenor's son Helicaon. The earliest surviving source for the present story is Lycophron 316 ff., fourth century. See also QS 13. 544 ff.

158 *took refuge by the altar*: that of Athene, which he had defiled (cf. Procl.); this action, and the consequent failure of the Greeks to punish him, merely increases Athene's anger.

the Greeks gathered . . . sacrifice to Athene: to appease her for the defilement of her statue. According to *Od.* 3. 136 ff., and the *Returns* (Procl.), the next poem in the epic cycle, this quarrel was incited by Athene; and it was conducted in an ill-tempered manner in front of the army while the troops were the worse for drink.

Diomedes . . . with only five ships: see *Od.* 3. 153 ff. and 276 ff.; for the subsequent history of Menelaos, see p. 164.

Mopsos . . . Manto: with this daughter of the seer Teiresias (p. 112) as his mother and Apollo as his father, Mopsos might be expected to surpass even Calchas as a diviner; his kingdom of Colophon lay south of the Troad in Lydia.

159 *When Calchas replied . . . without a doubt:* following the Sabbaitic epitome. The Vatican epitome reads, 'when he [Calchas] made no reply, he himself [Mopsos] said that she was carrying ten piglets, and that one of them was male, and that she would bring them to birth on the following day.' On this duel between the diviners, see also Strabo 14. 1. 27, where it is indicated that the fig-tree question came from Hes. *Cat.* (= fr. 278), and that the pig question was reported by Pherecydes (in a different form again, that the sow would give birth to three piglets, and one would be male).

Thetis: the goddess was his grandmother. In the *Returns* (Procl.) it was she who advised him to travel overland (see below), and the shade of Achilles tried to restrain Agamemnon and his followers from departing (for Agamemnon's sacrifice was insufficient to appease Athene and they would meet with storms at sea).

Athene hurled . . . was killed: cf. *Od.* 4. 499 ff., where Poseidon drives his ships on to the Gyraean Rocks, which are located by later authors either at the island of Tenos in the southern Aegean (the place of the storm in the present account), where there was a Mount Gyraios (Hesych.), or more commonly, at Cape Caphereus in southern Euboea (e.g. Serv. on *Aen.* 1. 45, QS 14. 568 ff.); here Aias was presumably wrecked at Tenos (for he was washed ashore at Myconos nearby), but in the *Returns* he was wrecked at the Capherides Rocks (Procl.). In the *Odyssey* Poseidon wrecked Aias, rescued him from the waves, but then killed him as here. Eur. *Troades* 75 ff. is the first surviving source for Athene's use of her father Zeus' thunderbolt.

Nauplios: see p. 62 and note; the earliest surviving source for this episode is Eur. *Helen* 766 f. and 1126 ff.

the intrigues of Odysseus: see p. 147.

160 *Aigialeia*: the wife of Diomedes, p. 43, king of Argos; her infidelity was also attributed to the anger of Aphrodite (e.g. Ov. *Met*. 14. 476 ff.), who was wounded by Diomedes during the fighting at Troy (*Il*. 5. 330 ff.).

wife of Idomeneus: the king of Crete, see p. 99 and note.

Xylophagos: literally 'Eater of Wood', i.e. of ships.

the country of the Molossians: Epirus, in north-western Greece. See also P. 1. 11. 1 f., and 2. 23. 6.

his father's kingdom: that of Peleus, at Phthia in Thessaly, which his father Achilles would have inherited if he had survived.

when Orestes went mad: after killing Clytemnestra and Aigisthos, see p. 163.

Hermione . . . at Troy: an allusion to the story that Menelaos had given Hermione to Orestes, but afterwards offered her to Neoptolemos if he captured Troy (see Eur. *Andromache* 967 ff.; some explain this as an accident, saying that Hermione had been given to Orestes by her grandfather Tyndareus at Sparta, and that Menelaos, who was away at Troy, remained unaware of it, e.g. sc. *Od*. 4. 4).

for the death of his father: Apollo, together with Paris, had killed Achilles, see p. 154, cf. *Il*. 22. 359 f.

by Machaireus: a name surely suggested by the *machaira*, or short sword (cf. Pind. *Nem*. 7. 42) used to kill him. It was also said (ibid. 40 ff.) that he was killed in an argument over the meat from his sacrifice (he objected to the Delphians appropriating such meat, according to Pherecydes in sc. Eur. *Or*. 1655). He was buried at Delphi and honoured there as a presiding hero (Pind. *Nem*. 7. 44 ff., P. 10. 24. 5).

161 *Gouneus . . . settled there*: there is a gap in the text here. This passage, which is prefaced, 'Apollodorus and the rest say this', is taken from Tzetzes sc. Lycophr. 902; the next two paragraphs are taken from ibid. 911 and 921 respectively. There too Apollodorus is probably Tzetzes' main source; he is referred to explicitly in the second passage.

Navaithos . . . Nauprestides: Navaithos is derived here from *naus*, ship, *aithein*, burning. Similarly, the Nauprestides were burners (from *pimpremi*) of ships. Cf. Strabo 6. 1. 12.

161 *Demophon*: a son of Theseus; the following story, of relatively late origin, was also associated with his brother Acamas (e.g. Aeschines *De fals. leg.* 31, apparently the earlier tradition).

162 *Nine Ways*: the earlier name of Amphipolis (Thuc. 4. 103); said to have been given that name because she ran down to the shore nine times when Demophon failed to return on the appointed day (Hyg. 59).

terror-struck: the reason is unclear; Tzetzes (sc. Lycophr. 495, following Ap.) says that he was 'overcome by a phantom' rather than struck by terror, but that may well be a mistake. The basket would have contained sacred objects used in the Mysteries of Rhea.

Amphilochos . . . killed one another: on this Amphilochos, a relatively late invention, see p. 114 and note. This story of a double killing was surely based on a similar story told about Amphilochos, son of Amphiaraos (Strabo 14. 5. 16, cf. Tzetzes sc. Lycophr. 440): after founding Mallos (in Cilicia) with Mopsos, he went to Amphilochian Argos for a year, and when Mopsos refused to accept him back as joint ruler on his return, they fought and killed one another in a duel (thus explaining the origin of the famous oracle at Mallos, in which both were involved, see Plut. *Moralia* 434d).

Locris was struck by a plague: yet another disaster provoked by the Locrian Aias' desecration of Athene's image, p. 158; the need to propitiate Athene provides a mythical explanation for the strange custom of the Locrian tribute, which is well attested (e.g. Polybius 12. 5. 7; the girls were chosen by lot from the hundred foremost families).

163 *after the Phocian War*: it ended in 346 BC; this could only mark the end of the thousand years if the Trojan War took place at an earlier period than the Greeks commonly assumed; see also Strabo 13. 1. 40.

was killed by Aigisthos and Clytemnestra: in the *Odyssey*, 3. 193 ff. and 4. 529 ff., Aigisthos kills him, in Aesch. *Agamemnon* 1373 ff., Clytemnestra; thereafter in tragedy they are often mentioned together, e.g. Soph. *Electra* 97 ff. Ap. is probably following the *Returns* here (for Proclus also reports that he was killed by both in his summary of the poem); if so, it is possible that the motif of the tunic, first mentioned in Aesch. *Ag.* 1382 ff., may also have originated in early epic. Aigisthos, the son of Thyestes, p. 146, came to Mycenae while Agamemnon was away at Troy and seduced Clytemnestra, *Od.* 3. 263 ff. In Aesch. *Ag.* Clytemnestra's action is provoked by Agamemnon's sacrifice of Iphigeneia (1414 ff.) and his infidelity with the Trojan captive women Chryseis and Cassandra (1439 ff.).

they killed Cassandra too: cf. *Od.* 11. 421–3; there she is killed by Clytemnestra alone, and that is the usual account (e.g. Pind. *Pyth.* 11. 17 ff.).

left Mycenae . . . killed his mother and Aigisthos: cf. *Od.* 1. 298 ff. and 3. 305 ff. There is no mention of Pylades in Homer, but in the *Returns* the murder of Agamemnon was 'avenged by Orestes and Pylades' (Procl.). On the whole affair, see Aesch. *Choephoroi*, and Soph. and Eur. *Electra*.

indicted by the Furies . . . acquitted: following Aesch. *Eumenides*; when the votes are evenly divided, he is acquitted on Athene's instructions (752 f.).

the land of the Taurians: the Crimea. Hereafter Ap. follows Eur. *Iphigeneia in Tauris*; for a divergent account of how the Taurians dealt with their victims, see Hdt. 4. 103.

164 *he himself married . . . father of Tisamenos*: such is the text of the Epitome, but Tzetzes (sc. Lycophr. 1374) states the alternative rather differently, reporting that he either married Hermione and had a son, Tisamenos, by her, or, according to some, he married Erigone and became the father of *Penthilos* (cf. P. 2. 18. 6, where he is said to have had an illegitimate son, Penthilos, by Erigone in addition to Tisamenos, his legitimate son by Hermione). The suggestion here that Erigone may have been the mother of Tisamenos almost certainly misrepresents the original text. This Erigone was the daughter of Aigisthos and Clytemnestra, p. 163 (not to be confused with the Athenian Erigone on p. 133). On Hermione, see p. 121. Tisamenos succeeded Orestes (who became king of Argos, and later succeeded Menelaos on the Spartan throne also), and he remained the most powerful ruler in the Peloponnese until he was killed and displaced by the returning Heraclids (see p. 94) and the Pelopid line was brought to an end.

Menelaos . . . treasure: see *Od.* 3. 276 ff.

only a phantom: see p. 147 and note.

went to the Elysian Fields with Helen: thus fulfilling the prophecy of Proteus in *Od.* 4. 561 ff.; they were sent there because Helen was a daughter of Zeus. Elysium was much like the Isles of the Blessed, a home for immortalized human beings vaguely situated 'at the ends of the world', ibid. 563 (although in the later tradition it came to be regarded as a region of the Underworld).

Explanatory Notes

166 *wolves . . . pigs, or asses, or lions*: in the *Odyssey* they are turned into pigs alone (10. 239, although some of her previous victims were turned into wolves and lions, 212).

167 *moly*: a mythical plant with white flowers, *Od.* 10. 302 ff., sometimes identified as a variety of wild onion; the details on Odysseus' use of it are not derived from the *Odyssey*.

Telegonos: important for his role in the *Telegonia*, the last epic in the Trojan cycle, as summarized in Epitome 7. 34–7; not in Homer.

The Sirens: cf. *Od.* 12. 49 ff. and 165 ff., where there are only two; their names, the statement that they were half bird, and the prophecy regarding their death are not derived from the *Odyssey*.

168 *cattle*: owned by the Sun and not subject to a natural death, see *Od.* 12. 127 ff.; Circe had warned that they should not be killed.

Latinos: not in Homer; in *Theog.* 1013 (part of a later addition to Hesiod's text, probably sixth century), he is Odysseus' son by Circe, and ruler of the Tyrsenians (i.e. Etruscans) with his brother Agrios. In the Roman tradition, where he is usually a son of Faunus, Latinus becomes an important figure as the king of the aboriginal inhabitants of central Italy when Aeneas arrived (e.g. Verg. *Aen.* 7 ff.).

for five years: in *Od.* 7. 259, seven years.

suitors: there is no catalogue of suitors in the *Odyssey*, although many are mentioned individually, and numbers are given for the suitors from each place (16. 246 ff.; only in the case of Ithaca does the number coincide with the total here).

169 *he wrestled with him*: in *Od.* 18. 88 ff., a boxing match, settled by Odysseus with a single blow.

170 *the land of the Thesprotians*: in Epirus, in north-western Greece.

propitiated Poseidon: for killing his son, the Cyclops Polyphemos, p. 165.

Teiresias . . . in his prophecy: see *Od.* 11. 119 ff.; Teiresias told him to travel inland until he found a people who had no knowledge of the sea and mistook an oar for a winnowing fan, and then offer up a ram, a bull, and a boar. But afterwards he was to return home to Ithaca and offer sacrifices there to all the gods (ibid. 132 ff.). In the *Telegonia*, however, the epic that took up the story of Odysseus where the *Odyssey* left off, the journey inland provided the occasion for a new series of foreign adventures.

Ithaca, he plundered . . . cattle: not realizing that he was in his father's kingdom; according to Hyg. 127, he was carried there by a storm, and was driven by hunger to ravage the land.

Explanatory Notes

from a stingray: added by Bücheler after *kentron*, translated as needle; this weapon (which was made by Hephaistos, sc. *Od.* 11. 134) was given to Telegonos by Circe (see Oppian *On Fishing* 2. 497 ff.).

Telegonos . . . married Penelope: the *Telegonia* concluded with a double marriage (Procl.) because he also took Odysseus' son Telemachos to Circe's island, and Telemachos married Circe! The departure of Telegonos and Penelope to the Isles of the Blessed is otherwise unattested, but the *Telegonia* is the most likely source.

seduced by Antinoos: the leader of the suitors in the *Odyssey* (where Penelope is a model of wifely fidelity).

gave birth to Pan, as a son of Hermes: see P. 8. 12. 6 for the local Mantineian tradition that Penelope died there. Pan was particularly associated with the wild country of Arcadia, where his cult originated. Herodotus (2. 145) talks as if the present account of his birth was generally accepted amongst the Greeks, but there were many others; he was often said to have been a son of Hermes by other mothers, and there was even a bizarre tradition that Penelope bore him to the suitors, causing Odysseus to leave home again in disgust (Servius on *Aen.* 2. 44). See also p. 31.

Amphinomos: in the *Odyssey* (16. 397 f.) he is cleverer and more gentlemanly than the other suitors, and thus earns a measure of approval from Penelope; doubtless conclusions were drawn from that.

as his judge Neoptolemos: cf. Plut. *Greek Questions* 14 (where Odysseus departs to Italy).

Thoas: leader of the Aetolians in the Trojan War, p. 148, see *Il.* 2. 638 ff., and 13. 216 ff.; the name of his daughter is unknown.

THE TWELVE GODS

FROM the classical period onwards it was commonly accepted that there were twelve principal deities. This idea, which developed from cultic rather than strictly mythological considerations, originated in the Greek colonies of Asia Minor, but by the fifth century BC altars had been dedicated to the Twelve Gods at Athens and Olympia. Athough there is some variation in surviving lists, the standard list in later times was: Zeus, Hera, Poseidon, Demeter, Hestia, Ares, Aphrodite, Hephaistos, Athene, Artemis, Apollo, and Hermes. Here we will exclude Hestia (who is of some significance cultically as goddess of the hearth, but has virtually no mythology because she never leaves home), and include Dionysos in her place. The group then includes all the Olympian deities who are most important in mythology and appear most frequently in the present work. At Rome, most were identified with local deities; the names of these are given in brackets.

Aphrodite (Venus). Birth, 29; incites love in Cleio, 30, in Dawn, 32; afflicts the Lemnian women, 50; transfers Boutes to Sicily, 55; mother of Harmonia, 101; gives golden apples to suitor of Atalante, 117; love for Anchises, 123, for Adonis, 30, 131–2; punishes daughters of Cinyras, 131; selected by Paris in judgement of goddesses, 146; saves him from Menelaos, but is wounded by Diomedes, 207.

Apollo. Birth, and arrival at Delphi, 31–2; kills Tityos and Marsyas, 32, the Giant Ephialtes, 34, the Cyclopes, 119; recovers his stolen cattle from the infant Hermes, and is given a lyre, 118; Zeus assumes his form, 115.

Grants divinatory powers to Melampous, 46, to Cassandra, 125; serves and helps Admetos, 48, 120; helps Argonauts, 55–6; arms Heracles, 72, meets him after he has caught the Cerynitian hind, 75, fights him for the tripod at Delphi, 85; fortifies Troy for Laomedon, but sends plague when denied fee, 79; shoots sons of Niobe, 105; his part in death of Achilles, 151–4, Neoptolemos seeks reparation, 160.

Loves Hyacinthos, 30, 119, Coronis, mother of Asclepios, 119; rejected by Marpessa, 39, Cassandra, 125; his children, Linos and the Corybantes, 30, Doros, Laodocos, Polypoites, 39, Miletos, 97, Eleuther, 117, Asclepios, 119, Troilos, 125, Anios, 148, Tenes, 150, Mopsos, 158.

Oracles of, 112, 114, 150; sends sign before fall of Troy, 157; sacrifices to, 149, 151; sanctuary of, 90; Manto dedicated to, 112; Zeus assumes his form, 115.

The Twelve Gods

Ares (Mars). Birth, 29; slept with Dawn, 32; enclosed in jar by Aloads, 38; conflict with Heracles over son Cycnos, 82, 90; spring and dragon of, at Thebes, and death of dragon at hand of Cadmos, 100; Menoitios sacrifices himself to, 110; tried on the Areiopagos for murder, 131; gave arms and horses to Oinomaos, 144.

Father of Oxylos, 39, sons by Demonice, 39, Meleager, Dryas, 40, Ascalaphos and Ialmenos, 50, 121, Diomedes of Thrace, 78, Cycnos, 82, 90, Harmonia, 101, Phlegyas, 104, Parthenopaios, 117, Alcippe, 130, Tereus, 132, Penthesileia, 154.

Grove of, at Colchis, 43; belt of, owned by queen of Amazons, 78.

Artemis (Diana). Birth, 31; shoots Tityos, 32; kills Orion, 32, a Giant, 35, the daughters of Niobe, 105, Callisto, 115; causes death of the Aloads, 38, Actaion, 102, Adonis, 131, Broteas, 143; angry with Oineus, and sends the Calydonian boar, 40, with Admetos, 48, with Heracles for catching hind sacred to her, 74–5, with Agamemnon, and causes sacrifice of his daughter Iphigeneia, but rescues her, 150; Atreus fails to honour vow to, 145, 150; makes Phylonoe immortal, 120.

Athene (Athenaia or Athenaie, contracted to Athene, or to Athena in fourth century Attic and later usage; at Rome identfied with Minerva). Birth, 31; discards flute, 32; and Giants, 34–5, 87; reared by Triton, and conflict with Pallas, 123–4; wins contest with Poseidon for Athens, 140; amongst the goddesses judged by Paris, 146.

Advises on the *Argo*, 49, on the ship of Danaos, 60; helps Perseus, 65–7; gifts and aid to Heracles, 72, 77, 78; returns apples of the Hesperides, 83; advises Cadmos, and confers kingdom on him, 100; gives Gorgon's blood to Asclepios, 119, dragon's teeth to Aietes, 53; involvement with the birth and rearing of Erichthonios, 132; purifies the Danaids, 62; blinds Teiresias, but grants him divinatory powers, 110; plans to make Tydeus immortal, but is deterred, 111; drives Aias mad, 155; angry with Locrian Aias and Greeks after her statue is defiled, asks Zeus to send storm, 158–9, propitiated by Locrians, 162.

Images of, 60, 158; sanctuary of, 88, 116, 132, 133; priesthood of, 134; wooden horse dedicated to, 156.

Demeter (Ceres). Swallowed by her father Cronos, 28; seeks for her daughter Persephone, received at Eleusis, 33, confers wheat, 33, 133; punishes Ascalaphos, 33, 84; bears horse Areion to Poseidon, 111; Iasion wants to violate her, 122–3; statue of her in Egypt as Isis, 60.

Dionysos. Birth and earlier life, 101–3; punishes Lycourgos, 102, Pentheus, 103, for rejecting him; transforms pirates, 103; drives mad the women of Argos, 47, daughters of Proitos, 63; gives vine to Oineus, 40, wine to Icarios in Attica, 133; grants powers to daughters of Anios, 148; father of Deianeira, 40, love for Ariadne and children by her, 140; brings mother up from Hades and ascends to heaven, 103.

The Twelve Gods

Hephaistos (Vulcan). Birth, 30; thrown from heaven, 31; and birth of Athene, 31; his forge on Lemnos, 32; kills a Giant, 34; nails Prometheus to Caucasos, 36; gives bronze-footed bulls to Aietes, 53, Talos to Minos, 56, a breastplate to Heracles, 72; makes castanets used by Heracles, 77, necklace for Harmonia, 101, armour for Achilles, 154; builds underground house for Oinopion, 32; looks after cattle for Heracles, 81; purifies Pelops, 144; dries up Scamander, 154; tries to violate Athene and becomes father of Erichthonios, 132; father of Palaimon, 49, Periphetes, 138.

Hera (Juno). Swallowed by her father Cronos, 28; marriage to Zeus, and their children, 29, given golden apples as wedding present, 81; suspended from Olympos, 31, 86; assaulted by Giant, 34; wins contest with Poseidon for Argos, 60; amongst the goddesses judged by Paris, 146; Thetis reared by, 128.

Behaviour to women loved by Zeus and their children: pursues Leto, 31; tethers Io as cow, sends gadfly after her, 59, asks Curetes to abduct her child, 59; delays birth of Heracles, 68, sends serpents against him, 70, a storm, 31, 86, drives him mad, 72, hinders him by inciting Amazons, 79, and dispersing cattle, 81, finally reconciled with him, 91; deceives Semele, 101, drives Dionysos mad, 102, and Athamas and Ino for looking after him, 43, 101; causes death of Callisto, 115.

Throws Orion's wife into Hades, 32; acts against Pelias for failing to honour her, 45, 46; helps Argonauts past Clashing Rocks, 53, Wandering Rocks, 55; sends daughters of Proitos mad, 63; sends Sphinx against Thebes, 106; blinds Teiresias, 110; assaulted by Ixion, 142; sends storm against Paris and Helen, 147; makes Menelaos immortal, 164.

Sacrifices to, 81; altar of, 57, 146; Ceux says his wife is Hera, 38.

Hermes (Mercury). Birth and exploits as an infant, 117–18; kills Giant, 35; recovers Zeus' tendons after they are removed by Typhon, 36; rescues Ares, 38; gives golden-fleeced ram to Nephele, 43; steals Io as cow and kills Argos, 59; purifies Danaids, 62; aids Perseus, 65–6; gives Heracles sword, 72, advises him in Hades, 84, sells him, 85; rapes Apemosyne, 98; gives moly to Odysseus, 167.

Appointed herald to the gods, 118, sent to Deucalion, 37, takes infant Dionysos to Ino and Athamas, 102, sent to Atreus, 145, takes goddesses to be judged by Paris, 146, Helen to Egypt, 147, Protesilaos up from Hades, 152.

Father of Eurytos, 49, Abderos, 78, Cephalos, 131, Myrtilos, 144, Pan, 170.

Poseidon (Neptune). Swallowed by Cronos, 28; given trident, and becomes ruler of the sea, 29; marriage and children, 33; fights Giant,

35; loses contest with Hera for Argos, 60, with Athene for Attica, 130; contends with Zeus for Thetis, 128; indicts Ares for murder, 131; fathers horse Areion by Demeter, 111.

Makes shelter for Oinopion, 32; gives a chariot to Idas, 39, powers of transformation to Periclymenos, 45; blinds Phineus, 52; sends flood and monster against Ethiopia, 66; makes Pterelaos immortal, 68; hides away Centaurs, 75; sends bull from sea to Minos, 77, against Hippolytos, 142; fortifies Troy, but sends sea-monster when denied fee, 79; gives Peleus immortal horses, 129; rescues Eumolpos, destroys Erechtheus and house, 135; makes Caineus invulnerable, 142; kills Locrian Aias, 159; angry with Odysseus for blinding Polyphemos, 165, sends storm against him, and petrifies Phaeacian ship, 168, propitiated, 170.

His children, Orion, 32, the Aloads, 38, by Tyro, 45, Phineus, 52, Belos and Agenor, 60, 96, Nauplios by Amymone, 61–2, Pegasos, 64, Chrysaor, 66, the Molionides, 87, by Atlantids, 117, Halirrhothios, killed by Ares, 130–1, Eumolpos, 135, Theseus, 136, Polyphemos, 165, others, 38, 50, 51, 68, 76, 80, 82, 86, 96, 110, 139; loves Pelops, gives him winged chariot, 144.

Sacrifice to, 49; sanctuary of 72; cult of Poseidon Erechtheus, 134, *Argo* dedicated to, 57.

Zeus (Jupiter). Birth, childhood, and ascent to power, 28; marriage to Hera, and children by her and others, 29–31; father of Dionysos by Semele, 101, of Hermes by Maia, 117; aids abduction of Persephone, 33; defeat of Giants, 34–5, of Typhon, 35–6; punishes Prometheus, 36, his release, 75, 83; separates Apollo and Idas, 39, Apollo and Heracles, 85, Athene and Poseidon, 130; places aegis between Pallas and Athene, 124; gives remedy to Athene, 111; adjudicates between Hermes and Apollo, 118; imposes servitude on Apollo, 119; contends with Poseidon for Thetis, 128; judges dispute between goddesses over Adonis, 131; causes oaths to be sworn by Styx, 29.

Transforms Ceux and Alcyone, 38, vixen and dog, 70, Nysian nymphs, 102, Niobe, 105; destroys Salmoneus, 45, Capaneus, 110, Lycaon and sons, 115, Asclepios, 119, companions of Odysseus, 168, causes death of Actaion, 102; punishes Sisyphos, 44, Ixion, 142; sends great flood, 37; grants Endymion unending sleep, 38–9; incites Oineus to passion for own daughter, 42; angry with Argonauts for murder of Apsyrtos, 54–5; orders purification of Danaids, 62; saves Heracles, 87; grants long life to Sarpedon, 97; gives Harmonia to Cadmos, 101, sends them to Elysium, 103; gives prophetic powers to Teiresias, 110; opens chasm for Amphiaraos, 111; helps Callirrhoe, 113; determines posthumous fate of Dioscuri, 122; abduction of Ganymede, 79, 123; grants Minos vengeance on Athenians, 137;

supports Atreus in claim to throne, 145; brings about the Trojan War, 146, reveals its duration, 149; has Helen sent to Egypt, 147; sends storm against Greeks, 159; made Aiolos controller of the winds, 166.

Loves Niobe, 58, Io, 59, Danae, 65, Alcmene, 70, Europa, 77, Semele, 101, Antiope, 104, Callirrhoe, 113, Callisto, 115, Maia, 117, Leda, Nemesis, 120, Aegina, 126; his mortal children, Aethlios, 37, Aiacos, 126, Amphion, 104, 117, Arcas, 115, Argos, 58, Asopos, 126, Atymnios, 97, Castor?, 44 cf. 120, Dardanos, 122, Epaphos, 59, Helen, 120, Hellen, 37, Heracles, 70, Iasion, 122, Lacedaimon, 118, Minos, Rhadamanthys, Sarpedon 96, Perseus, 65, Polydeuces, 120, Tityos, 31, Zethos, 104, 117.

Altars to, 90, 98; sacrifices to, 43, 82; sanctuary of, 117.

REFERENCES TO ANIMALS
AND TRANSFORMATIONS

Asses, companions of Odysseus turned into, 166.

Bear, Callisto turned into, 115; Atalante, 116, Paris suckled by, 125; Achilles fed on the marrow of bears, 129.

Bee, Periclymenos turns himself into, 45.

Birds, Melampous, 46, Teiresias, 110, come to understand their language; Stymphalian, killed by Heracles, 77; women mourning Meleager turned into, 41 (meleagrides, guinea-fowl, in other sources), and Aisacos mourning his wife, 124 (a diver, in the Latin tradition).

Bitch, Hecuba turned into, 158.

Boar, Calydonian, sent by Artemis, 40–1, further references to the hunt for it, 86, 116, 127, image on Tydeus' shield (which can be taken to be of Calydonian boar), 107; Erymanthian, caught by Heracles, 75–6; Adonis killed by a, 132; suitors of Alcestis to yoke a boar to a lion, 107.

Bull, Arcadian, killed by Argos, 58; Europa abducted by Zeus as, 96; sent up to Minos by Poseidon, 97, mates with Pasiphae, fathering the Minotaur, 98; Cretan killed by Heracles, 77, identifiable with Europa's or with that sent by Poseidon?, 77; Marathonian, identifiable with the previous, 77, killed Androgeos, 136, killed by Theseus, 139; bull sent against Hippolytos by Poseidon, 142; bronze-footed, yoked by Jason, 53–4; Talos a bull?, 56; Aison killed by drinking bull's blood, 56; Heracles takes and eats a bullock, 82, 89; Acheloos takes form of, when fighting Heracles, 88; Dirce bound to, 105.

Cattle, of Admetos, 120, of Aeneas, rustled by Achilles, 152, of Apollo, stolen by Hermes, 118, of Augeias, 76, of Electryon, stolen by sons of Pterlaos, 69, of Eurytos, 85, of Geryon, taken by Heracles, 80–1, of Hades, 80, 84, of Phylacos, gained by Melampous, 46–7, of the Sun, 34, 55, 168; Arcadian, rustled by the Dioscuri and Idas and Lynceus, 122; Theban tribute to Orchomenos, 71–2.

Cow, Io turned into, 59; guides Cadmos to site of Thebes, 100, Ilos to site of Ilion, 123; three-coloured, owned by Minos, 99; wooden, made for Pasiphae, 98.

Crow, turned from white to black by Apollo, 119.

Deer, Artemis turns herself into to cause death of Aloads, 38; Actaion turned into, 102; killed by Agamemnon, 150; substituted for Iphigeneia at sacrifice, 150; Athamas hunts his son thinking him a deer, 101.

Doe, Telephos suckled by, 88, 116.

Dog, unapproachable, guarding cattle of Phylacos, 46; of Minos, fated to catch prey, 70, 134, turned to stone by Zeus, 70; Molossian, kills son of Licymnios, 87–8; named Maira, leads Erigone to her father's body, 133; monstrous, Cerberos, 83–4, Orthos, 80; dogs of Actaion hunt their master, 102, catalogue of their names, 172.

Dolphins, Dionysos transforms pirates into, 103.

Dove, sent out by Argonauts to test passage between Clashing Rocks, 52–3.

Dragon, Delphyne, a she-dragon, 36; *see further under* serpents.

Eagle, eats liver of Prometheus, 36, shot by Heracles, 83; abducts Ganymede, 123; presages birth of Aias, hence his name, 127.

Fox, symbol of Messenia, 94; Teumessian, *see* vixen.

Gadfly, sent by Hera against Io as cow, 59, against cattle of Geryon, 81.

Goat, Amaltheia, whose milk is given to infant Zeus, 28. (Not explicitly named here as a goat; this can also be the name of the nymph owning it, cf. 89 and note.)

Goose, Nemesis turns herself into, hoping to avoid intercourse with Zeus, 120.

Halcyon (a mythical bird), Alcyone turned into, 38.

Hind, Cerynitian, golden-horned and sacred to Artemis, caught by Heracles, 74–5.

Hoopoe, Tereus turned into, 134.

Horses, immortal, given to Peleus by Poseidon, 129, lent by Achilles to Patroclos, 154; man-eating mares of Diomedes, kill Abderos, captured by Heracles, 77–8; winged horses of Zeus, 36; horses given by Ares to Oinomaos, 144, by Zeus (to Tros) and thence to Laomedon, 79; Lycourgos killed by, 152; of Rhesos, 153; Pegasos, 64, 66; Areion, offspring of Demeter and Poseidon, owned by Adrastos, 111; Wooden horse at Troy, 156–7.

Hydra, Lernaean, killed by Heracles, 74, its poison, 90.

Keux (a semi-mythical bird, translated as sea-swallow), Ceux turned into, 38.

Kid, Dionysos turned into, 101–2.

Lamb, golden, sent to Atreus by Artemis, 145, 150.

Lion, of Cithairon, 71, of Nemea, killed by Heracles, 73; Periclymenos turns himself into, 45; Atalante and Melanion, 117, companions of Odysseus, turned into, 166; suitors of Alcestis to yoke with boar, 107; on shield of Adrastos, 107.

Nightingale, Procne turned into, 133.

Owl, Ascalaphos turned into, 82.

Pigs, companions of Odysseus turned into, 166; Achilles fed on entrails of wild swine, 129.

168; snake in portent at Aulis petrified, 149; stones thrown by
Deucalion and Pyrrha turn into men and women, 37; the children of
Callirhoe turned into adults by Zeus, 113; Metis, 31, Nereus, 82, turn
themselves into many different shapes, Thetis into fire, water, wild beast,
128–9; the gods flee to Egypt through fear of Typhon and turn themselves into animals, 35.

Transformations of the gods: Demeter, 33, Apollo and Poseidon, 79,
into human form; Hera into an Amazon, 79; Zeus into a shower of gold,
to seduce Danae, 65, into Artemis or Apollo to seduce Callisto, 115,
Poseidon into the River Enipeus to seduce Tyro, 45; Demeter into a
Fury, 111.

INDEX OF NAMES

Content

The Library provides the fullest inventory of mythological characters and genealogies to be found in any single ancient source; in view of this, it was considered desirable that the index should be as full as possible, even if many figures may be obscure or otherwise unrecorded. All personal names are included, except for those listed in the following five catalogues:

The Nereids, p. 29.

The fifty daughters of Danaos and fifty sons of Aigyptos, and their respective mothers, p. 61–2.

The fifty daughters of Thespios and their sons by Heracles, pp. 91–2.

The fifty sons of Lycaon, p. 114 (one name missing).

The suitors of Penelope, p. 168–9 (one hundred and twenty-nine names).

Since virtually none of these figures appears in any other connection (and for the most part these catalogues are genealogical blind alleys), it is improbable that anyone would seek them individually in an index; but the few who do appear elsewhere are included.

The Spelling and Pronunciation of Greek Names

With a few exceptions (which are cross-referenced), the names are given in their original Greek form; please see p. xxix above for some brief remarks on this matter. It should therefore be remembered that the Greek diphthongs *ai* and *oi* will be found rather than their Latin equivalents *ae* and *oe* (thus Aigeus and Oineus rather than Aegeus and Oeneus), and that Greek *ei* will not be replaced by a long *i* (so if a name like Chiron or Tiresias seems to be missing, it should be sought as Cheiron or Teiresias).

In ordinary speech, it is usual for English speakers to pronounce Greek names in the way that seem most natural without attempting to reproduce the exact pronunciation of the ancient Greeks. This conventional (or compromise) pronunciation presents no great problems if a few rules are observed:

Vowels: There are no mute vowels. In particular, a final *-e* and the *e* in final *-es* should always be sounded, as in familiar names like Aphrodite and Socrates.

271

Index of Names

In Greek, *ae*, *oe*, and *oo* are never diphthongs, and each vowel should be sounded separately (e.g. in Danae, Iphinoe, Acheloos).

Of diphthongs, *ai* should be pronounced as in *high*, *au* as in *how*, and *oi* as in *boil*; and *eu* is commonly pronounced as in *eulogy*, or when followed by an *r*, as in *Europe*.

In names, *ei* is usually a diphthong, which can be pronounced as in *pay* (e.g. in Teiresias, Deianeira), but not always (especially at the end of names, e.g. Endeis, the Nereids).

Consonants: *C* is used for Greek kappa (although when transliterating Greek it is usual to use a *k*). This is properly a hard *c* (or *k*), but where it seems natural for an English speaker, it is often pronounced as a soft *c* (as in Alcibiades or Eurydice).

Ch is used for Greek chi, which represents an aspirated *k*. In names, e.g. Achilles, it can be pronounced like a *k*. It should *not* be pronounced like *ch* in *chapter*.

G is properly hard as in *gallery*, but again, where it seems natural (as with the name Aigeus) it is often pronounced as in *gin*.

N.B. Genealogical indications, most commonly a patronymic, are included for practical convenience, but it must be remembered that there are often conflicting traditions, and if it is stated, for instance, that somebody is the mother of a particular person, that may be only one of several traditions recorded (whether in the present work or elsewhere).

Information not derived from the text is bracketed.

Where there are more than two entries under a particular name, **bold type** is used to distinguish those which refer to mythical stories or passages which give biographical (rather than purely genealogical) information; and generally, where an entry is *italicized*, this indicates that it refers to the inclusion of the character in one of the four main heroic catalogues:

Those who joined the hunt for the Calydonian boar, pp. 40–1.
The Argonauts, pp. 49–50.
Helen's suitors, p. 121.
The Greeks who joined the expedition against Troy, page 148.

Index of Names

Achilles (*strictly* Achilleus), son of Peleus **129–30**, *148*, **149–55**, 157 **158**

Acrisios, son of Abas **62–3**, **64–5**, **67** 119

Actaion, son of Aristaios 102, 171

Actaios, father of Agraulos 130

Actaios, father of Telamon 126

Actor, father of Eurytos and Cteatos, 87

Actor, son of Deion 44, 49

Actor, son of Hippasos *49*

Actor, son of Myrmidon 38, 41, 127

Acousilaos (of Argos, historian, 6th–5th cent. BC) 58 (2F25a, Jacoby), 59 (F26 and 27), 63 (F28), 77 (F29), 102 (F33), 114 (F25b), 121 (F41), 126 (F21), 134 (F31)

Admete, daughter of Eurystheus 78

Admetos, son of Pheres *40*, **48**, *49*, 85 **120**, 121, 148

Adonis, loved by Aphrodite 30, 131–2

Adrasteia, nurse of Zeus 28

Adrastos, father of Eurydice 124

Adrastos, son of Merops 152

Adrastos, son of Talaos 42, 47, **107–9**, **111**, 112

Aegina (*properly* Aigina), daughter of Asopos 44, 126

Aello, a Harpy 29

Aellopous, a Harpy 52

Aeneas (properly Aineias), son of Anchises **123**, **152**, **153**, 157

Aerope, daughter of Catreus 98, **99**, **145**, 148

Aethlios, son of Zeus 37, 38

Agathon, son of Priam 125

Agamemnon, son of Pleisthenes or Atreus **99**, 120, **146**, **147–55**, **158–9**, 160, 163

Agapenor, son of Ancaios **113**, *121*, *148*, **161**

Agasthenes, father of Polyxenos 121

Agathon, son of Priam 125

Agave, daughter of Cadmos 101, 103

Agelaos, a servant of Priam 125

Agelaos, son of Heracles 92

Agelaos, son of Temenos 94

Agenor, father of Phineus 51

Agenor, son of Amphion 105

Agenor, son of Ecbasos 58

Agenor, son of Phegeus 113

Agenor, son of Pleuron 39

Agenor, son of Poseidon 60, 96

Aglaia, daughter of Mantineus 62

Aglaie, a Grace 29

Aglaope, a Siren 167

Aglaos, son of Thyestes 145

Agraulos, daughter of Actaios 130

Agraulos, daughter of Cecrops 130

Agrios, a Centaur 75

Agrios, a Giant 35

Agrios, son of Porthaon 39, 42

Aiacos, son of Zeus and Aegina 41, 49, **126**

Aias, son of Oileus *121*, *148*, **157–8**, **159**

Aias, son of Telamon *121*, **127**, *148*, **153–5**

Aietes, son of the Sun 43, **53–4**, **57**, 166

Aigialeia, daughter of Adrastos 43, 48, **160**

Aigialeus, son of Adrastos 43, 48, **112**

Aigialeus, son of Inachos 58

Aigimios, king of the Dorians 89–90, 94

Aigina, *see* Aegina

Aigioneus, son of Priam 125

Aigipan 36

Aigisthos, son of Thyestes **146**, **160**, **163**

Aigle, one of the Hesperides 81

Aigleis, daughter of Hyacinthos 137

Aigyptos, son of Belos 60

Aigyptos, sons of 60–2

Aineias, *see* Aeneas

Ainetos, son of Deion 44

Aiolos, keeper of the winds 165–6

Aiolos, son of Hellen 37–8, 43, 44, 120

Aipytos, son of Cresphontes 95

Aisacos, son of Priam 124–5

Aison, son of Cretheus 40, 46, 48, **56**

Aithousa, daughter of Poseidon 117

Aithra, daughter of Pittheus **121**, **136**, **138**, **143**, 157

Aithylla, daughter of Laomedon 161

Aitolos, son of Endymion 39, 49

Index of Names

Ajax, *see* Aias
Alastor, son of Neleus 45
Alcaios, son of Androgeos 78
Alcaios, son of Perseus 68
Alcathoos, son of Porthaon 39, 42
Alcatous, son of Pelops 72, 127
Alceides, earlier name of Heracles 73
Alcestis, daughter of Pelias 46, **48**, 85
Alcidice, wife of Salmoneus 45
Alcimenes, killed by Bellerophon 64
Alcinoos, father of Nausicaa 55, 168
Alcinous, son of Hippocoon 120
Alcippe, daughter of Ares 130–1
Alcmaion, son of Amphiaraos **42**,
    111–14, 162
Alcmaionid, the (an early epic) 42
    (fr. 4 Davies)
Alcmene, daughter of Electryon 68,
    69–70, 72, 92, 97
Alcon, son of Hippocoon 120
Alcyone, daughter of Aiolos 38
Alcyone, daughter of Atlas 117
Alcyone, daughter of Sthenelos 68
Alcyone, mother of Elephenor 148
Alcyoneus, a Giant 34
Alecto, a Fury 27
Alector, father of Iphis 108
Alector, father of Leitos 50, 121
Aleos, son of Apheidas 49, **88**, 92, **115**
Aletes, son of Icarios 120
Alexander, *see* Paris
Alexandros, son of Eurystheus 92
Alexiares, son of Heracles 91
Aloads, the (Aloadai) 38
Aloeus, son of Poseidon 38
Alphesiboia, mother of Adonis 131
Althaia, daughter of Thestios 39, 40–1
Althaimenes, son of Catreus 98–9
Amaltheia (a goat) 28
Amaltheia, daughter of Haimonios 89
Amarynceus, father of Hippostratos 42
Amazons, the **64, 78, 141**, 154, 172
Amisodaros, who reared the Chimaera
    64
Ammon, an oracle by 66
Amphianax, king of Lycia 62
Amphiaraos, son of Oicles *41*, 47, *49*,
    107–9, 111, 112, 121
Amphictyon, son of Deucalion 37, 132
Amphidamas, son of Bousiris 82

Amphidamas, son of Cleitonymos 130
Amphidamas, son of Lycourgos 116
Amphidicos, son of Astacos 110
Amphilochos, son of Alcmaion 114,
    162
Amphilochos, son of Amphiaraos **112**,
    121, **158**
Amphimachos, son of Cteatos *121*, *148*
Amphimachos, son of Electryon 68
Amphimachos, son of Nomion 153
Amphion, son of Zeus and Antiope
    104–5, 117
Amphios, son of Merops *152*
Amphithea, daughter of Pronax 47
Amphithea, wife of Lycourgos 48
Amphitrite, [daughter of Oceanos 28],
    29 (as Nereid), **33**, 135
Amphitryon, father of Iphicles 40
Amphitryon, son of Alcaios 68, **69–71**,
    72
Amphoteros, son of Alcmaion 113
Amyclas, son of Amphion 105
Amyclas, son of Lacedaimon 44, 115,
    118–19
Amycos, son of Poseidon 51, 79
Amymone, daughter of Danaos 60–1,
    62
Amyntor, king of Ormenion **90**, 92,
    129
Amythaon, son of Cretheus 39, 46, 63
Anactor, son of Electryon 68
Anaxibia, daughter of Bias 46
Anaxibia, daughter of Cratieus 46
Anaxo, daughter of Alcaios 68
Ancaios, son of Lycourgos *40*, *49*, **53**,
    116, 121
Anchinoe, daughter of the Nile 60
Anchises, son of Capys **123**, 152, **157**
Anchios, a Centaur 75
Andraimon, father of Oxylos 94
Andraimon, nephew of Oineus 40, **42**,
    148, 170
Androgeos, son of Minos 79, 80, 97,
    98, 136–7
Andromache, daughter of Eetion 125,
    158, 160
Andromeda, daughter of Cepheus
    66–8
Anicetos, son of Heracles 91
Anios, son of Apollo 148

274

Index of Names

Index of Names

Asterios, son of Cometes *50*
Asterios, son of Neleus 45
Asterodia, daughter of Deion 44
Asteropaios, son of Pelegon 154
Asterope, daughter of Cebren 124
Astraios, offspring of Ceios 29
Astyanax (son of Hector) 158
Astycrateia, daughter of Amphion 105
Astydameia, daughter of Amyntor 92
Astydameia, daughter of Pelops 68
Astydameia, wife of Acastos 128, 129
Astygonos, son of Priam 125
Astynoos, son of Phaethon 131
Astyoche, daughter of Amphion 105
Astyoche, daughter of Laomedon 124,
    161
Astyoche, daughter of Phylas 89, 92,
    148
Astyoche, daughter of Simoeis 123
Astypalaia, mother of Eurypylos 86
Atalante, daughter of Iasos or
    Schoineus 41, *49*, 116–17, 127
Atas, son of Priam 125
Ate 124
Athamas, son of Aiolos 38, 43–4
Athene, *see* 'The Twelve Gods',
    pp. 262–6
Atlas, son of Iapetos 29, 44, 83, 117,
    122, 168
Atreus, son of Pelops 69, 121, 145–6,
    148, 150
Atropos, a Fate 29
Atthis, daughter of Cranaos 132
Atymnios, son of Zeus 97
Auge, daughter of Aleos 88, 92,
    115–16
Augeias *or* Augeas, son of the Sun *50*,
    76, 81, 87, 92
Autesion, father of Argeia 93
Autolycos, son of Hermes 48, *49*, 71,
    85
Automedousa, daughter of Alcathos 72
Autonoe, daughter of Cadmos 101,
    102
Autonoe, daughter of Peireus 92
Axios, father of Pelagon 154

Bateia, daughter of Teucros 123
Bateia, wife of Oibalos 120
Baton, charioteer of Amphiaraos 111

Bellerophon (*properly* Bellerophontes),
    son of Sisyphos 44, 64, 96
Belos, son of Poseidon 60, 96
Benthesicyme, daughter of Poseidon
    135
Bias, uncle of Pylas 136
Bias, son of Amythaon 46–7, 63
Bias, son of Priam 125
Bilsates, father of Pylaimenes 152
Boreas (North Wind) 49, 52, 134–5
Boros, son of Perieres 127
Boucolion, son of Laomedon 124
Boucolos, son of Hippocoon 120
Bousiris, king of Egypt 82
Boutes, son of Teleon *50*, 55
Boutes, son of Pandion 133, 134
Braisia, daughter of Cinyras 131
Branchos, father of Cercyon 139
Briareus, a Hundred-Hander 27
Briseis, daughter of Chryses 153, 154
Brontes, a Cyclops 27
Broteas (son of Tantalos) 143

Cadmos, son of Agenor 53, 96, 100–1,
    103
Caineus, a Lapith 142
Caineus, brother of Ischys 119
Caineus, son of Coronos *49*
Calais, son of Boreas *49*, 52, 134
Calchas, a seer 129, 149, 150, 155,
    158–9
Callias, son of Temenos 94
Callidice, queen of the Thesprotians
    170
Callileon, son of Thyestes 145
Calliope, a Muse 30
Callirrhoe, daughter of Acheloos 113
Callirrhoe, daughter of Oceanos 80
Callirrhoe, daughter of Scamander 123
Callisto, daughter of Lycaon 115
Calybe, a nymph, mother of Boucolion
    124
Calyce, daughter of Aiolos 38
Calydon, son of Aitolos 39
Calypso, daughter of Atlas 168
Campe, guards the Titans 28
Canace, daughter of Aiolos 38
Capaneus, son of Hipponous 108–10,
    121, 172
Capys, son of Assaracos 123

276

Index of Names

Cassandra, daughter of Priam 125, **157, 158, 163**

Cassiepeia, mother of Atymnios 97

Cassiepeia, wife of Cepheus 66

Castor (of Rhodes, author of chronologies, 1st cent. BC) 59 (250F8 Jacoby)

Castor, son of Zeus *40*, *49*, 71, 120, **122**

Catreus, son of Minos 62, **98–9**, 145, 147, 159

Cebren, river, father of Asterope and Oinone 124, 125

Cebriones, son of Priam 125

Cecrops, first king of Attica 130–2

Cecrops, son of Erechtheus 134, 135

Celaineus, son of Electryon 68

Celaino, daughter of Atlas 117

Celeos, king of Eleusis 33, 133

Celeutor, son of Agrios 42

Centauros, son of Ixion 142

Centaurs, the 75, **128, 142**

Cephalos, son of Deion or Deioneus 44, **70**, 134

Cephalos, son of Hermes 131

Cepheus, son of Aleos *49*, 88, 115

Cepheus, son of Belos 60, **66–7**, 68

Cepheus, son of Lycourgos *40*

Cephisos, father of Diogeneia 134

Cerberos 83–4

Cercopes, the 85

Cercops (author of an early epic, *Aegimios*, also attributed to Hesiod) 62 (fr. 297 M–W)

Cercyon, son of Branchos 139

Ceteus, father of Callisto 115

Ceto, daughter of Pontos 29, 65

Ceuthonymos, father of Menoites 84

Ceux, son of Heosphoros 38

Ceux, king of Trachis 89–90, 92

Chalciope daughter of Aietes 43

Chalciope, daughter of Eurypylos 92

Chalciope, daughter of Rhexenor 136

Chalcodon, father of Elephenor 121, 148

Chariclo, a nymph, mother of Teiresias 109–10

Charopos, father of Nireus 148

Charybdis 55, **167, 168**

Chersidamas, son of Priam 125

Chersidamas, son of Pterelaos 68

Chimaera, killed by Bellerophon 44, 64

Chione, daughter of Boreas 134, 135

Cheirimachos, son of Electryon 68

Cheiron, a Centaur 29, 75, 83, **102, 119, 128–9**

Chloris, daughter of Amphion 45, **105**, 148

Chloris, wife of Neleus 105, 244

Chromios, son of Arsinoos 152

Chromios, son of Priam 125

Chromios, son of Pterelaos 68

Chrysaor, father of Geryon 66, 80

Chryses, a priest 153

Chryses, son of Minos 78, 97

Chrysippos, son of Pelops 104

Chrysopeleia, a nymph 115

Chrysothemis, daughter of Agamemnon 146

Chthonia, daughter of Erechtheus 134

Chthonios, one of the Spartoi 100, 103

Cilix, son of Agenor 96, 97

Cilla, daughter of Laomedon 124

Cinyras, son of Sandocos 115, **131**, 148

Circe, daughter of the Sun 43, **55, 166–7, 170**

Cisseus, father of Hecuba 124

Cleio, a Muse 30

Cleisithyra, daughter of Idomeneus, 160

Cleitonymos, son of Amphidamas 130

Cleoboia, mother of Eurythemis 39

Cleochareia, wife of Lelex 118

Cleochos, father of Areia 97

Cleodoxa, daughter of Amphion 105

Cleopatra, a Locrian maiden 162

Cleopatra, daughter of Boreas 134–5

Cleopatra, daughter of Idas 41

Cleopatra, daughter of Tros 123

Cleophyle, wife of Lycourgos 116

Clonia, a nymph, mother of Lycos and Nycteus 117

Clonios, son of Priam 125

Clotho, a Fate 29

Cloud, *see* Nephele

Clymene, daughter of Catreus 62, 98, **99, 159**

Clymenos, father of Erginos 72

Index of Names

Clymenos, son of Oineus 40
Clytemnestra (*properly* Clytaimnestra), daughter of Tyndareus 120, **146**, **150**, **160**, **163**
Clytios, a Giant 34
Clytios, son of Laomedon 124
Cnossia, a nymph 122
Cocalos, king of Camicos 141
Coios, a Titan 27, 28, 31
Coiranos, father of Polyidos 99
Comaitho, daughter of Pterelaos 70
Cometes, father of Asterios 50
Cometes, son of Sthenelos 160
Copreus, son of Pelops 73
Corinthos, father of Sylea 138
Coronis, daughter of Phlegyas 119
Coronos, father of Caineus 49
Coronos, father of Leonteus 90, 121
Corybantes, the 30
Cottos, a Hundred-Hander 27
Couretes, *see* Curetes
Cranae, daughter of Cranaos 132
Cranaichme, daughter of Cranaos 132
Cranaos, king of Attica 37, 130, **132**
Crataiis, mother of Scylla 167
Cratieus, father of Anaxibia 46
Cratos, son of Pallas 29
Creios, a Titan 27, 29
Creon, king of Corinth 57, 114
Creon, son of Menoiceus, of Thebes **69–70**, 72, 92, **106**, 110, 111
Creontiades, son of Heracles 72, 92
Cresphontes, a Heraclid 94–5
Crete, daughter of Asterios 97
Crete, daughter of Deucalion 99
Cretheus, son of Aiolos 38, **45**, **46**, **48**
Creousa, daughter of Erechtheus 37, 134
Creousa, daughter of Priam 125
Criasos, son of Argos 58
Crocon, father of Meganeira 115
Croesus 92
Cronos, a Titan 27–8, 29
Cteatos, son of Actor or Poseidon by Molione 87, 121
Ctesippos, son of Heracles 92
Curetes, the (Kouretes) **28**, **59**, **99**
Cyanippos, son of Adrastos 48
Cychreus, son of Poseidon 127
Cyclopes, builders 63

Cyclopes, Homeric 164–5
Cyclopes, sons of Ouranos **27**, **28**, **119**
Cyclops, a, *see* Geraistos
Cycnos, father of Tenes 150–1, 152
Cycnos, son of Ares 82, 90
Cyllene, wife of Pelasgos 114
Cynortas, son of Amyclas 44, 119
Cyrene, mother of Diomedes of Thrace 78
Cytisoros, son of Phrixos 43
Cyzicos, king of the Doliones 50

Daidalos, son of Eupalamos **85**, **95**, **137–8**, **140–1**, 172
Damasichthon, son of Amphion 104–5
Damasippos, son of Icarios 120
Damasistratos, king of Plataea 106
Damastes or Polypemon, killed by Theseus 138, 139
Danae, daughter of Acrisios 63, **64–5**, **67**
Danaos, son of Belos 60–2
Dardanos, son of Zeus and Electra 122–3, 135
Dascylos, father of Lycos 79
Dawn (Eos) 28, 29, **32**, **34**, **44**, **124**, **131**, **154**
Deianeira, daughter of Oineus 40, 88–91
Deicoon, son of Heracles 72, 92
Deidameia, daughter of Lycomedes 129, 160
Deimachos, father of Enarete 38
Deimachos, son of Neleus 45
Deino, daughter of Phorcos 65
Deion or Deioneus, son of Aiolos 38, **44**, 70, 134
Deiopites, son of Priam 125
Deiphobos, son of Hippolytos 85
Deiphobos, son of Priam 125, **155**, **157**
Deiphontes, husband of Hyrnetho 94
Deipyle, daughter of Adrastos 42, 48, 107
Deliades, killed by Bellerophon 64
Delphyne, a she-dragon 36
Demaratos (Hellenistic mythological writer) 51 (42F41a Jacoby), 105 (F56)
Demeter, *see* 'The Twelve Gods', pp. 262–6
Democoon, son of Priam 125

Index of Names

Index of Names

Evagoras, son of Neleus 45
Evagoras, son of Priam 125
Evandros, son of Priam 125
Evenos, son of Ares 39
Everes, father of Teiresias 109
Everes, son of Heracles 92
Everes, son of Pterelaos 68, 69
Evippos, son of Thestios 39

Fates (Moirai), the 29, 35, 36, 40, 48
Furies (Erinyes, the) 27, 163
Fury, Demeter as a 111; Alcmaion
   pursued by a 113

Ganymede (*properly* Ganymedes), son
   of Tros 79, 123
Ge (Earth) 27, 28, 29, 33, 34, 45, 59,
   81, 82, 115
Gelanor, king of Argos 60
Geraistos, a Cyclops 137
Geryon, son of Chrysaor 66, 80
Giants (Gigantes), the 34–5, 87
Glauce, an Amazon 172
Glauce, daughter of Creon 57
Glauce, daughter of Cychreus 126
Glaucos, son of Antenor 157
Glaucos, son of Hippolochos 153, 154
Glaucos, son of Minos 97, 99–100,
   172
Glaucos, son of Priam 125
Glaucos, son of Sisyphos 44, 64
Glenos, son of Heracles 92
Gorge, daughter of Oineus 40, 42, 148
Gorgons, the 29, 65–6
Gorgophone, daughter of Perseus 44,
   68, 119
Gorgophonos, son of Electryon 68
Gorgyra, mother of Ascalaphos 32
Gorgythion, son of Priam 125
Gouneus, father of Laonome 68
Gouneus, son of Ocytos 148, 161
Graces (Charites), the 29
Gration(?), a Giant 35
Gyes, a Hundred-Hander 27

Hades 87, cattle of 80, 84; cap or
   helmet of 28, 65–6; *see also* Pluto
Hagnias, father of Tiphys 49
Haimon, son of Creon 106
Haimonios, father of Amaltheia 89

Halirrhothios, son of Poseidon 130–1
Harmonia, daughter of Ares and
   Aphrodite 101, 103
Harpies (Harpuiai), the 29, 52, 134
Hebe, daughter of Zeus and Hera 29,
   91
Hecate, daughter of Perses 29, 34
Hecatoncheires, *see* Hundred-Handers
Hector, son of Priam 124, 125, 151,
   153–4
Hecuba (*properly* Hecabe), daughter of
   Dymas 124, 158
Heleios, son of Perseus 68, 70
Helen (Helene), daughter of Zeus and
   Leda 120–1, 125, 143, 146–7,
   149, 151, 155, 156, 157, 164
Helenos, son of Priam 125, 155–6,
   158, 160
Helios, *see* Sun
Helle, daughter of Athamas 43
Hellen, son of Deucalion or Zeus 37
Hemithea, daughter of Cycnos 150
Heosphoros, son of Ceux 38
Hephaistos, *see* 'The Twelve Gods',
   pp. 262–6
Hera, *see* 'The Twelve Gods'
Heraclids, the 92–5, 96
Heracles, son of Zeus and Alcmene
   30, 31, 34–5, 36, 40, 45–6, 48,
   49, 51, 68 (not named), 70–92,
   93, 115–16, 120, 124, 127, 134,
   141, 143, 148, 149, 155
Hermione, daughter of Menelaos 121,
   147, 160, 164
Herodoros (of Heracleia, mythological
   writer, late 5th–4th cent. BC) 56
   (31F41a Jacoby)
Herse, daughter of Cecrops 130–1
Hesiod (early epic poet) 64 (*Theog.*
   319)
Hesiod (from later works attributed to)
   42 (fr. 12 M–W), 52 (fr. 155), 58
   (fr. 160), 59 (fr. 124), 63 (fr. 131),
   105 (fr. 183), 114 (fr. 160), 115
   (fr. 163), 117 (fr. 72), 131
   (fr. 139), 171 (fr. 275)
Hesione, daughter of Laomedon 79,
   86, 124, 127
Hesione, wife of Nauplios 62
Hesperia, one of the Hesperides 81

281

Index of Names

Nice, daughter of Pallas 29
Nicippe, daughter of Pelops 68
Nicostratos, son of Menelaos 121
Nicothoe, a Harpy 52
Nile, the 59, 60
Niobe, daughter of Phoroneus 58, 114
Niobe, daughter of Tantalos 104–5
Nireus, son of Charopos 148
Nireus, son of Poseidon 38
Nisos, son of Pandion 136, 137
Nomion, father of Nastes 153
Nycteis, daughter of Nycteus 103
Nycteus, father of Callisto 115
Nycteus, son of Hyrieus or Chthonios 103–4, 117
Nyctimos, son of Lycaon 115

Oceanids, the 28
Oceanos, a Titan 27, 28, 29, 33, 53, 58, 80, 114, 117, 126
Ocypete, Ocythoe, *or* Ocypode, a Harpy 52
Ocytos, father of Gouneus 148
Odios, son of Mecisteus 152
Odysseus, son of Laertes 30, 120, *121*, **129**, **147**, *148*, **150**, **151**, **153–8**, **159–60**, **164–70**
Oedipus (*properly* Oidipous), son of Laios **105–7**, 108, 111
Oiagros, father of Linos and Orpheus 30, 49
Oibalos, father of Arene 119, 120
Oicles, father of Amphiaraos 41, 49, 86, 107, **113**
Oileus, father of Locrian Aias 121, 148
Oineus, son of Porthaon 39, **40–3**, 49, **88–9**, 92, 107, 108, **113**, 146
Oino, daughter of Anios 148
Oinomaos, father of Hippodameia 65, 117, **144**
Oinone, daughter of Cebren 125–6
Oinopion, son of Dionysos 32, 140
Olenias, brother of Tydeus 42
Omphale, daughter of Iardanos 51, 85, 92
Onchestes, son of Agrios 42
Oneites, son of Heracles 92
Opheltes (*called* Archemoros), son of Lycourgos 48, 109
Opis, a Hyperborean maiden 32

Orchomenos, father of Elare 31
Orchomenos, son of Thyestes 145
Orestes, son of Agamemnon 93, 94, 146, **160**, **163–4**
Orion 32
Oreithuia, daughter of Erechtheus 134
Orpheus, son of Oiagros **30**, *49*, **55**, 71
Orsedice, daughter of Cinyras 131
Orseis, wife of Hellen 37
Orthaia, daughter of Hyacinthos 137
Orthos, son of Typhon, a dog 80
Otos, son of Poseidon 38
Otrere, mother of Penthesileia 154
Ourania, a Muse 30
Ouranos (Sky) 27, 29, **34**
Oxylos, son of Andraimon 94
Oxylos, son of Ares 39
Oxyporos, son of Cinyras 131

Palaimon, *formerly* Melicertes, a sea-god 101
Palaimon, son of Hephaistos or Aitolos *49*
Palaimon, son of Heracles 92
Palamedes, son of Nauplios 62, 99, **147**, **159–60**
Pallas, a Giant 35
Pallas, daughter of Triton 123–4
Pallas, son of Creios 29
Pallas, son of Pandion 136; sons of 140
Pammon, son of Priam 125
Pamphylos, son of Aigimios 94
Pan 31, 170
Pandaros, son of Lycaon 152, 153
Pandion, son of Cecrops 135–6, 137
Pandion, son of Erichthonios 133–4
Pandion, son of Phineus 134–5
Pandora, the first woman 37
Pandoros, son of Erechtheus 134
Pandrosos, daughter of Cecrops 130, 132
Panopeus, a Phocian 70
Panyasis (epic poet, 5th cent. BC) 33 (fr. 21 Davies), 131 (fr. 22a), 172 (fr. 19b)
Pareia, a nymph 97
Paris, *usually* Alexander (Alexandros) **124–6**, **146–7**, **153**, **154**, **155**

286

Index of Names

Parthenopaios, son of Melanion or
Ares 108–10, 112, 117
Parthenopaios, son of Talaos 47
Parthenope, daughter of Stymphalos
92
Pasiphae, daughter of the Sun 43, 97,
98, 134, 172
Patroclos, son of Menoitios *121*, 130,
153–4, 155
Pedias, daughter of Mynes 132
Pegasos, offspring of Poseidon, a
winged horse 64, 66
Peiras, son of Argos 58
Peirithoos, son of Ixion *40*, 84, 121,
142–3, 149
Peisandros (of Cameiros, early epic
poet) 42
Peisidice, daughter of Aiolos 38
Peisidice, daughter of Nestor 46
Peisidice, daughter of Pelias 46
Peisinoe, a Siren 167
Peisistratos, son of Nestor 46
Peisos, son of Aphareus 119
Pelagon, son of Asopos 126
Pelasgos, son of Zeus, or earthborn 58,
114
Pelegon, son of Axios 154
Peleus, son of Aiacos *40*, *49*, 116,
126–9, 148, **160**
Pelias, son of Poseidon and Tyro
45–6, 48–9, 53, 56–7; funeral
games for 116, 127; daughters of
57
Pelopeia, daughter of Pelias 46
Pelopia, daughter of Amphion 105
[Pelopia,] daughter of Thyestes 145
Pelopia, mother of Cycnos 90
Pelops, son of Tantalos 68, 69, 73,
104, **126**, 127, 136, 139, **143–5**;
altar of 87; bones of 156
Peloros, a Spartos 100
Peneleos, son of Hippalcimos or
Hippalmos(?) *50*, *121*
Penelope, daughter of Icarios 120, **121**,
147, **168–70**
Penthesileia, daughter of Ares, an
Amazon 144, 172
Pentheus, son of Echion 103
Peparethos, son of Dionysos 140
Pephredo, daughter of Phorcos 65

Perdix, mother of Talaos 137
Pereus, son of Elatos 115
Periboia, a Locrian maiden 162
Periboia, daughter of Hipponoos 42
Periboia, wife of Icarios 120
Periboia, wife of Polybos 105
Periclymenos, son of Neleus 45, *50*, **87**
Periclymenos, son of Poseidon 110
Perieres, charioteer of Menoiceus 72
Perieres, son of Aiolos 38, **44**, 68, **120**,
127, 128
Perieres, son of Cynortas 119, 120
Perileos, son of Icarios 120
Perimede, daughter of Aiolos 38
Perimede, wife of Licymnios 69
Perimedes, son of Eurystheus 92
Periopis, daughter of Pheres 130
Periphetes, son of Hephaistos 138
Pero, daughter of Neleus 45, 46–7
Perse, mother of Circe and Aietes 166
Perseis, mother of Pasiphae and Aietes,
43, 97
Persephone, daughter of Zeus 30,
33–4, **84**, **131**, **143**, 170
Perses, brother of Aietes 57
Perseus, son of Nestor 46
Perseus, son of Zeus 29, 44, **65–8**, 70,
119
Peteos, father of Menestheus 121
Phaedra (*properly* Phaidra), daughter
of Minos 97, 98, **141–2**, 172
Phaethon, son of Tithonos 131
Phaia, sow of Crommyon, named after
the woman who reared it 139
Phaidimos, son of Amphion 105
Phanos, son of Dionysos 50
Pharnace, daughter of Megassares 131
Phegeus, father of Arsinoe 113
Pheneus, son of Melas 42
Phereclos, builder of ships for Paris
146
Perecydes (of Athens, historian, 5th
cent. BC) 32 (3F42 Jacoby),
33 (F53), 42 (F122a), 51 (F111a),
59 (F67), 71 (F69a), 89 (F42),
96 (F87), 100 (F22c), 101 (F89),
110 (F92a), 115 (F157), 126 (F60)
Pheres, son of Cretheus 40, 46, **48**, 49,
120, 130
Pheres, son of Jason 57

Index of Names

Index of Names

Sipylos, son of Amphion 104
Sirens (Seirenes), the 30, 40, **55**, **167**
Sisyphos, son of Aiolos 38, **44**, 64, **101**, 117, **126**
Sky, *see* Ouranos
Smyrna, daughter of Theias 131
Sparta, daughter of Eurotas 118
Spartoi (Sown Men), the 100, 109
Spercheios, son of Menesthios 128
Spermo, daughter of Anios 148
Sphinx, the 106
Staphylos, son of Dionysos *50*, 140
Sternops, son of Melas 42
Sterope, daughter of Acastos 128
Sterope, daughter of Atlas 117
Sterope, daughter of Cepheus 88
Sterope, daughter of Pleuron 39
Sterope, daughter of Porthaon 40
Steropes, a Cyclops 27
Stesichoros (lyric poet, 7th–6th cent. BC) 119, 172
Stheneboia, daughter of Apheidas or Iobates 62, 63, **64**, 115
Sthenelaos, son of Melas 42
Sthenele, daughter of Acastos 130
Sthenelos, father of Cometes 160
Sthenelos, son of Androgeos 79
Sthenelos, son of Capaneus 112, *121*
Sthenelos, son of Perseus 68, 69
Stheno, a Gorgon 66
Stratobates, son of Electryon 68
Stratonice, daughter of Pleuron 39
Strophios, father of Pylades 163
Strymo, daughter of Scamander 124
Stymphalos, son of Elatos 92, 115, 126
Styx, an Oceanid 28, 29
Sun, the (Helios) 29, *33*, **34**, 43, 50, 55, **57**, 76, **80**, 83, 97, 166, **168**
Sylea, daughter of Corinthos 138
Syleus, killed by Meracles 85

Talaimenes, father of Mesthles and Antiphos 153
Talaos, son of Bias 47, 107, 108
Talos, a man of bronze 56
Talos, nephew of Daidalos 137–8
Talthybios, herald of Agamemnon 148, 150
Tantalos, father of Pelops and Niobe 105, 143

Tantalos, son of Amphion 105
Tantalos, son of Thyestes 146
Taphios, son of Poseidon 68
Tartaros 35, 59; as place 27–8, 119
Tauros, son of Neleus 45
Tebros, son of Hippocoon 120
Tegyrios, king of Thrace 135
Teiresias, son of Everes **70**, **109–10**, 112, 114, **167**, 170, 171
Telamon, son of Aiacos *40*, *49*, **86**, 121, **126–7**
Telchis, kills Apis 58
Teledice, wife of Phoroneus 58
Telegonos, king of the Egyptians 60
Telegonos, son of Odysseus 167, 170
Telegonos, son of Proteus 80
Telemachos, son of Odysseus 147, 169
Teleon, father of Boutes 50
Telephassa, wife of Agenor 96, 100
Telephos, son of Heracles 88, 92, **116**
Telesilla (lyric poet, 5th cent. BC) 105
Telestes, son of Priam 125, **149–50**, 156
Temenos (son of Aristomachos), a Heraclid 93–4
Tenes, son of Cycnos 150–1
Tenthredon, father of Prothoos 149
Tereis, mother of Megapenthes 122
Tereus, son of Ares 133–4
Terpsichore, a Muse 30
Tethys, a Titanid 27, 28, 58, 126
Teucros, son of Scamander 123
Teucros, son of Telamon *121*, 127, 155
Teutamides, king of Larissa 67
Teuthras, king of Teuthrania 88, 116
Thaleia, a Grace 29
Thaleia, a Muse 30
Thalpios, son of Eurytos *121*
Thamyris 30
Thasos, son of Poseidon 96
Thaumacos, father of Poias 50
Thaumas, son of Pontos 29
Theano, wife of Antenor 152
Thebaid (early epic) 42 (fr. 8 Davies)
Thebe, wife of Zetheus 104
Theia, a Titanid 27, 28
Theias, father of Adonis 131
Theiodamas, father of Hylas 51, 88
Thelxiepeia, a Siren 167
Thelxion 58

290

The Oxford World's Classics Website

www.worldsclassics.co.uk

- Information about new titles
- Explore the full range of Oxford World's Classics
- Links to other literary sites and the main OUP webpage
- Imaginative competitions, with bookish prizes
- Peruse *Compass*, the Oxford World's Classics magazine
- Articles by editors
- Extracts from Introductions
- A forum for discussion and feedback on the series
- Special information for teachers and lecturers

www.worldsclassics.co.uk

American Literature

British and Irish Literature

Children's Literature

Classics and Ancient Literature

Colonial Literature

Eastern Literature

European Literature

History

Medieval Literature

Oxford English Drama

Poetry

Philosophy

Politics

Religion

The Oxford Shakespeare

A complete list of Oxford Paperbacks, including Oxford World's Classics, OPUS, Past Masters, Oxford Authors, Oxford Shakespeare, Oxford Drama, and Oxford Paperback Reference, is available in the UK from the Academic Division Publicity Department, Oxford University Press, Great Clarendon Street, Oxford OX2 6DP.

In the USA, complete lists are available from the Paperbacks Marketing Manager, Oxford University Press, 198 Madison Avenue, New York, NY 10016.

Oxford Paperbacks are available from all good bookshops. In case of difficulty, customers in the UK can order direct from Oxford University Press Bookshop, Freepost, 116 High Street, Oxford OX1 4BR, enclosing full payment. Please add 10 per cent of published price for postage and packing.